MW01612895

562 - 325 41 3

Untold

A Berringer Family Novel

Tamara Helene Arrington

dark wings publishing

ISBN: 0988491206
ISBN-13: 978-0-9884912-0-5

For my boys, Julian, Connor, and Parker
You keep me strong and proud, and you give me the courage to take
chances and follow my heart.
You inspire me.

CONTENTS

ACKNOWLEDGMENTS

Edited by R. Julian Gonnella

Contributed to by Ralph J. Gonnella

Special Thanks To:

My mom for always being there for my boys and me

My dad for passing on a love for books to me

Ma and Granny for being strong women in different ways and showing me what true strength is

Annette "Nett," Dinah "Ninah," and Laura for helping me during such a difficult time and giving me the chance to complete this book

Ron for giving us shelter and friendship

Beverly Simcic for believing in my abilities and supporting me throughout this journey

Justice Gorak for taking the time to help make this a reality

Introduction

 y the early 1960s Newport, Rhode Island had reestablished itself as a mecca for the rich and powerful. The Great Depression of the 1930s had wreaked havoc upon the wealth and wealthy of Newport. Many magnificent mansions built in the late 1890s by the rich and powerful had become mere gawking museums for visitors near and far who had come to Newport to be witness to the financial excesses of an era long past.

Slowly, Newport's majestic shoreline and rustic setting lured people of wealth back to the quaint metropolis where society and culture dominated the everyday atmosphere. The Kennedys, known as American royalty, summered often in Newport at their luxurious compound. It was at Newport that then Senator John F. Kennedy pursued and finally married Jacqueline Bouvier. John F. Kennedy was elected president of the United States in 1960, and the first family journeyed often to Newport for respite and relaxation from the pressures of the presidency.

Newport was a melting pot of old wealth, nuevo rich, and the pretend to be rich. The Vietnam War had not yet become the ugly spectacle that it was about to become. A pervasive air of optimism and prosperity infected the minds and spirits of the Newport society's chosen elite.

Margret Taylor Berringer had been a part of the Newport scene since birth. She was born into obscene wealth and grew up at Ocean Point Estate, her father's mansion overlooking the extraordinary Newport shoreline. While Margret was growing up, Ocean Point became a focal point for many of society's gala events. By the 1940s her father, William Taylor, had passed away, leaving her the Ocean Point Estate. Before her father's death, Margret married and became a Berringer. She continued to occupy Ocean Point with her new husband.

By contrast, the Berringers' existence at Ocean Point had become dark and secretive. The family and staff of Ocean Point slowly withdrew from Newport society and barely communicated with anyone outside of the iron gates that surrounded the deteriorating estate. Unconfirmed rumors swirled around the city that the Berringers were hiding many insidious secrets and were living with the torment of an ancient curse that was cast on the family many generations back due to the sins of their ancestors. The unkempt grounds of the estate lent credence to the rumors of financial difficulties, but little else was known about the Berringers and the secrets of their lives at Ocean Point.

The youngest member of this strange and reclusive family was Coral Berringer. The fourteen year old had grown up at Ocean Point. For all of her life, living in the mansion had been unremarkable except for the peculiar mothering ways of Margret Berringer. As a young child, Coral had experienced the deterioration of the estate, the reclusive nature of her family, and the bizarre discipline imposed by Margret, but had until recently assumed that these were the ruminations of a very private family.

Emerging from the innocence of childhood, Coral's curiosity dominates her thoughts as she pursues the discovery of whether her family exemplifies the conventional life or something more sinister and secretive than she could ever imagine.

As Coral grows from childhood to womanhood, the truths of the Berringer family emerge from the shroud of secrecy and abuse that has enveloped their lives for more than a decade. The journey of Coral Berringer is captivating, unbelievable, and at times disturbing. As the revelations of the sins of her broken family tree are revealed, everything Coral ever knew to be true is not what it may have seemed. Will the anger of the lies destroy her? Can she battle the demon that walks the hallways of Ocean Point? Can she survive the eerie castle that she fears is alive from an ancient curse? Will she be able to endure the torture and scars left by her mother's hands? Will she be able to hold on to the bittersweet love that she has longed for?

Will Coral be able to accept the UNTOLD truths?

When I was a girl, I would look out my bedroom window and wish that I could chase butterflies in the glorious gardens below me, but the gardens were neglected, and I was held captive. All I could do was watch the cocoons that hung from my window sill and patiently wait to see the exquisite wings emerge from their coma, allowing the fuzzy caterpillars to become divine creatures. I envied the butterflies. No matter what they were before, no matter what happened, they could just hide away and become beautiful and free then fly away completely untouched.

Wash My Sins Away

I sit in a bathtub of scalding hot water as Mother attempts to wash my sins away. Her coal black hair falls loosely around her face as she vigorously scrubs my tender, young skin with a bath brush. There is so much determination and rage in her eyes that I dare not fight this torture or even scream out. This cleansing ritual confuses me, and the pain that is being inflicted on my skin is almost unbearable.

It seems as if this agony will never end. My skin burns all the way to my bones as I grip the sides of the bathtub. Just when I fear that my shivering body can take no more, Mother throws the brush into the bathtub and rises to her feet. Her body hovers over me like a dark cloud covers a city before a hurricane. A look of satisfaction envelops on her

1

ᵣ face.

"Maybe from now on you will behave as a young lady should around members of the opposite sex. I will not have any sinning of that nature under this roof! Flirting with the delivery boys is and always will be unacceptable. Do you understand what I am saying to you Coral?" she proclaims as she taunts my name.

"Yes ma'am," I answer in almost a whisper.

Mother turns to the vanity mirror and begins to fix her hair into the tight bun that she wears every day. I know from past experience that I am not to get out of the bathtub until she leaves the room. If I stand, it will show a lack of respect for her and the punishment that she has inflicted on me. My skin still stings, and I long for the safety of my bedroom.

Sitting in the bathtub with my knees drawn to my chest, I wrap my arms tightly around my shins to try to cover my naked torso with my legs. I look up at Mother. She stands tall. She is a very tall woman, almost six feet tall, and her posture is so straight that it makes her appear even taller. She always preaches that good posture is a sign of self-discipline.

Mother has long, thin fingers. At times I think that she could snap me in half with them. Her hair is so black that if the light hits it at a certain angle it appears blue. Her nose is long and narrow, and it seems that where her nose ends her mouth begins. Her eyes are dark, but unlike the rest of her features, they are rather large and expressive. Towards me, they always seem to express anger and disgust. My nanny, Rose, tells me that what I see in Mother's eyes is pain. Rose says that my mother's eyes are dark because of the hard life that she has endured. Rose often says

2

kiddingly,

"I remember a time when your mother, the young Margret Taylor, had bright blue eyes, but as each year passes they seem to grow darker."

Over the last few years, I have questioned Rose often about my family and why Mother has had such a difficult life. She never gives me any answers. When I make the inquiries, she becomes anxious, and her eyes dance around the room to avoid eye contact. It is always the same answer.

"You are too young to understand life's complications." I remember once I asked her when I would be old enough to understand. She answered me with a remorseful tone.

"There are some things you are never old enough to understand."

I have always known that there is more to my family's past that is untold, but I have just accepted the secrecy. Now that I am growing older, curiosity consumes my every thought about my family's hidden secrets.

Mother spins her straight body towards me.

"Make yourself look presentable. Your father is coming home this evening," she hisses at me as she leaves the bathroom.

Amidst all of the pain that my body has endured, the thought of Daddy coming home fills my heart with joy. Slowly, I rise to my feet and step out of the ceramic clawfoot bathtub. It is still warm from the piping hot water that surrounds my body. As my leg crosses over the side of the bathtub, the pain from the stretching of my skin surges through to my spine. As I reach for a towel to dry myself, I catch a glimpse of my injured body in the mirror that hangs on the back of my bathroom door. My suffering body is blood red. In some areas my skin is rubbed raw, mostly on my inner thighs and around my budding breasts. I move my eyes away from my body and look at my face. I wonder who the girl is staring back at me.

I do not resemble Mother at all, but everyone says that I have many features like my father. My hair is slightly wavy and strawberry-blonde. In the summer when the humidity is present, it tends to become curly with long, wild ringlets. It is long past my shoulders. My eyes are a blue-green color, and the hue changes with my mood. I have a patch of faint freckles that lay across the bridge of my nose. I have always hated my freckles, but Daddy says that they are what give me character. He always knows what to say to make me feel special. Even though I favor my father, I definitely have a unique look of my own. I have always thought that maybe I look like one of my ancestors from the past that I am denied of knowing.

My eyes wander back to my body, and I can see the changes that are happening to me. Rose always says that I am filling out in the right places. All of the other girls in school have already begun to develop in the womanly way. Rose says that there is nothing wrong with me and that I might just be a late bloomer. She says that once bloomed, I will see life differently. The other girls in school have been wearing bras for several years now. I just now got to the point that I need to start wearing one.

As I continue to dry my body, I can vividly recall my last birthday when Rose came into my bedroom holding a pink, shallow box with a white bow on top of it. She handed me the adorable present and said,

"It's time you started dressing like a teenager. Besides, I see a flower almost ready to bloom."

I tore into the package with so much excitement that I almost ripped the box in two. Inside was my very own training bra. It was beautifully made with white lace. A pale pink bow sat in the center of the cups. It was the best gift that I had ever received.

I still retain the humiliation that I felt the first time I wore that pretty bra. It was the night of my birthday, and I wore it underneath one of the drab, old-fashion dresses that Mother allows me to wear. I remember feeling so beautiful and grown up. It was the first time I felt that I was growing close to becoming an adult and getting away from this crazy mansion to start my own life. I descended down the stairs, and it seemed as though I floated into the dining room like I was being carried by a beautiful, fluffy cloud that helped me make my grand entrance for my birthday dinner. I sat down at the dinner table across from Daddy. He noticed the silly grin that was plastered across my face.

"Why is my birthday girl glowing?" he asked as he smiled back at me and gave me a playful wink.

Mother was seated next to me, and I recall feeling the sting of her eyes when she looked towards my chest. It seemed that she had x-ray vision and could see straight through my dress to see my new bra, even down to the pink bow. My smile quickly faded.

"Go straight to your room and wait for me there!" she commanded.

As I left the dining room, I could hear Daddy pleading with her not to ruin my birthday. He does not and never has had any control over Mother. It appears that even he fears her just as everyone else in the house does.

When Mother arrived to my bedroom, she ordered me to remove my dress. I unzipped the back of my dress and let it fall down my body until it found its way to the floor. Her eyes peered ominously at my lacy bra. I could see rage brewing like a smoldering volcano behind her dark eyes. Fear filled my soul, and my once happy demeanor had disappeared. Her long arms reached towards me, and in one quick motion her long fingers snatched the bra right off my body. I stood there almost naked and humiliated. My stomach ached from embarrassment like I was unclothed in front of a room full of strangers.

"Young ladies do not wear enticing underclothes such as this undergarment. If I ever catch you wearing clothes such as this again, I will be forced to wash away your sins! Now put your dress back on and come down to dinner!" she commanded as if she was God himself on judgment day. I don't think that God could be this cruel to his worst sinners.

The next afternoon when I arrived home from school, Mother summoned me to my bedroom and shoved a shopping bag toward me. I reached for the bag, but before I even got to peer into it she sternly said,

"These will serve your purpose."

In the bag were several new training bras. Not one was made of lace or even had a bow on it. They were plain, white, and made out of scratchy cotton material. They looked more sturdy than feminine. She could see my disappointment.

"Coral, let me explain something to you. When a young lady wears clothing that flatters her female body parts and exposes excessive skin, the devil himself jumps into the minds of perfectly moral men and forces them to sin against young girls. If you wear clothes that entice the devil, then, my dear, you are just as much of a sinner as the devil himself!" She preached this to me as she paced the floor. Her eyes and thoughts seemed distant. Was she even speaking to me?

Still now as I stand in front of the mirror and remember that day, I can hear Mother's words echo in my memory. I stare at my naked body and empty eyes, and I feel dirty as if I have committed some atrocious sin. I try to snap my mind out of my disturbing memories and begin to dry my body again. Unfortunately, I cannot escape them as I view the old scars and marks from earlier cleansing baths. I have received scalding baths as punishment for as long as I can recall, and they never get easier. When I was younger, I did not realize that this punishment ritual was out of the norm, but now that I am older, I know that her methods are abusive. I have also realized that fighting back only makes things worse. For now, I tolerate my treatment and wait until I can leave this prison that I call home.

I slip on my robe and open the door into my bedroom. Rose sits on the edge of my bed. When our eyes meet, I see small tears in the corner of her eyes begging for permission to be released down her cheeks, but as usual, Rose finds the strength to pull them back.

Rose has been my nanny all of my life. She also grew up at Ocean Point. Rose's family has worked for this house for generations. Her father died in the Great Blizzard of 1919, but her mother remained a maid in the house until the day she died. Rose has continued her family's loyalty to mine ever since. Although Rose has been a servant at Ocean Point for all of her life, I have never looked at her as a servant. Rose is my family.

I have always viewed Rose as beautiful. She is a slightly plump black woman. I do not know how old she is because she does not have one wrinkle on her face which makes her age deceptive. Her smile can brighten any room, and her belly-laughs are contagious. When she is happy, her eyes seem to dance with innocent joy.

I often expressed to Rose how I long to be her daughter instead of Mother's. She tells me not to wish to be someone that I am not and that I should always be proud of who I am. She quickly explains that if I was her daughter, I would be a Negro like her. Rose tells me that being a white woman in today's world presents many opportunities that Negroes don't have and that if I put my mind to it, the possibilities for my life are endless.

"Miss Coral, I told you not to speak to the delivery boy again. I told you the first time that if your mother caught you speaking with him in that manner that she would blow a gasket!" Rose pleads with me to understand. The tension that I hold is too much to handle.

"I am so tired of living like a recluse in this old house! I was not flirting with anyone! I was just being polite! I want to run away! Why does Mother hate me so much? Why can't I live like the other girls at my school? They have slumber parties, listen to records, and have boyfriends!" The words that I speak make me feel even worse. The reality of my life is sobering and hopeless.

"Baby Girl, I understand your frustration, but you are still a young girl and cannot survive on your own yet. For now, you must follow your mother's rules, or you will continue to suffer. Sometimes in life, Coral, you have to endure the bad times to appreciate the good. I know that this is not easy to do, but you are growing up so fast. Before you know it, a knight in shining armor will ride up to the front door and take you away from me. I bet that he will make you the happiest girl in the world!" Rose says this as if I am a princess trapped in a magical castle, not the haunted one that secludes me from the normal world. "Come over here and let me rub some aloe on those burns. You must get ready. Your father will be home very soon."

Rose motions me to join her on the bed. I do as she wishes and sit down beside her. As she rubs the cool ointment on my back, my frustrations simmer to know that Daddy is coming home. I always look forward to the small amounts of happiness that he brings home to me.

My father is a biologist, and he specializes in marine biology. I am not sure exactly what he does, but he spends most all of his time studying sea life and fossils. He spends weeks at a time on a research vessel, leaving me here to be raised by only my mother. Often, I get angry at him for being gone all of the time, but he loves his work. I want him to be happy. He also tells me that his work is very important, and he boasts that someday his work may help create medicines to cure diseases. I suspect that he drowns himself in his work to avoid Mother.

He is so engrossed in his love for the sea that I was named in honor of the ocean. Daddy has always told me that nothing is as exquisite as a coral reef, and that is why he named his lovely baby girl after something so beautiful. I was not given a middle name. My name is simply Coral Berringer. Mother hates my name. When I was younger, Daddy would recite the story about how he chose my name, and she would always viciously say,

"When something is as beautiful as a coral reef, it is proper to only view it. If someone is foolish enough to reach out and touch its sharp edges, they will get cut and carry the pain with them forever."

Daddy would glare at her with so much intensity and anger. Unlike Mother, Daddy is only bark with no bite. Mother would just stand strong resembling an intimidating bull, but instead of being aggravated by the red cape being waved in her face, she would remain unaffected. I always knew that there was more meaning to this statement than I was ready to understand.

Mother hates Daddy's profession more than my name. She says that his work is not profitable enough and refers to it as a senseless hobby. Rose says that my grandfather, William Taylor, was a brilliant businessman and grew his inherited wealth by dealing in stocks and bonds. A few years after I was born, Mother let most all of the staff go. Now there is only Rose, Gretchen the maid, and Rollins the chef. I question Rose on numerous occasions as to why Mother let the once fancy castle deteriorate. Rose just shrugs her shoulders and says,

"I stopped trying to figure this family out many years ago." I believe that Rose knows all of the secrets of this old house but is trying to protect me and what innocence I possess.

My home, Ocean Point Estate, covers almost ten acres and sits high atop bluffs overlooking the ocean in Newport, Rhode Island. The mansion is enormous. I don't even know how many rooms reside inside the walls of this historic home. Years ago, Mother shut off the west wing of the house and forbade anyone to wander into it. The kids at school tease me relentlessly by saying that my house is haunted. Mother always says that the kids are jealous of the Berringer fortune, but there is no logic to her defense. I attend an all-girl private school, and there is blue blood pumping through all of their veins.

I understand why they believe that Ocean Point is haunted. Mother has not had a gardener in so many years. The grass has grown so high that the grounds are covered with weeds. She keeps the iron gates to the driveway entrance locked to all but family and servants. I struggle to envision the estate as it once must have been, but I have suspicions that at one time this dim mansion that I call home was a host to many cherished celebrations.

Occasionally when I wander into the kitchen for a snack, I sometimes catch Rollins, our chef, pretending to make a feast fit for kings. He is a very colorful character, and I enjoy watching him as he gives orders to dozens of imaginary staff members. It seems as though he is talking to ghosts of the past. When I was younger, Rollins would sometimes let me help prepare dinner. We would pretend that we were cooking a feast for the queen of England. I have asked Mother multiple times what parties Rollins always talks about, but her reply is always the same.

"Do not listen to that old, senile fool. He lives in a fantasy world."

Although Mother is stern with her convictions, I still believe that at one time the sun did shine brightly through our windows, and Rollins did coordinate hundreds of parties at the Ocean Point Estate. Today though, the mansion is always dark and dismal. In some of the rooms, there are layers of dust covering the furniture, and the air is stagnating. In the summer, it is hard to breathe because the air is so thick. Gretchen is the only maid left other than Rose. It is impossible for Gretchen at her age to keep the entire house clean, so in addition to closing the west wing, Mother designates only certain rooms to be occupied.

Every year as I have gotten older, more rooms have been shut down and banished from our lives. I am fourteen years old, have lived in this creepy old house all my life, and still have not seen the entirety of it. Despite what Mother wants to believe, we are far from living as royalty. I have cautiously questioned everyone in the house about my family and the estate, but it seems as if everyone has signed a pact of silence with the devil himself not to speak of Ocean Point's now secretive history.

Rose finishes rubbing the soothing aloe on my raw skin and excuses herself so that I can dress for Daddy's arrival. I open my closet and pull out a periwinkle-blue dress. I really enjoy this dress because it is not as drab as most of my others. It also makes me feel close to Daddy because it is trimmed with gold anchors around the conservative neckline and bottom hem.

I pull the dress over my head and inspect my hair and face in the mirror. I wish that I could wear my hair in the popular styles that other girls my age have the luxury of sporting. I am only allowed to wear it conservatively straight or in ponytails as if I was ten years old and not allowed to have all the cool up-dos that are popular. Mother insists that I still look like a little girl. I do not understand her fear of me maturing into a woman.

I pull my hair into a ponytail with a white ribbon and then slip on a pair of white bobby socks. I search through my closet to find my favorite oxfords. It is difficult to put my shoes on because my feet are swollen from the boiling bath. Finally I manage to get them on, but I am unsure if I can walk or not because my feet are so tender. With much determination, I waddle out of my bedroom and down the hallway.

What I am about to discover will change my life forever.

The West Wing

As I near the stairs that descend into the foyer, I can hear Mother's towering voice. She is scolding Gretchen. Quickly and carefully, I duck behind the shadows so no one can see me. I can view Mother walking back and forth in front of Gretchen and Rose as they stand at attention as a soldier in the military would.

"I thought I made it very clear to everyone in this house that no one under any circumstances is to go into the west wing or the areas that I have designated off limits!" Mother sternly speaks as her witch-like eyes stare straight at Gretchen, signaling that she is the perpetrator. I feel so much sympathy for her as she hangs her head and remains silent. Rose then speaks in Gretchen's defense.

"Mrs. Berringer, Gretchen simply got turned around and did not realize where she was." Mother shifts her eyes quickly to Rose and then back to Gretchen.

"I do not want to hear any excuses! This is the very reason that I let the rest of the staff go. Do you think that I enjoy watching this once prestigious estate perish right underneath my nose? No! I just cannot allow the past to be stirred up. Let the dead stay dead! If you are getting too old and absent-minded to find your way around this house, then maybe it is time I find a more competent and loyal replacement for you," Mother bellows at her.

Gretchen lets out a small cry and then scurries to her quarters. I can't believe how cruel Mother can be. I have accepted the infernal manner in which Mother treats me, but Gretchen has been with this family for almost thirty years. She is growing blind and is very fragile. Mother glares at Rose with intensity and then stalks out of the room like an alley cat that has just won a cat fight. Rose stays in the foyer for a moment appearing helpless and defeated and then walks towards the servants' quarters. I am sure that she is going to console Gretchen.

I stay with my body squatted in the shadows, holding onto the staircase as Mother's words echo throughout my mind and settle in my stomach. They leave an aching emptiness. What is this hold that Mother has over everyone? How could there be so much past in this house of which I am unaware? It is as if I am living amongst strangers in some other family's house. Let the dead stay dead? Was she speaking of my grandparents, or is there something else that this mysterious old house is host to? Curiosity races through me like a thoroughbred races for its honor.

Slowly, I rise to my feet and tip toe down the hall past my bedroom and towards the west wing. I don't know if it is courage that pushes me there or if it is something bigger. My feet are throbbing, and it is difficult to walk without sounding like a carload of clumsy clowns. I try to pretend that I am a ballerina that is gracefully gliding across a stage. The closer I get to the west wing, the darker it grows. It begins to get so dark that I can barely see my hand in front of my face.

My body trembles with fear, and I keep thinking that if Mother catches me in the west wing, the severity of the punishment will cost my skin dearly. Despite my apprehension at this moment, I do not concern myself with the consequences that might befall me. All I know is that I am tired of secrets and desperately need to know the truth about this spooky, old castle and the people that lived here.

My vision worsens. It is so dim that I begin to feel the walls to help guide me deeper down the long hallway into the forbidden west wing. As my hands run across the century-old walls, my fingertips touch what seem to be oil paintings. The paintings must be portraits of my deceased ancestors. I wish with all of my fearful heart that I could see them. Maybe there would be answers painted on the canvases.

There are layers of dust, and I can feel spider webs with each step I take. The air is musty, and the scent of mildew fills the hallway. It seems that no one has been here in hundreds of years. Just as I decide that it is going to be impossible for me to uncover all of Ocean Point's history and secrets in this overwhelming darkness, the hallway takes a sharp right turn, and I can see a light ahead.

Panic overcomes me. I want to turn and run, but curiosity urges me forward. The closer I get to the glow ahead of me, the more I can see that it comes from a room. The door is partially open, and I see that it is a bedroom. Part of the bed is visible, and it is covered with a white antique bedspread. The light that I see is a ceramic lamp sitting on a nightstand. I cannot believe my own eyes. This part of the house is supposed to have been deserted for more than a decade.

There are so many questions dashing through my mind. I desperately want to charge right up to the door and demand answers from whoever is inside, but something in my inner spirit stops me. I take a few steps closer to the ghostly room that appears to have a spell cast on me, and I can hear my footsteps echo down the hallway. I reach down and gingerly remove my shoes from my relentlessly aching feet.

I stand in the hallway in my socks and try to move forward, but the marble floors are slick. I fear that if I try to move closer, I will fall and frighten whatever is inside. As I balance myself against the dirty, old walls, I wait in hopes that I might catch a glimpse of the person inside. I can hear music playing from the bedroom that seems to be some sort of classical piece, and the haunting tune accelerates my curiosity.

Suddenly, I see a shadow travel against the walls and ceiling. I am petrified, and my legs tremble. The shadow is giant, and it is exaggerated by the flickering light bulb of the lamp. I can literally hear my knees knocking together. I can see the hallway much better with the light from the bedroom. It illuminates the walls. I now view one of the oil paintings that I could only feel before. The painting is of a man, and I cannot take my eyes off of him. He is a very handsome man about my father's age or maybe younger. There is so much resemblance between this man and my father that it is eerie. The man in the painting stares straight back at me, and it sends chills straight up the back of my neck. There is a plaque underneath the painting. It is most likely the name of this familiar man, but I do not dare to try to read it by moving closer.

Despite the shadowy figure moving around in the room in front of me, I cannot remove my eyes from this portrait. It is probably of a man whose blood pumps through my veins. Even amidst the extreme terror that I feel, anger finds a way into my soul. I wish that my ancestor in the painting could talk to me and tell me all about Ocean Point and the history that it harbors. I feel more cheated out of a normal life than ever before.

Instantly, the hallway is dark again. When I turn and look towards the open door, I can see that someone has walked in front of the light and blankets a shadow over the forbidden hallway. It is too dim to make out the mysterious figure, and I am so stunned by what my eyes are seeing that I cannot move. I wish to be brave and demand answers from the person standing in the doorway, but I am afraid to be seen. The presence appears for only moments, but as I am hunched in the hallway gripped to the walls of the west wing and trying not to make a sound, it seems like an eternity. All I can hear is my own heartbeat. It pounds so loudly that it could wake up my past family that once strolled down this hallway from the dead.

Abruptly, the bedroom door slams shut. It startles me, and I jump clear off of the floor. When my feet land on the hard, marble floor, I can actually hear every bone in my body reconnect. The music has ended. The only noise left is my thundering heartbeat and my rapid breaths. I am left alone in the darkness with oil paintings of dead ancestors and no revelations of my family's past.

I stand in the west wing and try to collect my thoughts and fears. I want to go further, but something deep inside me forbids my feet to move forward. The spell that I was entranced by is now broken. The pitch black hallway ends my investigation, and I know that by now someone must be trying to find me. If Mother learns that I am in the west wing, she will probably peel off my skin with her boney fingers. I bend over to put my shoes back onto my feet, and I see a quick flash of light hit the wall in front of me. It appears to be a flashlight. I can hear faint footsteps coming towards me, slowly getting louder and closer. Is it Mother looking for me, or is it the unknown presence in the doorway?

Terror envelops in me, and I begin to run. I do not have enough time to put my shoes on, and it is difficult to run on the slippery, dust-covered hallway floors with just socks on. With each running stride, I slide and can barely keep my balance. I have no vision of where I am running, and I keep bumping into a wall or falling on the floor. Whoever is behind me surely hears my every stumbling movement.

The hallway seems endless. I am not sure if my legs or heart is racing faster. I feel tears begin to well in my eyes. I finally see a light ahead, but everything is blurred from my tears. I pray that the glow that I see is a light from one of the designated rooms that I am allowed to be in and not that of the flashlight that I just saw deep in the west wing. My body begins to sting almost unbearably as my scalded skin stretches across my muscles and bones. Just as it seems that I can run no further, I see my bedroom. I reach for my door knob. As I grasp the brass knob, my sweaty palms just slide uselessly around it, and I cannot maintain a grip. After what countless attempts, the door finally opens. I stumble inside and slam the door behind me.

I lean with my back pushed against the door. I try to push the whole world out of my bedroom. I labor to catch my breath. My stomach is queasy. I can taste the dust from the abandoned west wing on my tongue. I attempt to regain my composure, but I cannot shake the vision of the man in the painting. My anxiety is heightened. At this moment, I know that my life will never be complete until I uncover my family's past no matter how disturbing it may be.

My dress is covered in grime. I rush to my dresser mirror and try to clean up before someone sees me. My face is so dirty that it looks like I have been working in a coal mine. The white ribbon in my hair has become dingy from the dust that hangs in the stale air of the west wing, and it now looks gray. A small spider web drapes from my hair and hangs in front of my right eye.

I dash around my bedroom removing all traces of the west wing from my timorous body. I tear my soiled dress from my body as if it is on fire and rush to the bathroom. I run a sink of warm water and collect a wash cloth from the closet. I scrub my face, neck, and legs, but no matter how franticly I clean myself, my thoughts continue to wander to the shadowy figure that I saw. Was it a ghost? Was it my mother?

After cleaning the grime off of my face and body, I return to my bedroom. As I enter the room wearing only my underclothes, Rose stands in the middle of the room holding my filthy dress. Alarm ceases my thoughts, and my mind searches for a lie to satisfy Rose. I look at her disappointed face, and I cannot lie.

"Coral Berringer, please tell me why your dress is so dirty." Rose acts as if she wants me to tell her a fib as the evidence of my disobedience hangs from her fingertips. I have always trusted Rose, and I believe that I can share with her my new revelation about this frightful house.

"Oh Rose, you're not going to believe what I saw!" I blurt out with excitement. Her eyes narrow, and her displeasure blankets my enthusiasm until I am silent. I begin to gaze at the floor in shame. She grabs my arm firmly and pulls me in front of the mirror.

"Dear child of God, I want you to look at your skin. Those scars may never go away. Your mother is very serious about her rules, and if she knew that you were in the west wing, I do not know if you could withstand the trauma that you would have to suffer as punishment," Rose sternly pleads with me.

"But Rose, I saw…" Before I can finish my sentence she intervenes.

"Listen to me Coral! You are too young to carry the pain of this family in your precious heart. Let me protect you for as long as possible. I know that you are growing up, but you are still not ready to understand what your family is all about. Please stay out of the west wing!" Rose releases my arm, and her expression softens. She cups my cheek with her hand. "Make yourself beautiful again. Your father is due home any moment."

She then turns and walks out of my room carrying my filthy dress as if she is going to get rid of the evidence that would convict me for life. Even though Rose is trying to discourage me from finding out the truth, her speech about being too young to carry the pain of the family proves that there is more to this estate and the Berringers than I have ever been told. I realize that Rose is trying to protect me, but I am mature enough to know the truth and even more. Somehow, I will find out all of the secrets that this mansion whispers in the night.

I change the ribbon in my hair and discard the stained one in the trash. In my closet of dull dresses, I search for the cheerful, little dress that I made in sewing class. I have been successful in keeping it hidden from Mother. Today, I feel brave and decide to take my chances. I spot the yellow dress and pull it away from all of the mundane colors that surround it. I hold the dress at arm's length with pride. The dress has small, white daisies scattered across the yellow fabric as if they are growing in the sunshine. Sliding my body into the dress, I inspect myself and hope that this joyful dress will conceal the horror that cultivates inside my consciousness from the unexplainable experience that I just escaped.

As I near the stairs that descend into the foyer, I can hear Daddy's voice. This wonderful sound makes me hurry down the stairs. Before he notices I am there, I see that he is talking to Mother, and the tone of his voice is cold and harsh. I reach the bottom of the staircase. He sees me, and a smile grows across his handsome face.

He is the most attractive man that I have ever seen. Someday, I want to marry someone just like him. His time spent at sea gives his face and arms a golden tan. His tanned face makes his eyes look even bluer than usual. Daddy brings the ocean back to me in his eyes. His wind-blown hair seems to be lighter from the bright summer sun. He wears a light blue shirt and khaki pants. The vision of him standing in front of me is exactly what I need right now.

"There's my girl, Coral," Daddy says as he opens his arms for me to run into his embrace.

I begin to run to him, but just as I get close enough to fall into the safety of his arms, Mother steps between us. I run straight into her stomach. Her body stands unmovable and unaffected by our collision. I look up at Mother's majestic physique, and then my eyes wander to her face. Her expression is rigid, and she stares straight down into my eyes as if she is staring into my soul and sees a demon straight from Hell. My first thought is that she knows that I was in the west wing, and I begin to mentally prepare myself for the punishment that Rose warned me about. My palms become moist from nervousness, and I look to Daddy for help. His smile has faded, and he seems confused.

"What is this dreadful garment you are wearing?" Mother questions me. The lump in my throat from her intimidation disappears, and I feel irritated as to how petty her concern is. Does this woman I call Mother have any mercy?

"This is the dress I made in sewing class at school," I answer with no hesitation.

"I do not remember giving you permission to buy this God-awful material, and the length is too short for a child of your age," Mother scolds as her eyes search the foyer for Rose to receive an explanation.

"I did not purchase the material. The school provided the fabric, and I chose the most conservative piece so that you would approve," I lie to her with impressive conviction to protect Rose. She purchased the stylish material.

"Margret, you are being ridiculous! This is a lovely dress," Daddy says as he wedges his body between Mother and me. He touches the bright yellow material and admires each white daisy that is scattered on the dress. "Coral did a fine job at sewing this masterpiece, and I believe that we should praise her talent."

His compliment brings a smile to my face and makes my heart want to melt. As I giggle, my eyes flirt with his. He then extends his arms around my shoulders and gives me a tight hug. When he embraces me, I let out a small shrill from the quick surge of pain caused by my freshly injured skin. He quickly releases me from his arms and looks at me with tender eyes. I look away to hide my embarrassment. He suspiciously turns my back towards him and unzips my dress. He can see the burn marks on my back. He realizes what has happened. If only I could show him my womanly parts. He might would get me out of this nightmarish mansion. I can see outrage brewing in his remarkably blue eyes.

"This has got to stop! Your actions are insane!" Daddy screams at Mother so loudly that it startles me. She looks at him as if he has not said a word.

"Joseph, you and Coral must retire to the dining room. It is time for dinner."

Daddy zips my dress back up and stands as strong and straight as Mother. He walks towards her and stays only inches from her. He stares straight into her eyes.

"If I see another mark on Coral, I will hold you and the demon that you speak of, which does not live in Coral but in the west wing, personally responsible, and you will pay!" He says this in a whisper as if he does not want me to hear, but I hear every word. He turns toward me and says,

24

"We are going out for dinner."

I am so impressed with the strength and boldness that he has just displayed. Mother does not even blink while hearing his stern threat. Daddy continues to stare straight at her until she becomes bored with the confrontation and leaves the room. He crouches down and gently puts his hands on my shoulders.

"Coral, are you alright? I will take you to the doctor if you want me to. I am truly sorry," he says this with so much sorrow in his voice that I want to comfort him.

"I am fine. All I want to do is spend the evening with you," I say with a loving smile.

"When did my little girl become so grown up?" He gives me a quick peck on my cheek. Daddy stands and regains his composure. "Hey, do you feel like walking?" he asks as he opens the door and we head outside.

"Oh Daddy, I would love it!" I shrill with enthusiasm.

I am so elated in anticipation of walking on the ocean sand with my daddy and the untamed wind blowing through my hair. As we descend into the backyard towards the ocean, my thoughts keep echoing Daddy's words. What did he mean by the demon that lives in the west wing? Is there really a ghost or monster after all? Are all the girls at school right about my house being haunted? A chill races up my spine and settles on the back of my neck. How will I sleep tonight knowing that there is a demon in the west wing that lives only footsteps from my bedroom?

I want to share with him what happened today and what I saw, but I do not want to make him unhappy again and possibly ruin our night together. I decide to keep my secret for now; it's only fair considering everyone else in the house has secrets. I push the bad thoughts out of my mind, and my soul begins to rejoice as we walk down the path in our overgrown lawn. The lawn is so unkempt that most of the weeds are taller than Daddy. I imagine what a delightful place this must have been when Mother was a young girl. I envision green grass, gardens full of colorful flowers, shrubbery lined paths, and huge trees to climb and escape underneath.

As I walk through the neglected lawn, I think about how easy it would be to get lost in all of these weeds. As we near the ocean, we pass another path which appears to be deliberately preserved. Daddy momentarily pauses in front of the path and stares down the narrow passageway. How had I never seen this before?

"What's down there?" I question him.

"Nothing, honey," he says without breaking his gaze.

His eyes are fixated and I can sense that his thoughts are distant as if he is in another time. I know that he is not telling me the truth. This path is a clue to this family's undisclosed history waiting on the other side of the overgrown weeds. I plan to travel down this path soon.

We tread closer to the ocean, and I can smell the fresh air. I can hear the waves crashing against the rigid mounds of rocks. Finally, all the misery of the mansion is behind me, and I am in full view of the ocean and all of its majesty. The sun slowly sets into the horizon, and the rays of sunlight struggle through the clouds. They light the sky with pink, purple, blue, and orange streaks. It feels as if I am looking at a painting. I would give anything to have the freedom to sit on this beautiful beach and paint every day.

Daddy reaches down and takes off his loafers. He encourages me to do the same, and I follow his lead. I love the feeling of the brown grains surrounding my toes. My feet become embedded in the sand. I wiggle my toes as the warm sand surrounds them. The wind blows my hair toward my face, and the cool evening air that encircles my body feels good on my battered skin. I push the hair out of my face and deeply breathe in the moist air. I feel so alive on the beach. I wish I had the freedom to spend more time here and experience the beautiful sunsets.

Our journey begins on the edge of the ocean where the waves chase our feet as they retreat back into the water. As we walk away from the estate, I look back over my shoulder at Ocean Point. It sits high on bluffs overlooking the ocean. I am not sure if it is my imagination, but the mansion seems dark as if a permanent black cloud hovers over the castle-like structure. I do not blame my classmates for saying that my house is haunted. As the years go by, and after what I have seen and heard in the last few days, I am beginning to believe that the rumors just may be true. Looking at the estate and thinking about the west wing makes me shiver. Daddy notices my shivering and asks if I am cold. We both silently stare at Ocean Point, and he recognizes what is giving me chills. I can sense the uneasiness that he also feels when looking at the overpowering estate.

We stroll down the beach until we stumble upon a quaint café not far from the ocean. I order a cheeseburger and fries. This is a treat. Mother only allows Rollins to prepare healthy meals. Daddy and I talk for what seems like hours. He tells me about his ocean adventures. I listen with all my attention focused on him. I become so interested in his stories that I almost forget about what happened earlier in the west wing. We talk and laugh. I wonder if this is how kids my age really live. Jealously seeks me out, and I struggle to chase away the negative feelings. I wish I could enjoy my night of freedom away from the imprisoning mansion and the cruel fingertips of my mother.

As the night draws to an end, we head back towards Ocean Point. Silence and dread surrounds us as if we are in a funeral march. The moon shines down onto the water, and its reflection casts small streams of light throughout the water, and it looks like crystals line the ocean floor. I cannot stop thinking about Mother. I want to hate her for how she treats me and denies me of being happy. She wants to keep me trapped in youth and held captive in a house that only has malice for me. No matter how cruel she is to me, I still long for her companionship. I daydream what it would be like to walk with her along the beach and hold her hand as she tells me stories of how she and Daddy met and fell in love. I do not remember her ever kissing or hugging me. The hunger for affection that I once craved has never been fed and has left me with a hollow feeling that I have learned to accept.

The closer we get to Ocean Point, the more hopeless I begin to feel. I dread the reality of being delivered to a mansion full of misery and ghosts from the past. As we approach the estate, I lose all maturity that Daddy has praised me for earlier. It seems that one of the demons that Mother always preaches about takes over my body, and I begin to sob uncontrollably.

"Coral, what is wrong?" Daddy asks as he kneels down to take me in his arms.

"I don't want to go back to that creepy old house! It is full of old ghosts, and the sun never shines through the windows. Mother doesn't love me, and I am so lonely! Please take me with you, Daddy!" I plead with him as I try to catch my breath from the sudden possession that has upset me.

"As much as I want you with me, I can't take you. You need to be in school and have a stable life. I know that your mother seems hard on you, but there are some things that you are too young to understand. I know it is difficult for you to believe, but she believes she is protecting you."

How can he say these things? Doesn't he see my skin? What is everybody protecting me from? I am old enough to understand. I deserve to know. This is my life! I feel so much rage and frustration. I begin to sprint towards the ocean. I want to escape from Ocean Point, Mother, and my life. The evening wind wildly takes control of my hair, and I can taste the ocean salt on my lips. Tears that stream down my face dry on my cheeks as I race to the water.

My feet touch the water, and I begin to run faster. I want to swim away from my cruel world. Silently, I pray that God will make me a beautiful sea creature and allow me to swim until I find peace and happiness. I want to swim to a place where no one can ever hurt me again. Waves begin to roll in towards the shore and crash against my body. I am surrounded in water, and I battle with the strength of the waves to descend farther into the ocean and farther away from my reality. The ocean salt begins to penetrate my recently wounded skin. The pain becomes overwhelming, and I have no fight left. I fall helplessly to my knees. The pain increasingly gets worse, and I begin to let out blood-curdling screams.

Daddy charges into the water and pulls my limp body out of the waves that have gained control over my exhausted, petite frame. He begins to run to Ocean Point with me in his arms. I can feel the weeds prick my face and arms as he races through the overgrown gardens. The pain from the saltwater has not let up, and I continue to scream out in agony. We arrive at the back door, and Daddy begins to shout for Rose. Rose quickly arrives.

"Oh dear God, what has happened?" she asks in a panic.

"Call an ambulance!" Daddy directs Rose. She rushes to the telephone and picks up the receiver. Mother appears next to Rose and takes the phone out of her hand.

"I will call Doctor Saunders," she announces.

"Rose, it burns! Please make it stop!" I cry out so loudly that I am sure the ghost in the west wing can hear me.

Rose instructs Daddy to take me to the bathroom. We arrive, and he lays me gently into the bathtub with my cheerful, yellow dress clinging to my damaged skin. It seems that even the daisies on my dress are distressed and are wilting. It all seems like a nightmare, but it is my reality. As my limp soaks in the cool water, the pain begins to ease. Doctor Saunders arrives and tells Rose to get me out of the bathtub. She helps me stand, and we remove my clothes slowly and wrap my trembling body in a towel. Daddy carries me and lays me gently down on the bed. The doctor examines my skin, and I can see that he is inflamed with anger. I am so exhausted that the humiliation of this intimate examination does not even bother me. I just want the pain to stop.

Doctor Saunders is a personal friend of my mother's, and he is the only doctor I have ever seen. He has seen these types of injuries on me my whole life. I recall when I was younger, and he would make a last-minute house call because the punishments went too far. I always thought that he was angry with me for being bad, but now that I am older, I realize he was disappointed in Mother.

He gives me a shot in my bottom to help numb the pain. I almost immediately feel sleepy. I lay in my bed naked and defeated. The day's events swirl in my head and get jumbled. I hear his footsteps travel out of the room, and I can faintly hear him talking with Mother in the hallway outside my bedroom door.

"Margret, this is the last time I am going to tell you that you are doing permanent damage to that girl! I have always been sympathetic to you for your misfortunes, but this is going too far! I could lose my license for not reporting this abuse to the authorities! I only come here because I know that poor girl will go untreated if I do not. You must stop this insanity. She is not the one you should punish!" He sounds very stern.

My eyes become so heavy that I give into the darkness that has crept its way into my mind.

My Scars

I open my eyes, and my room is very dark. The curtains are tightly shut, and I am not sure if it is day or night. I reach for my bedside lamp. I turn on the light and quickly reach for my clock. It reads that that it is four in the afternoon. I cannot believe how long I have been asleep. I almost slept the entire day away. Lying in bed, I still feel groggy. My body is moist from sweat, and my cotton nightgown clings to my skin. Rose must have dressed me after I fell asleep. My eyelids feel swollen, and I am exhausted. My thoughts are scattered, and my body aches.

Suddenly, my bedroom door abruptly opens, and my heart seems to skip a beat. My sleepy eyes try to focus on the doorway, but my body seems to be frozen from fear as I recall the frightful discoveries from yesterday. I cannot make out who is standing in my doorway. Is it the demon from the west wing that Daddy spoke of coming to get me? The figure steps into the room. My eyes finally focus, and I am relieved that it is Rose.

"I am sorry I startled you. You look like you have seen a ghost," Rose says to me. "How are you feeling this afternoon?"

"I am starving," I tell her.

"I will have Rollins make you up something real special," Rose says with compassion in her big, brown eyes.

I sit up in the bed and rub the sleep out of my eyes. Rose hands me a tube of ointment and tells me to apply it to my burns. She leaves the room. I get out of the comfort of my bed and force my stiff body to move. I go to my bedroom mirror and pull my nightgown over my head. I stare at my naked body in the mirror. I see fresh burn marks on top of old scars. Most of the marks are around my thighs and breasts, so luckily no one ever sees them. I cannot help but feel sad when I think about the day that I get married and how my husband might feel about my body. When I look at myself, I see ugliness. I cannot help but believe that my husband won't be attracted to my womanly parts.

In Ocean Point's study, I remember that there used to be old paintings of slightly overweight women that were almost completely naked. I used to look at their beautiful skin, and I could see how irresistible they must have been to men. I long to have an unblemished bosom like the women in the paintings. One afternoon, Mother caught me admiring the paintings. The next day, she took every single one of them down. She scolded me, explaining that the paintings were intended for being viewed as fine art and to exhibit the wealth of the family. She said that I had unclean thoughts when I viewed the half-clothed models. I have never seen those beautiful paintings again. They are probably buried in the west wing with the rest of the family's past.

I gently apply the cream to my burns, and my tender skin reacts to the slightest graze of my fingertips. I cannot stop thinking about the previous day's events. My mind repeats all of the things I heard. The man in the painting still haunts me. I can close my eyes and see every brush stroke that eventually became the picture of this unknown man. I know that I will not find peace until the truth of this house and family is unveiled. The secretive nature of everyone's actions and the mysteries of the past consume me. I begin to plan an investigation of my own. No one will tell me the truth, so I will have to find the answers by myself. I decide to start with the overgrown garden that seemed to seduce Daddy. I am not sure my aching body can take another round in the darkness of the west wing.

I get a clean nightgown out of my dresser drawer and slip it over my head. As the fabric finds its way down my body, the material slightly sticks to my skin from the cream. I straighten out my nightgown and put on a robe. Rose knocks on the door as she enters my room with a tray of food in her hands.

"Little Lady, jump back into that bed so you can eat this delicious food that Rollins made for you." She motions me towards my bed.

"Rose, would it be okay if I ate on the sun porch? I need some sunlight."

"Sure, let's get you settled on the porch." She walks onto the porch.

As I sit on the sun porch, I can hear the ocean crash against the rocks and smell the fresh ocean air through the screen of the oversized bay windows. The cheerful ocean wind plays with my hair as the cool breeze caresses my face. I cannot see the ocean, sand, or beautiful sky because the lawn is so overgrown that it obstructs the view. I am sure that at one time it was a spectacular view.

I sit at the small café-style table and devour my food without manners. My mind drifts to the enchanting, overgrown weeds. I wonder what secret must be hidden in these weeds. I imagine a tale of fantasy and drama with wild stories of deceit, love, sex, and maybe even murder. I am so caught up in my runaway thoughts and imagination that I do not even hear Daddy come up the steps from the side porch.

"You look a million miles away," he says to me with a smile across his handsome face.

"Where were you Daddy?" I ask with obvious suspicion.

I want him to tell me that he had been in the garden. His guilty eyes seem nervous as they dart around the sun porch, and he cannot make eye contact with me.

"I took a walk on the beach. It's a beautiful day," he answers.

I cannot help but notice he has on dress shoes and socks and not a morsel of sand has attached itself on him. He always wears loafers when he goes for walks on the beach. Even Daddy is lying to me now. Maybe he always has, and I was just too naive to see it. I deliberately look at his feet so he will know that I can see through his lies. I need to start demanding respect for the truth. My disappointed eyes stare at my empty plate.

"Well it looks like you cleaned your plate out. You know what that means don't you?" he says. I do not respond. "That means I can take you out for ice cream."

He seems to be having a conversation alone. I am gradually beginning to lose respect and admiration for him. First he lets Mother abuse me, and then he lies to me and acts like nothing has happened. I rise from the table and pick up my dirty plate.

"No thank you, I just want to go back to my room. I am not eight years old anymore," I say with a sarcastic tone and walk away before he has a chance to respond.

It breaks my heart to feel so much anger for Daddy, but I cannot manage how I feel. I even surprised myself by turning down a chance to leave this prison that I call home. I just know that I do not have the energy to hear anymore lies or play "happy little family." I arrive at the kitchen, and Rollins is hard at work preparing dinner. He sings and mumbles out loud. Usually, I would stay for a while to talk to him and listen to all of his stories, but today I do not have the patience and will not enjoy Rollins's quirky humor. On my way out of the kitchen, he notices me.

"Hello there, beautiful! You know you only have a couple of weeks before your big day. I have the menu almost complete for your approval," he says with a jolly voice.

"What big day, Rollins?" I ask him. He squints his eyes and cocks his head to the side as if he is confused.

"Well, it's Master Joseph's and..." Before he can finish his sentence,

Mother charges into the room and interrupts him.

"Rollins, you are such a senile, old fool. We are not having any parties or events. You are not feeding any kings or queens and certainly not the Kennedys." Her vicious words wound Rollins. He bows his head and looks ashamed. "Coral, what are you doing down here? Has Rose given you your medicine yet?" she asks as she stares at me. Her cold, ruthless lack of concern for me is expected but still hurtful.

"She gave me the ointment," I reply.

"No, you need to take the pain medicine," she tells me.

"I really don't need the pain medicine. The pain has become tolerable," I answer.

"That is nonsense. Dr. Saunders prescribed it, so you must finish the bottle," she commands.

Mother just wants me to stay unconscious from the pain medicine. I think she secretly hopes that it will kill me. I find Rose and take my medication. Afterwards, I crawl back into bed. I lie in bed and think about what Rollins had said. What is in a couple of weeks? Who did he think I was? From now on, everything I hear and see is a clue. Eventually, I will piece this puzzle together, but for now I will sleep. The small, white pills that I am forced to take crawl through my system and conquer my will to stay awake.

I sleep for almost two weeks. Mother keeps me sedated until the prescription runs out. My body seems weak even though I sleep for so long. I would wake up long enough to eat, use the restroom, occasionally shower, and then go back to bed. I almost sleep the entire summer away.

All of the pills are gone, and I hope that today I can stay awake. I roll out of my bed, and my stomach growls as if a lion resides inside of me. I go to my bathroom to take a shower. I so wish I could soak in a bathtub to relax, but I cannot bear a bath. Every time I take one it brings back the torturous memories of Mother's punishments. I can never imagine finding the peace to enjoy a nice, long bath.

The water is warm, and it feels good as it trickles down my body. I notice that my skin seems to be healing well. It is discolored, but it definitely seems to be improving. I notice that I have lost weight over the last few weeks. It discourages me because I am already so thin. I want to be curvy like the other girls my age. I get out of the shower and find Rose in my room changing my bed linens. On my closet door hangs a dress for me to wear.

"Good morning, Princess," she says. "I sure have missed you. I am so glad you have finished all of your medicine."

"Rose, Mother has drugged me for two weeks just over some burns. Do you really believe that is normal?" I ask this in a catty fashion with my hand propped on my hip.

"Little Lady, your mother is my boss. I do not have the authority to question her actions." She defends herself with an explanation of the tolerance she has for Mother's behavior. I know that she doesn't have a choice.

"Come on, Rose. I am tired of all of this. I am not a little girl anymore!"

"Well, I knew this would happen eventually," she states.

"What would happen?" I question her blank statement.

"All teenagers rebel against their parents, but Coral, your mother is not a normal parent. You don't know all that you are dealing with. Please be patient until your knight comes for you."

I stand in utter amazement. Rose wants to think that some dashing, handsome man is going to come and save me. Mother will never allow me to date or even meet anyone. Does she believe some random stranger is going to see me through the window and come rescue me? I go to an all-girl school, and I am not even allowed to leave the house unsupervised. I roll my eyes and shake my head in disgust.

"Is Rollins in the kitchen? I am starving," I ask as I begin to get dressed.

"Rollins has not been feeling well. He is in his quarters. I have been doing all of the cooking. I saved you a plate. I will get that heated up for you." She moves towards the door with all of my sheets bundled in her arms for the laundry.

"Hey Rose, do you think that Mother's master plan is to drug everyone in the house until she kills us off so she can be all alone?" I ask with sarcasm.

Rose leaves the room. I have defeated her with my abrupt honesty. I get up to go downstairs. As I descend down the stairway, I glance around the drab house and realize that it might not have been so bad to sleep most of my summer break away. At least when I am asleep I feel at peace. I enter the dining room, and Rose already has my food on the table. I sit down at the giant, formal table and begin to eat. I wonder who all has eaten meals here and if they were as lonely and sad as I feel. Once again, my mind goes to the thoughts of the past and inspires my curiosity. I feel if I can understand this family's past, then maybe I will understand my present. I need the darkness that I exist in to make sense to me.

Rose enters the room in hopes of approval of her culinary skills. I have always enjoyed her meals more than Rollins's. Mother does not think that Rose's creations are suitable for the Berringer family. Rose calls her food "soul cooking." She tells stories of her mother teaching her how to cook. Her face always lights up when she speaks of the time she had with her mother. It is as if her mind and thoughts go to another place, a happy place. I realize that her life has been difficult, but I still feel jealous of the family that she knew and the love they must have shared.

"Rose, I love your mashed potatoes," I say, feeling regretful about how I spoke to her earlier. A smile grows across her chubby face.

"Good, we need to put some meat on those bones. You are so thin, and men like a woman with curves," she says as she playfully strikes a model's pose. I giggle at her silliness and then ask,

"Where is Mother?"

"Your mother and father are both on business trips. I have to go to town and do some grocery shopping. Would you like to go with me? I will let you get that box of cupcakes you like as long as you promise me to eat all of them before your mother returns."

I almost answer yes. I would love to get out of this house for a little while, but just before the word rolls off my tongue, I realize that I would have the whole house to myself. I see it as a good opportunity to start my investigation.

"No, thank you. I have a book that I started a month ago that I would really like to finish," I lie to her. Rose sees the excitement in my face and questions my motives to stay behind.

"I see the mischief in your pretty, little face. I will let you stay behind if you promise me that you will not go into the west wing." She speaks firmly.

"I promise I will not go into the west wing," I say. I am not lying to her. I do not plan to go in the west wing. My next mission is the garden.

I return to my room. My bedroom is the only place in this house that does not feel like a foreign country to me. Rose says that this has been my room since I was a baby. She used to sleep in my bed, and there was a baby bed underneath the window that overlooks the ocean. Rose says that if I was fussy and she could not calm me down, she would lay me in my crib and open the window. She says that as soon as I heard the ocean waves and the beautiful sounds of the night, I would drift off to sleep like an angel.

My room is actually very beautiful. It still has a hint of a nursery even though the crib and baby toys are gone. The walls are painted a very light pink, and above each window there are hand painted bluebirds flying with their wings spread wide. There are white, fluffy clouds scattered across the walls, and on the ceiling there are scattered painted stars. Along the base boards and half way up the walls, there are beautiful painted white flowers that seem so realistic that you can smell them if you close your eyes. My bed is a white, iron canopy bed with bright pink material hanging from the poles, and it is covered with an antique, white lace. It has a few grape juice stains scattered across the expensive material. Rose tried to get the stains out so Mother would not see them and punish me, but no matter how hard she tried they were there for good, just like my burns.

I only get scalding baths as punishment when I have indecent thoughts or actions. My punishment for grape juice stains was that for a week I had to sleep on the marble floor with no covers or a pillow. I remember that week like it was yesterday even though I was only six. It was in the middle of the winter. The winters in Rhode Island are very cold, and usually the ground is covered with snow for months. Our house is not very heat efficient, and even in a warm bed it can still be cold. Mother says that every punishment I receive will have a lesson in it to make me a strong, respectable woman. The lesson in that punishment was to appreciate what is given to you and that you should take care of fine things. I think that is an important lesson, but when you are six you should be allowed to have accidents.

The only lesson that punishment taught me is that when I grow up I want to live somewhere warm. I would fantasize and draw pictures of sunny skies and warm beaches for years after that. One day, Mother walked into my room while I was drawing one of my masterpieces. She peered down at my happy portfolio of tropical themes.

"Coral, these are quite some pictures you are drawing," she said as she started going through each of my pictures one by one. "Where are these beaches supposed to be?" she asked as she studied each one.

I was so proud of my artwork. I was even more proud that she was interested in what I was doing. I spread all of the pictures across the bed and began describing each tropical paradise to her.

"This one is where I am going to live when I grow up, Florida. This one is Hawaii. This one is Jamaica." I went to each picture with pride and pointed as I explained each detail.

Mother silently listened, and when I finished, she snatched them off the bed in one swift motion and tore them in half. As I witnessed my work get destroyed, the pain in my chest was so strong that I then knew where the term "heartbroken" came from.

"You need to quit living in a delusional world, Coral Berringer! You are a Berringer, and it is your duty to take care of this magnificent home that my family worked so hard for you to live in. I will raise you to be a dedicated, respectable woman capable to run this home and business so that when I am dead and gone our family and house will live on!" she yelled at me as she stared straight into my tearful eyes, completely unmoved by my pain. "Get those tears out of your eyes! You are no longer a baby! It was bad enough that I had to listen to you cry when you were a baby, but now you are too old to cry. Strong women don't cry!" she lectured me.

I did not fully understand what Mother's message was, and I really still don't understand. I knew at that moment that she did not care about me, and at that point, I realized I had no control over my future. It was best just to wipe my tears and nod my head, and I have been doing that ever since. I keep my dreams of traveling the world and painting beautiful masterpieces all to myself.

As I sit in my window sill, I cannot help but be confused. Mother must have loved me at one time to have such a beautiful room specially painted for me. I wonder what I did to make her hate me so much. How could I be surrounded by such beautiful artwork but cannot make my own?

Where the Children Sleep

Rose finally leaves. I anxiously wait, as I watch the long, black sedan pull out of our circular driveway and through the iron gates. I want to hurry to my next investigation, but my mind tells me to be patient and wait until the gates close. My patience begins to wither, and my wait seems to last forever. In reality, it is only minutes. The gates finally close, and the car is well on its way down the road. I feel a mixture of fear and excitement. I attempt to talk the fear out of my head by rationalizing that the garden cannot be as bad as the west wing. I argue with my fear by telling it that I will be outside with the friendly sun shining down on me, and Mother Nature's beautiful creations will be under my feet and guiding me to the answers that I long for. I have no idea what the gardens have planned for me.

I rush down the staircase so hastily that several times I lose balance, and my feet slide down the stairs. I grip the railing for concern of tumbling down the massive, wooden stairs. I reach the bottom but fail to see Gretchen coming around the corner of the foyer. I almost run straight into our frail maid. I startle her, and she lets out a small scream. She begins to move as quickly as she can to get away from me. I reach out and lay my hand on her should in an attempt to calm her and let her know it is me. Old age has given her the ailment of poor vision. I am sure that she does not realize who almost plowed right over her.

"I didn't see anything. I promise! I won't tell. It's none of my business," she says in a frightened voice, attempting to shield her eyes to prove her honesty.

I stand in confusion as the tiny elderly woman tries to escape. Is Gretchen psychic and aware that I am planning to break a house rule? I pause for a moment and realize that this is impossible.

"Gretchen, it's okay. It's me, Coral," I say, trying to comfort her.

"Ma'am, I apologize. It's just the older you get, the more you look like your mother."

She leaves the room, and I shake my head and laugh to myself. She really is losing her vision to think I am Mother. I really do not blame anyone who suffers from anxiety in this house with Mother as our master. Her ludicrous rules and constant preaching of the devil living among us is enough to put anyone on edge.

It makes me upset to think about the condition that Gretchen is now in. Watching her decline in front of me brings gloom into my heart. She has worked in this house my entire life and many years before I was even born. I have fond memories of the times we spent together when I was younger, as was she. It does not seem like that long ago that she was a spry, little lady and not the confused and weak person that Father Time has created. I can remember that many times when Rose was ill, Gretchen would do her duties as well as her own which included caring for me. I recall her reading to me on the sun porch and singing me to sleep at nap time. It is quite upsetting to admit that our hired helpers have been more like mothers to me than the actual woman who gave birth to me.

I refuse to let anything interfere with my journey to the truth. I push my thoughts of sympathy for Gretchen away and continue forward. I have a limited amount of time to investigate, so wasting time obsessing over things that I cannot change will do me no good. As I enter the sun porch, I have so much enthusiasm brewing in my soul that I feel like Nancy Drew. I proceed down the stairs that will ultimately put me at the start of the overgrown path that I spotted on my walk with Daddy.

I feel the warm sun touch my skin. There is a slight breeze that flows off the ocean, and it gently ruffles my hair. I lick my lips, and there is a slight taste of salt. Part of me just wants to stop this investigation and find a secluded spot on the beach to take advantage of being outside; I want to let the warmth of the sun renew all of my hopes and dreams of a better day to be. The thought leaves rapidly as I see the ground below me. I step off the last stair and take a deep breath that I hope will fuel my courage. I continue onward with much determination as if my mind is forcing my body to move against its will. My arms swing back and forth, and my feet step with confidence.

I arrive at the path, and it seems even more overgrown than I recall. I dismiss my hesitation and step into the unknown. Fear breeds inside of me as I search for clear spots to walk. The further I go into the garden, the stronger my will becomes. Branches and bushes snag and pull my clothing and hair. Vines seem to reach outward and want to touch me. It seems that the weeds are trying to pull me back. I focus on the answers of my search and not the fact that all of the ticks and spiders are having their afternoon snack at my skin's expense.

As I continue to battle the wild foliage, the path seems to become easier to navigate and more groomed. Less shrubbery impairs my pace. I look down and see stepping-stones. The garden is now accepting me and inviting me in. I become surprised when I notice that there are footprints below me. Someone has recently walked the same brutal path that I just conquered. I am more positive than ever that there will be answers when these footprints end.

As I get deeper into the garden, I notice that the trees and bushes look to have obviously been maintained. The untamed vines have retreated and are peacefully wrapped around the tree trunks. I can now look up and see the azure sky over the mansion. Why would someone tend to the landscaping at the end of the path and not at the beginning? Why not take care of it all? I am puzzled by this finding. As I look at Ocean Point, it's a view that I have never seen. The residence is massive in size, and even though the house is frightening to look at now, I can see that it has good bones and could really be exquisite if someone would care enough to tend to it. It is a shame that Mother has let this family dynasty go to ruins. Mother is so arrogant and controlling that I am baffled that she does not mind our estate to be looked down upon in the community.

I see rooms that I do not recognize. I shield my eyes from the sun's glare and try to squint to focus. I try to identify with the layout of the house so that I can figure out where I am. I realize that I am looking at the forbidden west wing from the outside of the house. My memory shoots my emotions back to the panic I felt when stumbling down the hallways of the forbidden wing. Chills gradually inch up my spine despite the warm August weather. It is like someone is blowing a cold breath on the back of my neck.

I force the memories of the west wing out of my mind the best I can and concentrate on what lies ahead for me. I march onward. The path now seems to become some kind of maze that was deliberately planted for amusement, but it makes me feel like I'm doing circles. I begin to feel like a mouse stuck in a maze searching for a big hunk of cheese that he smells ahead of him. I can understand how that little mouse must feel, only my hunk of cheese comes in the form of answers.

I pass several colossal marble fountains that appear to have become planters for weeds. I see the remains of flower beds that are now overflowing with undomesticated plant species. The path takes a sharp turn and leaves me in awe as I stand in front of a white gazebo. The structure is enormous. Bright green vines climb the wooden posts as if their presence is intentional. Inside of it, there are benches that attach to the sides, and there are large pots with flowers in them. It is so odd, as the flowers have been cared for.

I walk inside the gazebo and kneel down over one of the pots. I cup one of the beautiful white flowers in my hand and breathe in the fragrance from the delicate petals. The smell engulfs me; it seems familiar. My memory is sparked, but I am left with an emptiness that resides in my mind because I cannot make any solid connection to the elegant flower. The scent gives me a feeling of peace and love as if I'm not at Ocean Point any longer. I start to daydream of a time when this dreary, old mansion could be full of happiness again, and the gardens could be my playground. I envision myself playing in the garden and being a jovial child.

These fantasies make me want to stay here forever, but I know that I have to move on. I find myself in another dilemma. I see three different paths. Which do I choose? I step out of the gazebo and walk to the opening of each path. I peer down to see if I can see anything in the distance, and I notice at the entrance to the second path that there are footprints similar to the ones I saw earlier. As I follow the footprints through the twist and turns, I can still smell the flowers that I'm leaving behind me. The scent follows me. The aroma of the flowers begins to become more robust the deeper I travel into the new path. I round another corner, and I cannot believe my eyes. I freeze in my footsteps.

I see a cemetery. There are twenty or so graves with tombstones jutting out of the ground. My eyes are drawn to one in particular. I see a grave that has a tombstone with a large, white cross. A pretty angel leans on its spotless marble surface. It is so delicate and feminine. In front of the stone, the same white flowers cover the ground where the person rests beneath. I stand in front of the grave and suddenly realize that these are the same flowers that are painted on my bedroom walls. What is the significance of these flowers? Why do I feel a sensation of calmness and love when I'm close to them?

I look at the cross, and there are only three letters engraved into the stone. It reads "C.O.B." Whichever relative of mine is buried here must have been very important, and it's apparent that someone still aches for them. Who in this crazy house travels down here and showers this grave with flowers? The more important question, though, is who is buried beneath these flowers?

I continue to walk through the small cemetery and read the grave markers, hoping that something I read will give me an insight. These graves are not tended to. It seems that each person buried here has been forgotten, and I feel miserable for these lonely souls and wonder if they roam the halls of Ocean Point to be heard and remembered. As I walk the gravesites of the neglected and forgotten, I see a row of smaller tombstones. I carefully step on the ground, being cautious as not to step on any of the areas my ancestors would be laying. I aim to get closer to the small stones. Before I reach the row of tiny stones, I find myself standing in front of what appears to be the largest tombstone in the cemetery.

It reads "Alan Jefferson Berringer." Suddenly, I am cold, and my muscles are tense. I feel a sense of gloom, and it seems that even the sky grows darker. This is my grandfather's grave, my father's father. I am sure that this is the man I saw in the painting in the west wing. Why does the grave of my own grandfather leave me with these unpleasant feelings? Why do I not know anything about him if he had such importance in this family to warrant such a lavish monument? My time in the gardens is giving me more questions than the answers.

I finally reach the row of smaller stones. Laying side by side, there are five small tombstones, and on each of them is just one name. The names engraved on the small, cross-shaped stones are Jefferson, Thomas, Annabelle, David, and Abigail. These must be children. Thinking of these children lying in the cold ground gives me great sorrow. I have always fantasized about Ocean Point being full of parties and grand balls, but if all of these children died in this house, it must be full of more pain and grief than I could ever dream of. The next haunting questions devour my thoughts. How are these children related to me? How did they die? Did this spooky house kill them? Or the most terrifying question of all, did Mother kill them? I wish these children could rise up from their graves and tell me what happened to them.

These horrid assumptions and questions consume me, and I cannot shut out these unsettling feelings. The sadness that I feel as I imagine their tiny little bones buried beneath my feet is overwhelming. I do not want to go back to the house. My imagination is out of control, and I envision the demons and ghost in the west wing. I worry. Will I be next? Why have they spared me for so long? I try to dismiss my supernatural thoughts and assume that Mother scalded these poor children in the bathtub just like she does me. This insight takes away my fear and replaces it with rage. Mother is the only demon in that house.

I have lost track of time, and I have to return to the mansion. I am unsure of how to get back to the entrance at the sun porch, so I turn towards the house and look up silently, asking the house to guide me. I attempt to use the placement of the windows as a guide to lead me in the correct direction. I have never seen this side of the mansion, and I reel of how huge it really is. My eyes scan the windows. I notice that one of the windows has the curtains pulled back, and there appears to be a person peering down at me.

Are my eyes playing tricks on me? I try to focus on the window, and abruptly, the figure changes from looking like a person to more of an animal figure. My legs become unsteady, and I begin to tremble from shock. I close my eyes and reopen them again. The figure is gone. Is it coming for me? I begin to run. I run as fast as I can. Oh my God, was it a ghost? Was it a demon? Or worse, was it Mother? Is that what killed the children? I begin to cry. I run and sob so heavily that I can barely breathe in the humid air. Branches and twigs scrape my face and legs. I am franticly running when the path takes a sharp turn, and I run directly into something or someone. The collision knocks me instantly to the ground.

I struggle to crawl away from whatever I just collided into. I can feel small rocks and dirt beneath my hands and knees. I am so petrified that the sharp pricks that the rocks inflict on my skin do not slow down my effort to flee for safety. I hysterically scream, and my eyes are full of tears and dirt. My vision is impaired. I hear the sound of someone running away back through the garden. When I believe the stranger is gone, I stop my frantic crawling. I sit on the ground and vigorously wipe my eyes for concern that the stranger will return. I feel something wet on my face. I take my hand and wipe the fluid off of my face. I look at my hand, and it is covered with some kind of sap that must have come off of the tree branches. I push my hair out of my face and stand to my feet as quickly as I can. I run until I find the safety of the house that I fear as well.

As I enter the back door, I pray that Rose has not returned. I look around and see that no one is in sight, so I rush to my bedroom. I arrive at my door, enter, and quietly shut it behind me. I have dirt, slime, and scratches on my face. I fetch a washcloth and start to scrub my face. My face is severely scraped, and it stings when I finish. I tear my dirty clothes off of my exhausted body and hide them in the back of my closet. I grab a new dress off of a hanger and slip it on as speedily as I can.

I am physically and mentally defeated. I plop myself down on the side of my bed. I put my head in my hands as the events of the day swim around in my psyche. Questions dominate my thoughts. Who was the person I ran into? Was it even a person, or did I run into something else and think it was a person? What was it that I saw in the window of the west wing? Was it a person or a monster? Who are those children, and how did they die? Who is "C.O.B?" Who is caring for the grave and lavishing it with white flowers? I am in a daze. Rose opens my bedroom door, and her presence doesn't even break my train of thought.

"Coral, what happened to you, Child?" she asks with concern. I don't even look at her. I ask in a very low voice,

"What kind of flowers are these painted on my walls?" There is a dead silence in the room. I can feel her eyes on me, but I don't even look up. I just sit there and patiently wait for an answer. Finally, Rose says,

"They are lilies. Why do you ask?" There is a suspicious tone in her voice. I ignore the negative feeling that fills the air like thick smog hovers over a big city. I causally say,

"No reason." Then, I rise from my bed like an emotionless robot. I go into my bathroom just to escape any more questions. I shut the door.

Surprisingly, Rose doesn't mention the incident for the rest of the day, and I act as if nothing happened. I think that we are both avoiding having to answer each other's questions. I am so frazzled from the experience in the garden that I decide that I am not going to do any more investigating for a while. A part of me is afraid to know the truth, and the other part is terrified that I may end up like those poor children buried in the garden. The images of their graves are engraved into my memory as deep as their names are carved into the tombstones. The assumption of what might have happened to them scares me almost as much as Mother does. I am overflowing with terror and sadness, but I know that my search is not over. I begin to pray nightly for the strength to handle what the house and my dead ancestors have in store for me.

The Demon in the Hallway

My summer break from school is nearing an end. Other than my unexplained moments in the garden and west wing, nothing exciting happened to me during the break. I cannot go back to school and brag to my classmates about an amazing family vacation or a spectacular party that I had to celebrate my fifteenth birthday. I turned fifteen during the time Mother was keeping me drugged. I barely saw Mother, and when I did she avoided all contact with me except an occasional nasty glance. Daddy would come home occasionally, but I am still angry with him and am not ready to forgive his ignorance and weakness. The older I become, the more I can see how pathetic of a man he is, and I think that I am slowly losing respect for him. I have concerns that my once tender feelings for him will never return. I do not understand why he does not fight for me. Why does he not stand up to Mother?

Today, Rose and I are going back to school shopping. I look forward to returning to school; at least I can get out of the house. Our first stop is the school uniform store where Mother pays the seamstress to lengthen my plaid skirt. Our school uniform is a white, long-sleeve button up shirt with a dark blue tie and a plaid skirt. The girls at my school tend to wear them short, but Mother is offended by the short styles that are now popular. The girls call them miniskirts, and I think they are cute. I wish I could wear the popular clothes that all the other girls my age take for granted.

I always feel out of place at school. I cannot say the girls at my school are mean to me, but they just don't talk to me. Many times when I walk in a room or by a group of girls, I can hear them whispering and giggling among themselves. I know it is about me. I think they may be scared of me. Maybe they think I'm a witch and will cast an evil spell on them. I have overheard them gossip about Ocean Point and how the house is haunted. There are all kinds of rumors about the mansion and my family, but most of what I have heard seem more like the creations from a child's mind. I do not blame them for their apprehension of befriending me or being frightened of Ocean Point. The place I call home terrifies even me.

To make my situation worse, Mother visits my school often. She and the dean are longtime friends, and he allows her unannounced visits to the property at any time. When Mother enters the school, a cloud of silence covers the chatter of teenage girls. As she walks down the hallways, the girls literally move to the sides as if they are deliberately creating a path for her. She strolls through the hallways like she owns the private school as she looks down her thin, long nose to everyone she passes. Her black hair is pulled back in its usual tight bun. It is so tight that her eyes appear to be slanted. She wears a long, black trench coat and black leather boots that point at the toe. She models this outdated ensemble no matter what season it is. The sound of her footsteps echo down the long hallways, and her presence is always known. When I am in class and hear her coming, I immediately become embarrassed as the girls stop their work and look in my direction. Sometimes I wish the rumors were true, and we were witches. She could just hop on her broom and fly quietly down the hallway, and no one would know she was there.

I desperately wish that my life could be normal. I wish I had friends. I have been sheltered in that spooky old castle for so long that when I overhear the conversations that the girls my age have, I usually don't even know what they are talking about. I am not allowed to listen to the same music, nor am I allowed to watch television, and under no circumstances am I allowed to talk to boys. Even if I was fortunate enough to make a friend, I would never be allowed to go to the drive in movies or a sleep over, and my refusal of their kind invites would probably hurt their feelings. I keep to myself and spare any humiliation that my secluded life will cause me.

Our last stop is the local school supply store where I get my textbooks, paper, notebooks, and pencils. Rose sends me to fetch pencils. When I arrive at the aisle where the pencils are displayed, there is a girl standing there picking out her pencils. I do not recognize her. She notices my presence, turns towards me, and cheerfully says,

"Hi, my name is Lucia Lombardi, but everyone calls me Lucy."

She is taller than me and slightly overweight. Her eyes are dark brown and full of sparkle. She has dark brown hair pulled into a ponytail, and curls fall loosely as a baby-blue ribbon completes the fashionable look. Her shirt is short and matches the baby-blue ribbon in her hair. She is wearing a white cardigan sweater, and it is unbuttoned all the way to where you can see her cleavage and white, lacy bra. She is well endowed and is much more physically mature than me. I cannot resist from being envious of her beautiful curves.

I am taken back by her friendliness, and the shy and reserved side of me takes control of what should be a pleasant experience. I meekly respond with a quiet "Hi," trying to avoid eye contact as I reach for a handful of pencils.

"Oh, that's great. The first person I meet that is my age is a snob. My brother warned me about the kids around here. I didn't want to believe him, but he was right! Fine, I don't want to be friends with you anyways!" she says to me with an angry tone, and her voice is louder with each word that flies out of her mouth.

This confrontation leaves me embarrassed and confused. I attempt to explain to her that I am not a snob, but I cannot get the words to come out. I stand fumbling pencils nervously in my hand. Lucy stands in front of me with her hand on her hip and a sassy expression on her face. It feels as though she will wait an eternity for my explanation. At this point, I know that I cannot recover from the humiliation, so I flee from the altercation, leaving her without vindication.

I search for the safety of Rose in what seems like endless rows of school supplies. I finally see her. She is speaking with a lady that I have never seen before. I run into Rose's view, and my arrival causes her to break her conversation. I am visibly distraught, so she politely pauses her conversation to console me. I feel so stupid and self-conscious that I do not tell her what has me upset. I just close my eyes, let out a small breath, and pull myself back together. I give Rose a look that I am okay. She turns back to the lady and introduces me.

"Coral, this is Mrs. Lombardi. She is the new maid at the Englands' residence next to us."

I am still shaken up and fail to realize that this woman has the same last name as the girl I encountered in the pencil aisle. I patiently wait for Rose to end her conversation, but I really want to shove her to the counter so we can quickly pay and make a swift get away before the loud, obnoxious girl finds me. I hear the polite pauses that signal the end of Rose's conversation, and I feel relieved. I relax a little to know that this nightmare will be over soon. I feel a tap on my shoulder. I turn and see the girl standing behind me. Instinct kicks in, and I slowly slink behind Rose like a timid five year old. The ladies see both of us but have no idea about our meeting in the pencil aisle. Mrs. Lombardi says,

"Lucy, did you meet Coral?" Lucy cuts her eyes to me and gives me a questionable stare. Then suddenly, her expression changes, and a big smile grows across her face.

"Yeah Ma, we met while getting pencils," she answers her mother as if we are already friends.

"I am glad to hear that. Coral lives in the residence to the east of us," Mrs. Lombardi explains.

"That creepy haunted house?" Lucy asks with a horrified expression.

I am sure she wonders how anyone would call Ocean Point their home.

"Lucia Lombardi, where are your manners?" she scolds Lucy.

"Sorry, Ma," Lucy nonchalantly says.

I am stunned by Lucy's carefree disposition when speaking to her mother. If I was to ever talk to my mother as Lucy does hers, I would be underground with the other children in the garden. Lucy moves close to me and hooks her arm in mine and says,

"Let's get out of here."

I look to Rose for permission, and she nods. She smiles and seems delighted that I have made a friend. I am very uncomfortable leaving the store with Lucy. We exit the store, and Lucy acts as if nothing happened between us and that we have been friends for years. Her cheery spirit puts me at ease. She speaks so fast that I can barely keep up with her, and it seems like she is having a conversation all by herself. She explains to me that the Englands hired her mother and are paying for her to go to private school. She tells me that her dad died a year ago, and her mom has to take care of her and her brother alone. Her family owned an Italian restaurant in Providence, but after they buried her father there was not any money left. They closed the restaurant and moved here.

"My older brother dropped out of school and kept getting in trouble. My mom was worried that he would get involved with the mafia like many of our other relatives. He is a good brother. He just took our dad's death hard, and it has changed him."

Lucy's story makes me feel empathy for her and her family, but Lucy is upbeat and tells me the intimate details of her family without remorse.

It surprises me that she is so open with a complete stranger. I have to sneak through a house and an overgrown garden to find anything out about my own family, and in five minutes I know more about this stranger's family than I do my own. I have questions for Lucy. What is a mafia? Is it a rock band? I decide to stay quiet and just listen for concern of saying something ignorant that would make her not want to be my friend.

Lucy still has her arm hooked in mine and begins to pull me towards a boy leaning against a building. He is tall and muscular. His skin is a dark olive color as if he sunbathes daily. His hair is dark like Lucy's, and it is thick and wavy. My feet begin to try to slow down Lucy's pace. I know that if Mother saw me near this handsome boy who looks more like a man that she would lose her mind, and my punishment would be more than I could tolerate. My attempt to detour Lucy in another direction has failed, and we stand right beside the attractive boy.

"This is my brother, Angelo, but we call him Angel," Lucy joyfully introduces us.

Both of us remain silent. Angel does not even look our way. He ignores her. He takes a long draw off the cigarette he is smoking and flicks the ashes. I am mesmerized by his beauty. I feel the palms of my hands begin to sweat, and I feel excited in a way that I have never felt before. Lucy continues to speak to Angel despite is obvious annoyance of our presence.

"Hey Angel, this is Coral. She lives in that creepy castle on the hill," she says to him so casually that I wonder if Lucy takes anything seriously.

At this very moment, I have never been more ashamed of Ocean Point and my kooky family. I feel like a freak. There is an awkward silence. He takes another long draw off of his cigarette and blows a smoke ring from his lips as if our company bores him. He finally looks at me and coldly says,

"Well, I am sure she doesn't have to sleep in the servants' quarters."

His sarcasm offends me, but his charisma captivates me. I want to fire back at him and tell him that my life is not as wonderful as he thinks, but I cannot compose myself enough to utter a word. I turn and begin to walk away feeling foolish and insignificant. Lucy comes running behind me.

"Coral wait up!" she says. I reluctantly stop and turn to her. "I'm sorry about my brother. He can be a real jerk! Once you get to know him you will like him," she says as she pleads his case. Part of me never wants to see this uncouth boy again, but I cannot deny that I am drawn to him. This leaves me feeling unsettled. "Meet me at the beach tonight after your parents go to bed," she tells me.

"Oh, I can't. I will get in big trouble," I answer, leaving out all of the horrid details of the penalties that I face when Mother gets angry with me.

"Then don't get caught!" she says in a mischievous whisper with a devilish grin.

Rose and Mrs. Lombardi come out of the store. Lucy puts her finger to her lips as if we have a secret to keep for life. She joins her mother, and I get into our car. I can hear Mrs. Lombardi fuss at Angel in Italian, and she grips him by the back of the neck and flicks his cigarette out of his mouth. She puts him into the car like she is a policewoman that just arrested a criminal. I giggle to myself, realizing that her firm discipline is very different than Mother's. I know that he is not in danger, but just his ego is a little bruised. Rose notices my fascination with Angel.

"He sure is a fine looking boy, isn't he?" she says with a coy smirk.

The rest of the afternoon I cannot stop thinking about Angel and Lucy. I am in an intellectual and emotional battle with myself in making the decision of whether or not to meet Lucy at the beach. I want to go so badly. I have never had a friend before, and I do not want to lose the possibility of friendship with someone my own age. I am concerned that if I don't show up, I will hurt her feelings, especially after we got off to such a rocky start. The other side of me cannot stop obsessing about what will happen to me if I get caught. I can close my eyes and hear Mother's preaching of the demon inside me. I can feel the hard brush on my skin, and I can feel the sting of the burning water. I can feel the blood trickle down my legs, and I can breathe the steam that travels up my body.

I decide that I am going to take a great risk and meet Lucy. I spend the remainder of the afternoon praying to God that I do not get caught. I plan to go for only ten minutes. I plan to lie so that the truth about my life is not uncovered. I am going to pretend that I have exciting plans and cannot stay long. I have sincere reservations that if the reality of my situation was to emerge that Lucy might believe I am crazy. I would rather lie to her than tell her the unbelievable truth. It is better than not showing up at all. I worry that I will lose the chance for her friendship for good.

The sun has set for the day, and the moon lights the night sky. I eagerly watch the clock on my night stand as the hands slowly tick. I put on my night gown and lie in bed. I wait to hear a quiet house. As I patiently wait to hear Mother retire to her bedroom for the evening, I cannot rid my thoughts of Angel. I wonder if he will be at the beach with Lucy. I remain perplexed as to why I seem not to be able to get this boy out of my mind. My nervousness increases with each minute that passes, but I also feel a thrill that I have never felt.

After what seems to be an eternity, I hear Mother's heavy footsteps descend down the hall. When I hear her bedroom door shut, I unexpectedly have second thoughts of my dicey plan. I need to find the guts somewhere inside of me to pull this off, but I soon realize that it is not guts getting me out of this bed. It is the immense curiosity and attraction that I have for Angel. I quietly slither out of bed, change into a sundress, and grab my shoes. I slowly creep through the house with my shoes in my hand. I can see my shadow illuminated on the walls, and it occasionally startles me. I feel a strange feeling that someone is following me. I stop several times and look behind me, but I see nothing. I conclude that this is paranoia and continue to sneak through the dark house. My dismissal of the disturbing feeling of being followed does not last long.

It returns and is stronger. I can hear a strange sound behind me. I know that this is not my imagination, and terror devours me. I stop moving. Who or what is following me? Please don't be Mother. I remain still with my back to the wall and let the strong structure support my body. I breathe as slowly and as quietly as I can. My eyes are closed, and my legs feel weak. I am afraid that they will give out from underneath me, and I will end up on the floor with a demon hovering over me and enjoying my torment. Whether this thing is a monster or it is Mother, the fear is equal. The consequences will be the same either way.

The strange noise seems to get closer, and I can feel its presence near. In spite of the uncontrollable fear, I muster up enough courage to open my eyes. I look to my left where I hear the sounds, and I see a shadow in the near distance. I cannot determine who or what this shadow is. Is this real? Is it possible that it is just the shadow of a piece of furniture? Is my mind playing tricks on me? The shadow is motionless, but I can still hear the noise coming from the hallway. Suddenly, I see the figure move with a swift motion. No matter how still I try to remain, my heart pounds, and my body shivers. The figure rapidly moves down the hall but thankfully away from me.

Moments go by, and the house is still. I slide down the wall and sit on the cold, marble floor. I come to the spine-chilling realization that this was real, not a delusion from a fearful teenager's mind. I also know that it was not Mother. If it was, I would already be boiling as a poor lobster would before he became a gourmet dinner. Was that the thing I saw in the room in the west wing? Does anyone else know about this person or creature? Maybe this house really is haunted. It is only a matter of time before it grows tired of me and my snooping and gives me a new home in the garden buried next to the other children.

Despite the unbelievable event that I just experienced, I decide that I have come this far, and I am not going to stop. It also crosses my mind that the creature might be waiting for me somewhere else in the house. At least I know I will be safe outside. I need to get out of this house and find a little hope that I might end up with a friend. The thought of seeing Angel again lingers in my thoughts, and my wonderment of this handsome boy is worth the risk in front of me.

I arrive at the back entrance of the mansion in the sun porch. I quietly open the back door and begin my descent down the stairs. I can feel the late summer's wind gently caress my face, and I can smell the glorious scent of the ocean. I cannot believe that I am escaping in the night. Where is this courage coming from?

My feet hit the earth, and immediately I feel free. I begin down the walkway that leads me to the ocean. I now pass the path that left me with so many questions. It is the same path that loaned me the feeling of peace and love but left me dirty, scratched, and terrified. I push out the bad memories and just concentrate on getting to my new friends. I draw near the entrance to the garden, and against my better judgment, I stop in front of the unruly trail.

I hear voices in the distance. I stand still and listen closely. They are not voices as if two people are talking. They are sounds of a group of beautiful female voices singing. The sound is gentle and sweet. The path attempts to seduce me. It calls to me. I have an overwhelming urge to enter the garden. I take one step into the garden, and the singing becomes louder. I feel entranced by the melody that calls me to come deeper into the path. It feels like I am in a trance.

The vines reach for me again as if to embrace me and tenderly pull me into the eerie garden. All of a sudden, a light flashes in the sky above me, and it breaks the spell that has been cast on me. The enticing music has stopped. I am troubled with the realization that I may be losing my mind with all of these unexplainable events. Is Mother secretly drugging me, and does this drug make me hallucinate? Is she trying to drive me mad? I see the quick flash of light again. It is coming from the beach.

I sprint towards the ocean. I climb a small dune, and I see two figures sitting on a rock. I assume that they are Lucy and Angel, and I begin to run towards them. I feel awkward as I run and hope that my overzealous mood is not too noticeable. The closer I get, I can see that it is them, and my heart begins to beat faster. What am I going to say? How should I act? I know from my shortcomings and sheltered life that I do not have any social skills, and I have often found it safer to remain quiet.

Lucy hops off of the rock and skips towards me while Angel remains sitting on the rock. She has a flashlight in her hand, and the light bounces wildly. She is out of breath when she reaches me just from the small jog that it took for her to get to me. She begins to speak to me so fast, and her train of thought jumps from one subject to another in a matter of seconds. As happy as I am to see Lucy, I cannot keep my eyes from wandering past her and gazing at Angel. The moonlight shines down on him, giving a perfect silhouette of his muscular body from a distance. All I hear are waves crashing against the shore as I struggle to take my eyes off of Angel. Lucy's words fall on deaf ears.

Lucy does not notice my disinterest in her nor my interest in her brother. I am amused by Lucy's enthusiasm and try to tell her that I cannot stay long, but she grabs my arm and starts pulling me toward Angel. He is perched on a large rock, and small waves roll back and forth beneath him.

"Look who I found, Angel," Lucy says as if she is bragging.

It makes me feel special. He pulls a cigarette out and lights it without acknowledging Lucy's announcement. Once the cigarette is lit, he takes a slow, long draw then exhales the smoke and turns to me.

"Wanna cig?" he asks as he shows me the pack of Winstons in his hand.

"No thank you. I don't smoke," I timidly answer.

"Yeah, I didn't think you did," he says in a sarcastic tone as he dismisses my presence.

"Give me a break, Angel. Not everyone is so delusional that they believe they are James Dean reincarnated!" Lucy says to him in my defense.

Lucy and I sit at the bottom of the rock and let our feet dangle in the warm water that flows back and forth below us. Lucy does not stop talking. She tells me countless stories and seems to never pause to even breathe. I can see why people may think she is annoying, but I find her interesting.

"Lucy, why don't you shut your big mouth and have your new little friend tell us something about her," Angel says in a belittling tone as he leans over the rock and lets his presence be known.

I search for words. I want to say something witty or cool, but my nervousness renders me speechless. I consider telling them about the apparition I just encountered, the graveyard in my backyard, or my callous mother. It would entice their attention, but it would probably make them think I am odd like the girls at school do. Or worse, what if they do not believe me?

"There is really nothing to say. I... I... I..." I stumble over my words until Angel crudely interrupts me.

"Why don't you start by telling us how rich you are? You can tell us about all the fancy trips you have taken. Or how about all the expensive jewelry your mother keeps in a safe behind a hidden door in your library?" Angel continues to speak in a taunting and demeaning manner, and his assumptions and words cut me like a sword.

I have become accustomed to brutal physical and emotional pain, but the sting of this boy's words is an ache that is new to me. I sit next to Lucy and feel my face grow warm. I am sure it is now a deep shade of crimson. I am thankful that the dim glimmer of the moon's glow reflecting off the water is our only light, making it so they are unable to see how his heartlessness affects me. Before I can respond, Angel throws one more dagger into my heart by saying,

"By the way, why do you wear those clothes? Are your parents Amish?" He lets out a confident chuckle and seems proud of his thoughtless behavior.

I now swim in my humiliation. I have no idea what to say or do. Tears start to fill my eyes, and this makes me even more ashamed. I panic and jump off the rock and begin to run. I franticly run to the house that causes me so much unhappiness, but I long for the familiarity of Ocean Point. The place that I loathe is calling me home and falsely making promises of safety to me.

I arrive at the border of our property and look up at the massive estate. Is this where I truly belong? Is this house just as misunderstood as I am? Or is this house going to torture me and slowly drive me insane? I know that the house does speak to me. Sometimes it is only a whisper, but I can hear it and feel it. I continue to the house, and as I approach the overrun path, I cover my ears so I do not hear the beautiful voices that call to me like the Sirens did to the sailors in ancient Greece before they gobbled them up.

I enter the house and quietly sneak back upstairs. With every turn and step, I watch for the demon or Mother. I do not wish to be caught by Mother or eaten by the mysterious beast that I shared a hallway with earlier. As I near my bedroom, I can hear Mother's voice. I want to stop to listen, but a little voice in my head tells me to go to my room. I am safe now. I did not get caught or eaten. No matter what the rowdy voices in my head are screaming, though, I slowly inch my way to Mother's bedroom door. My dangerous inquisitiveness is in control. As I stand outside her door, I can hear her words clearly. She is agitated and angry. It sounds like she is speaking to someone on the phone.

"We are going to have to handle this situation immediately," she sternly states.

I cannot help but assume that she is speaking about me. Has she found out about all of my explorations? Has she found out that I have snuck out? Does she know that I have had impure thoughts about a boy? Questions buzz through my mind.

"He is becoming uncontrollable. He has the strength of four men and breaks through the restraints." I am immediately put at ease. She has not found out about my mischievous behavior. "He escapes into the house, and half of the time he does not know who he is. I have spent years protecting him and this family. This is not going to ruin all of my hard work. I will not allow it! I need a solution to my problem, and I expect it by tomorrow!" she says in a businesslike manner and then slams the phone down to prove how serious she is.

I rush to my room and carefully shut the door. I then hear Mother's footsteps come down the hall, and I begin to panic. She must have heard me. I leap into the bed with all of my clothes on and shove my shoes under the bed. I roll towards the wall and cover myself up all the way to my head. I try to calm down and lie still. I hear the doorknob turn, and I shut my eyes, pretending to be asleep. I sense the hall light on my back. My body shivers from fear.

She lingers in the doorway for a short while. I can intuitively sense her suspicion. I know that all she has to do is pull my covers back, and my disobedience is will discovered. I do not want to end this awful day with a scalding bath. There is no doubt in my mind that will be my sentence for this act of disrespect. I can hear her footsteps come towards my bed. I prepare myself for the physical assaults that Mother's hands will inflict. She is so close that I can hear her breathing. I pray for her to go away. Unexpectedly, a loud groan comes from the hallway. Immediately, Mother hurries out of the room. A feeling of relief relaxes my body. I hear her footsteps hurriedly run down the hallway until they become faint. Then, I hear a door slam in the distance.

Who or what made that sound? Is that the sound of the shadow that stalked me in the hall? Who is Mother talking about on the phone? The only man that lives in this house is Rollins. Is she talking about Rollins? Was that his groan I just heard? I know his sleeping quarters are in the direction that Mother rushed to. She always complains about him becoming senile, but I have never seen him wander through the house. Is there a side to our peculiar chef that I do not know about? Is he dangerous, and if so, why is Mother protecting him? He must know something about her or this family that scares her. My mind spirals out of control trying to solve all of the mysteries. It seems that the conspiracies I play out in my head are ridiculous. Eventually, mind grows weary and gives in to my exhaustion, and I fall asleep.

Taking a Stand

oday is the first day of school. I look forward to being able to get out of this miserable house. I am so consumed with all of the secrecy that Ocean Point is host to that it is beginning to influence me. I know it is just a matter of time before my careless shenanigans cause Mother to discover my defiance. If I am at school, the house will not challenge me to uncover any Berringer secrets, and I will not hear the flowers' alluring voices tempting me to visit them in the garden.

I dread seeing Lucy at school because I really do not know what to say to her. I cannot defend or explain myself. I have done my best to push the thoughts of Angel out of my head. He is a very mean person, and his harsh words truly made my heart ache in a way that I have never felt before. No matter how hard I try, he creeps into my mind often, and sometimes he is all I think about. My obsession with him is draining and always leaves me unfulfilled. I do not like him and fail to understand why I have a fascination with him that I cannot dismiss. I dress myself for school and then make my way to the kitchen. Rollins is hard at work whisking a bowl of eggs. He looks up and pushes his tall chef hat back, giving me a quick wink. He affectionately smiles at me.

"Good morning, Good Lady! Your breakfast will be ready in a jiffy. Also, I need to know if you have decided on the quiches for your big day. I know your guests will love them. They always do. As a matter of fact, the Kennedys themselves ate the very same quiches at a charity ball that we hosted here some time ago," Rollins says with pride in his voice. I stand there, and I am very confused.

"What big day, Rollins?" I ask him. This is the second time he has referred to my "big day."

He stops beating the eggs and looks at me flustered. He stares at me so intensely that I begin to feel uncomfortable. His expression of confusion turns to regret. I realize that Mother is not around to interfere. I take advantage of her absence and begin to ask him questions.

"Rollins, who do you think I am?" He takes a moment and shakes his head.

"I apologize, ma'am. I thought you were your mother," he quietly says. I can see that he is frustrated with his blunder. I am not going to let this conversation end.

"My mother has dark hair and is very tall. How do you mistake me for her? Are you cooking for my *mother's* big day?" I question him. He puts his hand on his hip and begins to nervously rub his forehead.

"Yes, I am cooking for your mother. I have been cooking for this family for over sixty years." His voice grows sterner.

I begin to fire questions at him, and he now pretends not to hear me in hopes that I will tire of quizzing him. I interrogate him until I can see that the stubborn old man is now in his right mind. He knows who I am and knows to keep his mouth shut. I finally give up and go into the dining room.

When I enter, Mother is already seated and waiting for her breakfast to be served. She sits with her back as straight as a board and stares forward without acknowledging my entrance as usual. I sit down in my seat. Gretchen sluggishly makes her way into the dining room with our breakfast. She does her best to serve us in a proper and timely manner, but Mother has to belittle her by telling her how incompetent she has become. Watching Mother be this ruthless infuriates me, and her lack of mercy for Gretchen generates defiance in me that I soon regret.

"Mother, do you like quiche?" I calmly ask her as if I am her equal.

I calmly pick up my fork and take a bite of eggs. She looks at me like I am a foreigner and am speaking a different language. I am breaking a rule. Don't speak unless spoken to. This absurd rule is enforced at the dinner table more than anywhere else. I am sure that she is surprised that not only am I breaking a rule with deliberation, but I am doing it to ask a random question that to her has no meaning. Her eyes narrow, and she looks at me dead in the eyes. I can see fury in her eyes, but she remains focused on the game that we are playing. She feels challenged and curious.

We sit next to each other and are apparently having some kind of staring contest. She tries to make me cower with just one dominating look, but it won't work today. I have already come this far, and I am going to see this through no matter what punishment I may become victim to. She leans towards me. Normally, this move would make me flinch but not today. I am tired of her pushing everyone around in this house.

"Yes Coral, I do like quiche. Since you have already shown your mother so much disrespect, is there anything else you would like to ask me?" she says as she baits me. To my surprise, I continue to engage her with eye contact and say,

"Yes there is, Mother. Actually, I have many questions for you. I would like to know more about you, Mother. I would like to know more about our family and the history of this house, and I would like to know if you had quiche at your wedding with my father. I would also love to know why you hate me so very much. I would like you to tell me what I did to you to make you not love me," I say without breaking eye contact with her, showing no fear.

I am astonished that all of this actually comes out of my mouth. Mother slowly unfolds her hands and places them into her lap. A sinister smile comes across her face. It is not a genuine smile. It is similar to the warning signs that a volcano gives before it explodes. I know that I have gone too far and begin to prepare myself for the conclusion to the war I just started.

"To answer your questions, no I didn't have quiche at my wedding, and about me, let me see. I am an educated, God-fearing woman that has a very disrespectful daughter that I feel nothing for but shame and embarrassment. Your family, well, Coral dear, that will have to wait for another time because from what I know of you so far, you are not good enough to be a Berringer. You don't deserve to know about the blood that pumps through your veins because you were just an accident. You are just a true misfortune to this family, one too pathetic to be anything but a dirty, evil, and tarnished little girl. You should be lucky that I still let you live here regardless of your birthright. The only reason I allow you to stay is because I am too mortified of your existence to permit any association with this family in the outside world. I would rather hide you here than have the entire state know who you are. I regret daily allowing you to even attend school. Finally little Miss Coral, you want to know why I hate you? You want to know what you did to me?" Mother says to me in a calm, direct voice, and it feels as if she had planned this nasty speech in advance. Her voice grows to a loud scream. "YOU WERE BORN!"

She reaches towards me and grabs the back of my neck. Her sharp fingernails dig into my skin. Her strength is that of a giant as she lifts me out of my seat by my neck. She puts my face as close to hers as possible and begins to scream again.

"YOU WERE BORN!!!! YOU WERE BORN!!!! YOU WERE BORN!!!!" My face is sprayed with her saliva as the words bellow from her mouth.

She lets go of her grip on me, and I fall to the floor. Mother then bends down and straddles my body with hers as she pins my arms back with one hand and begins to punch and slap me in the face. She shouts about the devil and that I am a child of Satan. She has a crazed look in her eyes that tells me that some very dark part of her has power over her. She does not have control over her hysteria. Eventually, she stops hitting me and calmly stands to her feet. She kicks my body out of her way and brushes off the sleeves of her shirt as if touching me has tainted her. She pushes her black hair out of her face and tucks it neatly into the bun on the back of her head. In a rational voice, she says,

"It is time to go to school."

She walks to the intercom and calls for Rose to gather me and take me to school. She walks out of the room and leaves me on the ground like a piece of trash. I lie on the ground battered. She is bigger and stronger than me. She can hurt me and possibly kill me. This is the first time I have ever felt that despite her dominating me physically and leaving me on the floor bloody and bruised, I won. I triumph because I stayed strong and did not cower. There will be a day someday that her reign over me will be over. I refuse to live my life in her evil shadows like everyone else. Rose arrives and rushes to me. She helps me sit up. I look at her, and I can tell by her expression that Mother must have done quite a bit of damage.

"Oh Child, look what she has done to you," she says with sympathetic eyes.

I feel warm fluid trickle down the back of my neck. I wipe the fluid with my hand, and it is covered with blood. Rose immediately inspects my wound and begins to clean it with a wet napkin. I can feel my eye swelling and the scratches on my neck stinging. I rise to my feet and say to Rose,

"Let's go. I am going to be late for school."

She shakes her head and follows me to the car. The car ride to school is silent. Neither of us says a word. When our black sedan pulls up in front of the school, I get out of the car and grab my book bag. I do not even tell Rose goodbye as I shut the car door. I feel angry. I feel angry at everyone, angry at the whole world. I can feel the pain that I carry in my heart slowly turning into strength. I march into the school just like all of the other girls with the exception that their mothers probably did not beat them up at the breakfast table.

I pull my schedule out of my bag to find out where my first class is and begin to travel the long hallways to find it. I do not know if I am in denial over what had transpired between me and Mother or if I just do not care what people think of me, but I proceed down the hall as if my life is perfect. I can feel eyes all over me, and I can hear faint gasps and whispers as I pass my classmates. The more the girls react to my battered face, the more self-conscious I become.

The resilient girl that I pretend to be is getting lost in the crowd. I begin to wonder how appalling my beaten face really is. Am I disfigured? I haven't even stopped to look at the harm that Mother's hands left on me. I scramble to find the nearest bathroom. There are crowds of girls inspecting their make up in the mirrors and gossiping. I enter the room, and the injuries left from my assault shocks the self-absorbed girls. Instantly, the room clears out. My peers trip over each other as they try to escape the bathroom. I wonder how many seconds it is going to take for the gossip to begin about the weird girl that lives in the haunted house.

I do not immediately go to the mirror. I stand back against a wall and take the time to find the guts to see the results of the answers to my questions. I take a deep breath, stand up tall, and proceed to a mirror. I see a stranger looking back at me. I softly touch my skin and can feel the fluid swelling beneath the surface. Both of my eyes are bruised, and I have a large bruise on my jaw line. I look at the battered little girl in the mirror, and I do not feel sorry for her any longer. This beating is because I stood up for myself. It may not appear that way to anyone else looking in, but I knew what I was doing and survived. Yes, I look like a prized fighter that just lost the match, but I was in the ring for as long as I could handle. When I was knocked to the floor, I did not sob like a child. I took a beating without shedding a tear.

I realize that I cannot be at school with the painful truth of my life displayed on my face. I sneak out one of the side doors of the school and find a group of bushes. I travel around the well-manicured shrubbery to seek refuge out of everyone's view. To my surprise, I am not alone. Already hiding in the prickly, green leaves is Lucy. She looks up at me and says,

"What the hell happened to you? Do you have a boyfriend? Did he do this to you? My aunt, Jo, had a boyfriend that hit her once, and my cousin who shall remain nameless took care of him. Do you want me to call him for you?"

In usual Lucy fashion, she says all of this in one huge breath. At this point, I have to laugh. I begin to laugh out loud so hard that I cannot catch my breath, and my side begins to cramp from the strain of my uncontrollable laughter.

"What is so funny? Did that beating give you some kind of brain damage? Have you seen a doctor?" Lucy's questions shoot out of her mouth so quickly that I continue to struggle to stop my laughter.

"No, I don't have a boyfriend," I finally say with a moderate amount of composure. "Why are you hiding in the bushes?" I ask Lucy.

"Because this school is full of bitches!" she says and looks around to make sure no one heard her. I laugh again and say,

"Yes they are!"

"Let's get out of here," she says displaying excitement in the fact that she is not the only outcast.

"What do you mean? Where will we go?" I ask.

"Who cares? Let's go!" she exclaims and yanks me to my feet. Next thing I know, we are running off campus.

Lucy and I spend the day together at the boardwalk. It is the best day of my life. I do not feel uncomfortable with her now, and I am able to share with her what my mother does to me and all of the abuse that I endure. I tell her about the west wing, the garden, and the creature in the hallway. She listens and does not think that I am insane or lying. She is exactly what I need in a friend. This is the first time that I have ever spoken to anyone about the painful life that I am forced to endure. Being able to confide in someone and trust them is something that I never thought I would have

Lucy also shares with me that her mother is very worried because Angel disappeared again. She does not seem to be too concerned about Angel, though. I think that he has run away so often that she knows he will come back. She says that he just jumps on his motorcycle and speeds away. I am jealous of Angel. I would give anything to be able to leave my family, Ocean Point, the secrets, and the past behind me and never return. I am disappointed to find out that he is gone, and I desperately hope he returns.

Becoming a Woman

Lucy and I did not get caught skipping school. She is a clever girl. She wrote excuse notes to our teachers, and surprisingly they did not verify that they were actually written by our parents. Throughout the first few months of school, she and I would occasionally skip school and spend the day together at the beach or on the boardwalk. Breaking rules has become liberating for me. In the beginning, I was fearful that our missed days of school would be noticed, but as time has gone on it has become easier and less stressful. I rarely think twice when Lucy comes up with a new scheme.

She is teaching me so many things that a girl my age should know. We listen to music together, and she has taught me about all of the popular bands and shown me all of the teenage heartthrobs. They are handsome and all, but I have not seen one teenage idol that is as striking as Angel. I love the Beatles, and Lucy's favorite is the Supremes. She has taught me a fun dance to all of her favorite songs. We dance and laugh together, and for the first time in my life I do not feel so lonesome.

It has been months, and Angel is still gone. I am taken back that Lucy and her mother remain so calm regarding his absence, but Lucy says that her mother is tired and simply worn out. Angel is almost eighteen, almost a grown man. My anger for Angel's disrespect towards me has slowly dwindled away. Spending so much time with Lucy and understanding their background has given me insight to understand why he lashes out. I ask Lucy about him every chance I get, but I am very cautious with my questions and timing. I do not want Lucy to know this undeniable infatuation that I have for her brother.

Christmas is around the corner, and nothing extraordinary has transpired at Ocean Point. I hear an occasional strange noise in the night, but I just try to ignore it. Sometimes I am not sure it is real or just a dream I was having. I have been so distracted by my new friendship with Lucy that my fixation with the family and house has not been that important to me. I am still haunted by the things that I have seen and heard, but I try to keep it from taking any of the newfound joy away from me.

I am getting ready for the last day of school before the Christmas break. There is a party at school today. Mother does not allow me to attend the parties even if they are at school. She believes that school is strictly for learning and not socializing. This year, she has not even acknowledged the party, and she has not done her usual weekly visits to my school. She seems distracted, and I have hardly seen her at all lately. I am not going to complain.

Rose enters my room and lays a small gift on my bed. It is a small box and is wrapped in adorable royal blue wrapping paper with cute little snowmen dancing in the winter snow on it. I get excited when I see the gift.

"Is that for me?" I ask her.

"No, it's from you," she says and smiles.

"What do you mean?" I confusingly ask.

"Well, I have seen a different Coral since you have made a new secret friend. I assume you would want to get Lucy a Christmas gift," she says.

I am slightly shaken that Rose knows about my friendship with Lucy. I thought that I was doing a good job at hiding my new friendship. Has Rose known all this time? Does she know about us skipping school, the music, and the dancing? Rose can see that I feel uneasy with the possibility that the most important relationship I have ever had could be taken from me.

"Don't you worry your pretty little head. Your secret is safe with me." She comforts me with a quick wink. I am relieved by her reassurance that my friendship will remain a secret.

I am touched that she thought about Lucy and understands the significance of our relationship. I have never had a friend and did not even think to get her a Christmas gift. I am thankful to have Rose in my life.

"What is it?" I ask as I pick up the little box.

"It is a gold necklace, and it has a heart-shaped charm that reads 'Best Friends' on it," she proudly explains.

"Oh Rose, this is perfect! Thank you so much!" I reach out and wrap my arms around her neck.

"This is our little secret," she whispers in my ear. I know that my secret is safe with Rose because I know that she and everyone in this house has been keeping many secrets from me for years.

I arrive at school. I am full of anticipation to see Lucy and give her the gift. I skip down the hall towards Lucy when I see her at her locker waiting for me.

"Well you sure are all smiles this morning!" she says to me wondering why I am so happy. It is not my normal behavior to act playful and silly.

I reach into my book bag to retrieve her present. As my fingers search through my bag trying to locate the small box, I get a sharp pain in my stomach. The pain is sudden and distracts me. Lucy sees the stress on my face and puts her hand on my shoulder.

"Are you okay?"

Before I can answer, the hard, unbearable pain becomes so intense that I double over. I become concerned. My stomach is cramping like it did once when I had a stomach virus. That virus robbed me of any control of my bodily functions. I become anxious and need to go to the bathroom. I do not want to lose control in front of all of my classmates since they already think I am possessed. I feel like I am going to go to the bathroom in my panties, and I begin to sprint to the closest bathroom.

A thought crosses my mind. Did Mother do this to me? Did she poison me? Is she finally ready to get rid of me? Every time I do not feel well, I wonder if Mother is behind the discomfort.

I run as fast as my cramping stomach will allow. I slam the door open in a frenzy, and as always the room is full of girls checking their makeup and talking about boys. I am mortified by my dramatic entrance, but I know that I have no to time to worry about what they think. I find the nearest stall. I pull my panties down and feel fortunate that I made it in time. I am going to be sick, and I do not think I can hide what is going to happen. The fact that I am in this condition surrounded by a room full of catty girls is a miserable thought.

I sit there for a few minutes as my stomach continues to cramp, but nothing happens. I am sweating, and I feel very hot. The pain does not subside. It is excruciating, and I feel like I am going to vomit. My discomfort has reached a level of intensity to where the potential devastating reactions of my classmates have no importance to me now. I pray for my upset stomach to release and ease the stabbing pain, but it does not.

I look into the toilet, and the water is red. I am bleeding! I start to cry openly. I am petrified. Am I dying? Is this a curse? Did Mother poison me? I am going to bleed to death. I sit on the toilet horrified and trembling. Sweat drips down my face from my hairline. I hear one of the girls say,

"What's wrong with the freak?"

I do not even pay attention to the snickering and snide remarks I hear. The girls' nastiness is the last of my concerns with my pending death near. It is going to be atrocious when they find my dead body sitting on the toile. I hear a familiar voice.

"Coral, are you okay?"

It is Lucy. I feel solace to hear her voice, but I am also devastated. This is a disgusting way to die. Why could I not be poisoned like Snow White and just lie down and go to sleep? Maybe Mother is right. Maybe there is a demon living in me that is ripping me apart from inside with his long, jagged fingernails. Hasn't my life been full of enough gruesome violence? Is this how it has to end? Why does my death have to be so vulgar? I cry so forcefully that I almost begin to hyperventilate. In between gasps of air, I weakly say,

"No."

I am scared and cannot find a peaceful place in my mind to calm myself. I am finally finding tiny bits of happiness for myself, and now I am dying? I hear the bell ring, signaling that class is getting ready to begin. I hear the footsteps of the privileged girls scurry out of the bathroom. Lucy does not leave, and I can see her shoes from underneath the bathroom stall.

"Let me in," she insists.

"I can't! It's awful!" I say with a broken voice.

"Did your mother hurt you again?" she asks with a hint of outrage in her tone.

"I'm not sure."

"Let me in!" she demands.

I do not respond with hope that she will go to class and leave me here to die alone and spare me the humiliation of someone watching me slowly bleed to death. I hear a noise above me, and I look up. Lucy is standing on the other toilet in the stall next to me. She pulls herself up and climbs over the stall and then inches her body down to the floor where I am. She reaches under the stall and pulls her bag in the cramped space that we now share. I sit on the toilet bleeding to death, and she stands inches in front of me.

"What in the hell is going on, Coral?" she almost shouts at me. I can see she is becoming frustrated with my bizarre behavior.

"I am dying Lucy. Either the house has put a curse on me, or Mother is poisoning me," I say in a pathetic and defeated tone to express that I am accepting the fate of my mortality.

"What are you talking about?"

Lucy is confused and growing agitated. I find the strength to tell her that I am bleeding from my private area. I expect Lucy to be shocked, but instead she looks at me like I am crazy.

"Coral, have you started your period?" she asks.

"Period? What is that?" I ask.

"You know... Your menstrual cycle, monthly friend, Mother Nature?" she says slowly as if I am mentally impaired. I look up at her with a blank look. Lucy can see that I have no idea what she is talking about.

"Oh my, you don't know. I can't believe you are just now starting." she says nonchalantly.

What is she talking about? Starting what? Lucy begins to tear through her large purse and pulls out a plastic container. She opens it up and pulls out what looks like a miniature diaper. She hands me the tiny diaper and tells me to put it in my panties. I do as she says, and then she gives me some pills that she says will ease my stomach cramps.

"We are getting out of here, Girlfriend. We have a lot to talk about!" She shakes her head in disbelief. I do as Lucy says because I trust her. We leave school and begin to walk towards the ocean. She puts her arm through mine as we walk, and she says, "Coral, you really can be a drama queen!" and then chuckles.

The pain begins to ease, and the absence of it is a welcomed relief. The December air is frigid. We find a private spot under the boardwalk to escape the snow-covered ground and the wind. The wind is so powerful that its angry gusts feel like they make cuts on my face as we battles through their presence. We find a patch of sand and sit down. It is hard and frozen, but we overlook the discomfort and brave the elements to have the girl talk that I urgently need.

She explains to me that I have started my menstrual cycle, and she adds that I am a late bloomer. She got hers when she was only eleven years old. She tells me all of the details that I need to know regarding this awful experience that I now have to look forward to every month.

She decides not to leave any stone unturned and proceeds to give the talk about the "birds and the bees" to me. This is a conversation that Mother should have with me, but as usual she is not there for me as a mother should be. Lucy tells me all about sex, maybe more than I really want to know, but I am thankful that I have her and that she can share her knowledge. I cannot believe how the whole sex thing works, and to be honest I am a little grossed out. There is still a part of me that is curious, though. I ask Lucy if she has ever had sex, and she tells me no except for one time last year when Tommy Castello made out with her and felt her breasts.

I think that Lucy feels more empathy for me after going through this terrible experience. I hope that her witnessing this incident helps her have a better understanding of how bad my life really is. Yes, I am physically and emotionally abused, and now I realize how neglected I truly am. This neglect seems to hurt the most.

I enjoy spending this girl time with Lucy, but I still feel uncomfortable. I want to go home. I also miss Rose. I want to be with her and tell her what has happened, and maybe one of her hugs or sympathetic pats on my thigh will make me feel better. I tell Lucy that I want to go home.

Where Screams Cannot be Heard

We begin the long walk to Ocean Point. The wind remains brutal, and we walk straight into its path. My nose is numb, and my lips begin to get chapped. We march on through the bitter winter weather. After what is the hardest walk home of my life, I feel exhausted both physically and mentally. We stop when Ocean Point is in our full view but still far in the distance. We both silently stare at the stately castle.

"Wow, that is one big, creepy house!" Lucy says, trying to distract me from the sense of doom that slowly rolls down the side of the mountain that is the foundation of the place that I call home.

I want a place to come home to that has flowers in the windows, warm and inviting colors, soft and comfortable furniture that you just curl up on and watch television, beautiful artwork adorning the walls, and laughter, so much laughter. Instead, I have a dark, cold, dismal house that is full of screams, tears, and heartache. How did it get this way, I wonder? I do not believe that this house was built to be this way. Surely the hands that built this estate had better plans for the structure than the outcome created by Mother. I turn to Lucy and say,

"I wish you could stay with me." I look down at the ground saddened, knowing she cannot.

"I can sneak in if you want. Heck, that house is so big! How will anybody ever find me? Maybe if I go to the top of the tower a hot boy will come rescue me," she says playfully.

I have so much respect for Lucy's bravery and pure guts. For a moment, it actually crosses my mind to go along with another one of Lucy's risky plans, but no matter how much following in Lucy's daredevil footsteps liberates me, I cannot take the risk. I cannot endure another one of Mother's evil punishments in my current condition.

"I don't think it is a good idea," I state with firm conviction. I usually give in to Lucy's dominance, but I am attempting to display an adamant stance in hopes that she will listen. This is not a plan to take lightly and not the time to allow my usual meek disposition to surface.

"Hey Coral, won't you get in trouble for skipping school? It isn't even close to time for school to be dismissed," she questions me with concern for my safety. She is right. Mother will have no sympathy for my situation. Why can I not have a mother when I desperately need one the most? "I have a crazy idea," Lucy says with mischief in her voice. "Why don't we sneak into the garden and go visit the secret graveyard. I can help you investigate, and maybe together we can figure out what is going on with your kooky family. No offense."

Just the mention of the graveyard gives me an unnerving feeling, but there is also a sense of comfort and love that I feel when I am near those beautiful lilies. It is like they whisper to me and tell me that everything is going to be alright. How can the memories of the flowers instantly make me regress? I cannot believe that I am actually entertaining Lucy's idea. It is so dangerous. What if something bad happens? What if the gardens take away the only friend I have? On the other hand, Lucy gives me courage and strength that no one else can, and having her by my side may push me to find out the true answers, not just the silly theories that come into my mind when I am frightened. I argue myself with logic. There is a long pause as I contemplate her generous offer.

"Lucy, do you have any idea how dangerous this idea is?" I ask, trying to make her understand the horror that waits for us.

"Yes I do! That is why it is going to be so fun! Come on, let me help you. I am tough! I will protect you, and I bet with me being there it won't be even near as scary as you remember. I promise we will be quiet. Your mother will not even know we are there!" she says and tugs my arm in an attempt to persuade me to follow her plan.

"Okay, well what about the creature that I have seen? What if it smells us and comes for us?" I throw an exaggerated argument back at her and wait for her to back down.

"Please, I am not scared of a creature! Do you know how ridiculous that sounds? It's not that I don't believe you saw something creepy but a creature? Really? Coral, now you're just being dramatic again," she says and rolls her eyes.

I become slightly miffed at Lucy for reducing my experiences to childish daydreams, but I cannot blame her doubt. I second guess myself daily and feel at times that I am just crazy, but I know what I have seen. It is stamped in my memory. I feel challenged by Lucy's shallow understanding of the horrors that surround me.

"Okay, but Lucy, this is serious! If we get caught, my mother will hurt me badly!" I sternly say to her, hoping that she will understand the grave danger in what we are getting ready to do. She begins to jump up and down like a toddler and clap her hands enthusiastically. "Lucy, this is what I am talking about! You cannot act like this once we get to the estate!" I say once again to try to intimidate Lucy, hoping that she will heed my warning of the danger that waits for us. She smiles and then whispers,

"I understand." She puts her finger over her lips.

Despite the immense concern that I have of Lucy not actually being able to control herself, we begin to battle the snow-covered ground as we make our way to Ocean Point. We agree that the best way to keep ourselves from being seen is to enter the property from the side of the gigantic hill that borders the side of my house. Even though this is the smartest way for us to sneak onto the estate without being seen, we now have to fight the icy-white hill that feels more like a mountain.

The snow is tall and cold, and it makes our hike slippery. It is deep, and in some spots on the hill it reaches all the way to our knees. I think to myself how ludicrous it is for us to fight so fiercely to reach a place that looks down at us and wishes us discomfort. After a long, treacherous battle against the elements of a northern winter day, we arrive at the top of the hill. We are both depleted of energy and struggle to breathe at a normal pace. We sit down in the freezing snow to regain our strength.

When we both feel ready, we sneak to the back of the house and hurry to the overgrown path that waits to guide us to the secret graveyard. We arrive at the entrance to the path, and even though it is in the middle of the day, the passageway is dark and haunting. I look at Lucy to silently confirm that she still wants to enter. She nods her head indicating that she does. She does not take her eyes off of the hollow trail in front of us. I step onto the path first, and Lucy follows me.

Lucy and I walk side by side and hold hands. She looks at the sky through the occasional openings that the snow-covered tree branches allow. With winter now here, the wild weeds and flowers that impaired my vision before are now dead and frozen in the harsh winter snow. Even with the absence of the wild foliage that seemed to attack me with every step, the path is still just as aware of my presence as before.

The trees seem alive even with the cold snow and ice taking the warmth from their frozen limbs. They own this part of Ocean Point and will not hesitate to claim their territory. Lucy grips my hand tighter with every turn that the path forces us around. She is fixated on the dismal mansion that watches us as we trespass through the secret garden. With each step into the garden, Lucy's bravery is slowly sucked out of her, and the mansion is amused by it.

Even with the path more visible, it still leaves us confused of our location due to the blanket of snow that tames the unruly grounds. Despite the undeniable emotion of pure fright that the passage instills in my heart, the garden is quite beautiful with the trees covered in snow.

There is an array of sizes of icicles that dangle from the tree branches that reach into the maze. They give the appearance that the trees were deliberately decorated by the winter sky. We make a sharp turn, and the gazebo is in front of us.

"Wow, that is the biggest gazebo I have ever seen! It's as big as my old house in Providence was!"

Lucy's elation over the structure seems to have simmered her once apparent fear, and she runs to the gazebo. She goes to the middle of the gazebo and leans her head back, holding her arms out with her palms facing the white sky. She begins to turn her body in circles. Snow falls from the sky, and she looks like she has been placed in the center of a snow globe. I can hear the childlike music that snow globes usually make. I watch Lucy play in the gazebo. This is how I envision children playing on these once glorious grounds. I wonder if the children buried beneath my feet lived long enough to play in and enjoy this garden. I imagine them stepping their bare feet on the lush, green grass and smelling the fragrance of the brightly colored flowers that grew throughout the magnificent garden. During a winter day like this one, I see them bundling up in winter clothes and making snowmen with fancy top hats and carrot noses.

I have to believe that there were blissful days and happy memories once made in this now unwelcoming lawn. I am pleased to see how delighted and carefree Lucy is, but I am aware that her childish fun will get us noticed. I join her and ask her to sit down. She stops spinning, but she stumbles from the dizziness. She reaches for the safety of a nearby bench and sits down.

"You are going to have to let me get married here! It is groovy! Your mom really must have some serious issues to let this place go," she says.

I smile and say that she can get married in the gazebo just to pacify her interest, but I have no intentions of being anywhere near this house when it is time for her to get married. I sit on the bench, and to my amazement I can smell the white lilies again. How is this possible in this bitter, cold air? The flowers have frozen, and the fragrance should have disappeared. I look around the gazebo to see if the beautiful flowers are magically growing, but I see nothing but snow and icicles. I guess my memory is triggered by being where I first discovered them. I realize that with all that happened today I never gave Lucy her gift. I reach into my backpack and pull out the dainty, little present. I hand it to her and smile.

"Wow, you got me a gift?" she says as she rips the delicate snowman paper off of the tiny box with much enthusiasm. She opens the jewelry box, pulls out the fragile necklace, and says, "Coral, I love it! Thank you so much! You are my best friend too!" She puts the necklace around her neck and fastens the clasp.

We leave the gazebo and make a plan to visit the graves of my ancestors, but on our way Lucy notices an oddly shaped door on the side of the house. It is cracked open.

"Where does that door go?" she asks curiously.

I do not know. I have never seen it before, but I do know that it is attached to the house. We do not need to take such a gamble. Before I can voice my opinion, Lucy starts to make her way towards the house. I cannot stop her because I am afraid if I yell to her that I will be heard. I have no choice but to follow after her. The door is wooden and has carvings embedded in it seeming to be of a religious nature with crosses and symbols. The top of the door is circular, and it reminds me of something you would see on an old medieval castle. Lucy runs her fingers across the carvings on the door and seems to be mesmerized by the art. She looks at me and says,

"Are you ready?"

"Ready for what?" I ask, but I already know the answer. She wants to go into the room behind this frightening door. "No Lucy, we shouldn't. It's too dangerous!" I say. I have immense hesitation about what is in store for us inside. I do not have a good feeling about this.

"Come on, we have already come this far!" she says as she does the Catholic cross movement across her head and chest. Before I can stop her, she opens the door and is inside. I hesitate, and then I copy her Catholic prayer across my head and chest and quickly follow behind her.

Lucy stands in the room and is motionless. Her body is so rigid that she looks like a statue. Even with the small amount of light that the partially opened door lets in, the room is still dark. It is hard to see the entire room. I can see a small, antique-looking lamp sitting on the dirt floor. I bend down and attempt to turn it on. To my surprise, the old lamp works. It radiates a dim, amber glow that vaguely lights the room.

"Holy shit Coral, this is a torture dungeon!"

I cannot believe what we see. There are chains attached to the walls with shackles. There is a stained mattress in the corner of the room. There are no windows, so no natural light can enter.

"Did your family have slaves?" she asks, trying to come up with a possible explanation of why this room is in my house.

"I don't know," I say, wondering myself.

I do not think with my family living in the north that we would have had slaves. I move closer to the chains that are firmly attached to the stone walls, and I can see drawings that have been etched into the stones. Unimaginable horror consumes me when I realize that the chains have to be for children. They are attached so low to the ground that there is no way a grown person could physically be chained at this height, and the drawings in the walls look juvenile like a child has created them. All I can think about are the children buried outside of this room. Is this where they were kept? Is this how they died? Were they tortured to death, starved, and treated like animals? I ache for them even though I'm not sure if this is what really happened in this room.

I take a closer look at the drawings. I run my fingertips across the markings in the stone and retrace the artwork of a child who must have suffered as much as I have. I feel a connection that I cannot explain. Some of the sketches are of normal, childish artwork with puppies, flowers, and trees, but there are some disturbing images left behind by a child's hand that are chilling. There are drawings that look to be of monsters, demons, and the devil. Words are scattered among these pictures. They read, "help," "hungry," "scared," "hurt me," and the scariest one of all reads, "She is coming." Oh my God. This child is speaking of Mother! It says that *she* is coming, not that *he* is coming. Did Mother torture these children down here? I have never been as afraid for my safety and future as I am at this very moment.

I inch my way to the thin mattress that lays on the dirt floor. It is filthy and covered with dirt. There are rips in the material and stains on the fabric. I am sickened to imagine the suffering that these innocent children must have gone through. I picture the small children sleeping on this disgusting mattress all cold and alone. My heart is heavy, and this new revelation is a burden that I am not sure I can keep inside. I notice a book in the corner. I pick it up. It is worn and tattered. I open the torn leather cover and discover that it is an old Bible. I am now convinced that this room was made with Mother's hands after discovering the Bible.

I turn to look at Lucy, and she has moved towards another door. It is visible that at one time the door was locked with a huge, rusted chain and old-fashioned deadbolt lock the size of my hand. The lock lays on the floor, and the chain suspends on the door handle as if it is exhausted from working so hard to keep the precious children in prison. Lucy attempts to open the heavy door.

"No, Lucy! We do not know where that door leads or what could be behind it!" I whisper with as much sternness that my soft voice can put out.

Lucy ignores my plea and pushes the door open. It creaks loudly. I am sure that if someone is inside that he or she knows of our presence now. I move to the door that she just forced open and can see that behind it is a passageway of stairs that goes straight up. Unlike the other room, there are windows in this hallway. I think I am in the west wing because from the windows I see a view that I have never seen before. The hallway is dusty and full of spider webs. Lucy begins to enter the hallway, but I grab her arm. I plead to her with my eyes to stop. I squeeze her bicep to try to get her attention. She grabs my hand firmly and pulls me into the hidden passageway with her. She does not seem afraid as if something has possessed her and is coaching her on where to go and what to do. She seems emotionless.

We slowly begin to climb up the steps guided by the small amount of sunlight that creeps through the windows. After eight to ten steps there is a landing, and at the landing there is a door. The stairs then continue in a curved, circular fashion to another landing. There are several of these landings, essentially creating a massive spiral staircase. Each door is chained and locked just like the door that we entered from once was. I question if all of these rooms are the same as the room we just left. There were five gravestones with children buried beneath, so is there a room for each of these children? Nothing makes sense, but I also know that nothing about this is right either. Something very terrible took place here, and I can feel it. I want to stop and go back to the garden. I want to hear the white lilies sing to me. I want to sit in the gazebo and act like we never found this passageway or torture room. I try to pull Lucy towards me indicating that I want to leave, but she selfishly ignores my request.

I lose track of how many flights of stairs we climb, so I inch myself towards one of the tiny windows and look out. I cannot believe that we have climbed almost to the top of the mansion. I know that we have to be close to the level I live on, but because the passage goes in a circle it is confusing. As we arrive at the next landing, we hear a noise on the other side of the door. We both are startled and stand as still as we can. It is difficult to breathe in the dusty passageway. I can feel the dirt travel through my nostrils and search for my lungs. We hear another loud bang as if someone is slamming something down. Then, we hear the one sound I dread hearing the most, my mother's voice.

I squeeze Lucy's hand as tight as I can. Mother's voice is towering, and she taunts the person that she speaks to. I can hear her preach to the person of the Bible and all the fire and brimstone scriptures that I have heard ever since I could walk. I can hear her boots pace the floor as she screams about sin and the devil to this person. Who is in there with her? Suddenly, we hear the sound of someone being whipped. The sound of the whip is muffled by the noise of a piercing scream that is so distorted that it does not even sound human.

Lucy lets go of my hand and takes off running and stumbles down the stairs. Her departure is so without grace that I know Mother and whatever is being enslaved in there can hear her bang against the walls as she tries to escape the castle's secret passageway. I stand alone in the darkness, too afraid to move or breathe. Tears stream down my face, and I uncontrollably shake until I have to sit.

The whip stops, and the loud howls of pain reduce to whimpers and slow sobbing. I hear Mother's footsteps again. She comes close to the door that I sit right next to. The footsteps stop. I hold my breath and use every muscle in my body to remain still. She hovers in front of the door for a few moments as if she is listening through the door to hear the intruders. After a moment, she walks away. I can hear her tell the person,

"Okay Sinner, back to your lesson for the day." She begins to whip the person again, and the screams return.

I have been saved. She has dismissed the noise that she heard, and now I have to escape. I remain on my bottom and carefully use my arms to scoot down the stairway as quickly as I can. The screams and cries echo behind me. They become faint, so I know that I am almost to the bottom of the stairs. When I get far enough down, the sounds of torture are gone. I rise to my feet and dash down the stairs as fast as my shaky legs will move. I reach the bottom of the stairs, and I keep running. I charge through the room of torture and straight outside. I do not even stop. I slam the small wooden door closed, and I am breathless. I lean my back against the hand carved door and try to regain my senses.

I close my eyes and hope that when I open them again that this was just a dream, and I will wake up in my bed. I open my eyes, but it is not a dream. I scan the property to see if I can find Lucy, but she is nowhere to be seen. I am so angry at her for dragging me into the scary, little room and then pulling me up the stairs just to leave me there alone with Mother on the other side of the door. At the same time, the concern that Lucy will not want to be my friend any longer troubles me more than my fleeting anger. I cannot say that I would not blame her. Who would want to be friends with someone like me? I am sure she thinks that my entire family is completely insane.

I look around the garden and try to stay as small as I can so that I am not seen. I can see the top of some of the tombstones in the distance. All I want to do is find those white lilies that give my spirit peace. I have taken my last risk today, and I am fortunate that my poor judgment has not already revealed my rebellious actions. Since Lucy is nowhere to be found, I want leave the garden. I have had one of the worst days of my life, and my stomach is beginning to cramp again.

It is time to call it a day. I push myself off of the door that I have been leaning on, and I see movement out of the corner of my eye. Instinctually, I look to see what it is, but there is nothing there. I assume that my eyes are playing tricks on me. I bend down and pick up my book bag that is now covered in grime from being dragged down the dirty stairs. As I adjust the bag across my shoulder, I see a small cottage in the distance. I have never seen the little house before. As I inspect this new discovery from afar, I think that I see a person standing on the porch. Is it Lucy? Has she found a safe place for us to hide? I am so happy that she did not leave me. I start to jog towards the cottage, but the closer I get, I am able to recognize that the person on the porch is not Lucy.

It is a man. I stop instantly in my tracks and look right at this stranger from a distance. He is wearing some kind of hat that impairs my ability to make out who he might be. It appears that he does not see me. Who is this man? Why is he on our property? Suddenly, he notices me and leaps off the porch and out of my sight. Is that cottage not owned by my family? Is that someone else's residence? This does not make sense to me. The cottage is obviously on our property. The man apparently wishes to do no harm to me. I do not get the sense that he is a threat to me, so I decide to let this man continue to run away from me while I run home. As unusual as this new revelation is, I have already had enough unwelcomed surprises today.

I slink around the house like a burglar would after stealing prized jewelry. I search for a way to get to the sun porch without having to go through the garden. It has to be possible. I come to a dead-end where the huge trees and shrubbery are so thick that I would have to have to chop down everything in front of me with a shear just to walk.

I look around trying to place myself in hopes that I can quickly find one of the paths that will lead me home. I navigate around the yard, and I soon find one. I know that this is not the one that I usually travel, but I will take the first escape that I can find. I hope that they all connect in some way. The wind gets stronger and blows against the trees. The frozen branches look brittle with the snow and ice encasing them. I am cold and tired, and it seems that I have been on this path for an eternity. I am not sure that I am making any progress. It is as if the paths are alive and continue to change directions to keep intruders lost and disoriented. The malicious trees laugh at my confusion.

My feet are so cold that they are becoming numb, and my steps are uncoordinated. I pause to rest. I reach towards one of the trees and place my hand on it for balance. The weight of my body causes the tree to sway. I hear a clanging sound, and instantly large icicles begin to dive down like daggers. The ice stabs the ground all around me. Large icicles actually spiral from the sky and pierce into the ground straight up as a knife would. The rainfall of frozen ice continues and strikes me. The sting of the trees' attacks urges me to run. I hurry through the path, and the icicles continue to fall from the trees.

The ice continues to batter me and hit me on my back. It slams roughly on the top of my head. The jagged ice pierces my feet, and the only safety my toes have is the protection of my shoes. I twist and turn, feeling like I am just going in circles as the passageway punishes me for infringing on its land. I see a small clearing in front of me and sprint to safety. I exit the trail breathless. After an abrupt stop, I place my hands on my knees and struggle to accept the air into my lungs. I peer over my shoulder. There is no ice pouring out of the sky. The wind isn't gusting against the trees. The path is calm and serene. It has the pleasant image of a wonderful winter day that you would see on a Christmas card. Am I losing my mind? Is there something mentally wrong with me, and I just do not realize it? I know what just happened to me, but it does not seem possible.

I stand and begin towards the back door so I can sneak in. I see the stairs that lead into the sun porch in the distance. I hope that Mother is so preoccupied with torturing that person that she overlooks me tonight. I feel terrible for thinking this way, but I honestly do not think that my body and mind can endure anything else today. As I climb the stairs, I hear a car engine start. I stop and crouch down to watch the car leave the driveway. I am overjoyed to see that it is Mother leaving. I enter the house and franticly search for Rose. I loudly call out her name as I enter each room. I hear her come down the hall, and I run in her direction. I get close to her, and she stops my movement by grabbing my shoulders. A look of panic is on her face.

"Child, are you alright? I have been worried sick!" she says desperately. She grabs me tight and pulls me into her chest. This overwhelming display of affection leaves me wondering how late I really am. "Your school called today and said that you weren't in any of your classes, and some girls reported to the teacher that you were in the bathroom screaming. I have spent my whole day looking for you!"

I immediately know what is in store for me when Mother comes home. Rose can read my concern from my expression and reassures me of my safety. She tells me that she intercepted the phone call and that Mother knows nothing about my absence. Relief washes over me, and I am so thankful that I fall into her chest as a sign of thanks.

"Child, tell me what happened and where you have been!" she demands. Her concern grows into anger.

"Did one not bother to think that she should tell me about getting my period?" I ask her in a spoiled, snippy tone. My entire disposition changes from longing to have Rose help me through such a traumatic experience to being irate for her dismissal of such an important event that every woman goes through.

She appears ashamed and stumbles over her words as she begins to try to give me an explanation. I do not even wait for a feeble excuse. The mood between us changes from relief to disappointment. I just shake my head and exit the room.

I arrive at my bedroom, and I feel dirty and unclean. All I want is a shower. I wish that I could stand under the warm water and wash this day away. I know that this is unattainable since Mother has been trying to wash my sins away for years, and nothing has changed. I stand under the water, and it feels good as it flows across my naked skin. I look down at my stomach, and it is swollen and tender to the touch. I really wish that someone loved me enough to prepare me for this gross monthly ritual.

I do not want to think about the dungeon below me. I do not want to close my eyes and hear the sobs of the trapped children, and I definitely do not want to think about who or what that was screaming on the other side of the door. Right now, I do not care who lives in the cottage and do not want to know why the trees tried to kill me. I do not want to face the reality of this secretive house.

I enter my bedroom, and laying on my bed is a pink box. At first, I think that maybe Rose left me a gift because she feels so terrible about not taking the time to explain the menstrual cycle to me. I pick the box up and am disappointed to see that it is just a box of tiny diapers like the ones Lucy gave me. I take the box into the bathroom and take out what I need. I then shove the box in the closet and try to forget monthly visit that is now a part of my life.

I hear the intercom buzz, and Rollins's voice radiates throughout the house. He informs everyone that dinner is ready. Hearing his voice is a pleasant sound for me, not because I am hungry but because I love hearing Rollins and his accent. It takes me back to a time when I was innocent and did not realize how bad my life really is. I guess ignorance can be bliss sometimes.

I dress and leave the comfort of my bedroom even though my stomach feels queasy. All I want to do is crawl into bed, pull the covers over my head, and pretend that the world does not exist outside of my bedroom. I do as a well behaved girl would and make my way to the dining room despite how horrible I feel. I want to avoid any possibility of being punished today.

As I near the entrance of our lifeless but once elegant dining room, I hear that Rose and Mother are in the middle of a heated conversation. I stop behind the wall before I become visible and eavesdrop, hoping that Mother did not find out about my reckless afternoon adventure with Lucy. It is apparent as I eagerly listen that Rose has informed Mother that I have started my period. I am sure that the discomfort and nastiness of this ridiculous condition that I am in will please Mother.

"I knew this day would come. We have been lucky that she is so awkward and underdeveloped that this hasn't happened sooner. I thought that one of my nightly prayers had been answered, that she would not be able to reproduce and continue to bring unclean and unholy children into this world," Mother says as I can hear her franticly pace the floors.

Why does this normal womanly function put Mother in such a

worried state? Her voice seems different as if she is not in control. Even though I am hiding behind a wall and cannot see the two of them, it sounds like she is just speaking out loud instead of engaging Rose in an important conversation about her daughter. I try not to let her hurtful words affect me as I discreetly listen.

"It is now more important than ever that Coral is watched and her every move is monitored. She is now biologically able to bring forth a child. This family's curse cannot be carried on through this worthless girl. I won't let it happen. This ends with her, and I don't care what I have to do to ensure that it does!" Mother speaks fast. She does not handle herself in the same controlled demeanor that I am accustomed to. I have to admit that I enjoy the thought of Mother being distraught even if it is over something that I do not understand.

"Margret, with all due respect, Coral is growing up, and you cannot stop nature from taking its course. She is becoming more of a woman and less of a child on a daily basis. She is a smart girl, and at some point she will take a stand. She isn't like the others. She has fire in her just like…"

"DO NOT SAY THAT NAME IN THIS HOUSE!" Mother screams at Rose. I have never heard Rose call my mother by her first name.

"All I am saying is that you will not be able to keep her here under your control forever," Rose says seeming not to be affected by Mother's rage.

"Don't underestimate my ability to keep this house and everyone in it under my control! Look at what I have accomplished so far," Mother proudly states. After a few moments of silence, she begins to speak again. "This is what has to happen. Coral will not go back to school. She will be schooled here by me, and I am going to add four hours a day of religion. She needs to have the Lord's word injected into her brain daily to combat the evil inside of her. There will be no more visits to the town. She will now stay inside within these walls where the evil and shame is contained." The desperation in her voice is a side of her that I have never seen.

"Margret, you cannot hold her prisoner here. This is insane talk. People will begin to ask questions, and I don't think you want that to happen. Besides, don't you think you have your hands full right now?" Rose says, trying to persuade her to be reasonable.

"Let me worry about what people might think or say. My money has kept many mouths shut, and this time will be no different," Mother pretentiously states.

"You need to think this through, Margret. I am afraid that you are opening up very old wounds, and I really don't think you are prepared to face the consequences if this plan of yours fails. Besides, Coral will be eighteen before you know it, and I am sure after the treatment you have given her that she will leave Ocean Point as soon as she can," Rose continues as she tries to make Mother see that her plan is flawed. Mother's mind is so focused on keeping me hidden from the world that she does not listen.

"Rose, Rose, Rose, you are so simple minded. That ignorant girl doesn't know a thing about life. She doesn't know how things work, and she definitely doesn't know her legal rights. I have done a good job of keeping her as simple minded as you! All I have to do is keep her confined, and nothing will change," Mother says and laughs wickedly. Her continuous insults do not change Rose's stance.

"I am aware that it is my job to follow your rules. I will continue to do so within reason, but you also need to understand that I have never lied to that girl and never will. She will start to ask questions soon, and she deserves the truth. She deserves a life outside of these walls. She did not do this to you or this family. Not one woman who has ever stepped foot in this house is responsible for the sins that you preach of that have destroyed the Margret that I used to call my friend. That girl is no different. You are making her and everyone else in this house pay for the sins of a man! I have gone along with this cruel scheme of yours because we were once friends, and I know your pain. I understand your pain. I have gone along with this against what I truly believe is right, and I am warning you. I am nearing the end," Rose says to Mother in such a calm voice that it seems she has had these words trapped in her mind for decades.

Is my hearing failing me? Is Rose actually standing up to Mother? I feel so proud of Rose but also a little afraid for her. There is a tense silence in the room that I can feel through the wall. I hear Mother's footsteps again, and then I hear something break. Did she hurt Rose? I want to charge into the room to Rose's rescue, but I do not. I remain on the other side of the wall like a helpless coward.

"If this is the way you feel, then I think it is time for you to go! I can't have this kind of disrespect in my home, especially now that the devil has returned and walks among us. We have a host living here to give birth to another abomination into this family. I want you packed and gone by sun up tomorrow!" she commands.

So much of what she says sounds like the rants of a deranged woman, but what I do hear, and what matters the most, is for Rose to be gone. I am still concerned that Rose is hurt, and Mother is standing over her unresponsive body bellowing out demands. I fight back the urge to cry from knowing that my Rose is leaving me. I cannot survive without Rose. Finally, I hear Rose's voice, and she is still as calm as before. I am relieved.

"Okay Margret, remember the day that you and I were best friends? Well, let me tell you, I cherish who you were then. That woman is still the woman I love. I will not give up the hope that she lives somewhere inside of your damaged soul and that you just refuse to let the past go and find a shred of peace and happiness in your final years. So out of respect for what our relationship used to be, I will leave at sun up, but I will take Coral with me. You will write me a large check so that I will have the proper means to provide for her. I think that this will be best for everyone."

"Are you out of your mind? YOU WILL DO NO SUCH THING! Even if that girl's blood is tainted with evil, she is still a Berringer! If you were from the same class as me, you would understand the loyalty that supersedes the bad deeds that this family may experience," she says to Rose without even considering the conditions that Rose has set forth.

I do not understand why Mother would not be ecstatic with my absence from the family. Does she not realize that by releasing me from her tight grip that the devil she fears will leave her precious Ocean Point as well?

"Okay, then I guess I am not leaving because I will not leave this residence without Coral!" Rose fires back at Mother but remains centered and level headed.

"You have no right to make those demands. I will handle this now. I will call Sheriff Calloway and have you removed, and you will not be packing for Coral!" Mother states.

I hear footsteps, and then I hear someone pick up the phone. I cannot believe what is happening. I want to race into the room and scream at Mother. I want to tell her that I am leaving with Rose, but something inside of me keeps me in the shadows. I feel a gentle tug on my shoulder, and I hear a soft whisper in my ear that tells me to wait. I do not know if I am delirious over the stress of the confrontation or if it is over losing Rose, but I remain still.

"Before you make that phone call to the sheriff, you might want to consider one thing, Miss Margret. I will have a long ride back to Providence with the sheriff. I wonder if he would find any interest in what you have hidden in the west wing. I assume that he would want to contact one of his friends who work for FBI once he hears what I know and am no longer afraid to reveal." Before she can finish with her threats, Mother slams the phone down.

"Fine. You stay, but Coral stays confined in this house!" Mother says out of desperation. I hear her pointed black shoes stomp on the expensive marble floor toward where I am hiding. I slowly tip toe backward until I retreat into the darkness of another room to hide my presence. I hear a second crash, and it sounds like something shatters into pieces as Mother leaves the dining room. "Rose, I am not feeling much like having dinner now, so tell Coral that she will be dining alone tonight. By the way, make sure you clean up that broken glass. We wouldn't want anyone to get hurt now, would we?" Mother says in a sarcastic manner.

When I see that Mother is a safe distance away, I hurry into the dining room. I want to go give Rose an enormous hug, but when I enter the room and see Rose on her hands and knees picking up the broken glass I hesitate. I decide not to tell Rose that I overheard the argument. I do not know why I choose to keep my knowledge quiet. This would be the perfect way for me to get the answers I need, but something stops me and tells me that right now is just not the right time. I stoop down and carefully help Rose pick up the broken vases that Mother so carelessly destroyed.

I sit at the dinner table alone, but I do not mind the solitude. I am definitely not in the mood to look at Mother. I sit alone and think about all that I heard between Mother and Rose. I did not hear any big secrets that would give me all of the answers that I have been searching for, but I do know I am not crazy. There are secrets. There are painful, sinful, and menacing secrets. After hearing the heated altercation, I know that my presence in this family and house has something to do with the strange, eccentric life that all that live here are forced to lead. I did see a side of Mother that I have never encountered, and her undeniable aversion is disconcerting.

I try to rest my weary mind from my eventful and heart-wrenching day, but no matter how many broccoli spears I shove in my mouth, my heart is heavy. I feel empty inside. I am devastated to know what my life is to become now. I am going to be caged in this house like an animal.

The thought of my isolation brings my spirit down to such a low that I am concerned for my ability to cope with it or even attempt to find the strength to crawl out of it. The part that makes me the saddest is knowing that my friendship with Lucy is never going to be the same. She might have already decided that my family drama is too horrendous. I had a glimmer of hope that she would still be my best friend until now.

As much as I do not want to admit it to myself, I also feel a vacancy inside of me from knowing that there will never be a possibility to get to know Angel. No matter how unkind he has been to me, I am still enchanted by him. I think of him every day and wonder where he is. I question if he could ever see me as anything more than a weird, rich girl that dresses odd.

These are things that I know I cannot change. Mother is the ruler over Ocean Point and everyone trapped in the secrets that these walls enclose. I know that in order to survive I have to comply with her rules and decisions. This is not a life. This is an incarceration, and the sentence that Mother has executed will be my demise.

Isolated

It has been over a year since I entered the prison that I call home. Christmas came and went, and as usual there was no Christmas tree, decorations, twinkling lights, or presents. That was the first year that our lack of joyful spirit did not bother me. I did not feel much like celebrating. Father did come home for a few weeks during the holiday, but our relationship has been so strained. It is partly because he stays gone more now, but I am still angry with him. He knows this and has just chosen the coward's way. Instead of trying to improve our relationship, it is easier for him to just not to be around.

I do not even affectionately call him Daddy any longer. I refer to him as Father. I do miss those warm and happy feelings that I used to get when I would see that handsome man, but now that affection is gone. It might be because I am older and that it is a normal part of maturing, but the main reason is because he is not saving me. Daddies are supposed to protect their little girls, and he has failed at that task for too many years. His denial has destroyed any respect I ever had for him.

After Christmas went by, so did Valentine's Day, Easter, Fourth of July, Halloween, and yet another Christmas and Valentine's Day. Not one of these occasions was recognized, and they definitely weren't celebrated. When I turned sixteen, I did not get a sweet sixteen ball which is customary with the families in our social class. I did not get a shiny, new car like all the other girls around here do. I even missed out on getting my driver's license. I have learned to stop complaining about my misfortunes, though. I just live with them.

I have watched the seasons come and go from the seclusion of my bedroom window. The clocks haven't stopped, but my life has. I have become a shell of a person only functioning to stay alive. I am bound to the house, and every step I take is watched, studied, and evaluated. I have no privacy any longer. In the night when I go to sleep, my bedroom door opens every hour for a bed check like clockwork.

When Mother started this ridiculous system of domination, I would be so tired during my homeschooling that I would struggle to keep my eyes open and keep my yawns under control. Mother would take a ruler and smack my hands as hard as she could if I seemed not to be paying attention or dozing off. I wanted to stand up and yell at the demented woman that if she did not wake me up every hour that I might be more alert in her makeshift school. As an obeying prisoner does, I remained silent and took every slap to the wrist. Over time, I adjusted to the nightly check and eventually became a heavy sleeper.

Mother hired a nun and a priest to come to Ocean Point and give me four hours of Bible lecture daily. Not one lesson delivered to me was of love and hope, the way I believe God is, but of fire, brimstone, and eternal damnation. After the first hour of every lesson, it seemed that everything that came out of their self-righteous mouths was just repetitive. I got very good at pretending to pay attention but not hearing a word that they arrogantly preached.

As each day, week, and month passed, I would grow more despondent and severely depressed. There were several times that I found myself planning to end it all. I thought that death had to be better than walking around purposeless. I felt dead already. I was numb inside. I had no real emotions any longer, and that fire that Rose always speaks of was blown out by Mother's spiteful breath. Mother was getting what she wanted. I lost my will to live, and as each day passed I became less of a person and more of a doll that she just plucked off of a shelf. She could make me do whatever she wanted. I grew used to being Mother's puppet. She pulled the strings, and I let her manipulate my lifeless body in whatever direction she wanted. It was simple. I just existed.

Surprisingly, my punishments eventually ended. Mother could see that her diabolical plan had worked. She administered every move I made, and promptly, became the little robot that she wanted me to be. The strange part is that I was not acting this way to please Mother. It was not because I feared her or her punishments. It was not because she finally convinced me that I was wicked and immoral and that I was obeying because I wanted to cleanse my spirit of the evil. I was acting this way because I did not care anymore. This is what I had become.

I could tell that the transformation in me bothered Rose. In the beginning of my slide into hopelessness, she would try to pull me out of the deep depression. Her compassion, kind words, and attempts of encouragement felt like home to me, but the misery was the victor. Coral was truly gone. As much as it upset Rose that I was not mentally well any longer, I think she was relieved that the new me was not physically or verbally abused. What she did not understand was that my new punishment of seclusion was worse than any sharp word that rolled off of Mother's tongue, any temperature of hot water, or any slap my face could receive from Mother's long, boney fingers.

Mother knew that her plan worked, and there was no need to show dominance any longer. It was understood that she was my master, and I was her filthy slave. Even though my behavior satisfied Mother, she still has no love for me. She truly loathes me. Abiding by her rules and pretending that she was my God did not change the pure hatred that she has for me in her heart. She just can deal with my existence now.

I would go to my window and see if I could locate Lucy or Angel on the beach below me, but I never did. I wonder if Lucy thinks that this creepy castle swallowed me whole. Maybe she thinks that Mother killed me. Either way, it does not matter. I am gone and have been for so long that I am sure she does not even think about me anymore. I think about her and Angel every day, and I miss her companionship more than I can convey. Losing Lucy's friendship has left me grief stricken and alone.

I wonder if they still live next door. I wish I knew if Lucy finally got the boyfriend that she desperately wanted. It would be so great if we could run under the boardwalk again and she tell me all the romantic details, but knowing Lucy they would most likely be steamy stories that once would have embarrassed me. I wonder if Angel ever came home or if he ran off and joined the Italian mob like his mother feared he would.

He is a man now, and for all I know he fell madly in love with another girl and is happily married. These questions will probably never be answered, so I have put Lucy and Angel in a special place in my memories. They are the only good memories I have.

I not only have changed mentally, but I also have changed physically. After I started my period my breasts grew large, and my hips widened. Rose had to buy me three different bra sizes in only two months. My body finally looks like a woman's body. I am still petite and look somewhat fragile, though. Rose says that I am what you call small-boned and tells me how many women would kill for a figure like mine. She leaves out the fact that no woman would ever wish for the gruesome scars that I live with.

I often stare at my developing figure in the mirror. The body I now have is the one that I dreamed of having when I was a wide-eyed fourteen year old full of aspirations of happiness and love. What a silly girl I was to think I could ever be normal. The scars on my skin will show anyone how bizarre I really am. They have not faded with the years; they are a part of me now. I have accepted this, and I rarely even think about them anymore. I used to be afraid of what my future husband would think, but that was just a young girl's fantasy. I laugh at the idea that any man would ever want to marry me.

I do not even think about the secrets of the house anymore. I still hear the screams from the demon that lives down the hall. I can still smell those lilies and hear them whisper to me. I still ache for the children that lived behind the round door, but these things do not consume me anymore. I just let all the ghosts, demons, and memories live together in this house just like they have for many years before me. They live within me now, and I guess we have always been soul mates. Ocean Point owns me now.

It is a usual Saturday morning, and I sit at my window and listen to the ocean. I open my window and close my eyes. The ocean breeze finds its way through the crack, and the fresh scent fills my room. I can hear the waves crash against the bluffs and retreat back. I sometimes spend hours doing this and thinking of nothing. I let the grief and pain go somewhere else. I just breathe and feel peace. I remain still in my mind and body. I read somewhere that in other countries and religions they do this and that they call it meditating. I like to call it escaping.

I do my ritual mediation, but I cannot rest my mind as I usually do. I feel very unusual today. I do not feel as morose as I normally do, but by no means am I happy. I keep having thoughts of Lucy and Angel. My unexplainable fixation on the two is distracting. There must be a reason that they constantly occupy my thoughts.

I open my eyes and look down at the beach. I hope to see them sunbathing on the beach or hanging out with friends. I scan the beach, and other than a few seagulls, there is nothing there. My room is so high up, and the house is such a distance away that even if they were on the beach I would not know if it were them or not. They would just look like tiny people from my view. I attempt to relax again and try to push what I truly long for out of my psyche and regain the amazing self-control that I have mastered, but all I can concentrate on is how wonderful it would be to have my feet in the warm sand and to breath in fresh air instead of the stale, musty air that circulates through this house. My bedroom door opens.

"Good morning, Sunshine. Are you ready for some breakfast?" It is Rose.

"No, I am not very hungry this morning," I say despite the fact that I would fancy the rich taste of Rollins's eggs benedict.

I would rather go hungry than share another meal with Mother today. I need some reprise from her authority. I spend almost every waking moment with her. Between my homeschooling and Bible class, I have no desire to spend any more time with her than required. Rose knows my reason for wanting to skip breakfast and goes on to say,

"Your mother left this morning. She is going to be out of town for business for a few days. Are you sure you don't want to come down and eat? Rollins has that kitchen smelling like Heaven. He has cooked eggs, sausage, hash browns, and I picked up some fresh fruit at the store yesterday."

Just hearing her talk makes my stomach growl from hunger. The best news is that Mother will be gone. I rejoice inside to know that I will not have to lay eyes on her for days. It has been so long since she left town. This news gives me a sense of contentment that I have not felt in over a year. Rose and I walk through the mansion together towards the dining room. As we draw near, I feel dread with the thought of the silent and unpleasant meals that I am forced to share with Mother.

"May I have permission to eat my breakfast on the sun porch?" I ask her. I revel in the idea of enjoying my meal in the sun-lit room instead of the ominous dining room that is filled with so many God-awful memories.

"I think that is a splendid idea. You run along now, and I will join you momentarily with your breakfast." She nudges me forward.

I take a seat at the small wicker table that I wish still had a view of the ocean. In winter when the plants die, the foliage clears up just enough to be able to see the blue water. I can hear the waves in the distance and the seagulls flying above me. It is distressing that I sit here surrounded with God's beautiful creations, but I am confined to this glass box. Rose wheels in a food cart. I am delighted to see two plates, two sets of silverware, and two glasses of orange juice.

"Miss Coral, would it be okay if I joined you for breakfast?" she asks. Rose and I used to sneak to the sun porch or have picnics in the living room together when I was younger. Those are wonderful memories.

"I would enjoy that very much, Miss Rose," I say in a playful and sophisticated voice.

Rose puts our plates on the small table and sits across from me. I devour my food. I do not receive the eggs benedict that my stomach is craving, but the array of breakfast items that fills my plate is pleasing to my palate and empty stomach. As I shovel the eggs in my mouth, Rose begins to talk in a very curious voice.

"Yesterday when I was at the market I ran into Mrs. Lombardi from next door." Her eyes do not look up from her plate. She speaks to me as if she is giving me a hint or telling me a secret. I stop eating with my fork still in my mouth. "She was gathering groceries for Lucy's birthday party that is this evening," she continues to tell me.

Why would Rose share information with me that she knows would just cause me heartache? She must know how much I wish I could attend such a special day for my friend. She looks up at me. I am sure that my anguish from missing Lucy and not being able to attend her party is obvious. With a lack of sensitivity, she continues speaking.

"The celebration is going to be on the beach tonight." Her words and thoughtlessness make me feel like a knife has been inserted into my back, and every detail she reveals twists the knife until I cannot breath. I put my fork on my plate and rise to my feet.

"Rose, I think I have lost my appetite," I say in a tone that shows how irritated she has made me. As I leave the room, she does not acknowledge my annoyance or even the fact that I am leaving and continues the conversation as if I am still sitting across from her.

"The party is going to start at five o'clock tonight. To me, that is terribly late to begin a party. By that time I will be in my nightgown snuggled up with a new book that I have been dying to read, and you know how I get once I start reading a good book. I just shut the world around me out. I get so interested that I don't hear a thing that goes on around me. Also, with your mother out of town, she won't be running me to death. I am really looking forward to starting that book," she peculiarly says.

I am bewildered for a brief moment, but then I finally understand why Rose is saying these things to me. She is encouraging me to go to Lucy's party. She is cluing me in that it is safe for me to sneak out in some kind of secret code. Rose continues to eat, and then says,

"When you get a chance, you might want to look in your closet. You have a good day now, Child." She turns and smiles at me with a playful expression on her face. I smile at her and say,

"You too, Rose."

I bolt to my room and open my closet. All of my drab clothes are pushed to the left side of closet, and displayed alone is a new sundress. It is white and has small straps that crisscross in the back. This dress is not long like all of the others hanging in the closet; it is short. I pull the classy dress out of the closet, and I run my fingers across the expensive fabric. I instantly rip off the scratchy, gray dress that I am wearing and slither my body into the new, chic dress.

I make a dash to the full-length mirror that hangs on my bathroom door. I see my reflection in the mirror, and I feel pride. The dress fits me perfectly. I turn from front to back, looking at all angles of my body in this charming dress. I hear the door knob to my bedroom door turn, and I instantly feel anxious. Did Mother come home early? If she were to see me in this dress, all of my hard work at obeying her would be ruined. I am too close to a bathtub to allow her to see me now. The door slowly opens, and I am thankful that it is Rose.

"Well look at you. You have grown into one gorgeous woman, Coral Berringer," she says.

"Oh Rose, I love it! This dress is exquisite!" I say without taking my eyes off of the mirror in front of me.

I continue to observe the dress at different angles. I really have allowed the dark aura that lives in this house to drink me in and keep me drowned in sorrow and self-pity for so long. I truly thought that my existence in this world would stay in a state of dread and gloom forever.

I am taken back by the reality that one simple dress can change my sadness into joy, even if for just a little while. Rose moves toward me and hands me a present. It is a medium sized, flat present with light pink wrapping, and it is tied by a large, white ribbon with bright pink polka dots.

"This is a birthday gift for Lucy. It is a diary," she informs me.

"Oh Rose, this is so wonderful, but you know I can't..." Before I can complete my sentence, she places her finger over my lips to silence me. I stop speaking. She then turns to leave. She looks over her shoulder at me and says,

"I don't know what you're talking about, Coral. I hope you have a wonderful day." She closes the door and leaves me with so many emotions that need to sink in.

I sit down on the side of my bed, and I begin to feel nervous. As much as I would love to go to Lucy's party, I am fearful that she may not want me there. It has been over a year since I have seen or talked to my best friend. The last time we saw each other, we were crouched in the grungy torture dungeon in my house. What if she thinks I am a freak just like everyone else does? The thought of her thinking poorly of me will crush me. She could have replaced me. The possible reality that she may have a new best friend and that I am now an outsider makes the delight of my new dress slowly disintegrate. These fleeting moments of happiness are not enough to fuel the battle against the darkness that now owns my heart.

I stand up and begin to remove the dress from my body. My assumptions and fears have left me defeated. I slip the hideous, old fashioned dress back on. I pull the hanger out of the closet and carefully place the new dress back on it then return the dress to the closet. The delicate, white dress is still showcased alone because my other clothes are still pushed to the side. I peer at the ravishing dress, and my heart aches.

I make believe that I am at Lucy's party. I pretend that when she sees me she charges the beach to reach me, leaving all of the other guests to realize how important I am to her. She and I would spend the entire party laughing and chatting as we always did before. Time would have stood still during our separation, and nothing would have changed between us.

As my imagination continues to run rampant, my thoughts venture to Angel. In my made up story he has come back and has been waiting for me to escape the dungeon that I have been trapped in. He sees me from afar in my new, white dress, and he does not make fun of my clothes. He cannot take his eyes off of me and my new figure in the grown-up garment. It is childish and naive to have faith that any of my fantasies could actually come true. I stopped believing in fairy tales a long time ago.

I cannot look at this dress anymore. What moments ago had given me such sweet hope is now causing me to spiral back down into the pit of despair that sucked me in so long ago and has been slowly feeding on me since. I regretfully begin to push my acceptable clothing back to the center of my long closet. With each piece of clothing I return to its original spot, I become more miserable. Tears begin to travel down my cheeks, and my woe quickly turns into rage. In a hysterical frenzy, I pull the bleak dresses out of my closet and throw them to them floor. I weep loudly and have lost control. In my state of fury, I lose my balance and stumble into the long closet. I reach to stop myself on the wall inside of the closet. As my hand forcefully slams against it, I hear a tearing sound. I regain my balance, and I look at my hands. To my surprise, they have gone into the wall. I pull my hands back, and I see the impact of my weight. My hands pushed through the wallpaper that lines the interior of my closet.

How do I have the physical strength to punch through a wall? Is my anger this powerful, or do I possess superpowers that I have not yet discovered? Is Mother right? Do I have a demon living inside of me that just made its first appearance?

I inspect the damaged wall and can see that it is not really a wall. I slightly pull back the torn wallpaper, and I can tell that there is a door behind it. My first thought is that this door must lead to the stairway that Lucy and I discovered together. The layout of the mansion would not make this assumption possible, though; my room is very far from where we found the secret passageway. Is this house full of tunnels and hidden stairways?

I am intrigued, but I know that if I tear the paper completely off that my discovery will be noticed. I retrieve scissors from my bathroom and carefully cut the paper off at the border of the ill-concealed door. I try to open the door, but the decorative door knob that was probably once there is missing, probably so that it could have been covered with wallpaper. I scrounge for a bobby pin in my dresser drawer. I locate one and rush back to the door. After poking and jabbing at the old lock for some time, I hear a click. I actually did it. I unlocked the door.

The door slowly opens without even a push. The door invites me to pass through, but I dread what is on the other side. I finally build up the courage to bend down and walk through the door, thoughtful not to tear anymore of the wallpaper so that I can manage to cover up my break in when I am finished.

It is so dark that my vision is blinded. I slide my feet around on the floor to make sure that the surface is flat and that there are no stairs or objects that would cause me to trip. It is, so I cautiously move forward. I can see a dim illumination ahead of me. I follow the light, and it draws me into a room. The light is actually the sunlight that strains to penetrate the heavy curtains. I go to the window and pull the dust-covered drapes back to assist the sunlight in filling the mystery room with light. I turn and look at the hidden room, and I cannot believe what I see.

It is a larger duplicate of my room. The same white lilies are painted on the walls and ceilings. The walls are the same color except a slight shade darker. There is an enormous canopy bed. Spread across the elegant bed is a thick, cream-colored bedspread that is adorned with feminine, violet-colored pillows. There is expensive lace material draped around the bed that flows down the iron bars. The bed is so romantic and whimsical. I walk to the bed and run my fingers across the fabric. I do not recall ever being in this room, but it has such a familiar feeling. I know that the familiarity can be because of the similarities to my room, but there is an awareness that is heightened as the tips of my fingers graze the fabric. All of the drawers in the antique furniture are empty. The large walk-in closet has hangers that dangle from the rod, but they are lonely and without clothes.

I enter the bathroom. It is huge, probably the size of my entire bedroom. There is a large clawfoot bathtub that is on a marble platform with large, roman-styled pillars surrounding it. I picture soothing and tranquil baths and not the terrifying ones that I get from Mother. There is a long vanity that is decorated with a massive antique mirror. I can envision a beautiful princess brushing her long, lustrous hair while gazing at the mirror.

The room is deserted. It does not look like anyone has been in here for years. The most peculiar thing about this room is that there is no door. The only entrance is through my closet. As my investigation of this hidden room continues, I can see that there was once a door to the hallway, but it has been sealed off. Whose room was this? Was this Mother and Father's room when they had me? It makes sense considering that the rooms are attached. Does this mean that there was a time that Mother loved me? She would have had to have loved me to spend so much time and attention to detail to create such an elegant, loving environment.

Something very heinous had to have happened to her for her to go from painting pastel colors on the walls to wearing black, witch-like clothes. Am I what Mather claims I am? Did I do something sinful to her as a child and just do not remember? Am I full of the devil like she says I am? I cannot fathom how a child could do this much harm. The most I can comprehend is a devilish, mischievous toddler who is difficult to handle at times. This discovery has me puzzled but at the same time hopeful that there was a time that Mother did love me. Was I a bad baby? Did I cry too much? I have so many unanswered questions and wish that just one person would tell me the truth. Maybe I could understand if I knew the truth. Maybe I could forgive her and everyone else who has aided in holding me hostage in this miserable house.

Again, my imagination begins to conjure up ideas. Did something bad happen in this room? Did a horrible crime happen inside the walls that I stand between? Did one of my deceased ancestors die here? I have so many questions, but the room is stripped bare of any answers. I have been in very few rooms in Ocean Point, but this one is unlike any room I have ever encountered in this stale residence. It is warm and graceful. I can picture this charming room inviting visitors of the mansion to enter and make themselves comfortable.

As much as I try to make this room a scary and creepy place like the garden, hidden pathway, torture chamber, or neglected graveyard, I cannot. I feel protected and loved in this room. I feel at home here, and I have never felt at home in this eccentric house, not even in my own bedroom.

I approach the enticing bed, and I cannot resist lying down in it. I lie back onto the lacy pillows, and there is a familiar fragrance. It is not the old, musty smell that all of the other rooms have. Instead, it is sweet and fresh. It is engulfing and fills me with a warm, cozy feeling. I want to fall asleep in this welcoming bed and have sweet, tender dreams. I suddenly realize that the fragrance that has me entranced is the scent of the white lilies. I am not alarmed by this revelation, though. Instead I feel comforted. I can feel the petals of the lilies wrap around me and keep me calm.

The serenity that this room lends to my discontented soul urges me to drift off into a pleasant sleep. My eyes grow heavy, and I feel my normally tense body relax. I tell myself to get up and go back to my room. Even without Mother lurking around every corner stalking me with her sinister eyes, it is not wise for me to be found here.

There is a reason this room has been sealed up. Rose has been so kind to me. I do not want to do anything that will cause her hardship, and if Mother knew that I entered this room while I was solely Rose's responsibility, she would go mad and might would do something to hurt Rose. I keep telling myself to rise, but my eyes close. I fall asleep.

Protection from the Storm

I open my eyes and faintly see a beautiful woman lying next to me. We are face to face with each of us on our side. She has beautiful, long hair and tender, green eyes. She smiles at me with admiration and softly strokes my hair. Surprisingly, I am not afraid of this stranger that is lying next to me. Instead, I feel calm and content.

As I grow more conscious, the lady disappears, and I assume that I was dreaming. I stretch my arms and sit up. I realize that I am in the hidden bedroom. What time is it? Has Rose been looking for me? I hop off of the tall bed and rush to the window. I can tell that it is late because I can see the sun beginning its decent over the sea. I reach up to close the drapes, and something shiny on the floor catches my eye. I reach down and pick up what seems to be a dainty bracelet. As interesting as my new find is, I do not take the time to observe it. I shove it in my pocket and swiftly close the drapes.

Since it is later in the day, the glow that guided me into this amazing room is much dimmer now. The setting sun has left me little to no light to guide me back to my closet. I have to reach my arms out and feel the walls. I am grateful that I had such a fascination with this deserted room and spent so much time inspecting it. It gave me a good awareness of the room's layout, so I am able to navigate myself back to the door in my closet that separates these two worlds. I pause before entering my room. I am terrified that someone is on the other side of the door waiting to scold me for my unacceptable actions. I slowly pull the door, and a gentle feeling circles me. I hear a soft voice tell me to stay.

I slip into my closet, and my room is silent. I watchfully tip-toe through my closet and peer out of the door. I do not see anyone. I turn to the door and close it carefully behind me. I push the torn wallpaper back over the opening and pull a handful of my clothes in front of the secret door in hopes that it will keep the wallpaper concealed until I can properly repair it. I am pleased to see that my plan works. I step out of my closet, and I have to maneuver over and around all of the clothes that I had thrown on the floor during my temper tantrum. I pick them up and hang them back in my closet. I get everything back in order and turn to peer around my room.

The tender, soothing feeling that the mystery room gave me is now gone. I am left with an overwhelming feeling of emptiness again. It feels like I just lost something special to me. These random, unexplained emotions have power over me. I do not think that I can conquer the constant despair that reigns over me. As long as I live under this roof, the dark energy will continue to seep into me and take every piece of happiness that I will ever find.

I sit down on the edge of my bed and continue to feel pity for myself. The white dress catches my eye. It hangs elegantly next to dark gray, muted brown, and navy blue clothing. It seems so out of place hanging in my closet. It is like the pretty dress got put in the wrong bag by accident at the clothing store and ended up in the wrong closet with the wrong owner.

My thoughts are on Lucy and her party. I want to see her so terribly. Am I going to let fear and depression run my entire life? Will I let Mother win? I have the opportunity to have a fabulous evening with my best friend that I miss so dearly without the risk of getting in trouble. Am I that weak? How can I sustain so much abuse my entire life and am afraid to see my own best friend? I feel disappointed and foolish.

I pull the shiny bracelet that I found out of my pocket. It is a platinum bracelet that is tastefully adorned with small diamonds. There are three delicate strands of metal that connect the sparkling stones. This must be a child's bracelet. Was that room a child's room? Were my assumptions wrong? Did I possibly have a sister, and we had connected rooms? I wrap the fragile strands around my wrist. Whomever this belongs to must be loved very much.

I close the clasp around my wrist and instantly feel a need to shake off these gloomy feelings and get dressed to go see Lucy. This meaningless bracelet that a stranger once wore fuels my valor to put aside my insecurities and take a chance.

I jump off the bed in a frenzy. I know from the position of the sun that the party has already begun. I look at my clock, and it is after seven.

I gather the beautiful dress from my closet and slip into it. I hustle to the mirror to inspect every inch of myself before I leave.

The nap that I took was beneficial. I look well rested and relaxed. I study my face. The freckles that once were scattered across my nose and cheeks have disappeared and left my skin tone a light ivory color. I gaze intently at my features and how they are positioned on my more mature face. I recognize that I do not favor my father as much as I once did. It is evident that I am his daughter because of similarities, but there is something about my appearance that separates me and gives me a unique look all of my own.

The curls in my hair hang wildly around my face. I grab hair barrettes in an attempt to tame my locks. I clip the untamed strands up, and they now fall loosely around my face and down my back. The humidity must be high for this many curls to seize my usually wavy hair.

I am as ready as I will ever be. I grab Lucy's gift and head out of my room. I am hesitant to leave the bedroom, troubled that people may have been looking for me while I disappeared during my accidental nap in the picturesque bedroom. I hastily dismiss the concerns and scurry through the house. I am already so late that my sense of urgency over shadows the details.

The house is calm. The disguised heartbeat of the house that keeps my life in chaos seems to be vanquished. Without Mother here to absorb its sinister desires and continue the tradition of sadness that is house enjoys, it is hushed.

As I near the sun porch, I cannot help but recall the last time I snuck out of the house and the unexplained shadow that was following me. I remember being confident that it was a demon. I now dismiss the embellished mind of a scared girl. Even with the doubts that my maturity discards, I still glance over my shoulder every few steps. Besides, who knows what truly is possible when evil is given the environment to thrive? I guess demons can come in all shapes and sizes. Ask Mother. I am one.

I exit the back door and charge down the stairs. I giddily skip towards the beach. I am beside myself with excitement. I refuse to let the notion that Lucy will reject my friendship take me over, and I plan to take a gamble to get my friend back. When I reach the entrance to the overgrown path, I slow down. I have not even been in this backyard in over a year, and the last time I was in the garden's pathways I was assaulted by the snow-covered trees and attacked by icicles.

I stop where I would usually enter. The sun has set on the horizon, but there is still enough daylight for me to see. The snow and ice is gone, and spring has given birth to flourishing green leaves and colorful, wild flowers. Undisciplined vines seem to rule over the other foliage as they creep into its space and wind themselves selfishly throughout the passageway. The path is painted in bright, merry colors, not the ice cold white that my memory was left with from that traumatic winter day. This does not look so scary. Did my mind play tricks on a petrified little girl by exaggerating the frightening path?

A gentle wind blows through my hair and the garden. The vibrant, wild flowers sway in the breeze, and the leaves growing on the tree branches gently shiver as if they are cold. I am mesmerized by the walkway, and for some odd reason I want to enter the maze. Why does this garden enjoy seducing me? My body moves forward, but my mind says no. I look up at Ocean Point and can feel that the house is displeased with my newfound will power. Its reign over me will cease if only for one night.

I walk away from the garden, pathway, and house. I do not look back. I arrive at the beach, and I feel the warm sand under my feet. It is just as I remembered. It has only been just over a year since I have had sand between my toes, but it seems like much longer. The waves are at high tide and roll onto the beach with avid force. They crash so loudly that all other noises are drowned by the mighty sea.

I begin to walk toward the Englands' residence. The beach is covered with scampering crabs. I have to watch my step and cannot sprint to Lucy like I did in my daydream. One absentminded step could cause me to get snipped by the sharp, little claws of these beach dwellers. Despite the immediate danger that my appendages may be in, I quite enjoy watching the little, white creatures scamper throughout the sand.

I can see a fire ahead and assume that it is Lucy's party. The closer I get, the more my heart becomes heavy. There is no one here. I am too late. My hesitation to see her has paid me back. I continue to walk toward the bonfire that is slowly burning down. I want to savor the limited amount of time that I am allowed out of my cage that Ocean Point keeps me entrapped in.

I look around at the deserted party site, and I am annoyed with myself for being so childish and weak. I missed my chance to make things better again between Lucy and me. I turn and begin my dreaded journey back to the estate. I am positive that the house will be pleased that I am returning devastated. I once read a line in a book that said something like, "Tears are for when you hurt so deeply that there are no words." I hear a voice behind me call my name. I instinctively turn without apprehension, and standing behind me is Angel.

"Is that you, Coral?" he asks.

I am caught off guard and just stand there in front of this man that I have thought about daily for so long. I have no words. During this awkward moment of silence, Angel slowly looks at me from the ground to my eyes. His eyes drink in my new womanly figure. He stares at me and has an intense look in his eyes that I am sure Mother would say is inappropriate. I feel embarrassed by his intensity, and he senses my discomfort. He politely brings his eyes back to mine, and I become lost in his gaze.

"You have changed," he says, seeming surprised that I am not the inept, old-fashioned dressed little girl that he first met. His noticeable fascination in my transformation makes me fidgety. I skim the ground, trying to avoid eye contact with this gorgeous man.

"Do you know where Lucy is?" I ask nervously, scanning the area and pretending to look for her.

"Yeah, they all took off to the boardwalk. They left a little bit ago," he says. I hold her present out towards him, inviting him to take the package. My nerves cause my hands to be jittery, and the small book shakes in my grasp.

"Can you give this to her for me?" I meekly ask.

He takes the package. I can still feel that his eyes are concentrated on me. I turn and begin to walk away from him. I feel self-conscious and shy. I missed Lucy's party. To make it worse, even after all of the fantasies that I have had about Angel he was standing right in front of me, and I had no idea how to conduct myself.

The tide has calmed down, and the waves now leisurely roll to shore. I travel down the beach at the break of the waves, letting the water surround my feet before returning back to the sea. I stroll through the sand at a leisurely pace. I do not want to return to the mansion in a hurry as it would give it the delight of me not finding any indulgence outside of its borders.

"Hey, you don't have to go. You can hang out with me."

I turn and look over my shoulder, and I see Angel standing in the distance. The light from the moon casts a glow around his muscular body. He is looking in my direction, but I cannot see his face. The night has casted a shadow that conceals his handsomeness. I am amazed that the man that has been filling my mind with curiosity and intimate feelings actually wants to hang out with me.

I want to stay with him so badly, but I am apprehensive of my ability to not make a fool of myself. I do not think that I can bear the thought of him thinking that I am still just a little girl underneath the womanly body that God has blessed me with. I cannot even find the strength to speak to this man, so I just shake my head and continue to walk away from him.

As much as I loathe it, I also keep hearing Mother's sermons in my head. Her constant rants about boys and how they have unclean thoughts flood my mind. It is as if she has programmed me without my permission. These thoughts of sin and temptation seem to reside in my mind like natural thought progression. After seeing how Angel lustfully looked at me just because I grew breasts, I question that Mother may be right. I need to avoid these feelings of being torn between my uncontrollable desire for Angel and the imprinted mindset of unholy thoughts and actions.

I hear movement behind me. I turn and see Angel jogging towards me. I stop walking out of politeness, but I really just want to take off running like a gazelle being chased by a famished tiger. My emotions are so mixed up and intertwined.

"Come on, just for a little while," he says in a sweet and alluring voice.

Why is he all of a sudden interested in me? Is he so shallow of a man that because I have grown breasts and have on a fancy dress that he wants to be nice to me now? He can sense that I am on edge. He reaches down and grabs my hand.

"Come on, I just want to show you something."

He eagerly begins to pull me down the beach. Angel dragging me down the sandy beach reminds me of how Lucy used to persuade me to join her in adventures. Temptation takes over, and all of my previous feelings disappear. I go with him.

We run down the beach as the water gracefully rolls over our feet. The moonlight guides us as we go hand in hand. We both become tired from running and change our pace to a casual stroll. It takes me a little while to realize that Angel is still holding my hand. Butterflies are not fluttering in my stomach. They are performing suicide bomber maneuvers.

I pull my hand away from his and pretend that I need to push my hair out of my eyes. He can see how uneasy I feel with him. He grabs my arm to stop me from walking and positions himself in front of me.

"I want you to know how sorry I am for being so rude to you when we first met. I was going through a lot of rough things, and I was basically a big jerk." His apology helps to ease my worries. I humbly smile at him, letting him know it is okay. "Also, I want you to know that Lucy told me about your mother and what she does to you," he sympathetically says.

I immediately feel humiliated and ashamed. I do not want him to know these horrible things about me. I begin to shake my head with immense regret for letting anyone this close to me. I start to run back towards Ocean Point. Knowing that he knows my secrets and about my lurid existence is too much for me to take in. I run as fast as I can. My shame is chasing me, and I cannot outrun it.

Angel sprints after me. He runs faster than I do and passes me then positions his body in front of mine. He stops which forces me to slow down. I try to stop, but my momentum causes my body to slam straight into his. He catches me and holds me, preventing me from falling. I am in his arms, and his eyes are fixated on mine. His eyes are soft and tender. I am completely spellbound as I look into Angel's brown eyes. His eyes plead for forgiveness and acceptance. I force myself to look away. He pulls me tighter to him and whispers in my ear,

"It's okay. I don't care about any of that. We all have secrets. I just want to be your friend. I think you need one."

His words allow my tense body to relax in his arms. It feels magical to be in Angel's strong arms. I have a safe and protected feeling. His embrace makes me feel like he would fight the demon that lives in my house just to keep me safe. Angel releases me from his tender embrace.

"Now quit being hardheaded. I have something amazing to show you," he says and then smiles at me.

I have never seen him smile. He has the most unremarkable smile. This man could ask me to go anywhere with him now, and I would follow as baby ducks chase after their mother.

We continue. It seems as if we have been roaming the beach for hours. He assures me that we are almost there, sensing that I am growing tired. The sky is becoming very dark very quickly. It appears that a storm is brewing at sea. For a brief moment, I think of my father and worry about his safety with him being alone at sea. Angel stops walking, and I follow suit. He points to a lighthouse in the near distance. It looks abandoned and has a nostalgic look to it.

"Do you see that? Lucy finds enjoyment in going to parties and hanging out with her friends. I find enjoyment in discovering," he says excitedly. "Come on!" He grabs my hand again, and we run towards the old, abandoned lighthouse. When we arrive, Angel opens the rickety door to the lighthouse. I hesitate to enter and ask,

"Are you sure it's okay for us to go in here?" He gives me an evil grin and pulls me by my hand, dragging me through the door. I giggle at his daredevil attitude.

"Wait until you see the view from up there," he enthusiastically says as he points to the top of the structure.

The building appears that it has been unattended to for years. The bottom floor looks like a small, cozy house. It is equipped with everything one would need to live. Maybe I can run away and live here. Who would find me here except Angel? It is absolutely filthy, but I could clean it. I feel at home here. I now become excited about our adventure.

"Come on!" Angel yells as he stands in a doorway with his eyes fixated upwards.

He takes off running up the stairs. They wind in circles that never seem to end. The structure is similar to the secret passageway in the west wing except not threatening. We climb and climb towards the sky, and the higher up we get the louder the sound of the ocean waves crashing against the lighthouse become.

We reach the top of the building, and Angel demands that I close my eyes. I do as he asks, and he moves behind me and covers my eyes with his hands to prevent me from peeking. He pushes me forward with his body pressed against mine. He is so close to me that I can smell his cologne, and it is intoxicating.

He walks me to the edge of the lighthouse and removes his hands which signals me to open my eyes. My eyes are wide, and the view in front of me is absolutely breathtaking. I look at the ocean, and it seems to never end. I can see down the beach in both directions. I walk around the circular tower, capturing a view of everything that surrounds us. My enjoyment quickly fades as my eyes reach Ocean Point.

The house seems to be alive and stares straight back at me. It breathes into me and fills me with indescribable shame. Angel notices my mood change from joy to sorrow. He stands close to me. We stand together in complete silence and stare at the haunting sight. Storm clouds are migrating from the sea and are resting above Ocean Point. It is an eerie and dark scene. We are both absorbed with the energy that the mansion radiates.

"Lucy told me about the things that happen in your house and all of the secrets that your family is hiding." Is there anything Lucy has not told him? He pauses as if to distract me from being upset. "I have an idea." He runs back down the stairs. I wait for a while, and then I hear his steps come back up the stairs. He returns with binoculars. "Here, you can see into the windows of your house with these."

He hands the bulky object to me and coaches me on how to use them. I immediately start to scan the windows of the mansion. Most of the windows are covered with curtains, but there are a few that I can see in. It is amazing how clear and far I can see. There is no movement in the house, and just as I decide to give up, my eyes come across a lit room. I can see plainly into the room. It is my room. Has Angel been watching me from up here? Has he seen my most private moments? I turn to him and look straight into his eyes.

"Do you watch me when you're up here?" I ask, not believing how bold I am being.

He becomes nervous and will not make eye contact with me. This is a side of him that I did not imagine existed. Where is that brash, arrogant Italian boy?

"Yes, I watch you," he says sounding ashamed.

I have odd, mixed emotions. I fear that he has seen me naked. The thought of it violates me to my core, but at the same time I feel aroused. I remain speechless not knowing how I should react.

"I watch you at your window, and you seem so sad. I have seen your mother as well, and she is one scary chick! No offense." His comment about Mother breaks the uncomfortable silence, and I let out a small giggle.

"Have you seen me... um... um..." I scramble for words to ask if he has seen me naked.

"No, I have not. I know when to stop looking. I may not act like it, but I'm actually a very respectful person."

I feel relieved. I cannot handle the thought of Angel seeing my scars. Angel and I continue to stand at the top of the lighthouse in silence, enjoying the tranquility of the night. The sky is growing wickedly black, and it is evident that a very bad storm is on top of us. The sky grumbles and alerts us that we should take cover.

"I need to get home before this storm hits," I reluctantly say.

"Okay, I will walk you," he gentlemanly offers.

Before we can even reach the stairs to descend down the lighthouse, the sky falls down on us. The rain pours on our bodies so strongly that it hurts. The wind is robust and pushes our bodies wherever it wants us to go. Lightning rules the sky, and thunder roars at us to warn us not to interfere with its fierce rage.

We slip and slide across the wet, narrow floors. I hang on to the ledge and try and catch my balance. Angel firmly grips my arm and pulls me into the doorway to shield me from the dangers of the violent storm.

Once I am safely inside he slams the door, and our bodies collide into each other. In an attempt to catch each other's fall, we are in a close embrace. We stand face to face, and neither of us moves a muscle. The sound of the treacherous storm is our background music.

Our hair is soaked, and water drips off of our faces and bodies. Angel's eyes linger to my breasts. My eyes follow his, and I notice that he can see straight through my wet sundress. Every inch of my body is visible for him to see. My dress clings to my body. It looks like I am naked. I panic. I do not want him to see my ugly scars. I want him to continue to desire my body as he did on the beach, not be disgusted with my disfigurement.

I pull away from him. I foolishly open the door and run back into the storm. The wind beats me and pulls me as Mother does. It feels like she is standing above me afflicting punishment for my sins with the man that was just holding me. I slide around the slick, circular tower and stop my movement by gripping the railing. I use my strength to pull myself to my feet while Mother Nature takes her wrath out on me. The only thing that I can see as I hang on to the side of the lighthouse is Ocean Point. The house is punishing me. It is sucking the only happiness and freedom I have had since I have been imprisoned in its evil, selfish walls. I begin to scream at the house like a crazy person. My emotions overwhelm me.

I feel my body being lifted and carried away from the edge of the lighthouse. Suddenly, the rain is not pelting my body, and the sound of the storm has grown quieter. Angel holds my entire body in his arms, and he sits on the floor in the stairway. My seemingly naked body is stretched across his lap, and I am hysterically crying. He touches my face to calm me down. His eyes look at mine and not my exposed body. I begin to compose myself, and my cries subside. He slowly lifts my face by the back of my head to his.

I feel his lips on mine. I can taste the ocean salt on his lips. His kiss is long and lingering. The kisses become more passionate. I do not even think about what I am doing or if I am doing it right. My desire for Angel escalates, and my shame of my body's discolored scars diminishes. I feel his hands run down my body, and a sensation of desire rushes over me and takes charge. Abruptly, he stops kissing me and takes his hands off of my body. I do not want him to stop. I look at him in confusion.

"I'm sorry," he says and has a look of guilt on his ruggedly handsome face.

I want to ask him why he stopped. I want to tell him not to. I know that I do not understand my feelings or exactly what just happened, but my need for him to be close to me is fervent. It feels like I will die without his hands on me. Is this the devil jumping inside of me? Is this what Mother has been preaching about? I am being a victim of the serpent himself, but I feel no disgrace in wanting Angel. How could this be so evil when it makes me feel so alive?

I remain silent because I trust Angel. As much as I want him to continue, he is more experienced than I am, and I respect his knowledge. He wraps his arms around me and holds me close to him. The storm's rage increasingly worsens. No matter how loud the thunder bellows or how dangerous the lightning appears, as long as I am in Angel's arms I feel safe. The storm is frightening and dangerous, but there is a huge part of me that never wants it to stop because I know that once the skies are quiet and tranquil I will probably never see Angel again.

Two Doors Shut

After my evening with Angel, something has changed inside of me. I hurt more than I ever have before, but it is a different kind of ache. When Mother burns me, the sting eventually subsides. Her harsh words wound me, but eventually I just file them in the back of my mind. Father hasn't protected me. He left me lonely, but I grew up. Losing Lucy's friendship disappointed me, but I accepted it. The emptiness of not having Angel in my life is a constant, throbbing ache that nothing can replace. Even with the anguish that I constantly feel, the moments that we shared woke something up within me.

It has been months since our evening in the lighthouse, and he is still the first thing that I think about when I open my eyes and the last thing that I think over before I close them at night. I cannot concentrate on schoolwork or Bible class because my mind is with Angel. I can still feel his touch on my skin, smell the cologne on his neck, and taste the salt that covered his lips. I wonder if he thinks about me as much as I think about him. I pray that he will not fall in love with another woman before I can escape this horrid house.

Many nights before I go to sleep, I go to my window and look at the lighthouse, wondering if he is watching me. Sometimes when I am at my window, not even knowing if he is in the lighthouse or not, I will slowly undress for him. I will stand visible to anyone who looks up at my house, nude with no shame or regret. I want him to know that I want him even though we cannot be together now. I give him all I can give him from afar.

I know that he can see my scars, but I have accepted that they are a part of who I am. They are a part of my deplorable past that I cannot change. I can only have faith that he will someday fall in love with my pain as much as he falls in love with me.

Nothing has changed in the house. I am still held captive and force-fed radical religious beliefs and notions. Mother's demented thoughts and fears seem to accelerate daily; she has become more erratic and distracted.

I now know that Mother is mistaken to classify all men in one category. Not all men have ill intentions. The devil does not jump into the minds of boys and make them do sinful acts. What happened between Angel and me in the lighthouse was not inappropriate or immoral. It is the only thing that has ever felt right.

My time with Angel has given me something to look forward to. I do not even think much anymore about this bizarre house or the secrecy that it thrives on. My obsession of discovering the truths of my family has become uninteresting. I care more about my future than everyone else's past.

All that matters to me is being close to Angel again. I want to run away with him and begin a new life. I do not want to be a Berringer. I just want to have a normal life where misery is not all that I can feel, where I can touch and smell flowers and watch the wings of butterflies flutter as they fly from flower to flower. I want to breathe fresh air and sleep contently without constant paranoia of who or what is going to open my door. I really do not believe this is too much to ask. Is it?

I have uncovered a new strength to get through the day, and it is not a strength that I have to force. It is a strength that has cultivated within me from love. I do not slumber around in a state of hopelessness as before. I hang on to a thread of belief that someday I will find myself entangled in Angel's strong arms again. I am not so naïve that I do not acknowledge that it is more realistic that I will never feel his lips pressed on mine again, but for now I am going to live in delusion where I feel awake.

I am still full of anguish, though. It is a part of who I have become. It may never completely leave, but I have found a way to control the feelings without them controlling me as before. Maybe someday the joy I feel with Angel will balance out the struggles of the past and make me a whole person for once.

I aimlessly wander the halls of Ocean Point purely out of boredom. I hear a heated conversation coming from the kitchen that grabs my attention. I revert back to the days when I would creep around the property like a silly detective looking for clues. I slowly edge myself towards the disagreement that is transpiring. I hear my name.

"I'm not at peace any longer with Coral in this house. Have you looked at that girl lately? You know who she looks like, and she is in danger! We have all stayed quiet and watched this curse breed under this roof for years. I am an old man, and my maker will be calling me home soon. I will not leave this earth with these sins stamped to my heart. This ridiculous family's sins are now our sins!"

It is Rollins. He is not talking in circles and confusion as he usually does. I question if his senile behavior has been an act all along to protect himself from Mother's brutal treatment of the staff and to derail my suspicion. Who do I look like? Who will hurt me? I am in danger? He must be referring to Mother. Does Rollins know that my time here nearing its end? Is Mother getting ready to do me in like the other children buried in the graveyard?

"Rollins, be patient. The time for the truth and disclosure is near. I feel it in my soul. You need to hold on for just a little bit longer. Coral needs us. I understand the guilt you feel. I feel it too, all the way to my bones, but I have learned to sleep at night knowing that if all of us had left that poor, sweet girl she would be dead already. Margret is not going to be able to continue on with her schemes as she wants. I have noticed a change in her, Rollins. This agony inside of her has been eating at her for decades, and I truly believe that it is gradually devouring her from the inside out. She is going to break sooner than she even knows," I hear Rose plead.

"What about the west wing? The immoral is growing stronger. I hear it every night, and before long nothing and no one will be able to contain it," Rollins argues back.

The new Coral wants to stomp into the room and demand them to tell her what is going on, but I know that this will do nothing but silence them. My intrusion will make them even more cautious with their conversations. I need to wait this out and see what transpires. If I am in jeopardy now, it will only increase if Mother knows that I am suspicious. I will be in even more danger. She may excel the date of my demise.

The conversation has come to a conclusion, but I am not sure who won the debate. I slink back through the house and continue to ponder the west wing and the evil that is supposedly growing there. Is Mother some kind of mad scientist, and I am not aware of her talents? Maybe she is harvesting evil pods in the west wing like they would in a science-fiction horror novel. I chuckle at my vivid imagination. There has to be a logical explanation.

I decide that I am going to march right to the west wing and bang on every door until the demon that everyone speaks of answers and invites me in. I stampede toward the west wing with determination. I arrive at the entrance of the wing and look down the veiled corridor. The fright that I felt years ago when I secretly traveled down the wing comes flooding back to me. The hairs on my arms stand straight up from goose bumps. The memory still haunts me.

I want to turn the lights on and ambush the wing until I unveil the secrets that have affected and ruined so many lives, but I doubt my conviction. What if there is a demon in one of the rooms? I do believe that there is evil in this world and most definitely in this house. It is possible that this house, person, or creature is possessed and that this is its home as much as it is mine. I stand at the edge of the threatening darkness, and all of my previous findings on this estate come chasing after my courage.

I recall the screams from outside of the door that Lucy and I heard, the children's graves, the violent garden that is home to trees that tried to kill me, and the figure that I saw in the window. For so long, I was drowning in frustration and searching for the truth. I let my spirit perish and became accepting of the unknown. Now I have allowed love to cultivate in my heart, and it has become more important than the secrets that surround me.

I think back to what Rose said to Rollins about "the time being near" and "being patient." I decide that even if he is not going to take her advice that I will. I return to my room and retire for the evening.

The morning comes, and I am surprised to see that it is later than when I usually wake up. Rose did not give me my usual wake up visit. It is passed the time when breakfast is usually served. I rise from bed and dress myself. I am intrigued in finding out how this house that is always ran like clockwork is actually behind schedule. Something must have happened. I make my way to the kitchen, and Rose is franticly cooking breakfast.

"What's going on?" She looks at me and has a frustrated but sad expression.

"Rollins resigned this morning," she says.

"Did Mother kill him?" I say, surprising myself with my question. The first thought that came to my mind slipped right out of my mouth.

She lets out an overzealous belly laugh and says,

"No Child, he was just tired."

I know why he left, and so does she. He could not take the guilt that Ocean Point bestowed in his conscious. I am beside myself that he did not even tell me goodbye. I have known Rollins since birth. He is my family, and I am going to miss him greatly. I reach for a spatula and begin to help Rose prepare breakfast.

I hear Mother's footsteps drawing near. It is the sound that I imagine I will hear the day that death knocks on my door except she is even more menacing than the Grim Reaper himself. Anticipation bounces between Rose and me as we hear her get closer. She rounds the corner and sees us making omelets. This infuriates her, and she screams at me.

"Coral Berringer, what do think you are doing? You are not a servant, Young Lady!"

She comes around the counter and pulls my ear until my feet begin to move. She leads me around by my ear as if I am a rowdy toddler. She guides me by my ear into the cold and daunting dining room. She then returns to the kitchen and begins to yell at Rose. She is so heated that I can hardly understand her words. Her fury is out of control. Her shrieks sound ludicrous. If she was not such an intimidating and physically strong woman, I do not think I could control my amusement over her behavior. Rose is correct. She is losing it.

I am concerned about her escalating behavior. When I was younger, I did not know that her treatment towards me and everyone else was wrong. I did not know any better, but something inside of me always knew something was not right. I think that Mother gets frustrated that I have never been the cookie-cutter image of her and have not joined her religious cult. I sometimes feel that I have a cherub sent from the heavens that sits on my shoulder and confirms that she is the one with the tribulations, not me.

What does Mother's evident descent into absurdity mean for Rose, Gretchen, and me? She has always been self-deceptive, but her decline is evident. I can tell that she is livid over Rollins's departure. Not only does she now have no one to cook for her, but now someone with valuable knowledge about her and her precious family is not under her thumb any longer.

I have overheard conversations in the past of her saying that once the staff is gone, she will not hire replacements. Of course she cannot hire a new staff. No one in their sane mind would work for Mother, and the wickedness that Ocean Point exudes would have them running for the door before the interview even began.

I know that the occurrences that I have endured during my life here in the mansion are real. I am sure though that when I was younger my encounters seemed so much more chilling and terrifying. Regardless of what is reality or fiction, I know that there are untold secrets in this mansion that have employed every person in this house to remain silent. The sinister secrecy of this ominous estate is the king and ruler over everyone who enters. It dominates and has power over all of us. Whether it makes us insane, evil, scared, meek, or angry, the influence of the secrecy has driven the past and present and is now steering the future. I hear Mother's footsteps again and prepare myself to be the punching bag that she needs to release her anger.

"Go get yourself prepared for Bible study. Sister Anna will be arriving soon. There will be no breakfast this morning," she says. She is visibly flustered. "Make sure that you bring your rosary beads. Today's lesson is going to be about praying for your forgiveness."

My forgiveness? Is she blaming me for Rollins's departure? I guess that she is right. He left because of his regrets and apprehension of the future and called me by name. I am clueless as to how my presence in this family dictates other's decisions, but I do relish in watching how out of sorts Mother has become. Her rage is attempting to mask the panic that is overwhelming her.

I return to my bedroom to get my materials for class, and when I open the door, there is an envelope laying on the floor. I open it and pull out a single, folded piece of paper. I unfold it, and it reads,

"I'M SORRY.

All My Best To You,

Rollins"

My heart falls to the bottom of my stomach. He is really gone. I envy him for escaping all of the turmoil in this house. I wish that he would have taken me with him. As much as I will miss him, I am delighted that he gotten out of Ocean Point. I will live with contentment knowing that his final days of life will not be serving my family but healing the wounds that he has been burdened with.

For the rest of the day, I am in the library hearing the same lectures and lessons as the day before. Every ten minutes we break and kneel to pray for my immoral sins. I am required to clutch the crucifix attached to the rosary beads in a manner that proves my sincere apologies for transgressions that I have committed. I have no idea what I am asking forgiveness for, but as usual I play the part that these self-righteous servants to the Lord command of me.

How did Mother find these religious maniacs that undoubtedly believe I am as unholy as she does? Do these religious freaks actually think that they are going to mold my mind and release the serpent that slithers within me? Do they actually think that they are making a difference in my life or even teaching me anything?

The only thing their lessons and sermons tell me is that I am going to Hell after what I did with Angel. I will not accept this as fact no matter how many testaments they recite to me. Angel's touch was not the touch of evil. It came from a pure and loving place. What these two radically God-fearing servants do not know is that I have been in Hell ever since the first day I was born. The only piece of Heaven that I have ever experienced was Angel and the intimate moments that we shared at the top of the lighthouse.

My Bible lectures are over, and I am so relieved. My knees are sore from the frequent kneeling onto the hard marble floor as I repented my transgressions. The priest and nun have left, and now it is just Mother and me alone in the library.

I am tired, and my body is giving me signs that I am going to yawn. I fight back the urges that will expose my weariness. Mother paces back and forth in front of me, lecturing on the history of the Civil War for the millionth time. A trained, professional teacher would be amused by the short lists of subjects that Mother teaches to me. She does not put forth the energy to do any research or come up with lesson plans to give me a broad range of knowledge. She only teaches about the things she already knows. She does not care if I get a top-notch education or not. This is just her way of keeping me in this penitentiary and under her authority.

I cannot restrain the yawn that is eager to break free. I prepare my body for the sting that the ruler is about to impose on my hand. She leisurely taps the palm of her hand while she stalks back and forth in front of me jabbering times and dates that have no significance. Just at the right time, the door swings open, and Rose is standing in the doorway.

"Rose, how many times have I told you not to interrupt me during my lessons?!" she bellows.

"Forgive my intrusion, but I must speak to you in private," Rose submissively replies.

"Can't your trivial needs wait?" Mother responds.

"No ma'am, it is an emergency."

"Fine!"

Mother slams her ruler on the table and storms out of the room. The door slams behind them. What has happened now? I hear their subdued voices behind the door but cannot comprehend what they are saying. I hear their footsteps depart. I sit in the library for over an hour waiting for Mother to return or for someone to tell me what the emergency is. My bottom is sore from sitting in an uncomfortable chair for so long. I stand to stretch my legs.

I nonchalantly stroll around the room and happen to glance out of the window. I see an ambulance pull into the driveway. Who in this house is hurt? The only people left living here are Mother, Rose, Gretchen, and me if you do not count the demon in the west wing. The emergency workers get out of the truck, but they do not seem to be in a hurry. They pull a stretcher from the back of the vehicle. I watch them come inside the house, and I hear the mobile bed thump the floor. Then, I hear wheels roll down the hallway.

Oh no, it is Gretchen. Something has happened to her. I debate with myself whether to exit the room and go to her side or not, but I know that will displease Mother. I am afraid I will face the wrath of a lunatic.

I pace back and forth trying to choose my fate. I need to see Gretchen before she leaves. I want her to know how much she means to me and how much I care for her. I am afraid that at her age she could be seriously ill and pass away at the hospital and that I will never be able to tell her goodbye. I hear the wheels from the gurney travel back down the hallway towards me. I have to go to her no matter what the consequences may be.

I jerk the door open and dart into the hallway. The paramedics are wheeling someone down the hallway. When I see that there is a sheet that completely covers their passenger, I become immobile from the instant realization that Gretchen is already dead. Mother and Rose walk behind them somberly. I become visibly distraught, and I drop to my knees and begin to sob as I watch precious Gretchen being wheeled out of the house.

Mother sees my public display of emotion which is frowned upon as a

Berringer. It is not acceptable to express your feelings in front of others, especially strangers. It is a sign of weakness. At least that is the belief that Mother has tried to instill in me. Despite this, I cannot hold back my sorrow.

Mother is enraged and begins to come towards me in an aggressive approach. She is so focused on getting to me that she carelessly bumps into the stretcher causing the top half of Gretchen's body to fall off. I see her lifeless body hang. She is blue, and her eyes are open and fixed. From the position she is in it seems like she is looking straight at me. Her comatose eyes pierce though me and leave me with the taste of death in my throat.

I scream at the top of my lungs and put my face into my knees as I squat on the floor. Rose lets out a yelp of shock and surprise. Instinctively, she attempts to come to me and shield me from the ghastly sight. Mother does not even acknowledge what she just did to Gretchen's dead body and continues to march towards me. She is so motivated to get to me and shut me up that she shoves Rose to the side. Mother moves past Rose in one swift motion, causing Rose's objective to protect me to be vanquished.

I am on the floor and am inconsolable. I know that Mother is standing over me. Despite the severe, mournful state that I am in, I can still feel her wrath close to me. Predicting my fate, I put my hands over the back of my head for protection from Mother. She bends down and puts her face near mine. She reaches into the curled space that my body has formed and clinches my face with one hand. She forces it to hers and says in a low, threatening tone,

"Coral, you shut up that crying and stand to your feet now."

Her voice is not screaming, but her eyes are. I slowly rise to my feet. Mother has now placed her hand on my shoulder and grips it so hard that it is as if she is holding my collar bone in her hand. We face the paramedics as they continue to roll out of the mansion with Gretchen. Someone has repositioned her body, and she lies flat again with the sheet draped across her body and face. As the last paramedic exits, Mother says to them in a calm, emotionless voice,

"You gentlemen have a pleasant day."

Rose closes the door behind them. Instantly, Mother's arm is high in the air, and with one rapid motion she backhands me. I stumble to the ground. Even though I am older now and my body has filled out, I am still petite and dainty. Mother is still able to physically overpower me. I lie on the ground in physical and emotional agony. Mother straightens up her clothing as if nothing has happened and walks away.

"Take care of that weak, useless thing on the floor," she calmly tells Rose as she struts by.

Rose races to me and lifts my upper body off of the floor and cradles me as I sob. She cries as well. We both loved Gretchen. After a short time, Rose and I rise off of the floor. There is a mirror hanging on the wall, and I glance in its direction to see how badly my face is injured. Mother's handprint is already marked and swelling. Rose inspects my face and shakes her head.

"Miss Coral, this is all going to end soon," she says like she is confessing undisclosed information that only she knows.

I hope that her words become a reality and that this nightmare will just be a part of the past. Rose walks me to my room and tells me that she is going to bring me something to eat. I am not hungry, but I am in such a daze with my grief-stricken heart that I let her leave without argument.

I sit on the edge of my bed and reminisce about Gretchen and all of the times that we spent together. I look out my window and think of Angel. I look towards the lighthouse in hopes that he is waiting for me. I want him to see how much I am hurting. I want him to rush to me and climb the mansion to rescue me. I want to feel safe and protected as I did the night that he held me in his arms. I want his strong arms to seize me and lift me out of this castle and into the night.

I go to the bathroom to get some tissue, and I see a sparkle in the back of the bathroom closet. It is the delicate bracelet that I found in the room behind my closet. I reach for it and place it in my hand. There is an unexpected feeling of tranquility that washes over me. I desperately want to wear this beautiful piece of jewelry, but I know that if anyone sees it on my wrist that there will be questions.

The sparkly bracelet reminds me of the secure and loving feeling that the room on the other side of my closet gave me. I long to be in that big, elegant bed again curled up with the soft, fancy pillows and the air filled with the scent of fresh lilies. I dare not to sneak into the concealed room today. With all of the drama surrounding me, my actions will be exposed. Even though I know that the room is off limits and buried behind flimsy wallpaper, I have an undeniable need to be close to it.

I enter my closet and inch my way to the poorly camouflaged doorway. I press the front of my body against the torn wall paper and close my eyes. I wish that the kindness of the room would seep through the door and lift my pain away. Tears flow down my face for the loss of Gretchen and Rollins. I feel a gentle touch on my shoulder that leaves me with the sensation that someone is attempting to soothe me. It startles me. I turn quickly to see who is behind me, and no one is there.

The closet fills with the smell of a bouquet of lilies. I feel a breeze around me that is cool but refreshing, not the bone-chilling sensation that I usually experience in this house. The closet is full of a captivating aroma of the precious, white flowers, and the small space that I stand in seems to be filling with some kind of fog. It is not the kind of fog that you would see on an eerie night in the garden but more like a fluffy cloud that scatters across a blue sky.

I hear someone coming down the hall, and instantly the mist that is sharing the closet with me vanishes. I do not have time to contemplate what the mist that surrounded me was or if it was a figment of my imagination. I quickly leave my closet and shove the bracelet into the pocket on my dress. Rose enters the room with a tray. She brings me soup and a sandwich. She places the dinner tray on my dresser and tells me that she will be back to check on me. I do not even touch the food.

I pull the bracelet out of my pocket and put it securely back in its hiding place. I put on my nightgown and lie down. I leave my curtains open tonight. I want the moonlight to shine down on me, reminding me of the happy moments that I had with Angel. I close my eyes and drift off to sleep.

Touch of Evil

I am not sure how long I have been asleep when I feel a presence near me. I open my eyes, and the room is pitch black. Who closed my curtains? I try to see something in the blackness that fills my room, but it is too dark to even see my own hand. I hear nothing. I am so exhausted after such an agonizing day losing people that I hold dear to my heart that I cannot collect the energy to do anything but disregard the unsettling feeling and close my eyes again.

My eyes are closed in an attempt to give my mind some respite. I doze back off. I awake abruptly again, and I feel a warm body lying against my back as I lie on my side. I hear a muffled sound. I feel hot breath on my neck and shoulders as I become more conscious coming out of sleep. Someone touches the material of my nightgown, and now I know that I am not dreaming. I try to scream, but nothing comes out of my mouth. I try to move, but my body is motionless from overwhelming fright.

I hear raspy words that are so distorted that I cannot understand what this stranger in my room is saying. I struggle just to lift my little finger off of the bed where my hand rests. It feels like weights are holding me down. I cannot move or cry out for help.

I continue to attempt to scream, but not one peep comes out of me. I am petrified. I feel a hand slide underneath my nightgown and slowly travel against my body until it rests on my bare breast. At last, a sound of horror travels from deep within me, and I let out a blood-curdling scream. I scream and do not hold back my frantic pleas for help. Once my vocal cords melt from the fear that freezes every tiny muscle in my body, my screams do not stop.

I thrash about, trying to shove my attacker off of me. I push myself up onto the palms of my hands and scramble to escape the strong hands that attempt to hold me down. I manage to kick and hit and drive my back against the headboard of my bed. The assault goes on as the invisible figure continues to reach for me. I still cannot see him in the darkness that surrounds me, but I can feel his arms swinging as he tries to catch me. The noises from the assailant become deeper and louder. Combatting the figure frustrates him, and this makes his effort to capture me become even more forceful. I still scream and fight with all of the power I can find in my frail body.

This assault seems to never end. My bedroom door opens, and a dim light comes in from the hall. I can see the outline of the assailant. He begins to howl like a rabid animal. Is this the demon that lives in the west wing? I am so petrified that I close my eyes, cover my ears, and continue to scream. I do not want to see or hear him. He has me trapped, and I can do nothing else.

Suddenly, someone grips my body, and I begin to jerk and buck my body with optimism that whoever has a hold of me will let me go. Amidst the sounds of grunts and groans, I hear Rose's voice. I realize that Rose is trying to save me. I reach for her, and she pulls me off of the bed and carries my fatigued body out of the bedroom and briskly guides me down the hall.

I can hear Mother's voice. She is yelling at my attacker, and his sounds continue on. The echoes of the altercation resonate down the hall and throughout the house. Does she know who the assailant is? As Rose and I search for refuge with the danger being only footsteps away from us, I notice that the walls of the hallway that we are fleeing from look strange. As we franticly search for safety, it seems that the walls are moving. It appears that the walls are bulging out and then pulling back in as if the house is alive and breathing. Have the vile thoughts of the attacker awoken this corrupt and wicked house, or has the house manipulated this stranger to carry out its sinful desires?

Rose pulls me into one of the bedrooms and rushes me to the bed. She does a quick inspection of my face and body and then sits down next to me. She cradles me in her arms to shield me from any danger. My screams turn into uncontrollable sobs. I cannot speak, and I labor to breathe. I become anxious as I begin to hyperventilate. Rose attempts to calm my rapid breathing by stroking my back. The sounds of a gruesome battle continue to come from my bedroom. I am trembling and disoriented. I eventually regain enough presence of mind to speak.

"Rose, shouldn't we help Mother? Shouldn't we call the police?" I ask, surprised at my concern.

"No Child, your mother can handle the situation," she assures me.

What situation? Who or what is that? Did I finally meet the demon? Was that an intruder who broke into the mansion? Rose shivers as much as I do, and the look in her eyes is chilling as if she had just been attacked herself.

After a short time, the noises suddenly cease. The house is quiet. Every time I ask Rose questions about what has just happened, she sternly silences me. We hear a commotion in the hallway, and I jolt, remembering the attack that I just endured. Rose pulls me tighter to her and begins to run her fingers through my hair to sedate my disquieted mind. There are footsteps and dragging sounds coming from outside of the door. I hear more than just Mother's footsteps. Someone else is in the house. Someone is helping Mother, but whom? Rollins left yesterday, and our precious Gretchen just died.

Rose and I are in the bedroom for hours, and I grow very tired. My screams, cries, and sobs have conquered me, and I cannot keep my eyes open despite the extreme state of anxiety that I feel. I lie back on the bed and curl my body into a fetal position to protect myself if the monster comes back for me. I try to rest my mind and body, but every time I close my sleepy eyes, the ghastly noises that the beast made come flooding back. I can still feel his vile hand fondling my breasts.

Abruptly, the door blasts open, and it startles me. I spring up from my child-like position. Without even verifying that I may be in immediate danger, I begin to scream again thinking that the intruder is coming back to make me his prey. I am in a daze after being woken from a restless sleep. I regain my wits and see Mother. She charges toward me with a demented look in her eyes.

"Were you touched?!" she screams.

I am afraid to answer, and the thought of the hand touching my private areas has left me feeling dirty and unclean. I am horrified and ashamed. This is what Mother has been preaching and warning me about. I am concerned that Mother may have been right all along.

"Were you touched?!" she screams again, becoming extremely hostile.

"Yes," I say. My voice cracks and my lips tremble as the word comes out.

"Where?" she demands.

I say nothing and stare at the floor. I cannot say it out loud. I wish that the floor would come alive as the walls in the hallway did and suck me in, hiding me from the monster and Mother. She rips me off of the bed and slams my body firmly to a standing position on the floor. As my feet are forcefully planted on the floor, I hear the bones in my body connect from my feet to the top of my spine just like when I snuck into the west wing. I continue to look down, and my tears begin to flow again. My chest begins to heave as I try to restrain my weeping.

"Where were you touched, you dense girl?!" she yells at me.

I still cannot look at her. With my eyes still fixed on the floor, I slowly point to my breasts. I was touched everywhere, but this is all I can reveal. Mother reaches out and grips my arm. Her fingernails dig into my flesh. I feel moisture as the sharp pricks from her nails penetrate my skin. She begins to pull me into the hallway. I realize that she is going to punish me. She yanks me toward my bedroom, and I know that she is going to give me a scalding bath.

"I did nothing wrong! No Mother, please!" I beg.

She ignores my pleas. I begin to resist her, and the tussle between us results in me plummeting to the floor. I fight so fiercely that I do not even feel the impact from landing on the marble floor. She drags me down the corridor by my hair and wrists. I try to dig my heels into the floor to stop her, but my feet slip across the wood. I exert every ounce of strength that I have left in my worn-out body to resist Mother's punishment. My body slams back and forth against the walls as if I am the tiny ball in a pinball machine. The trauma inflicted on my head causes me to black out several times.

Her strength is unstoppable, and she overpowers me. She pulls my body into the bathroom. I continue to jerk and pull, trying to release her grip from me. She snatches my hair so hard that it feels like she has ripped my scalp off of my skull. Her seize over my long hair prevents my escape. She lifts my upper body off of the floor and forces my head towards the hot water that she has managed to turn on even with me flipping on the bathroom floor like a fish that was just plucked out of the sea.

I can feel the steam on my face as it rises from the water. Blood drips off of my face and tints the blistering water red. The tip of my nose touches the water. I close my eyes and hold my breath, preparing for my face to be submerged in the torrid water. Suddenly, I feel the might of Mother weaken, and she releases me from her grip.

I pull myself back over the side of the bathtub and spin around. I see that Rose has pulled the insane woman off of me. She has Mother's arms pinned behind her back, and Mother cannot move. She twists and turns her shoulders but is unable to slip through Rose's clutch. Mother screeches like the demon jumped out of me and into her.

"Go, Coral! Go!" Rose screams at me. I hesitate. I should help her. "Go! Go! Go!" she screams at me again as she struggles to keep Mother's arms confined.

I begin to run. I run through the house and out of the back door. I dart past the overgrown garden and do not stop to look down the path or smell the lilies. I run as if I can feel the surge of wind that Mother's arms produce as she reaches for me.

I sprint barefoot on the sand, and it makes my footsteps heavy. I have to use all of the force I have left in me to move through the sand. My ankle is throbbing and making my escape physically grueling. I must have injured it during the struggle with Mother.

I have on only a flimsy, white nightgown and panties, but I do not care how exposed I am. I am so fatigued that I do not think I can make one more stride with my weak legs. My getaway seems impossible as I fall into the coarse sand. My face takes a dive into the brown grains, and it gets buried in the sand. I pause and wipe my face with my sand-covered hand, and it just makes it worse. Regardless if I can see clearly or not, my determination to flee the suffering waiting for me at Ocean Point inspires me to try to stand. The strain in my ankle exudes up my leg, and I am unable to put weight on my injured foot. My head throbs from being pounded into the wall. I refuse to give up, so I start to crawl. I toil through the sinking sand but do not stop. It seems that I am wiggling through quick sand. The earth pulls me and slows me down.

Just when I do not think I can continue on, I see the lighthouse in the near distance. I need the shelter of the building and the protection that I hope Angel will give me. I begin to slither through the sand like a soldier in battle lying low and moving towards the enemy target.

I crawl to the door of the lighthouse and use the structure to aid me in standing on one foot. I rest all of my weight on the door and turn the doorknob. The door swings open, and I fall inside.

The Lighthouse

I must have passed out. My unconsciousness is broken when I faintly hear voices. I open my eyes, and I can still feel grains of sand in the corners of them. My vision is blurry, and the room is spinning.

I lie partially inside the lighthouse with my lower body remaining collapsed in the sand on the other side of the door. The voices come closer to me. I can hear footsteps descend down the winding staircase of the lighthouse. I desperately hope that it is Angel. I regret him seeing me in this condition, but I have to disregard my pride because I am severely injured and need help.

My hearing seems to be impaired because the voices I hear are distorted like my head is partially submerged under water. I strive to raise my pounding head. I manage to lift it enough to see Lucy playfully bouncing down the stairs. Her focus is on someone behind her. She does not even notice me lying in the doorway.

I have wanted to see her for so long, but this is not how I pictured our reunion. She playfully trips off the last step, and then I see a boy embrace her from behind. They joyfully collide into the wall and begin a passionate kissing session.

I try to raise my body off of the cold floor and make my presence known, but I cannot move. I lie on the floor and watch the two lovebirds kiss and grope each other in a very clumsy fashion. I feel like I am intruding on a very private moment for the two of them, but observing their actions tells me that this is not an encounter of any importance to either of them.

The boy has a bottle in his hand and does not put it down during their graceless romp. He swings the large bottle back and forth near his leg. They pause from their sloppy kissing long enough for each of them to take a big swig out of the bottle. It is evident that they are drinking alcohol and that they are drunk.

Lucy giggles and slurs her words. The boy does not seem to want to talk. He appears to be more interested in her breasts. The encounter between the two intoxicated, insincere lovers progresses, and he begins to unbutton Lucy's shirt. I feel uneasy that I am viewing this gawky scene, and honestly I do not want to.

I make an effort to rise again, but my attempt fails. They still have not noticed me. I begin to slam my hand on the ground repetitively until I can manage to make the impact loud enough for them to halt their casual romp and become aware of my comatose body lying only a few feet from them. It takes a few slaps to the ground beneath me, but Lucy finally hears my signal for help. I see her nudge the boy off of her bosom to see where the noise is coming from. She gets a glimpse of my battered body lying helpless on the ground and lets out a loud squeal.

The boy backs away from her and scans the room, confused by her unexpected outburst. He sees me lying on the floor, and I hear him insensitively respond in viewing my condition by saying,

"What the hell is that?"

Lucy shoves the boy off of her. He stumbles back and loses his balance, but even with losing his footing he still manages to take another drink out of his bottle. Liquid from the bottle spills on his shirt. He seems more concerned about the stain left behind by his careless drunken state than he is about the wounded girl lying on the ground.

Lucy dashes towards me, but from the liquor swimming in her blood stream, she is impaired with her movements and loses her pace. She steps sideways then back but eventually finds her way to me. She drops inelegantly to her knees.

"Coral, is that you?" she asks as she makes an effort to push my hair out of my face to confirm my identity. Her judgment is off, and her hand slips, carelessly poking me in the eye. "Oh my God, it is you Coral. You are bleeding!" she says. I can hear shock and horror in her voice.

"What a buzz kill," I hear the boy say.

"Tommy, get the hell out of here! Your party is over for tonight!" Lucy says.

The boy stands in front of us and looks down at me while his body sways from side to side. He inspects me like I am road kill and is fascinated with the gruesome sight left in the wake of a speeding car. Lucy attempts to lift me off of the ground, but she struggles with my dead weight. I am unable to assist her. She looks over her shoulder at Tommy and says with a frustrated tone,

"Damn it Tommy, either help me or get out of here!"

She is able to lift my shoulders up slightly with the goal of rolling me on my back. As she lifts me, the front of my nightgown is visible, and the blood-covered garment alarms the callous boy.

"I'm out of here!" He steps over me as he flees the scene. His desertion does not seem to affect Lucy.

"Coral, I will be right back. I am going to get help."

She jolts to her feet, cautious not to step on me, and runs out of the door. I try to tell her not to get my mother, but I cannot stop her. I am sure that she knows that Mother did this to me, though. She is gone for so long that I fear she maybe got as unnerved by my condition as Tommy did and is not going to return. I calm my insecurity of being abandoned by slowing down my erratic thoughts long enough to remember that the lighthouse is quite a distance from any of the residences on the beach.

I hear footsteps come towards me. Has Mother found me? Has the demon who laid his unwanted hand on me escaped Ocean Point and found me by my scent? I gaze upwards, and I see Mrs. Lombardi.

"Lucy, help me," she commands as she rolls my shoulders to my side and then lifts my back. Lucy has a hold of my feet and gently assists my legs while they follow the movement of my upper body.

I feel my body being lifted off of the dirty ground. The manhandling hurts, and I let out a small cry. I am embarrassed by the vulnerable and weak condition that I am in. Lucy and her mother tow my body to the small, worn-out mattress in the corner of the quaint living quarters.

As my suffering body is placed on the old, soiled mattress, I hear someone else come through the door. Panic strikes me, afraid that this time Mother has come to retrieve me. I fear that Mrs. Lombardi called her not understanding that she is the monster who did this to me. I try to rise up in delusion that if she has come for me that I have the strength to make another getaway. It is a failed attempt. Again, my injuries have defeated me.

Mrs. Lombardi places her hands on my shoulders, silently telling me to lie still. Out of the corner of my eye, I see Angel. I turn my face towards him, and his expression speaks to me and confirms my assumption on how dire my injuries are. He looks stunned and horrified as he gazes down at me. I want to cry from humiliation, but there are no tears left in me. I feel completely depleted. He seems so concerned, but he obviously does not know what to do. He wrings his hands and seems to be tortured by my condition. Mrs. Lombardi looks down, and she notices how exposed my body is underneath the flimsy, white nightgown that clings to my body from the sweat that my body produced during the horrendous events at Ocean Point and my physically grueling escape through the sand.

"Angel, hurry to the house, and bring me blankets and some water!" she tells him.

She is attempting to respect my modesty and aids me to salvage what little dignity that I have left. I also am sure that she sent Angel to prevent her son from seeing a scantly clothed girl. A mother would think that my revealing position is inappropriate for her son's eyes. She begins to inspect my injuries. She follows the trail of dried blood that leads to my ear. She gently moves my head from side to side, and she tenderly runs her fingers across my scalp, feeling all of the lumps that are swelling. She looks at my legs and sees all of the scrapes and bruises that Mother's brutality left behind. She notices my injured ankle. Her face exudes worry as she moves my foot to diagnose the severity of my injury. Even from the slightest movement I flinch in excruciating pain.

Just as she completes her thorough inspection of my beaten body, Angel returns. He totes blankets, pillows, and a container of water. Mrs. Lombardi hurriedly takes the pillow from Angel's bundle and cautiously places it under my head. She assists my neck as it falls back onto the pillow. She takes a blanket from the stack in his hands and covers my exposed body.

She hands me the container of water and supports my head as she lifts it off of the pillow so that I can take a drink. The water is so refreshing, and I am parched. I begin to drink the water too quickly to satisfy my overwhelming thirst, and I begin to choke. She removes the container and allows my head to naturally fall back on the pillow.

My vision begins to improve, and I can see clearer. I inspect Mrs. Lombardi's face. I see so much resemblance of Lucy in her. She has a chubby, round face with expressive, chocolate-brown eyes that emit a feeling of kindness. Her distinctive, brown eyes ease my anxiety and encourage me to trust her.

She has dark brown hair that is the same shade as Lucy's. I cannot tell how long it is because it is pulled on top of her head in a conservative bun. She is a little chubby, and I bet when she was younger she had a curvaceous figure like Lucy's. I envision that this is what Lucy is going to look like when she grows older.

She shakes her head as if she is trying to process the appalling state that Mother's ruthless anger left me in. She begins to talk to Lucy and Angel as if I am not even in the room. She speaks with a strong northern accent. She has the sort of voice that can be the sweetest sound but can change when needed to keep her children in line.

"We have to get this girl to a hospital," she firmly states.

When I hear her plan, the fear of my certain demise takes over. I cannot go to the hospital. They will just send me back home to Mother so that she can finish the war we were engaged in. Once she discovers that my condition has been publicly disclosed, it will enrage her even more. I should just give Angel directions to the secret graveyard to pick a spot out next to one of the children and dig my burial hole. I try to rise up and speak. The water quenched my thirst and soothed my throat enough that words are now able to leave my mouth. I faintly begin to plead with her not to send me to hospital.

"Please don't. They will just send me back to her, and I know she is going to kill me."

I am sure that Mrs. Lombardi must think that I am nuts and talking craziness from the damage to my head. She tries to calm me by placing her soft hand on my cheek and compassionately stroking my face. I feel envious of Lucy and Angel for having the privilege of being given such a kindhearted Mother.

"Coral, you have a busted eardrum, possible concussion, and maybe a broken foot. You need professional medical attention," she says trying to convince me that her diagnosis is accurate. Lucy loudly speaks from across the room. Her words run together and are almost inaudible.

"Yeah Ma, her mama is crazy! She will kill her!"

I look at Lucy, and she is obviously still experiencing the effect of the liquor. She stumbles around as if she has two left feet. Mrs. Lombardi watches Lucy's uncoordinated movements and becomes aware of her altered condition. The tough Italian mother comes to the surface. She displays evident disappointment in Lucy's irresponsible behavior.

"Lucia Lombardi, you need to get your bottom to the house now. Go sober yourself up, and go to bed! I should ground you! If only your papa could see you now. Girl, you are going to be the death of me, and you better not be bringing any babies home for me to raise! Get outta here!" she says, scolding Lucy.

Lucy listens to her mother's orders, but she does not seem the least bit concerned about her disapproving tone. She just giggles and jabbers something about a baby and then blows her a kiss and waves goodbye, leaving the lighthouse.

"With all that is going on here she wants to act childish and foolish. I am going to have a head full of gray hair before I can get that sister of yours raised. I thought that the Lord would only punish me with one unruly child, but he sent me two of you!" she says to Angel lightheartedly and gives me a quick wink just like Rose does.

Seeing her wink makes me think of Rose, and I have immeasurable concern that Mother has harmed her for interfering during my punishment and assisting me in escaping. I want to tell them about my apprehension, but first I have to persuade them not to take me to the hospital.

She begins to discuss a plan with Angel on how they will transport me to the hospital. She talks over me and has disregarded for my pleas. I rise off of the pillow as much as I can manage. I begin to beg her for mercy and secrecy. There is irony in me begging for them to keep a secret for me when the things that have haunted me my entire life are secrets. Now I am asking for someone else to keep one for me.

"You are badly hurt, Baby Girl. It would be neglectful of me to let you lie here and suffer any more than you already have," she says as she attempts to sway my wishes.

"I can take it. I have taken worse!"

I become convinced that she is not going to listen to me. I can see in her eyes that she is not buying my tough-girl persona. Out of desperation, I hastily pull my nightgown down and expose my bare breasts that are marked with scars from the deep burn marks that one of Mother's punishing baths left behind. I do not even consider that Angel is standing near and can see my naked bosom and unsightly scars. Instantly after my hasty display of desperation I feel horrified and search the room to find his whereabouts. Fortunately, he is away from me and is preoccupied with pacing back and forth like he is cultivating a plan in his head.

Her eyes widen, and I sense that my scars have taken her back. After the initial shock dwindles, she becomes aware that I am lying with my bare chest uncovered. She swiftly pulls my nightgown back up and replaces the blankets back on top of my shivering body.

"I am very sorry Coral, but I cannot take on the responsibility of caring for you. If you are discovered, I will lose my job and get arrested. You are still a minor," she explains to me with sorrow in her voice and empathy in her eyes.

I nod to her to signal that I understand and then look away because I know that my eyes are beginning to fill up with tears, and I do not want her to see my tears. No matter how much I feel that my life is in jeopardy by being delivered back to the arms of my heartless mother, I do not wish to be a burden.

I foresee the wicked delight that Ocean Point will rejoice in when I am back under its roof. I can already smell the stuffy, thick air that fills the rooms like a layer of fog ascends on a murky lake at daybreak. I can hear the unearthly sounds that the demon screams. I am optimistic that Mother is so incensed over my escape that she slays me quickly. I do not want to live in this constant physical agony and mental anguish any longer. This last confrontation has drained the last smidgen of capacity left in me to survive her and Ocean Point. I lie here and have come to terms with my fate. Angel speaks from across the room.

"I will take care of her," he says with a matter of fact tone.

Angel has not said one word since my injured body was discovered laying limp on the ground. The lighthouse is silent. His proclamation seems to have hushed even the waves that break against the rocky shore that the foundation of the lighthouse rests upon. Sensing his mother's hesitation in supporting this dicey arrangement, Angel begins to argue his case.

"Mother, I am a grown man now. I can take care of her and help her heal. She can stay here. No one will think to look here at least for a while. I know that this is a temporary fix, but let's just get her well. I can clean this place up. The living quarters are a little primal, but it is better that she is here than in that house being tortured." He argues with his Mother without her saying a word. Mrs. Lombardi shakes her head and says,

"You are just like your father. There's no need in me trying to change your mind. You Italian men are so stubborn."

She pretends that she is annoyed at Angel, but I can tell that she is full of pride. It has to be gratifying as a mother to realize that despite the trials and tribulations that every family has she has raised an honorable man. The reality of the difficult situation is that there really is not any other option to ensure I will be safe.

I am touched so profoundly by Angel's sacrifice and risk to keep me safe and with him. I really am not sure if he feels the same way for me that I do him, but I do know that there is a connection between us that is undeniable. Now I feel justified in my irrepressible desires to be close to him. I want to reach out and hug him tight and never let him go, but my weary arms are now useless.

"Okay Angel, go to the house and get some food, drinks, and supplies that you will need here. It is most likely going to take weeks for her to regain her strength, so plan accordingly. Also, have your belligerent sister send over some of her old clothes for Coral to wear," she says as she gives us her blessing and support. I am overwhelmed with her kindness. I reach toward her face, and I say sincerely,

"Thank you, Mrs. Lombardi. Thank you."

She smiles and then begins to clean my wounds while Angel leaves to gather the things that we will need for our cozy, little hide out. For the first time in my life, I feel truly blessed. God took away two people that I absolutely adored, but he also sent me angels of mercy to protect me and support me.

Mrs. Lombardi is silent as she cleans the wounds on my afflicted body. The thought of someone inflicting this amount of harm on his or her only child disturbs her so greatly that she has a loss for words. I perceive my reasoning for the silence by the way she is caring for me. As she doctors my wounds, I can see her silently grieving for me. It is impossible for her not to run across an old scar. Every time her gentle fingers graze my mutilated skin, her expression darkens. As she nears the completion of cleaning the last deep scrape on my leg, I see tears glisten in her big, brown eyes. I realize that Mother's crimes against my young skin have made an emotional impact on Mrs. Lombardi. If a stranger to me can see that this treatment is wrong and cry for my suffering, then why is my own mother so callous to it?

Angel's timing is perfect, and he arrives back at the lighthouse just as Mrs. Lombardi is done. She fumbles through the things that he retrieved from their home and finds some of Lucy's old clothing. She aids me in getting the blood-stained nightgown off and assists me in getting properly dressed. She slips a pair of cotton shorts on me and then helps guide my upper body into a soft, comfortable t-shirt. I have never had on a t-shirt or shorts before, and even with the dull ache of my body casual clothing makes me feel better.

She stands up from the bed, and I notice the hesitation that she has from leaving us alone. She is obviously fretting over the possibility that we will be discovered. Angel senses his mother's apprehension, and he goes to her side and puts his arm across her shoulder and says,

"Ma, we will be fine. I will take good care of her. You know that I may not have made the best grades in school, but I am street smart just like Uncle Vinny." She throws her hands into the air as a sign that she has lost the battle and heads towards the door. She looks at me and says,

"Feel better, Coral. You are a very strong young lady." Her words of encouragement make me feel special. It is nice to think that as pathetic as I am laying here looking frail and bruised that she can see past the external scars and see the strength that lives inside of me. "By the way Angel, I expect you to be a gentleman!" she warns him, reverting back to the stern Italian mom.

"Ma, go!" he says to her with slight frustration in his voice.

She cracks the door and peers out, making sure that it is safe. She exits in hopes of avoiding any suspicion that our trespassing in the abandoned lighthouse may render.

Angel tensely unpacks and organizes the things that he brought from his house. It appears that he is trying to make himself look busy so that he does not have to look at me in my current condition. I do not blame him. I know that I cannot possibly look attractive lying here bruised and dirty. My heart is home to so much sorrow thinking that he may never see me the way he did when we weathered the violent storm together.

I scan the small room and see little things that I did not notice the first time I was here. There is a tiny galley kitchen that you can walk through. It seems to have the appliances that we need, but the only problem is that there is no electricity in the abandoned building. The room is now lit by lanterns that Lucy and Angel had previously brought to their secret playroom, but I notice that Angel brought an additional light source of candles and a flashlight.

There is a small couch in what the last resident considered his living room, and sitting in the corner is a television. I so wish that we did have electricity. I have never watched television before, and what a treat that would be. There is a bathroom behind me with a miniature standup shower. It is so small that I do not think Angel would even fit in it. If he did, his head would surpass the faucet.

The one thing that I am thankful for is that we do have access to water. I overheard him tell his mother he had found the main switch for the old lighthouse and turned it on himself when he snuck back to the house to pack our necessities. He is very clever and street smart just like he told his mother.

The little house is filthy. Grime and dust have dominated every corner and object in this quaint hideaway. I am not stressed about the condition of my new temporary living quarters. I can clean it when I am well and safe. I would rather sleep in soot than be under Ocean Point's roof within Mother's reach.

The nervous silence is about to drive me insane. Even though Angel is in all of my thoughts every waking minute of my days, I still feel uncomfortable around him. We had an exciting and intimate moment together, but it was brief and only once.

"Angel," I say softly. I wait for him to acknowledge me and look my way. He looks at me, and I pat the bed giving him the sign that I want him next to me. He still fumbles with the supplies and takes his time to answer my request. "Angel, please. It will be okay," I say again and then pat the bed for the second time.

His expression softens, and he comes to my side. He doesn't sit on the bed next to me, but he kneels next to me. I pat the bed again, wanting so desperately for him to hold me as he had before and take this aching away from me.

"No Coral, I am afraid that I may hurt you." He looks meaningfully into my eyes, and his concern for me warms my heart and makes me believe that he has been longing for me as much as I have for him. "I am not going to let anyone hurt you ever again," he proclaims and then lightly kisses my forehead.

I want to reach up and grab his face and bring his lips to mine. He lays his head next to my shoulder, and I can see that this is as close as he is going to get to me now. I feel that sees me as a china doll that is stored high on a shelf in an expensive department store and that he is concerned I will easily shatter. The sun is beginning to rise, and streams of diffused light sneak through the stained-glass windows. I watch as the sun becomes strong and brighter as it rises above the sea.

The small windows that surround the little house are adorned with vibrantly colored glass. The windows cast an array of beautiful colors and designs that surround us in our little hideaway. The sight is breathtaking, and I am entranced with the flamboyant colors as they dance on the walls of my new home. I foolishly consider that the dazzling and bright hues of the jovial sunshine that trickle into room are a sign of many happy and bright days to come. The disturbing reality is that my future is predestined and out of my control. I know that plans are being formulated as I lie here that will bring a veil of darkness into my life where no lights will shine, and the evil will rear its ugly head and change my life forever.

I hear the sounds of the waves as they crash into the foundation of the lighthouse. They assure me that they will give me peace and protection as the powerful water surrounds the circular building even if it is for just one night.

I grow tired and find it impossible to fight sleep any longer. I fall asleep with more love and peace than I have ever known. In my shattered soul I know that this is not forever. I am burdened with the fear that this will end with more grievance than one person can survive.

Falling in Love

I wake to curious sounds in an unfamiliar place. I open my eyes, and I become instantly unnerved. I am still disheartened from the latest incident with Mother and the beastly being that snuck into my room. I am not fully awake from such a restful sleep. I let out a small whimper for help, and I see handsome Angel walk towards me. I recollect my memories and now can perceive where I am.

"Well hello there," he says.

I wipe my eyes and yawn. It is freeing that I can actually yawn without being swatted with a wooden ruler. I am not sure if I should feel delighted that I have the freedom to do the simplest things such as yawning without fret or be mournful because I have lived my entire life being punished for such insignificant acts. I look around the room, and I am amazed that the dirt and grime is gone. The small area is spotless.

Even Mother's ridiculous white glove test would pass the humble home.

The living area has been decorated with colorful pillows laying on the petite couch, and a bright red shag rug has been placed in front of it. The once dull corner of the room is now a darling little sitting area. As I look around at my new home, I see dishes on the shelves in the kitchen and a shower curtain hanging in the miniature shower. The floor has been cleaned immaculately, and there are large, brightly colored throw pillows scattered throughout the entire little space. I can visualize myself curled up on one of the huge downy pillows with a book and not being afraid of who or what is coming down the hallway. There are velvety pastel blankets draped across the couch and pillows to provide us with warmth on the chilly Rhode Island nights. Seeing the newly decorated and cleaned room gives me a feeling of euphoria and a renewal of energy.

The undisturbed sleep has helped my afflicted body, and I think that I am able to sit up. I push myself up. It takes great effort, but I fight through the soreness. I sit up, and I am baffled when I get a second glance of the room. When did Angel do this, and how did I sleep so soundly that I didn't hear him bustle around me in his apparent cleaning frenzy?

"How long have I been asleep?" I ask. He chuckles and looks down at his watch before he answers me.

"Hmm, in two hours it will be two full days, so forty-six hours and three minutes." I cannot believe what he is saying. I have slept for two solid days. He sees my disbelief in what he told me. He bends down and says, "You needed the rest."

It takes almost two weeks for my injuries to subside enough for me to be comfortable. Angel is so wonderful to me. He is loving, caring, and attentive. He makes me feel safe when anxiety about being discovered creeps into my programmed mind and steals my contentment. He cares for me emotionally and physically throughout my recovery.

I experience the sweetest kind of relationship with Angel. It exceeds all of the fantasies and daydreams that I had in my mind while being imprisoned in Ocean Point. We spend endless hours talking, and we never run out of things to talk about. He is not only the man that I crave romantically, but he is also my best friend.

There are days that we make an area on the floor with all of the colorful pillows and blankets. He stretches out across our little makeshift bed, and I lie with my head on his chest as he reads the most amazing stories to me from the collection of books that we find in the old lighthouse. Those innocent moments where I can hear his heartbeat through his chest while my face rests on his muscular physique are magical.

For those two weeks, I still find it difficult to walk without experiencing pain. At sunset, Angel carries me to the top of the lighthouse so we can watch the sun gradually disappear into the sea. The spectacle of pinks, purples, oranges, and golds paint the sky with the dimming rays from the sleepy sun. Some evenings when we know the weather will be pleasant, Angel lugs some of our pillows and blankets to the top of the tower, and we camp out all night and talk the evening into morning waiting for the sun to make its glorious return. The vision of the ocean at daybreak is breathtaking. The sea is completely dark, and all at once the massive sun peaks across the horizon. The tremendous, golden beams from the sun's arrival light the water. The dolphins sometimes play in the water, jumping and doing flips for our amusement. The seagulls fly around us and squawk all of the time.

These unforgettable times that I share with Angel allow me to let go of my insecurities and let trust into my heart. The uneasy feelings that I used to have when I was near him vanish. As each day passes, I grow closer to this man who is my savior even if it is only for a brief time. We share an intimacy that few will ever know.

We are trapped in this tiny space with no electricity or modern conveniences. I have not left this building since I arrived, fearful of being noticed. Angel leaves occasionally to go to the store for us, and even though he is gone for only a short time, I miss him.

I have now been living in the lighthouse for almost a month. I try to keep the negative thoughts and feelings of Ocean Point out of my mind. I know that my time here is not forever, but I do not want to waste a second of my blissful time here and allow the sinister house to take it from me. I miss Rose and hope that Mother did not harm her. I feel like I abandoned her, but I know that this is truly what she wants for me. I wonder if Mother is glad that I am gone and has washed her hands of her unholy little girl or if there are policemen on every corner hanging up flyers with my picture in hopes of receiving clues to my whereabouts.

I am finally able to put pressure on my foot and walk with ease. I undoubtedly only sprained my ankle. If I had broken a bone I could not have recovered so quickly. My hearing is still hindered. I may have suffered permanent hearing loss, but the gurgling sound that has been obstructing my hearing has subsided.

Angel and I are cuddled up together in the tiny bed that we have been innocently sharing when we hear a bang at the door. I am concerned that Mother has found me. Angel motions for me to hide. I slip behind the door that leads to the stairs. I crouch down and put my hands in the prayer position, and I begin to pray. I pray for God not to take me away from my new life and all the happiness that he has blessed me with. I pray for protection of Angel and myself. I am so concentrated on my desperate pleas to God that I have heard nothing from the other room. I peek through the crack where the door is hinged, and I see Angel move the chair that we propped against the doorknob to keep intruders from entering our little sanctuary.

He opens the door wide enough for someone to slide in sideways. I relax when I see that it is Lucy. I haven't seen her since the day I fell face first into this place. It has bothered me that she has not wanted to spend time with me and make up for the time that we lost during my incarceration.

Lucy seems to have changed a lot, and I am not sure if the person she has evolved into is someone that I would find enjoyable to be with. Angel told me that she got involved with the wrong crowd just like he once did. He pretends that her harmful lifestyle does not concern him, but I sense that it worries him greatly. He just does not want to admit it. The two of them have weathered a lot together due to the loss of their father at such young ages. I leave my hiding spot and enter the room. Lucy plops down on the bed and looks around.

"I like what you guys have done with the place."

She seems half sincere and half sarcastic. I am unable to read her intentions. She chews gun and blows bubbles that pop on her lips. She continually licks the bubblegum residue off with her tongue. It is difficult to have a conversation with the constant distraction of her chewing. She is wearing the shortest shorts that I have ever seen and a skintight shirt that is the same length of her shorts. There is a horizontal pattern of stripes that cover the shirt. Her hair has been straightened and then violently teased at the roots and deliberately raised inches off of the crown of her head with some sort of stiff substance. The color is not the rich chocolate brown that I once admired; it appears lighter.

"So, have you guys done it?" she impolitely asks.

At first, my naive mind does not understand her question. Angel tells her to shut up and dismisses her raunchy question. It seems that whatever comes to Lucy's mind just flows out of her mouth without her even thinking it through. She has always been this way, but I used to find amusement in her loose lips and enjoy her honesty. What I once found endearing I now find unrefined and vulgar.

"What do you want, Lucy?" Angel asks her with irritation in his voice. She seems to not hear her brother and then says,

"How much longer are you guys gonna be shacking here? I miss being able to bring hot guys here." It seems to infuriate Angel that she can be so tactless.

"Lucy, why don't you just leave? Isn't there some boy waiting in the backseat of a Camaro for you?" She snickers at his insult.

"That was a good one, Bro. Hey, quit being so mean. I came here to invite you guys to a party tonight on the boardwalk. I figure it will do you two good to get out of this box for a little while and join the rest of us living."

"Absolutely not! That is a terrible idea and way too risky for Coral," he says shutting her invite down.

"Oh come on, it will be fun! I bet Coral has never been to a party." She argues her case and then turns to me, wanting me to take her side in the debate with her strict brother. Her focus is now on me. "I can come over and bring you some hip clothes. I will fix you up all groovy for your stuffy boyfriend." She is trying to entice me.

Her obvious manipulation is working. The thought of getting dressed up for Angel like I did before excites me. All I have had to wear for the last month is Lucy's hand-me-downs. I have been strutting around in baggy t-shirts, shorts, and capris that are too big because of our size difference.

My face must show the stimulation that Lucy's precarious invitation gives me. Angel sees my fascination, and his expression turns defensive. He slowly shakes his head, signaling to me that he is not going along with Lucy's plan. I have never been to a party or on a date, and this is probably as close to a date that I will ever have with Angel. As much as I love being secluded in this lighthouse, it would be nice to be able to leave it even for a little while. I know that there is a possibility that leaving here may put me in danger, but I question if Mother even cares enough to seek me out. Lucy's attention span is miniscule, and she becomes tired of the argument that really does not mean much to her. She stands up and says,

"Fine, I've got better things to do than sit around here with you two lame cats." She begins to walk towards the door, and against my better judgment I quickly follow her.

"Lucy, will a lot of people be there?" I ask with hope that my desire to go will be validated.

I nervously look at Angel knowing that he does not approve, but I hope that maybe he has had a change of heart and might consider the excursion. His expression remains unyielding. I know that Angel has my best interest at heart. In reality, I know he is right, but I wish that he would just take consideration in the life I have had. I have never had the chance to experience what every other person my age has taken for granted. Being with him has given me the feeling of security. I am at peace with taking chances because I know that he will be there for me if I fall.

"I don't know, the usual people from school. It's no big deal. It's just a chill party on the beach. It's not like we will run into any of your insane mother's friends, and besides, after I am finished dolling you up no one will even recognize you. You already don't look like the girl that you did a year and a half ago, and now that you don't have to wear all of those scratchy, puke gray clothes, you are unrecognizable," she says.

Her explanation of why it will be okay makes sense, and I am now on her side. I look at Angel, and without words my eyes cry out to him for understanding. It is unwise, but I have never once in my life had anyone my age not look at me like I was a weird freak. Over the last two years, I have grown into a much different person. My time here with Angel has freed me in so many ways and has made me feel normal. Even if it is for only one night, I would love to look like the other girls, talk like the other girls, and feel like the other girls.

"No, No, No!" he says. It seems that he has left no room for compromise. I walk towards him and reach for his hand. He pulls it back. I reach again, and this time he allows me to grasp it.

"I know it is hard for you to understand, but one night like this would mean so much to me. I would really like to take the risk. I want to go, Angel," I tell him.

The whole time, he avoids eye contact afraid that if he sees my pleading eyes that his position will weaken. His eyes dart around the room. I move my face to his until our eyes meet. He shakes his head and releases his hand from my hold.

He starts to rub his hands together as he always does when he is nervous. His usual monotonous pacing begins. He walks the floor as if Lucy and I are not even in the room. We watch him silently pound out the pros and cons with each footstep he takes. It seems that Angel circles the room forever, but it is only minutes in reality. Suddenly, Lucy boorishly says,

"I do not have time for this. I have to go get ready for the party. Hell, I don't know what you guys are so worked up about. It's just a party." She has her hands on her hips like we have just wasted hours of her precious time. She has come to the conclusion that we are not worth the effort. "Hey Angel, maybe this will help you make your decision. Maybe if you get Coral drunk you can finally get some," she says jokingly.

Neither Angel nor I think that her crass comments are amusing, and both of us shoot her a look of annoyance. I see how upset he is growing with his sister, and I do not want a sibling brawl to ruin my chances of being able to experience my first real party. My mind scrambles to try to figure out how to simmer the brewing war that I see heating between the two. I turn towards Lucy and ask,

"Can you please wait one second," knowing that as soon as she walks out of the door that the possibility is gone.

She gives me a look of boredom and then blows another bubble with her gum. I walk to Angel and grab both of his forearms, forcing his frantic pacing to cease. He gazes into my eyes, and I can tell that he is sincerely worried.

"Angel, please just one time. We will be careful. You know how to keep me safe," I beg.

"Okay Coral. We will do it just this once, and we will do it my way! Do you hear me?"

He gives into my wishes. I grab him and hug him tight. A huge smile forms on my face, and I begin to jump up and down like the little girl that I was when Lucy and I were friends. I skip over to her, and for one moment I wish that things were the same between us as they were then. She could share my excitement, but those days are gone. She looks at me like I am bizarre.

"Okay, I will be back in an hour to fix you up," she says and then leaves.

Angel leans the heavy chair back against the doorknob to keep us safe. I am sure he wishes that he could rearrange the door so that we were actually locked in and could halt the threat that this meaningless party could bring into our unnoticed residence of the lighthouse.

I enthusiastically jump into our miniature shower. Taking a shower in the lighthouse is quite amusing. It is so small that when in it you cannot turn around or stretch your arms. I do not complain. I feel fortunate just to have running water. I stand in the teeny shower and wait for the chilly water to rain down on me. It usually takes a few minutes once you turn the lever for the water to start squirting out of the showerhead.

I brace myself, waiting for the ice cold water to come rushing down my naked body. We are lucky that Angel was able to figure out how to turn on the water, but the downside is that we only get cold water. I ran away from my home where I lived in a cold, unloving environment and was tortured with scalding hot water, and now I am in a warm, loving home and tortured with frigid, cold water.

The icy water begins to shower over me, and I cleanse my body as fast as I can to shorten my time under the nippy water. I dance with my feet to combat the overwhelming chill that the water covers my body with. Angel and I have made a game out of timing each other in the shower to see who could last the longest in the freezing water. He always wins. His amount of will power impresses me.

In my usual time of approximately eighty-five seconds, I leap out of the little shower and wrap the nearest towel around my goose bump covered body. As I dry off, I wonder what Angel is doing. I become concerned that my insistence on going out tonight may have upset him to the point that he may be angry with me. The thought of him being displeased by me is troublesome.

I wrap the towel around me and walk out of the bathroom. He is still pacing relentlessly. I can see that accepting Lucy's invitation is pestering him greatly. He hears me and looks up from the floor that his eyes and feet have been burning a hole through.

I stand with only a towel wrapped around me. My skin is wet, and my hair drips water down my face. He looks toward me and immediately stops pacing. I recognize the look that develops across his once harsh face. He stares at me with the same lustful need that he had when our bodies were entangled together during the storm. His stare is passionate. It makes feel like I am his victim, but I am not scared. I am so relieved that he looks at me the way that he did once before. I have yearned for him to want me romantically every day that we have been stowed away together.

During our time in the lighthouse together, we have grown very close. We have had affectionate times sharing each other's hopes and dreams, but we have not been physically intimate like the way we were on the top of the lighthouse. We have fallen asleep snuggled up together on our tiny bed, but the nights have not been entertained with powerful lingering kisses or touches.

I stand in front of this man that I have fallen deeply in love with, and all I want at this very moment in time is for him to take me in his arms and kiss me so intensely that I forget about the party. I want this man to do things to me that Mother says are sinful. I want to be a sinner. I want to sin.

Angel recognizes how aggressive his gaze is and dismisses his hunger and desire. I do not want these feelings of desire for each other to end. He turns his head away and he withdraws from me. Why is he working so hard to contain his hunger for me? I know that he craves me as much as I do him. Will Angel never touch me the way that I need him to ever again?

This denial of my physical needs gives Lucy's promised makeover even more importance. I want to show him that I am not the damaged little girl that stumbled helplessly into the lighthouse. I am a woman ready for him to love and take me as his own. My optimism of tonight helps me cope with Angel's rejection.

There is a knock at the door, and I am delighted to see Lucy come bouncing in with a slinky red dress on and carrying a large bag. The dress is so tight-fitting that her breasts are pouring out of the bodice like they are being tortured and trying to break away from the restraining fabric.

Lucy tells Angel that he needs to leave for a while so that we can have girl time. I have not been impressed with the person that she has become, but I do appreciate that she wants to give me the opportunity to look pretty for Angel. Angel is still not at ease with our plans but agrees to leave. He instructs Lucy to put the back of the chair against the door to keep us safe while he is gone.

Lucy does as he asks and then puts her bag on the bed. She begins to pull out clothing, hairbrushes, makeup, and shoes. I am grateful that she put so much thought and time into helping me. I am overflowing with anticipation to see the end results of my makeover.

Lucy wastes no time getting started with the attempt to transform me from plain, strange Jane to a woman that Angel cannot resist. She seems to be in a hurry. I am sure that she has some cute but insignificant boy

waiting somewhere to grope her full breasts.

I worry about Lucy and her ability to see that the choices that she is making are detrimental to her. I have concerns that if she continues to allow boys to treat her body like a play toy that she will never be able to have or appreciate the kind of relationship that Angel and I share. I know that Lucy and I will never be close again like we were before. I guess it was unrealistic to think that she and I could see each other again and just pick up where we left off over a year ago. While I was being held hostage like Rapunzel, she was out enjoying life, making friends, and growing up.

My life stood still, and I lived in daydreams and fantasies without having a chance to make decisions based on my experiences as she had. I hope that I would have made different choices than Lucy has, but there is no way to ever really know. There are always reasons that people act the way they do and make poor choices. Maybe losing her father has made her reach out to every boy who looks her way. I am deciding to stay optimistic that she is just being a typical teenager and will grow out of this wild, selfish phase.

Lucy sits me down in a chair and begins to apply makeup to my face. I have never worn make up before. It feels funny as she brushes color onto my ivory skin. She continuously complains about the dim light from the lantern and burning candles impairing her vision. Each time I feel the brush covered in makeup stroke my cheek, I feel more alive.

By the time that she has finished painting my face to her satisfaction, my hair is finally dry. It is unruly with curls that seem to be alive and twist and turn in every direction. Being so close to the ocean makes my

hair unmanageable. The moisture in the air attacks my hair. I usually just pull my rowdy locks into a ponytail. I don't know how to do anything fancy anyways.

She looks at my hair and tries to figure out how to calm my rebellious mane without the modern technology of electricity. She explains to me that the normal girl cannot survive without a hairdryer and rollers. I giggle at her remark, not because it is funny, but because of how shallow women must really be that they could not survive with the materialist equipment that they need to make themselves pretty.

She becomes perturbed as she begins a battle with my curls. She has a large brush and forcefully attempts to discipline my hair by combing it roughly and trying to make it straight. Her aggravation of losing the war that she and my curls seem to have been engaged in shows. She lets loose of the long strands of my hair and grabs a small comb.

She lifts my hair by the root on the top of my head and then uses the small comb to tease my hair up into the same style that she is sporting. Her aggressive teasing hurts, and I flinch several times. She is focused on the end result, and I think that my disorderly curls have frustrated her to the point that she just wants to be done.

She picks up a can and begins to spray the roots of my now poofy hair. She then stands back and sprays the mist in a circular motion around my head careful not to miss one strand. At first, I think that she is spraying a household cleaner on my head.

For a brief moment, I wonder if Lucy is playing a joke on me and if her interest in my appearance is just to humiliate me and make me feel foolish. I remain silent and wait hoping that my assumptions are

presumptuous. She sets the can on a table next to me. I pick up the can and read the label.

"Hairspray

The Ultimate Strength To

Hold Your Hair In Place All Day"

I am relieved but feel guilty that I have turned out to be so distrusting that I thought that Lucy would intentionally hurt me. I feel silly for my concerns and know that she is not malicious. Even with her now narcissistic mentality she would not try to hurt me.

After she gets to a place that she thinks she has done her best with my uncooperative hair we migrate to the bed that is covered with an array of dresses, skirts, and shirts. Lucy is a lot heavier than I am, but luckily for me, I do not think she realizes that she wears her new style of clothes a couple sizes too small which fit me perfectly.

She picks up a black mini skirt and holds it in front of me in my towel as if she is picturing the teeny skirt on my body. She looks at me and recognizes that I need undergarments. She tosses through the clothes deliberately scattered across the bed until she finds bras and panties. She selects a bra and displays it to me, holding it by its delicate straps. I am awestruck when I see the bra that she chose for me. Hanging from her fingers with freshly painted hot pink fingernails is a white lace bra with a pink bow in the center of the cups. It is exactly like the one Rose gave to me that Mother snatched off of my body years ago. I am mesmerized by the coincidence. I am thrilled that I will be able to put the gorgeous garment on my body, and no one will stop me from feeling feminine and beautiful tonight. Lucy looks at me like I am idiotic and says,

"Here, take it and put it on. What is wrong with you? Did your mother put LSD in your cereal?"

She shoves the stunning bra at me so casually. It means nothing to her, but it is everything to me. I catch the bra in my hands as she slings it in my direction. I have not taken my eyes off of the lovely material since I first laid my eyes on it. I disregard her apparent insult because I do not even understand what she is saying. What is LSD? I feel the lace with my fingertips and gaze at the fabric as if it is my new born baby that has just taken its first breath.

"Coral, put it on you goof!" she says with her patience growing thin. I turn and start towards the bathroom with intent of putting the bra on in privacy. "Where are you going? Put it on here. We are running out of time. I have to get to the party before all of the liquor is gone," she says hastily and motions for me to come back towards her as she continues to dig through the mountain of clothes that she dumped on the bed.

I feel so ill at ease knowing that Lucy expects me to drop my towel in front of her. Is it normal of girls our age to undress in front of each other? Of all of the times that I have imagined what it would be like to attend a slumber party with girls my age, never did I picture them all running around unclothed and exposed for each other to see. Is that what teenage girls actually do? Regardless if this is normal between girlfriends or not, I cannot allow her to see me naked. She will definitely notice the scars burned into my flesh beside my private areas. Lucy has turned out to be so inconsiderate. If she says one unpleasant thing about my body, I am sure that it will make me feel even more self-conscious.

I walk back towards Lucy. I just stand in front of her holding my towel tight underneath my arm. I am not sure how to handle the situation. She is being so kind to me, and I do not want her to think that I am being difficult or stupid. She notices me standing next her as still as a statue that would decorate the streets of Paris.

It finally dawns on her why I hesitate to follow her command. She stops shoveling clothes and places her hand on her hip in the sassy way that she always does. She pauses and then stares me dead in the eyes. I know the words that are getting ready to leave her lips will not be the halfhearted comments that she usually makes. I feel like she means business and is going to scold me.

"Coral, look. I know you have scars. I know your kooky mother beat you and did unimaginable stuff to you, but it's time you grow up and get over it. We are almost eighteen, adult women. You are only going to be young once. All of us will grow old and ugly someday, so stop letting those stupid scars mess with your head. You have scars. So what? Deal with it. It could be worse. You could be flat-chested!"

Unexpectedly, she yanks the towel off of me, and I stand in front of her naked. She removes my towel so swiftly that I have no time to hold tight to the terry cloth material covering my body. When I fully acknowledge that I am standing completely naked in front of another person, and even more traumatizing, a girl who has flawless skin, I am mortified.

Lucy inspects my naked body like she did after she finished applying the makeup to my face. Her eyes move up and down my body occasionally focusing on my scars, but her expression remains relaxed and not altered by the sight of my mutilation. She grips my hand that holds the tantalizing bra and pulls it to my face. The bra dangles in my face. I clutch the lacy strap so tightly that I think I have cut off the blood circulation in my fingers.

"Okay, I have seen your awful scars. Are you done freaking out? Now put the bra on. We have to get you dressed," she says. My emotional issues are putting a strain on Lucy's usual complaisant mentality. I am speechless. "By the way, you have great breasts! You need to stop getting caught up in the small stuff. Guys won't care about your scars after they see those. Just do it in the dark or by candlelight," she says and smiles at me.

I try to sort through the strange interaction that Lucy and I just shared. I am so angry with her tactless and insensitive treatment of my modest ways. I am more infuriated by the relaxed manner that she speaks in when talking about what I have endured. She does not understand. She has a mother who loves her and will never harm her. I now come to terms with Lucy's shallow views of my condition.

I see how flawed she really is. I guess she always has been this way, but I had always overlooked her short comings. I was so infatuated with her because she was my first and only friend. Hearing her compliment my breasts makes me feel appealing, and even though her words sound offensive, harsh, and unsophisticated, she is right. I need to learn to accept my scars.

Even though Lucy has lost interest in my bosom, I fasten the pretty bra on as quickly as possible, still not feeling at ease with my nudity. I slip the matching pair of white, lacy panties over my thighs. The enticing underclothes make me feel like a princess. Lucy throws me the black miniskirt. The speed of this makeover has accelerated. I know that I must be satisfied with anything that she chooses, or I will be left trying to piece an outfit together alone. I step into the mini skirt. It is so short that you can see the scars that are on the inside of my thighs from where Mother would scrub my skin.

Despite Lucy making me feel like an obligation that is ruining her plans, I am worried that all of the trendy clothes that she was kind enough to share with me will be too short and reveal the results of my unfounded sins. I bring to her attention my grave concern about the little black number that she has chosen for me. Lucy does not panic and get worked up like I always seem to. She just grabs the hem of the skirt and pulls it down until my scars are hidden. The elastic band rests on my hip bones.

She slings a royal blue sweater at me, and I fumble to catch it. Her impatience and anxiousness makes me edgy. I slide my arms into the sweater and then button up the front. Lucy turns to look me over. She looks me up and down again like she did after she ripped the towel off of my nude body. Her eyes arrive at the brightly colored, soft sweater that hugs my breasts. She promptly sets free the pearl-like buttons that presently conceal the white, lacy bra. She undoes enough buttons until the white lace is visible and my cleavage is exposed and looking for attention. I look down and feel ill at ease and afraid that my scars may be revealed with this much of my advertised skin, but to my dismay the scars hide beneath the beautiful bra.

Lucy has me turn in circles as she confirms that her job is done. She smiles and begins to bundle the rejected clothing into her bag. When she finishes packing she jets out of the lighthouse like she has an emergency to tend to, but I know that it is about a boy. It seems that everything is about a boy with Lucy.

I slip on comfortable shoes. Unfortunately, due to my injured ankle I cannot wear any of the cool shoes that Lucy brought. She says that they are called platforms. They have a very tall wooden base, and even if my ankle was not an issue I do not think that I could conquer one step while wearing the elevated, trendy shoe. I have no doubt that I would end up on my bottom, and my incoordination would spoil my new grown-up persona, that my overzealous ambition may not be able to pull off. I head to the bathroom mirror to see how I look after Lucy's makeover.

I arrive at the tarnished mirror and look at my reflection. I see a woman staring at me through the glass, and I am awestruck with the vision that I see. My curls are relaxed and wavy as they flow down my back. The thickness of my hair cups my face and compliments the subtle makeup that Lucy applied to it. From the aggressive teasing that she performed on my strawberry blonde hair, it is left tall on top with a lot of volume. At the roots, it looks like it is plastic.

I touch the fake-looking hair, and I am surprised to feel how hard it is. The fumes in that can of hairspray do peculiar feats. I look at myself bewildered but not because I find myself unbelievably beautiful. I stare at myself because I feel as if I have seen this image before. It is an unexplainable and extraordinary feeling.

I hear the hinges of the door squeak as the door to the lighthouse is opening. Usually when Angel and I hear any commotion outside of the safety of the lighthouse I hide until he confirms that everything is okay, but I am so excited for Angel to see me that I barge out of the tiny bathroom without hesitation. Standing in the doorway is Angel.

I am now in his view and waiting for his approval. He is silent, and I cannot read his thoughts on his expressive face as I normally can. I wait 22for him to say something, change his expression, or make a movement. He gradually strolls towards me. I feel jittery, concerned that he does not like my new look. He stops in front of me and looks my body over. He reaches for my sweater and fastens two of the buttons that are to blame for my breasts overflowing beyond the material. I find it enduring that he respects me and my body enough to want to hide my womanly figure. Later in life as I grow older and wiser, I am sure that I will look back on this simple action from Angel and realize that he does not want anyone else to see, lust after, or enjoy what he now has claimed as his.

I stand in front of him eager to hear approval of my new womanly look. He does not say anything. I begin to feel insecure. Angel is not the kind of man that throws compliments around to woo potential dates. He is a man of little words. He shows me how he feels by standing beside me when I need him and protecting me when no one else will.

Even with knowing that his characteristics are more honorable than most, I still want confirmation that he finds me attractive. I do my best not to seem upset by his lack of attraction to me. My disappointment must be noticeable. I begin to walk away, pretending to prepare for our departure, and as I turn my back I can feel my eyes become moist. I do everything in my power to keep my disappointed tears inside. He reaches for my hand and pulls me back to where I am facing him again. He touches my cheek and says,

"You look very pretty, Coral."

He smiles, and the sting that his delayed flattery inflicted is gone. Angel changes his clothes and reluctantly escorts me out of the door. This is the first time that I have left the round building in over a month. As much as I love our little hideaway home, it is so nice not to feel like a hidden fugitive.

We sneak through the sand hand in hand. Angel constantly looks in every direction to make sure that we are not spotted. We arrive at his motorcycle. He straddles the bike and tells me to jump on behind him. I want to take a moment to admire him on his bike. He looks so powerful and handsome, but he is already uptight concerned that we might be noticed. We are close to Ocean Point and fearful that Mother may see us. The evil castle could see our happiness, come alive with fury, and suck me back inside of its dark, cold interior.

I climb on the big engine and wrap my legs and arms around Angel. He starts the motorcycle. It is loud and exhilarating. We speed off into the night. My hair flies wildly into the wind. Even after all of the time that Lucy spent making it perfect, the robust wind whipping through my hair is such a liberating feeling that I do not care if it gets messed up. I hang on to Angel as we speed down the dark back roads to avoid any attention. I have never felt this enlightened in my whole life. I lay my cheek against his back and squeeze his torso tightly. I do not want this ride to ever end.

We arrive at the boardwalk, but Angel comes in the back way. We park at a distance from the party discreetly behind some bushes and small trees. He has carefully planned our journey to the final detail, to ensure that our presence will be minimal. Angel has put so much thought into making sure that we will remain out of harm's way tonight. I touch my hair, and it still stands straight up from the hefty amount of the hair glue. I mat it down the best I can with the palms of my hands.

As we hold hands and sneak towards the beach, I feel such pride. I am proud of my appearance, my new life, and mostly that this incredible man is holding my hand. As we get closer, we can hear music playing, and I see a blaze of fire that is surrounded with party goers. Our feet hit the sand, and Angel remains cautious as he peers through the crowd of jovial teenagers.

It is strange that now that we are now at the party that I begged to attend, I look around and realize that even with my new look, life, and boyfriend, I still have nothing in common with the girls my age. The excitement that I once felt vanishes. I just want to jump back on Angel's bike and ride far away from here.

He can see that I am on edge, so he begins to guide me towards a huge rock near the break of the waves. He wants to salvage the evening with at least us being able to put our feet in the salty water while the moon shines down on us, lending us a romantic setting. As long as Angel and I are together, we do not need anything or anyone to entertain us. We get so lost in each other that the contentment is enough. I wish I had acknowledged this before we came to the party. I would have never wanted to leave the lighthouse.

As we make our way to the rock, we have to navigate through crowds of drunken teenagers that slumber from being impaired. I smell something peculiar in the air. It has a strong odor as if a skunk had run through the crowd and sprayed all of the happy-go-lucky partiers. The smell is so pungent that I feel a little queasy. I look around to distinguish what the odor may be, and I see a group of teenagers. At first glance, I think that they are smoking a cigarette, but the closer I look I know that it does not resemble the cigarettes that Angel inhales. I feel juvenile for not knowing what the strange cigarette is. I do not want Angel to realize how child-like my mind really is when it comes to all modern customs that I have never been exposed to. I do not want him to see my innocence and be turned off towards me, so I dismiss my curiosity.

The teenagers are loud. They shout across the bonfire at each other and randomly dance in the sand. It appears that there are no strangers at the gathering except for Angel and me. Everyone is grouped together mostly in one area laughing, talking, drinking, and smoking the mysterious cigarettes.

As we weave our way through the masses of carefree teenagers I spot Lucy. She is hugged up with a boy on a blanket in the sand. They seem to have been attempting to find a private place. They are moderately concealed by a hefty rock, but their fierce make out session is far from discreet. Anyone who walks by can see the two of them intertwined in each other. It looks as if I am the only who is engrossed in their explicit romp. I try not to look at Lucy with her tongue shoved down another boy's throat, but it is so risqué to me that I am enthralled. She does not even notice us as we continue on to our destination. Angel seems sickened by his sister's erotic display and looks the other way. Just as it seems that we have dodged the last drunk teenager, I hear a girl's loud voice say,

"Coral, is that you? Coral Berringer?"

Angel hears it as well, and he pulls me behind his back for protection like I am his child that he is shielding from a moving car. We try to continue to migrate towards the rock, but the girl follows us and her voice is accelerating in volume. She attracts attention to us, and other people stop their activities, interested in what the girl is saying. Our intentions to inconspicuously spend some time at the beach together are now flawed. We have been noticed, and I have been called by name.

The girl that I recognize from school is relentless and will not leave us alone. We turn back in the direction of the congested event with the objective of getting back to our safe lighthouse. We are blocked in by the swarm of noisy teenagers that heard the commotion. Angel still holds me behind his back, aiming to get me away from the persistent girl.

The loudmouth girl reaches for Angel's shoulder attempting to push him to the side and get a better view of me and confirm my identity. Angel jerks his shoulder to shake her hand off of him and warn the inebriated girl to back off. She does not acknowledge his signals and keeps saying my name. She travels around Angel's arched and defensive shoulder to get to me.

We cannot even make one step towards a getaway. She leans in near me, resting her upper body on Angel. She uses him as a brace to prevent herself from falling. She makes an effort to point her finger at me, but the uncontrolled appendage remains curled and shakes from the lack of manipulation of her motor skills.

"My God, it is you," she says. She waves her friends over and boisterously shouts, "Hey everybody, it's the freak! We thought your mother killed you and cooked you up like a rabbit."

She laughs, and it prompts the others to do so. I remember this offensive girl from school. She was one of the pretty and popular girls. Recalling my time at the private school brings back the feelings of insignificance and of being an outcast. The other girls were not mean to my face, but they whispered behind my back daily which was as damaging as if they said it out loud. I have always assumed that they were so scared of me because of the rumors that circulated about my family and house that they hushed their insults. I guess now that we have all grown up that this girl is not as afraid of my magical powers.

At this very moment I wish that all of the gossip was true and that I could cast a mystical spell against this crowd of uncivilized kids, freezing them in time so that Angel and I could break away from the chaotic scene. After he and I were safe and sound back at the lighthouse, I would wipe their memories clean of my sighting.

The girl continues to ridicule me, but I am so intimated with the crowd that now surrounds me with laughter that her voice is drowned in the hysteria. Anxiety takes over my logical thinking ability. I look at the people who surround me, and their faces become distorted as if their flesh is blending into the fire burning next to us. They move in the same wavy motion that the fire burns. Am I imagining this, or is it possible that the menacing spirit of Ocean Point followed us to the boardwalk? Has the demon in the west wing possessed the bodies of all who encircle me?

I close my eyes hoping that the beastly faces are just an illusion that my irrational mind has conjured up. I pray that when I find the bravery to reopen them that everything will be normal again. Before I find the courage to open my eyes, Angel turns around and lifts me up under his arms. As he swoops me off of the sand-covered ground, our bodies come pressed together chest to chest and face to face. I wrap my legs around his waist to ease the load of my weight. I hang on to him with all of the physical strength that I have. He holds my bottom and back and begins to rush through the crowd like a football player who has the ball and is sprinting for the winning touchdown. I feel his body twist and turn as he merges through the drunken bodies in his path. My petite frame makes Angel's strides through the crowd seem effortless.

I am hysterically crying. I am devastated, partly because of my delirious visions and partly because I am mortified from the girl's vicious comments. As Angel once again is being my savior, I am still so wrapped up in my own head of childish fears that I ignore the real concern that I should have. This incident is a threat to our safety. My apparent emotional immaturity is now my enemy, not the drunken kids, not Mother, not Ocean Point. I have become my own enemy.

Angel places me on the back of his motorcycle, and we speed away. I hang onto Angel so snugly that I can feel the vibration of his heartbeat on the palms of my hands. I dreamed that this night would give me the feeling of being normal and the freedom that I have always been denied, but instead it brought back the bitter truth that there is something wrong with me. I now know that I will never be normal. I cannot just dismiss my past because I put on makeup, borrowed clothes, and sprayed my hair with hairspray.

As we round the curvy roads that take us back to the safe lighthouse, I dread the moment that the motorcycle stops. I want to tell Angel to just keep driving and not touch the brakes until we are far away from everyone and this island. As usual, I do not have the backbone to protect him as he has protected me.

Even with the truth staring me in the face telling me grow up, I still focus my concerns on the thought that after what Angel heard the vicious girl say about me that he will think poorly of me. I regret my behavior because I acted like a frightened child who was convinced there were monsters in the closet. I am consumed with apprehension that Angel will stop caring for me, or look at me like I am immature, or find me unattractive. These insecurities are driving me mad. Is it possible that I am mentally ill?

Possibly my worst nightmare has come true, and Mother has been right all along. Is it viable that the devil does live inside of me? Will he slowly climb to the surface of my soul until he consumes me completely? Was that the devil in me tonight? Did he promote my selfishness? Did he cause my delusions? Did he tempt me to throw Angel's life aside and care more about myself than the only person who has given me protection?

The bike stops, and Angel jumps off hastily as if he is still fuming from the harassment that we just drove away from. I have never seen him with this kind of demeanor, and it startles me. I begin to step off of the motorcycle by swinging my leg over, but before my foot hits the ground he lifts me off of the seat. He grabs my hand tight and pulls my body until we are in a full blown sprint. He doesn't cautiously peak around every corner as before.

I look at his face, and he has a concentrated look that frightens me. Is he angry with me because I coaxed him to attend that disastrous party? Is he humiliated at my absurd behavior at the party? Is he so concerned that we are going to be found that he wants to get us inside as quickly as possible?

We enter our once tranquil hideaway. Angel's movements are so forceful that I am confused. Is he so angry with me that he is going to punish me like Mother? Could the loving hands of this man turn violent like Mother's?

He slams the door shut behind us and in a swift motion pushes my back against the door. He presses his body against mine and begins to kiss me more passionately then he did at the top of this lighthouse. My body relaxes into his, and I feel like butter as I slowly melt into him. His strong kisses wake something up inside of me that I have never felt before, and my body wants more. This is what I have craved for so long, and he is finally showing me that he wants me.

Angel abruptly stops kissing me. I move my mouth back towards his, begging him not to stop. He puts his finger over my lips as if he is telling me to hush. My first thought is that I am doing something wrong. I feel insecure and panicked. Angel is the only man that I have ever kissed, so I am sure that I am doing something wrong. I just hope that he is patient enough to teach me what I need to do to satisfy him.

"Coral, you do not need all of the artificial makeup and clothes. You are beautiful just the way you are. You are the most beautiful woman I have ever seen, and I want you. I want you and only you all for myself. I fell in love with you so long ago watching you in your window. Even from a distance I could see your heartache, and all I wanted to do was take it away even before I even knew you. I will never let anyone hurt you again. I will chase those demons away from you, and as long as I am alive no one will ever put their hands on you again. This is my promise to you. I am going to get us out of here. We are going to leave tomorrow. It's not safe for us here any longer. I love you, Coral." His eyes are watery and sweet. I am overwhelmed with the loving words. I have waited so long to hear them.

"Oh, Angel..." I attempt to tell him how much I love him as well, but before I can finish my sentence he begins to fiercely kiss me again.

He lifts my yearning body off the ground and carries me to our small bed. He lays his body across mine. His kisses become soft and tender, and he looks into my eyes as his lips touch mine. His kisses cause me to lose myself in him even deeper, and my body wants to be closer to him. My desire for him is a reaction that I cannot control. He reaches his hand under my back and pulls my trembling body into him.

I lovingly gaze into his eyes, and they tell me that he wants me. I hold his body so tight. I never want to let him go. My body and mind are asking for something that I cannot conceive, but I know that if this sensation is not satisfied that I will go insane. I think I will stop breathing if this man stops touching me.

Angel pushes my shoulders down to the bed and forces me to release my intense embrace. He rises and proceeds to aggressively rip his shirt off over his head. My hands aimlessly reach for him, wanting his body back on my mine. Even during the second that it took for him to become bare-chested, the absence of feeling his skin against mine is agonizing.

He answers my pleas and returns his tan, muscular chest to mine and resumes the fiery kisses that I never wish to end. Our kisses pause. I see his eyes look down at my soft, blue sweater. During our passionate movements of our love making, the buttons that he had fastened earlier have popped back open, and the white, lacy bra is permitting my voluptuous cleavage to be revealed. The look in his eyes is that of a thirsty man who desperately needs a drink of water, and my body is the drink he needs.

He runs his hand down my chest until his fingers touch the white buttons that contain my bosom. As he unbuttons each one of the little pearl-like buttons, the sensuous, lacy bra is revealed to him. The delicate lingerie seems to fuel is his desire.

He gently cups my breasts and then begins to kiss me hard. His body begins to slowly move. He rises up again and runs his fingers across the bra until he finds the clasp between my breasts. He fumbles to unsnap it. The clasp unsnaps, and the thought of my scars suddenly enters my mind. I do not want him to stop what he is doing, but I fear that if he sees my deformity that he will not want me anymore.

I pull my arms to my chest to shield my breasts from being exposed. He knows the shame that I feel and begins to kiss me again. His kisses soothe my anxiety, and the passion returns. He reaches down and grabs one of my arms that are being used as a barrier to keep his eyes away from my horrid scars.

He lays my arm to the side of my head and applies force. I am unable to move my restrained arm. His face travels back to my breasts. I cannot resist him. He has me pinned, and I am at his mercy. Angel's ambush and control over me does not frighten me. It makes my body need his even more. His assertion stimulates me and makes my hunger for him overpowering. The intensity that I feel for Angel results in tears flowing down my cheeks.

I can feel his breath on the skin of my bare breasts. My eyes wander down and see that Angel's eyes are entranced by my bare skin. His warm mouth tenderly grazes my skin, and my body begins to scream for him to kiss and caress my bosom. He ignores its requests, and instead he moves his lips away from the tips of my breasts and begins to kiss the horrendous scars that surround them.

His act of pure kindness and love brings down all of the insecure walls. I fall even deeper in love with Angel. He looks up at me after seeing and kissing my scars and whispers,

"You are beautiful."

I begin to pull his face into my breasts. His hand begins to touch them, and his mouth travels to every inch of my skin. I have to have this man. I have to be closer to him. I am not sure what I am doing or how to satisfy this yearning that has taken home inside of me. My passion and need for Angel navigates every inch of my body. I experience sensations and urges that I do not comprehend and have never felt before. I know now that Angel loves me, so I easily surrender myself completely to him. I draw my body into his and use my eyes to beg him to give me all of him.

I run my hands across his back and feel his now nude, strong body. Our bodies are intertwined, and nothing can interfere with the carnal passion that rages between us. I continue to pull myself to him, not understanding what my body wants and painfully needs. I feel Angel's body closer to me, between my legs, and my arousal becomes difficult for me to harness. His embrace becomes more firm, and his body tenses.

I can feel his muscles constrict, and then I feel a sudden discomfort that quickly subsides. An unbelievable rush of ecstasy surges from the tips of my toes and passes through my entire body until it is exhausted and I am breathless.

I realize that Angel and I are making love. Our bodies have become one. He aggressively clenches my face with his hands and begins kissing me again. His kiss is deep and untamed. His body is tight and increasingly more forceful until he feels the same rush of pleasure that I did. His sweaty body falls onto mine. We now lie in bed motionless.

Angel finds the energy to move beside me. He lies behind me and wraps his strong arms around me. I inch my body backwards into the curve of his torso. My body dissolves into his until every inch of our skin is touching. We lie undressed in each other's arms, and we soon both drift off to sleep.

Held Captive

There is a violent bang at the door. Angel and I startle and wake from our pleasure-induced sleep. We both abruptly jump into a sitting position. Before we have the opportunity to get out of the bed, there is a forceful crash, and the door is shoved open so ferociously that it slams into the wall. Angel's chair does not deter the unexpected intruders.

I instinctively yank the covers that Angel and I have been snuggling underneath towards my bare body to conceal my indecency. Policemen come piling in the door in an aggressive and threatening manner. They shine flashlights into our faces that blind me. It is impossible for me to see anything front of me, but I hear footsteps and rustling noises encircle our little home.

It all happens so fast that I do not even have a moment for it to sink in and be scared. I am groggy. I can tell by the darkness outside that we have not been asleep for long. I am not even sure if I am having a devastating nightmare or if this is really happening.

A police officer comes from behind us and pulls Angel's arms back. The officer drags him off of the bed and onto the floor like he is a criminal. Angel begins to resist the officer's restraint as he is pinned to the floor. There are now two police officers straddling him with one of each of their knees restraining his arms to his back. He bucks his body like a wild horse whose owner is attempting to tame him as he tries to fling the policemen off of his back.

He is overpowered. I look down at him. The intense brightness of the flashlights is shining directly at his face. He squints his eyes, attempting to see. I know that he is angry, but I can also sense that he is as afraid as I am now.

"Ma'am, you need to step out of the bed," I hear a man say in an authoritative voice.

I am petrified. I do not move. He says it again but this time more commanding. I look at Angel, and his cheek is now being pressed to the floor by one of the officer's hands. I have gotten use to looking to Angel to guide me, but he is now trapped on the floor. I have to handle this intimidating situation by myself.

I have been programmed to obey and keep silent, and without Angel being able to handle the devastating circumstances I only know how to comply with the officers' commands. I wrap the covers around me as I would a bath towel and begin to stand as I have been instructed to do. I hear a different voice.

"Ma'am, you need to put the blanket down," he says sternly. Because of the extreme brightness of the flashlights, I cannot see anyone in front of me. I begin to run my hands across the bed as I search for clothing to cover my nudity. "Ma'am, I need you to drop the blanket and put your hands over your head where we can see them," the voice says again.

I am mortified. If I follow the orders from the officers, I will be standing nude in front of what sounds like a room full of men. The harsh instructions that the concealed voice states enrage Angel, and I hear a scuffle on the floor near me. He is using all of the power in him to lift his body up. The two policemen begin to press their weight onto his back with full force. He is full of determination, and his will to stop the degrading command that the authoritative figures are demanding me to do is unbelievable. Angel has the might of ten men, and the officers struggle to keep him under control.

I try my best to remain strong, hoping that Angel will calm down. I am concerned of what harm they may inflict on him if he pushes the officers' patience too far. I timidly ask,

"Can I please put some clothes on?" I shiver from the defiling feeling that the officer's order injects into me.

"You will be allowed to put on clothing after we know that you are unarmed," he firmly states with no room for negotiation.

I cling to the blanket like I am a toddler that is afraid of monsters under her bed. I am still trying to find the moxie that I need to become uninhibited and spare any more trouble for Angel. I am hopeful that if I handle this situation in a more mature manner and do not fall into pieces like I normally do that it may ease the pressure that he feels to be my constant savior. If I can find a way to comply with the demands of the officer no matter how disturbing and inappropriate they may be, it will make things easier for both of us. I call out to the strong spirit that must live within me and rediscover the place that I used to go to endure Mother's insanity. I have to do this and have faith that he will not get as distraught if he knows that I am okay than he will if I break down. It is time that I become brave for him. This is not the time to pity myself. I did this to us. I did this to him.

"Ma'am, I am going to ask you one more time to drop the blanket. Let's not make this any more difficult than it has to be," he calmly states, but even with a coolness in his voice I can tell that he is serious and that I should do as he says.

I uncontrollably tremble from absolute degradation. My hands shake as I release the blanket from my grip. Angel sees my unclothed body and begins to become combative again. Other officers are summoned to assist in keeping him seized and immobile on the floor. Angel's strength is fueled by anger and his need to protect me. My attempt in heroism is not enough to keep his rage subdued. I just gave myself to him, and now I am forced to stand in front of a room full of men completely stripped with flashlights shining all over me. It seems that I am giving myself away again to a room full of strangers, and it makes me feel like filth.

I expected that once the blanket touched the floor that the officers would immediately analyze the situation and see that I have no weapons and am not a threat. On the contrary, I stand unclothed, and the background noise that I once heard is silenced. I cannot see faces, but I feel their eyes on my skin. I am aware of their enjoyment in humiliating a young runaway. There is no telling what lies Mother has told them, and they seem to be taking their time with returning me home.

Angel has almost become irrepressible. Four men have to tame him. I wonder how many policemen are actually in this tiny hideaway. The longer I stand with the lights shining all over my body, the less embarrassed I become. My discomfort turns into anger. I do not think about my scars, and I do not care if any of these strangers see them. All I care about is how Angel sees me. Even with the resentment that I have for these inappropriate officers, I know that I am helpless and cannot change the outcome of Angel's or my situation. We are both doomed. At this point, we are going to fall victim to Mother's influence, so I strive to cooperate in hopes that we will escape this losing battle unharmed. Finally, I hear the same voice again.

"Ma'am, you can put your clothes on now."

I begin to walk towards the little dresser drawers that we keep our clothing in. I am sensible enough to know that if I was to arrive back at Ocean Point dressed in Lucy's outfit that I wore to the party tonight that Mother would eliminate me without delay, possibly even in front of the police. Her wrath toward me will be irrepressible. I hear the same stern voice again.

"Ma'am, you need to stop and come back into our full view." I try to explain to the officer that I need to get my clothes from the drawer. "No ma'am, you need to put on the clothes that are closest to you. You must keep your hands visible at all times."

Meanwhile while we discuss what clothes that I am allowed to put on, openly and without control. This is all my fault. Angel has done nothing but treat me with love and respect, and now he is in trouble because of his noble intentions.

He begins to scream, trying to tell the policemen how much danger I am in, but no one listens. The more frantic he becomes, the crazier he sounds. These servants of the law perceive us as two defiant kids who disrespected their parents and authority just to have a casual romp in an abandoned lighthouse.

I abide with the officer's demands and go with the policemen. I cannot remove my eyes from Angel. I have a horrible feeling that I will never see him again. I do not stop looking at him until his suppressed nude body is out of my view. The further I travel, the louder his screams for me become. It is like our world together is being ripped apart. My heart breaks into so many pieces, and I know that no one except Angel will ever be able to put all of the shards that my heart just shattered into back together. I have a horrible feeling that this is the last time I will ever see the man that I cannot exist without. I welcome death by Mothers hands if I will never be in Angel's arms again.

The officers put me in the back seat of the squad car and shut the door. I watch the lighthouse as we drive away, and I see my happy home become just a memory. All I have left are the bitter sweet memories and a longing for the man that I now know I have lost.

We only have to drive a very short distance. I find it ironic that the entire time I have been missing I have only been a long walk from Ocean Point, and no one knew. I am sure that the wicked house did. Not one day went by that I did not feel its eyes on me. I am sure that it is

I am still exposed in front of a room full of men. I feel like they are prolonging this just to watch me suffer. It seems they are trying to feed some sick fantasy that they hide from their wives.

At this point, I just want my uncovered body to be protected from the undeserving eyes of these strangers. Mother is going to assassinate me regardless of what condition I am in. Knowing this reality is how I justify my promptness to dress and obey the uncompromising policeman. Mother most likely has fumes that have been burning inside of her for so many days now that her insides boil with rage.

I hastily snatch up the bright blue sweater and skirt that I previously wore to impress Angel and attempt to fit in with my peers that are laying at the end of the bed. I tuck the clothing under my arms and proceed to madly search for my underclothes. In the heat of Angel's and my love making only hours ago, clothing was removed and tossed without thought, and now in the darkness of the room and distracting blaring spotlights that are pointed at me, I am disoriented and cannot see the white, lacy material. I am aware that I must be cautious as to not make any sudden movements that may heighten the absurd watchfulness that these authoritative figures feel is necessary.

"That will do fine, ma'am. Just put those on," he declares, referring to the sweater and skirt. I dress and wait to hear the now impatient voice direct me on what to do next. "Okay, it's time to go, ma'am." Those words are my death sentence.

I begin to make my way towards the blinding lights that the unsympathetic voices hide behind. I look over my shoulder and see the man that I love in custody on the floor like a criminal. I start to weep feel their eyes on my skin. I am aware of their enjoyment in humiliating a young runaway. There is no telling what lies Mother has told them, and they seem to be taking their time with returning me home.

Angel has almost become irrepressible. Four men have to tame him. I wonder how many policemen are actually in this tiny hideaway. The longer I stand with the lights shining all over my body, the less embarrassed I become. My discomfort turns into anger. I do not think about my scars, and I do not care if any of these strangers see them. All I care about is how Angel sees me. Even with the resentment that I have for these inappropriate officers, I know that I am helpless and cannot change the outcome of Angel's or my situation. We are both doomed. At this point, we are going to fall victim to Mother's influence, so I strive to cooperate in hopes that we will escape this losing battle unharmed. Finally, I hear the same voice again.

"Ma'am, you can put your clothes on now."

I begin to walk towards the little dresser drawers that we keep our clothing in. I am sensible enough to know that if I was to arrive back at Ocean Point dressed in Lucy's outfit that I wore to the party tonight that Mother would eliminate me without delay, possibly even in front of the police. Her wrath toward me will be irrepressible. I hear the same stern voice again.

"Ma'am, you need to stop and come back into our full view." I try to explain to the officer that I need to get my clothes from the drawer. "No ma'am, you need to put on the clothes that are closest to you. You must keep your hands visible at all times."

Meanwhile while we discuss what clothes that I am allowed to put on, handle this situation in a more mature manner and do not fall into pieces like I normally do that it may ease the pressure that he feels to be my constant savior. If I can find a way to comply with the demands of the officer no matter how disturbing and inappropriate they may be, it will make things easier for both of us. I call out to the strong spirit that must live within me and rediscover the place that I used to go to endure Mother's insanity. I have to do this and have faith that he will not get as distraught if he knows that I am okay than he will if I break down. It is time that I become brave for him. This is not the time to pity myself. I did this to us. I did this to him.

"Ma'am, I am going to ask you one more time to drop the blanket. Let's not make this any more difficult than it has to be," he calmly states, but even with a coolness in his voice I can tell that he is serious and that I should do as he says.

I uncontrollably tremble from absolute degradation. My hands shake as I release the blanket from my grip. Angel sees my unclothed body and begins to become combative again. Other officers are summoned to assist in keeping him seized and immobile on the floor. Angel's strength is fueled by anger and his need to protect me. My attempt in heroism is not enough to keep his rage subdued. I just gave myself to him, and now I am forced to stand in front of a room full of men completely stripped with flashlights shining all over me. It seems that I am giving myself away again to a room full of strangers, and it makes me feel like filth.

I expected that once the blanket touched the floor that the officers would immediately analyze the situation and see that I have no weapons and am not a threat. On the contrary, I stand unclothed, and the background noise that I once heard is silenced. I cannot see faces, but I infuriated that I escaped its horror and found a love that took away the blackness that it embedding within me.

I look down at my clothing and try to prepare myself for Mother's torture. I do not have on panties or a bra. Some of the buttons on my sweater snapped off last night during Angel's and my forceful and passionate embraces. My breasts are nearly completely exposed. If I make a careless movement, my breasts will come right out of this sweater, and my womanly features will be revealed.

Once she lays eyes on me, she is going to go ballistic. I am not physically strong enough to escape her punishments. She is just too powerful for me to fight back. I know that if I defend myself she is just going to hit harder. It took me almost a month to recover from her last attack, and I did not even do anything wrong. Now she has valid reason to reprimand me, and in the time that I have been hiding I am sure that her rage has been cultivating daily. Her strength will be irrepressible. There is no uncertainty in my belief that this is my last day alive.

I want to persuade the policeman driving the car not to take me home. I want to explain to him that I fear for my life and how sadistic Mother is. I am confident that he just sees me as being a common delinquent teenager who defied her Mother to run away and have sex with a boy. I know that my words will not be heard and that he will dismiss my pleas, so I remain voiceless.

The vehicle comes to a stop sign. As the wheels stop rolling, I irrationally contemplate opening the car door and running. I reach over to where the door handle usually is, and there is nothing there. It is impossible for me to open the door and flee. Even if I am able to cleverly divert the officers and trick them into opening the door, as soon as they realize that I am attempting a breakout they will most likely shoot me. After weighing the odds of which deaths I could choose from, the sudden and sharp pain of a piercing bullet or the slow and agonizing torture at the hands of Mother, I would choose the bullet without question. Even if it was to enter my body and mutilate my insides until I slowly bled out it would be less suffering than if Mother was my executioner.

I am completely trapped. The car makes a turn onto Ocean Point's long, winding driveway. I can feel the bumps as the car travels on the neglected road, hitting the potholes that are scattered throughout the winding driveway. I want to tell the officers that they are delivering me to my funeral. My mind anxiously searches for the words to say to sway the officers to my side and turn the car around. After running through so many scenarios that I conjure up to convince the uniformed men, I finally decide not to even bother. They will never accept my stories as true.

As the house comes closer, I can feel it peering down on me. I can hear its condescending laughter, and I can smell the musty smell of the interior. I can hear the creaks that the floors make when the demon wanders the halls at night. I can feel the steam that is rising out of my bathtub, just waiting to boil Angel's scent off of my skin.

I see the enormous mansion, and chills crawl across my skin. The castle-like structure exudes dominance and possession. It owns me and everyone who has ever slept under its roof. The evil is trapped inside of the house, and it festers and grows inside of the souls of those who reside at the majestic estate.

I visualize myself standing at the entrance with a giant, lit match. I put the flame on the brown bricks that stack together and form the structure of the house. I watch the bricks catch fire and burn one by one until the blaze is irrepressible. I see the ghosts, spirits, and demons flee from the roof as the flames chase them out. I watch the house burn to the ground and end the secrets and pain that it creates.

Unfortunately, this is only in my imagination. As we pull up to the front of Ocean Point, it stands sturdy and unharmed. It is hard to believe that for over a month I have been living in a space that is only half the size of one of the suites of this estate. This house is so enormous in comparison, but there was more love filled in the living quarters of the lighthouse than even one of the house's closets. I could only imagine how much love could grow inside such a big structure if allowed.

The officer opens the car door and commands me to step out. I place my feet onto the tiny pebbles of gravel that are scattered in the driveway. The tiny rocks pierce my bare feet. I look up at Ocean Point, and it seems to smile at me, welcoming the sinner home. I have a hunch of what is in store for me, but the house already knows my fate. My fate has been planned out and Ocean Point is the host to the horror that will soon become my existence and most likely my long suffering demise.

The officers escort me to the front door and ring the doorbell. The loud, blaring chimes signal the end for me. I hear the familiar footsteps of Mother come towards the entrance. My first instinct is to hide myself behind one of the officers and anticipate being immediately assaulted. As I attempt to shield myself behind the uniformed man, he snatches me by the arm and jerks me until I stand straight in front of the door. I will be the first thing Mother sees as the heavy door opens. I will be in arm's distance of the strong blows that her hands will not be able to resist when she views my risqué appearance.

The door opens. I am terrified to look up at Mother. I stand in the doorway with my eyes down. My hair is tussled and falls into my face. I am barefoot and half-clothed. I am being held in place by the policeman's grip on my upper arm. I feel like one of the turkeys that I used to watch Rollins sling around in the kitchen by its legs then slam into a roasting pan and shove into the oven to bake until tender. I will not be baked. I will be boiled. I can already feel the steam seeping into my nose and eyes.

There is a silence. I am limp, and I hang from the officer's grip. He waits to pass his criminal to the warden. I smell the scent of the stuffy house ooze out and eliminate the smell of the fresh, outside air. I feel nauseous from the stale odor. I feel Mother's disapproving eyes pierce through me. I feel the heat that her body exudes surround me as her usually cold blood begins to boil.

"Mrs. Berringer, is this your daughter?" the officer asks to confirm my identity.

"Yes, it is," she says in almost a hissing tone.

As I hear her raspy, hissing voice, I visualize her as a snake with a long, thin body that wraps around me like the vines in the garden and squeezes me until she crushes every bone in my body and then devouring me whole. Before the officer can escort me into the house, she reaches out and clinches my loose arm. She rips me from the officer's firm grip. The force of her pull causes me to trip as I cross the doorway, missing the small step up.

"Thank you, gentlemen. That will be all," she says in a businesslike manner and then attempts to quickly close the door. She is so anxious to begin running the hot water that has filled her thoughts while awaiting my return that she does not spare a moment for small talk.

"Mrs. Berringer, there is some paperwork that we need you to sign so that we can complete our report," the officer says trying to stop her from shutting the door. She sticks her head through the remaining opening and says,

"Thank you for your time gentlemen, but my daughter is in need of my attention now. I will call the sheriff tomorrow and handle all necessary documents. Now, you gentlemen have a pleasant evening."

She shuts the door. Any chance of me escaping Mother is now over. I still have not looked up at her. She releases my arm from her hold and begins to circle me and inspect every inch of my body. Her fiery eyes are on my bare flesh, and I anticipate that the fire smoldering behind her judgmental eyes will shoot out and burn me with more agony than the searing fires of Hell.

I hear small footsteps shuffle down the corridor. I pray that it is Rose and that she is alright. I move my eyes toward the rapid footsteps without raising my head, and I see the beautiful, chubby woman coming towards me.

"Oh Coral, I have been so worried about you."

Rose rushes to me and begins to attempt to take my quivering body into an embrace, but as her arms extend towards me Mother reaches down and removes my body from her reach.

"Don't touch this jezebel! We don't know what filthy diseases she has now!" she says, cautioning Rose to keep her distance. Rose is undoubtedly disturbed by Mother's preposterous words. She narrows her eyes at Mother and shakes her head. "Watch this indecent whore while I call her doctor. She needs to be examined. Even though she is a child of the serpent, there is no need to spread immoral diseases throughout this house."

She lets go of my arm and wipes her hands on her long, black dress as if she is removing infectious germs and then stomps out of the room. Rose reaches for me and takes me in her arms regardless of the rants of the mad woman. She holds me tighter than she ever has before, and I do not want her to ever let go of me. I strive to express to her my worries regarding Angel's safety that are eating me alive, but before either of us can say a word, Mother stomps back into the foyer. She does not seem to notice that Rose has ignored her command not to touch me. She now seems in a hurry and preoccupied.

"Ma'am, I will take Coral upstairs and prepare her for Dr. Saunders's arrival," Rose says to Mother.

"That will not be necessary. I will be escorting her to the hospital, and Dr. Saunders will be meeting us there."

Rose and I look at each other surprised by Mother's statement. I have never been to a hospital in my entire life. Dr. Saunders always does house calls for me. Mother has never wanted the community to see the condition that her punishments and rage leave me in. I do not understand why she now will not be humiliated by the way I look and the lewd alignments that she is convinced I am afflicted with. I am bewildered that she is going to be seen in public with me as uncovered as my body is. I am stunned that she does not even take a moment to have me change clothes, to protect her family's reputation.

She grabs my arm again. Her hold is firm and strong. She tows me out of the door and through the sharp stones that scrape the bottom of my feet. She shoves me into the back seat of the car with great force as if she is pushing me down a dark hole that leads me to the depths of Hell.

The car starts, and we begin to leave for the hospital. As we drive away, I look out of the back window, and Rose is standing in the doorway with her hands covering her mouth as if she knows that something bad is getting ready to happen. I am still having a hard time understanding why Mother is in such a hurry. Is she that ridiculous to think that I have come home with an infectious disease and must rush to rid it instantly?

The vehicle descends down the curvy driveway, and Rose fades into the background until her image disappears. All I can see now are the pointy towers of the wicked house. I can hear its loud, sinister laughter again. It radiates through me and is deafening. I cover my ears and want for the noise in my mind to stop.

The car comes to a sudden stop. I turn and redirect my view to the front of the black sedan. I see a suspicious car parked on the side of the road in front of us. I am puzzled as to why we have stopped near this unknown vehicle. I see both of the car doors open from the dark colored car in front of us. Two tall figures get out. They are completely dressed in black. They begin to urgently walk towards our car. The closer they get to us, the more I can see that they are wearing black ski masks.

I assume that we are going to be robbed or kidnapped, and I begin to scream at Mother to drive. She sits still and does not look at me or say a word. The men split up as they reach the front of our car. They now stand in front of the back doors where I am. The robbers are blocking the doors, and there is no way for me to make a getaway. They have me blocked in, and Mother remains motionless.

They aggressively sling open the doors and climb into the back seat with me. I begin to scream at the top of my lungs and begin to combat with one of the masked strangers and try to crawl across him. I fight and squirm over one of the men's laps as I attempt to exit the car. I experience the sharp pain of a prick in my neck. I instantly feel strange. The noises around me slow to muffled sounds, and I feel my arms and legs relax until I can barely move them. My head is heavy as if someone is pushing it to the ground. I feel my head fall gradually onto the masked stranger's lap. Everything goes black, and the noises stop.

I try to open my eyes, but they seemed to be weighted. It feels like silver dollars are resting on my eyelids. Through the slits of my defeated eyelids, I see a glow that gives off an amber hue. The dim light moves back and forth. I make an effort to raise my arm, and I can lift it a few inches off of the surface where I am laying. I exert all of the strength I have, but my arms just plop back down on the surface listlessly.

I have no feeling in my legs. I try to wiggle my toes, and I can feel them slightly rub against their counterparts. I move my head from side to side and strain my eyes trying to develop a clear image, but all I can see is the amber radiance that surrounds me.

The previous events from the night are jumbled in my mind. I can visualize pictures of Angel, Mother, Rose, police cars, Ocean Point, and the masked men, but I cannot put any of these images in order. What is happening to me? Am I finally losing it? Am I going insane? I work tenaciously to put the pieces together in my psyche, but they are all like strewn puzzle pieces that will not fit together.

I can feel my body drift in and out of consciousness. This cycle seems to repeat itself over and over again. This relentless cycle is not in my control. My struggle to regain reign over my own body and thoughts seems to go on endlessly. The frustration to seize one clear thought is exasperating.

I am unaware of how much time has passed. At last I can open my eyes, and the strain has ceased. It takes a few minutes for my eyes to adjust and navigate through the thick, yellow luminosity that appears to be the only light present. I lie flat on my back. Even with the glow filling the room, it is dark when I look up.

Now that I have regained power over my hindered vision, I challenge my arms to find the muscle to bear weight and assist me in sitting up. I pull my arms to my body and am pleased to see that my motor skills have returned. In one motion, I push myself up into a sitting position using the returned strength of my arms. I feel something cold and hard against my hip. I look down and find that my wrists are in shackles. The shackles are attached to a bulky chain. I franticly try to move my arms, but they immediately jerk back being the victim of the chain that restrains them.

My vision remains impaired. I cannot see any amount of distance in order to discover out where I am, but I can see the rusted shackles that are wrapped around my wrists. My mind is still scattered, but I know that I have seen these restraints before. I begin to jerk my arms hoping that maybe one of the links in the chains will break, but they are sturdy and keep me where they want.

Suddenly, I realize that I am in the torture room that Lucy and I found years ago. My nightmares are becoming my reality. I was not a harebrained little kid when I believed that children were held hostage here. This is where the children buried near me took their last breath.

The events that took place now come back to me. I now comprehend what Mother had arranged. I think it was last night, but because of my state of confusion I do not know how much time has passed since the masked men entered our car.

She set all of this up. The sharp prick that I felt was a needle. They injected me with something to sedate me and make their job easier. Does Rose know that I am here? There is no way that Rose would let this happen to me. I know this after seeing her stand up to Mother and physically restrain her to aid in my previous escape. Mother was not in a hurry to rid me of disease, she was in a hurry so her plan of kidnapping me would keep with the assailant's schedule. She did not call Dr. Saunders to meet us at the hospital. She called the masked men to alert them that we were on our way.

I close my eyes and begin to cry knowing that this is the beginning of my demise. Angel will never find me here. Lucy is so self-absorbed and foolishly intoxicated most of the time that I cannot imagine her remembering this room and concluding that I am being held captive. She has probably thinks that our discovery was just childhood silliness.

I cry because I know that I will never be able to tell Angel how sorry I am. I will never feel his soft lips on mine again. I will never feel his strong arms hold me or carry me away from danger again. I will never hear him tell me that he loves me again. I will never be able to tell him how much I love him and appreciate the constant kindness and protection that he gave me.

I still wear the fragments of clothes that I left the lighthouse in. I pull my feet to my chest and try to wrap my arms around my bent knees. I lean my head back and begin to scream to the heavens. I scream at God and ask Him to make me understand why He allowed me to be born into this evil, wicked family. I scream to Him that if Mother is right, and I am born from Satan's command, then why let my conception come to term.

I beg God for answers. I plead for mercy and for Him to make my death by the hands of my own mother quick and painless. I scream to God, and the room remains silent. Does He not hear me? Does He not love me? Was I born unholy? Why is He not here for me? I curse him and overflow with resentment for the God that I want to believe created me.

I suddenly feel a cool breeze surround my body. I hear faint voices. They are softly singing. What is the song I hear? It seems that all of the voices sing different songs and struggle to make it one. Despite the confusion of the melodies, the sounds are magical. The gentle sounds are familiar. I close my eyes and recall the beautiful lilies. I have not heard the voices of the white, delicate flowers in so long. As haunting as their voices are, they provide me with a sensation of calmness and affection. I open my eyes, and the cool breeze grows stronger. I am concerned that the drugs that Mother had her goons injected in me are causing hallucinations. I question my sanity.

I see a face that I have seen before. At the end of the thin mattress suspended in the amber glow is a ghost-like vision. Floating above me is a beautiful face and upper body of a woman. She has bright blue eyes that are filled with so much gentleness that one glance from her fills me with a warm sensation. She wears a white dress, and the material flows behind her and blends into the fog-like substance that surrounds her. The elegant, white lilies that I saw in the garden surround her and are scattered amidst the fog. Tiny butterflies flutter their wings above the flowers and bounce from flower to flower trying to get a sweet taste of nectar. Is this real? Am I viewing a real-life apparition? Am I hallucinating? I acknowledge that I have been heavily drugged, but this vision seems as real to me as the shackles attached to my wrists.

I am astounded that I do not fear this presence that floats above me. There is somewhere inside of me that is connected to this familiar spirit. I recognize this woman. She is the woman who slept with me in the sealed bedroom that is on the other side of my closet. Is God sending me an angel? I pleaded for Him to help me and cursed Him for my pain. Did God send me this angel to show me that He is here and watching over me? Is He proving Mother's accusations wrong and confirming that I am not a child of Satan?

The beautiful fog vanishes, and the voices are silenced. The fluttering butterflies have flown away, and I am left alone in the dark. My thoughts are so cluttered. I labor to decipher what is real or imagined. I block out the eerie glow and the musty, thick air that seeps into my lungs. I find a center inside me among the trauma.

The door opens, and I still toil to see clearly. I can see that it is dark outside. Is it the same night, or did I sleep for days like I did in the lighthouse? My fuzzy vision is adjusting to the tawny lighting, and it is evident that the drugs are slowly leaving my system, making me more alert.

I see Mother step into the room, and behind her are the men who attacked me in the car. They step beside her. One of the masked men heaves a huge trunk into the little dungeon. Seeing the threesome makes me want to let out blood-curling screams, but I know that no one will hear my cries from down here. What good will my desperate outburst accomplish with me hidden at the bottom of the forbidden west wing?

Possibly the demon will hear my cries, but he is the last creature that I wish to see in this little room where I am detained, especially since I am helplessly chained to a rock wall. These demented people are going to do whatever they want to me anyways, so I remain hushed. I question if one of these concealed men is the stranger who crawled into my bed and is the reason that all of this has happened to begin with.

What is in the trunk that sits only a few feet away from me? Is it full of weapons to carry out hours of torture? Is Mother going to make me suffer for days before ultimately slaughtering me? Is she going to put me in the trunk after I have taken my last breath to hide her crime? Mother looks to the disguised assailant who hauled in the trunk. She snaps her fingers and points to the bulky container. He obeys her command. Did Mother hire more servants just to help her kill me? He opens the large box, and she reaches in and pulls out a large pair of scissors.

I look at her face, and she does not look like the woman I know. She has always been wicked, but this look that she has is much more terrifying than I can describe. With the scissors in her hand, she begins to come towards me. A normal person at this point would begin to let out earsplitting screams from witnessing an insane woman coming for them with a pair of scissors, but I do not even let out a whimper. I have accepted my fate and prepare myself for a gruesome assault.

She reaches behind my head and takes a hand full of my long hair. She pulls it so tightly that I am unable to move without my hair being ripped out by the roots. I relax my body with her grip and hang like a worn out rag doll, tattered and stained. She violently pushes me on the bed and puts the scissors between my legs. I feel the cold metal on my private parts. Oh my God, she is going to cut me in half. I close my eyes tight. I have to feel my body rip in two, but I definitely do not want to witness the bloody scene. I feel the sharp ends of the scissors move off of my skin, and I hear a ripping sound. I keep my eyes closed until I feel the sharp ends of the knife graze my throat.

I cautiously open my eyes and hesitantly look down. I lie here shackled and completely naked. She has cut my clothing off of my body. She returns her concentration to my head and snatches a hand full of my hair again. She tugs on my hair, brutally pulling me upward until I am in a sitting up position. She begins to cut my hair. I can see long strands fall all over my naked body. She cuts my hair so hysterically that she appears to be playing the role of a sadistic barber. She chops my hair off so close to my scalp in some spots that I am sure I appear bald. Her manic disposition has left her hands shaky, and many times the tips of the scissors nip my scalp leaving a warm drizzle on my head.

She runs out of long strands of hair, and her rampage with the scissors ends. I sit with my own hair blanketing my body. Instinctually, I want to reach up and feel my skinned scalp, but I withhold my urge and besides I am not even sure that the chains would permit it. She struts away from me with a slow walk of satisfaction. I am bewildered by the strange ritual that she seems to be performing. I remain silent and let her spiteful plan come to fruition. I have no clue of the level of disgrace that my Mother has arranged on her only child, but I imagine that I soon will face her resentment towards me on a level that sinks to a depth of brutality that I am unaware exists.

She stands at the end of the smelly mattress and again snaps her fingers for her dedicated criminals to come forth. All three of them stand in front of me and peer down on me like I am an animal that they just caught in a trap. She obliviously calculated this plan down to the very last detail and had meetings with her new servants to effortlessly execute the steps of the sinister plan in advance. They know what she wants with just a snap of her fingers.

"Coral, my dear, isn't this what you want, to show off your naked body to men? Show these men your body," she orders me.

I reluctantly do as she commands. I release my embrace from my knees and display my nude body. I have no idea where this demeaning exhibition is leading. I am in survival mode and obeying for self-preservation. I want this to be as physically painless as possible. I sit with long strands of my strawberry-blonde hair surrounding my naked body, and the stare of the masked men's eyes disgrace me. All I can think about is Angel. I only want him to see me like this. I feel like I am doing something wrong to him even though Mother is forcing me.

"Coral, I failed you. I have spent so much of my precious time and energy to educate you about how weak men are. Men are like open wounds susceptible to any disease that comes near them. Men are so vulnerable to the temptations of the long hair that lays around you now, the skimpy clothing that I cut off of you, and the curves of your body. Satan has an open invitation to enter a man's heart when he sees an improper girl like you. The evil jumps into his body and forces him to do things to women that he doesn't really want to do. I thought that I taught you that. I failed you, Coral. I failed you," she says as she paces the room and pretends that she is actually capable of guilt.

She performs as if she is on a stage in an award-winning play, and there is an audience full of adoring fans. Frightening enough, I truly think that she believes her outlandish theories.

"I failed you because no matter how hard I tried, you still became a whore! You are a Berringer, and whether your stupid little mind knows it or not, that means something. To think that a Berringer was found naked in a bed with a filthy Italian is repulsive! Even with you being nothing but a common, dirty slut, that boy is still not in your class." She grows more irate with each word leaves her mouth. "You probably think that you are something special just because you can get a boy to want you, lust for you, and lie to you about loving you just so he can get between those legs, don't you?"

Her words do not even make sense to me. She does not know what Angel and I have together. I shut her words out and hope that this display of lunacy ends soon. Whether she kills me or leaves me alone here naked in this chilling room, I just want this to end.

The men's eyes are focused and have not left my body. The intensity that is building in the room is beginning to make me nervous. All I can see is the white of their eyes fixated my nudity.

"I think it is time that you learn a lesson you unholy, filthy little girl. I tried to tell you what men will do to you. That just didn't work, so maybe it is time that I show you."

She speaks so calmly, but I know that the rage is controlling her and is slowly building up the steam to discipline me in the raunchiest manner. I am aware that Mother has a plan, and her words are like clues to the reveal. She steps in between the two men that she seems to have complete discipline over and says words that will haunt me for the rest of my life.

"Okay gentlemen, go show this whore what men will do to her if she continues to entice them with her body."

The strange men crawl onto the mattress where I am chained and restricted. One shoves me back, and my naked body lays powerless. The other masked man is on his knees and begins to touch my body. He touches me in places that only Angel has ever touched. The two perverted assailants continue their assault by revealing their private body parts to me. My silence ends, and I begin to beg them to stop. My resistance does not slow down their perversion. It instead seems to fuel their illicit desires.

Mother watches them molest me and appears to receive pleasure from the sickening actions that these men are doing to me. She pulls out her rosary beads, and from a distance I can see them clutched firmly in her hand. She holds them close to her face and begins to pace around the repulsive scene that she has orchestrated. I hear her arrogant prayers to God and a number of saints.

I focus on Mother, knowing that I cannot bear to see the nauseating acts that these animals are dominating me. I want her to look at me, make eye contact with me. I want my eyes to ask her for mercy. I have to consider that somewhere inside of her there is love for me. If her heart has become barren of love for me, surely there was a day when I was an innocent, helpless baby in her arms that she connected with. I need to remind her of that. I need her to make these men stop. I want to see the blue eyes that Rose says she once had. How did she become the vicious woman that I know? Did my father make her this way? Is this the way that he made love to her? Is this what happened to her once? There has to be a way that I can get her to snap her fingers and have these monsters cease this attack.

I open my eyes as wide as I can and push the pain, fear, and humiliation that I have now and have been storing inside of me for so long to the surface. I scream "Mother" continuously until she looks at me. I look in her eyes and whisper,

"Please make them stop."

For a brief second, her gaze softens. I can see that my strategy has been effective, but it only lasts for mere seconds. She catches her weak moment, and in order to regain the control she turns her back to me and says,

"Gentleman, remember your orders of no penetration. I will not have another child of Satan born under this roof."

After hearing that command, I realize that she is not going to end this lesson that she believes I need to be taught. I stop fighting, and I just close my eyes and lie still. The men continue to do things to me that I know are evil and immoral, but this is not the way men really are. This is not what Angel did to me.

The assault goes on for a long time, and I think that they will never stop. I would rather have gotten another scar from boiling water than have these men touch me so intimately. I belong to Angel. I know that I cannot ever tell him about what these men are doing to me. He would never look at me the same again. He would see me as unclean and filthy just like Mother does. My body begins to hurt due to the careless groping hand. I do not think that I can handle this much longer. Finally, I hear Mother's frosty voice.

"Okay that is enough, gentlemen." The sexual invaders obey Mother and bring their sick pleasure to an end. I am left physically sore. I do not even understand the things that they did to me. I know at this very moment that I will never be the same. "Okay, prepare the room."

Mother makes her final demand for the evening. I am sure that she is instructing the men to prepare to finish me off. I hear the trunk open again. I am so exhausted that I do not even look to see what they will do to me next. After what I just experienced, I wish that they would kill me. Angel will never want me now, and even if he did I do not know if I could suppress the images and feelings that these men left me with. I am unsure if I could even allow the man I love to touch me where these predators have left their fingerprints.

I feel tarnished, marked, and dirty now. Mother forced me to become what she has been shrieking I am for years. She won. Her fears and paranoid beliefs are now true. She made me what she truly wished I was. Now that I finally became the rubbish that she has wanted me to be, she is justified with every slap to my face, punch to my eye, every drop of hot water, and every uncaring word.

The pretty, blonde woman that I envisioned earlier was not an angel sent by God to watch over me. She, the singing lilies, and the tiny butterflies were just a drug-induced hallucination. She did not guard me from the vile hands that stained my body. She was not real. The malicious hands were. I can still feel them. Mother comes near and peers down at me. Her expression is of satisfaction.

"Now Coral, tell me. Have you learned your lesson?" she asks me. I do not answer her, and instead I turn my face away from her. This angers her, and she reaches down and grabs what hair I have left and pulls my head back. She lowers her face to mine. Her reaction prompts me to respond.

"Yes, I learned my lesson," I quietly say.

"Well you better be grateful of me for stopping them when I did. Next time you want to go walking around dressed so obscene, remember that I will not be there to stop them," she says as if she did me a favor. Does this woman actually think that she has saved me by not allowing her followers to penetrate me? She firmly plants a silver bucket onto the side of the flimsy mattress and callously says, "This is for your bodily functions. I will be back in a few days and see to it that you get some food."

She and her two secretive servants leave, and I hear the heavy door lock behind them. I look over at the bucket and cannot believe that this is actually happening. My mind wanders to the little children that probably called this their bedroom before me. Was she this cruel to them as well? Even with all of the personal angst that I am experiencing, I still have an ache for the ones before me. Their grave plots were so small. They must have just been little kids. It pains me to think that such small, innocent children faced the same doom as me. I wonder how she actually killed them. Did they starve to death? Did they die of dehydration? Did she beat them unconscious? These are question that I doubt I will ever know until the moment that I draw my last breath in this dungeon and join them in death.

It is hard to know how much time passes secluded in this dark room. There is no light of day, and the isolation and boredom becomes monotonous. I force myself to sleep as much as possible just to escape the reality of my life. Sleeping is always interrupted by the rats that seem to think my feet are their midnight snack. They scurry around me and treat me as an intruder. Being chained to a wall makes me easy prey for them. I am covered in bite marks and scratches from the foul little rodents.

Spiders build their webs above me, and I spend hours watching them weave their little traps. I used to be terrified of them and want to knock down their little masterpieces with concern that one of the black, creepy bugs would end up on my head, but the lengths of the chains that hold my arms hostage are too short. Now, the eight-legged little crawlers and I have come to an understanding. There are many times that I talk to my little roommate as he hangs suspended from the thread. I really believe that at times he hears me.

The room is beginning to smell from my bucket. Even though time has gotten away from me, I know that it has to be days since Mother and the masked men left because I am so hungry that my stomach aches. My mouth is dry, and my lips are chapped. The once soft skin of my lips is cracked and painful to touch.

I hear the door rattle, and I do not know if I should be excited at the expectation of food and water or be dreading the possibility of another attack. The door opens, and it is again dark outside. Mother prances into the room without a concern in the world. She acts like this entrapment is perfectly normal.

She treads heavily towards me and sits a bag on the floor. The bucket that she is carrying is full of something heavy because she labors as she hauls it towards me. She makes an impolite expression, signaling that my odor is pungent. She uses both of her hands to toss the contents of the bucket over me. Ice cold water pours over my body. The freezing water drenches over me and soaks the flimsy mattress.

"You smell rancid," she says with no remorse for my condition that she has created.

I do not say a word. She pulls a few pieces of bread out of the bag and throws them at me. She begins to dig in the bag and pulls out a red apple and flings it thoughtlessly on the bed. I am so hungry that I just want to attack the slices of bread and inhale them in one bite.

Not knowing what cruel activities Mother has planned for me next, I choose to wait until she leaves before I eat the slices that my stomach begs for me to eat. She pauses and looks down at my still nude and shivering body that has heaps of my cut hair stuck to my skin. The water acts like glue for the butchered strands. They adhere to me as if they are lost and trying to crawl up my body to find their home that they were cut from.

She opens the trunk that is placed near me and reveals a small blanket. This light brown blanket that hangs from her fingertips has been this close to me for all this time. I have spent endless hours ferociously shaking from the cold temperatures of this dismal room. I have been so cold that I have pleaded with my new spider friend to weave me a blanket, and during this entire time of suffering there has been one locked away only feet from me. She pitches the blanket to me.

"I can't stand looking at your immoral flesh any longer!" she barks at me.

I take the scratchy blanket and lay it across my cold, wet body. The blanket is small and does not have enough length to cover all of my body, so I just cover up my private areas the best I can. I hear a knock at the door. The knock is a deliberate code. The door then opens, and one of the men comes walking in. Panic sits in the pit of my stomach. I am concerned that Mother is going to allow this man to torment me again. Thankfully, he just is here to complete a chore that Mother has for him. He sits down a new bucket and removes the one that was left for me to relieve myself in. He also delivers a pitcher of water. He leaves and shuts the door behind him.

Mother proceeds to sit down on the trunk next to me. I see a familiar look on her face. It is the look that she displays when she is about to teach me a mind-numbing, religious sermon. She gracefully crosses her legs and places her elbows on her knees, clasping her hands together.

"Coral, I remember a day a few years back that you were insistent that I tell you some things about your family," she says with a sly, crooked grin spread across her pale face. Her recalling that day, tells me that my defiance at the breakfast table has been hanging in her memory since.

A part of me becomes excited that she is going to share the secrets that I have longed to understand for years. A few years back, the little girl that I used to be would be sitting on the edge of her seat absorbing every word like a sea sponge. I am hopeful that her words make me understand why she detests me and has made me her prisoner.

"Well, let me start this lesson that you seem not to ever comprehend. Men are weak. They are all spoiled little boys that only want from you when they want it. They will use you, lie to you, betray you, and then leave you when things get tough. They expect you to clean up the messes that they make," she says like she is giving me information about my family, but really she is just rattling off nonsense like she always does. "I will give you an example of how weak men are. Let's talk about your father," she says, knowing that this will spark my interest. She is correct. She has my attention, and I look up at her. "Do you know that your 'Daddy,' as you call him, has not worked in over ten years?" she says, taunting me. "He has been lying to you all of this time. Do you remember all of his outlandish stories of living on the ocean in a research vessel? Ha! That pathetic excuse of a man has been worthless all of his life. The most amusing part, dear Coral, is that your daddy doesn't even love you enough to care for you the way that I have. I have dedicated my life to providing you shelter, food, clothing, and education and have done my best to rid you of the serpent that resides inside of you, but looking at you, I know that I have been defeated by Satan. The serpent is too potent for me to cast him out alone. Your evil is just too prevailing." She reveals the heart wrenching lies, and I do not want to believe her. Even with the emotional distance between my father and me, if this is the truth it will crush me. "While I have sacrificed to deliver God's word, your daddy has been hiding out only feet away from you this whole time. He has been living on this property in the gardener quarters all this time," she says with pride.

She delivers this distressing information to me and is so twisted that she still preaches to me about my evil ways and confirms her sacrifices for me. She is oblivious and does not even care that this news of my father's lack of commitment to me is painful. This is not a lesson about men. This is just another way to destroy me and expand her corrupt punishments.

My memory takes me back to the day that Lucy and I discovered this very room that I sit in. I recall seeing an unknown man standing on the porch of the quaint cottage at the edge of the property. That man was my father. My father has hid from me for all of these years in my very own backyard. He relaxed in his private cottage evading Mother and me, and meanwhile he abandoned me to suffer at the hands of a religiously corrupt psychopath. It is unforgivable that my father can look out of the window of his tranquil cottage and actually see the door where I am being held captive and tortured. I wonder if he knows that I am here.

She can see that sharing this information has affected me. She seems to enjoy the moment as if there is a contest of which is the better parent. It astonishes me that my mother is so ill that she believes she has been a good parent but failed because my evil is too powerful for her to conquer. Evidently, she has given up propelling the demon out of me and now feels the need to hide me in this dungeon. I am not fixable in her mind. I am her lost cause. Just as I think that the painful information meeting that we appear to be having is over, she smiles wickedly and continues her pursuit to completely devastate me.

"Well we just have to put the past behind us and move forward," she counsels me. "You do not need to think about all of these worthless men. Your father is too useless to do you any good, and I have taken care of your foul Italian." Hearing her say that she has "taken care" of Angel petrifies me. What did she do to him? Did she have her goons beat him up, or worse, kill him? Her enjoyment escalates when she notices my tears after she mentions Angel. "You did not think that I would allow this man who spat on God to not pay for his sins, did you?" she says. She rises to her feet and begins to pace back and forth in front of me. She puts her arms behind her back and clasps her hands together. She is gearing up to deliver another deranged lesson. "That boy kidnapped and raped a minor, and dear Coral, that is against the law. Did you honestly think that I would trust you to stay away from that trash? Did you think that I would allow you to breed with a crude Italian that is not even good enough to clean my toilets? The seed that the two of you would bring forth would grow into a hideous creature that should never take one breath of life."

My Angel is paying the price for being the only person who has ever protected and loved me. This is all my fault. How will I ever forgive myself?

"Did you really believe that man was worthy of you spreading your legs? Let me tell you a little something about your prince charming. He's no prince at all you stupid little girl. Not only is he jailed for a very long time because the transgressions that he inflicted on this family, but he was already wanted for many crimes. Now he is where he belongs, jailed with all of the other immoral indigents."

She has so much pride as she delivers her news. She has taken a criminal off of the streets and appears to be such an upstanding citizen. Meanwhile, she has her daughter chained to a wall unclothed, dirty, cold, and hungry. I would rather befriend the rank rats and give them permission to feed off of my flesh than listen to one more word that comes out of Mother's mouth. She feels satisfaction with destroying me once again and leaves to let the darkness devour me.

The days, weeks, and months go by, and she still does not murder me. Slowly, I feel the life get sucked out of me. With each day that passes, I lose my desire to survive. Mother visits me only in the night. This tells me that no one knows I am down here. She needs the night to cast shadows that she can camouflage herself as she sneaks in and out of my jail cell. I only see her and her masked helpers occasionally. She comes to throw me a few pieces of bread, water, and if I am lucky I occasionally get fruit.

The infrequent times that a layer of peanut butter is smeared between the stale slices of bread are a treat. I was already thin, but now I have become skin and bones. I am sure that at this point I am malnourished. It will only be a matter of time before my body cannot feed off of itself any longer and gives up. I have become so thin that even the rats are not interested in taking a bite out of my puny body any longer.

The little room stinks from the bucket that I am forced to use as my toilet. The masked men usually empty it but not often enough. I need a bath so badly that I would even be accepting of another scalding bath. At least I would be clean after the burns subsided. The only cleaning that I receive is a bucket of freezing water dumped on me every once in a while. The frequency is hard to decipher. The absence of sunlight makes my days and nights run together, and time is now a nonissue. The water from the bucket that gets insensitively dumped on my scrawny body soaks into the already grubby mattress, and now a potent odor of mildew fills the room.

I often wonder if the other poor children who had faced the same fate as me had these same experiences. Sometimes when I am dozing off, I feel the shackles around my wrists and imagine what their tiny, little wrists looked like trapped in the very same device that I am confined in. Sometimes when the night is the quietest and the isolation begins to overwhelm me I can hear children's voices asking me to come play. I do not know if it is delirium that causes me to hear the precious, voices echo throughout the dark confinement or if the children's spirits still reside here with me and are reaching out to comfort me and counting the days until I can join them and play with them in their darkness.

At one point the amber light burns out, and for days I sit alone in the dark. All I can hear is the scurrying paws of my rat family. The inability to stop my brain from thinking and the numbness that exudes from my toes and creeps to my arms become unbearable. I realize that staying in one position for long periods of time results in an aching body. I am unable to position myself to view my body, and I cannot see what causes the tremendous pain that shoots from my bottom. I find myself insanely screaming for God to take me. I live the life that I would imagine a prisoner of war would, but the difference is that there is not an army looking for me. There is only one person who would fight a dragon to find me, but he is caged as well.

It has been a while since I have had a visit from Mother, and my stomach growls and grumbles. I am so hungry that I feel nauseous. I peer down at my stomach, and I notice that something has changed. My stomach seems to be swelling. I have become so malnourished that I am beginning to resemble the starving children that live in third world countries. Seeing my bulging belly evokes seeing the pictures of the little children who live in misery. When I was allowed to attend school, one of my textbooks had pictures of the countries and the underprivileged residents. I can vividly remember feeling so much pity for the suffering little ones that I saw in the pictures. I would have never imagined that we would have so much in common.

Days seem to go by, and I do not receive as much as a slice of bread. My nausea increases on a daily basis. I have begun to use my bucket more to vomit in than for any other bodily function. I do not know how much longer my mind or body can continue on. My strength is depleted, and my will to survive is diminished. I hope every night that Angel will come into my dreams and hold me tight. I hope that he will tell me that everything is going to be okay like he did when the lighthouse was our home.

Some time goes by, and I am given very little to eat. Every time that I am given even a slice of bread though, it does not stay down long. I vomit daily, even when I have no food in my stomach. Those times are the most uncomfortable. I wake at night and have a strange sensation in my stomach. It feels like the butterflies that once fluttered over my infatuation for Angel have returned.

I rub my swollen stomach, and as I lay my hand on my abdomen I instantly realize that I have not once had my monthly visit since I have been held a prisoner. I recall the apprehension that I had when the certainty of my fate sunk in after I was kidnapped and left in this place to rot. It actually crossed my mind about how disgusting I would become once my time of the month would arrive, but I have been so preoccupied with trying to tolerate my bleak living conditions that the concern of Mother Nature has not entered my mind again.

My hand rubs my hard belly, and I wonder if I may be carrying a child, Angel's son or daughter. The thought both terrifies me and makes me joyous. There is nothing that I would want to do more than have the baby of the man I love, but we are both in prison. My sentence will eventually come to an end. Unfortunately, it will not be because I will be released but because I will be assassinated and join the family of dead children that visit me when I am at my weakest. We will not be able to share our baby, and I am not sure that I can do it alone even if Mother allows me to live. With my hand on my belly, my concentration is no longer on my survival or wish for a quick and painless death. It is on my poor baby. With the state that I am currently in, I do not see how a fetus could possible thrive and grow to be healthy. I hardly receive enough nourishment to sustain my own life. How can this unborn child have even a chance of taking its first breath?

If Mother is to find out that I am carrying a baby I can only imagine how infuriated she will become. I foresee that this new revelation will push her to the brink of pure insanity and her demented behavior will consume her and then destroy me. I can picture her coming at me with the large scissors, and instead of cutting my hair off she would cut the baby out of me and sacrifice it to God. The only thing worse to her than me being brought into this world would be a child of my own. She is determined to stop the legacy of immorality within me.

There is no way for me to know for sure if I am with child or not, but I know that my suspicion very well may be a reality. I will have to do my best to keep my stomach hidden from Mother's judgmental eyes. I now depend on the small, scratchy blanket that she once threw at me like she would throw a dog a bone. Without the uncomfortable blanket there is no way to hide my developing stomach since I have been left unclothed for all of this time.

Over the next month or so, there is no longer a question of whether or not Angel's child grows inside of me. As time inches by, my stomach grows larger, and the butterflies grow into tiny punches and kicks from inside of the womb that my poor baby is trapped in. There is no doubt that I am with child.

I worry daily about the health of my growing fetus. There is no way that a few pieces of bread a week will be enough to feed a growing baby, but if I reveal my little gift from God to Mother both my child and me will be slain. The growing child inside of me gives me the will to want to live again. I will not be like my mother. I will fight and protect my child until my life is taken from me.

My desire to have Angel by my side increases as each day passes. Our child grows stronger even despite the poor conditions that it is given to develop in. The absence of him is insufferable at times. I reach to the depths of my inner strength to find the courage to continue on. I am a mother now, and my sole purpose is to bring this baby into the world with love and protection.

A few more weeks go by, and since I have accepted the truth of my baby living within me my senses have heightened. My thoughts have deepened, and I have intuitive experiences that I cannot explain. So many times as I lie in my one position and wiggle my body into as many different spots that my chains allow, I feel surges of pain. During these troubling moments I hear strange chants and brutal screams.

In the beginning I think that they may be the noises of the children that surround me, but I am sure now that it is something different. These screams are much more mature and lack the innocence of the voices of playful children. These sounds seem ritual and malicious. I feel like I am surrounded by angry spirits. When the chanting sounds fill the room and bounce off the grimy stones, an overwhelming, foul smell drifts throughout the dark dungeon. The smell is so pungent, that it usually leaves me with my face buried in the silver bucket left by my bed and vomiting the scraps of bread that sit in my empty stomach. I question how much wickedness has filled this room. I know how powerful Mother is, but these new sounds seem ancient as if they are from another time.

I have not ruled out the possibilities that these new noises can be the results of uncontrolled hormones or that my body working is so hard to keep the life inside of me viable that the lack of nutrition is causing me to become delirious. Regardless if the voices that I hear are imagined or real, they are very disturbing, and the individuals that these sounds come from are filled with pain and evil.

One evening, I do not hear the door open which is very unusual. Since

I have been locked in here, the least amount of sound wakes me, but I feel so weak lately that I spend most of my lonely days asleep. My body is depleted from trying to keep my baby alive. I often abruptly wake and reach for my stomach. I place my hand on my firm belly and hope that I feel my little one squirming around inside me. If I do not immediately feel a little foot or a petite punch, I desperately shake my abdomen in hopes that my baby is just napping.

Many times that panic takes hold of me when I do not feel movement. I spend hours crying and talking to the unborn baby, fearful that it just cannot make it another day. Sometimes after hours of angst I finally feel a dainty flip or turn. These small movements are all I live for these days. I have fallen deeply in love with the gift that God has given me, and now I cannot live without my child.

I am unexpectedly woken as Mother recklessly grasps the poorly cut hair attached to my scalp. Her exertion to find strands long enough to grip shows on her face. Since becoming pregnant my hair has attempted to rejuvenate itself, but the roots have been fighting a losing battle. The lack of vitamins and protein that my baby and I urgently need causes my hair to continue to fall out from the root. She jerks my body into a sitting position and shoves my head toward my naked stomach. I did not have the blankets positioned to conceal my expanding stomach. Mother now knows that I am with child. The force of her brutal shove leaves my head almost touching my stomach.

"Tell me what that is in your stomach!" she screams in a crazed voice louder than I have ever heard before.

Dark rage has taken her over. I have remained silent since the day that

I was propelled into this darkness. I have strived to prolong my life and lessen the abuse imposed on me, but now I must speak. My unborn baby does not have a voice, and now I need to fight to keep it safe.

"Please Mother, do not hurt my baby," I beg of her as I try to push my head back against her vigorous hold to make eye contact.

Surely she would not want to hurt her own grandchild. Somehow I am able to overpower her seize on my head and stare directly into Mother's bitter eyes. I am uncertain of how I am able to override her force especially with her temper more turbulent than I have ever seen before. It feels as if a force beyond my drained body has taken me over.

"Mother, please do not hurt your grandchild," I plead with her, hoping that if she realizes that this baby is also a part of her that she may spare us both. She yanks my head back and slaps me across the face so severely that my lip splits. I can taste the blood fill my mouth.

"THAT IS NOT MY GRANDCHILD! Never speak those words to me again! That thing you have growing in your womb is an abomination and needs to be removed!"

She shoves my body onto the bed. Her eyes seem to be possessed. What is she planning to do to my baby and me? When I imagined her cutting my baby out with the large scissors it was just an exaggeration that my terrified mind created. Is she so sadistic that she could do this to my unborn baby? Is this even possible?

I become frantic and begin to tug and pull at the shackles around my wrists in an attempt to escape. I am being irrational. I have tried this a hundred times before. In my frightened state I have to protect my baby, so I foolishly try again. Even if by a miracle from God the shackles suddenly release, Mother will never let me escape this room. My new motherly instincts take control, and as senseless as my struggle is I still attempt the impossible.

"This will have to be taken care of tonight and no later! This is no longer a seed that can be easily removed. It has already grown into a swine whose indecent blood is that of the devil!" she screams at me and then charges out of the door.

She is so beside herself with insanity, she fails to lock the door behind her. Again, I aimlessly attempt to break out of the restraints. If I can be released, I can run for the door and make an escape. Even if I have to run through the garden and fight the malicious trees and aggressive vines, I will fight them and anything else that will stand in the path for me to reach the other side.

After what is probably hours of attempting to squeeze through the restraints, I am exhausted and drop my hands to my sides. The metal has dug into my skin, and both of my wrists are bleeding substantially. I begin to cry. I begin to call to the children who have shared this space with me, petitioning them to help me get the shackles off of my wrists. Surely their tiny little fingers could slip through and pick the lock just as I did when I found the secret room in my closet.

I cry out to the rats that live in the old walls to please come and chew the metal in half with their razor-sharp teeth. I search for my little spider friend and attempt to persuade him to build a web with strands so strong, that if wrapped around the chains that the rusty links would sever into. I hear nothing, and I see nothing. I am alone, and there is no way that I can win this battle against Mother. Lifting my arms takes every bit of strength that I have, and I am useless. How did I ever think that I could save my baby when I have never even been able to save myself from Mother?

I place my bloody hands on my stomach and begin to rub my belly. I try to soothe my baby and let it know that everything will be alright, but I know that this is the first lie that I tell my child because nothing is going to be okay ever again. Blood from my wrists slowly drips on my stomach, and I fear that this is just the beginning of my bloodshed. I scream for Angel. I am aware that he will not hear me, but I am exhausted and feel my body drifting away. Have I lost too much blood? Has my body fed off of all of the fat I had left? Am I actually going to die of starvation? My head spins, and my vision becomes diffused. I argue with sleep until I have nothing left.

Unsure of how much time has passed; I am stirred out of my unconsciousness by the noise of the door rattling. I want to scream out at the top of my lungs with hope that my neglectful father may hear my cries for help, but I have no fight left in me. My entire body is heavy, and I cannot even move my toes. My screams for help will not override Mother's authority over my baby and me. Even if someone could hear my shallow screams for mercy, I do not think they could save us from Mother's wicked government.

The door opens. The amber light that is usually a constant glow now flickers. I am not positive if this is my weakened vision or if the light is getting ready to burn out as it did once before. Is it possible that the spirits of the children are inconspicuously warning me of the sinister treat that the visitors. I see two figures standing in the doorway. I can make out Mother by the outline of her body, and the other seems to be a man. I hear footsteps travel towards me. As the two approach me, I am able to distinguish that the male figure is Father Paul.

Relief washes over my body just like the ice cold water from the bucket drenches me. Mother has had a change of heart and is bringing the priest to help me. He is here to bless my child and use the Lord to renew the strength that has been taken from me so that I can carry my baby to life. My relief comes to an immediate end when I hear Mother's words, the words of an absolute maniac.

"See Father, she is being controlled by the devil! We must rid this unholy spirit from her and have God put an end to the evil spawn that is living inside her!" she commands.

Are they going to attempt to perform an abortion by exorcism? Is this Priest as demented as Mother?

I attempt to focus on the priest's face. Once I am able to clear my blurry vision slightly, I see an expression of horrid shock and amazement as he looks at me shackled naked to the wall. The grimy, brown blanket has been tossed to the side of the mattress, and once again I lie naked in full view of anyone who enters. He can see the blood smeared across my growing belly. My haircut looks as if it has been tended to by a chainsaw. I am visibly dirty and malnourished. He performs the Catholic symbol of a cross across his face and chest the same way Lucy did before entering this very room.

"What have you done, Margret?" he asks in a remorseful and somber tone.

"I have done nothing! This is the work of the serpent himself! Now go rid my daughter of all of the evil that lives inside her including that bastard child!" she commands.

Mother shuts the door to the room. I know that my only hope is this man of God who stands before me. If he does not help me, I know there is no God and that my fate is condemned. I have to believe that there is a great spirit above though. He blessed me with my baby. My little miracle punches and kicks resiliently inside me. I am sure the turbulent waves that my belly is displaying are visible to Mother and Father Paul. It seems that even my baby knows that it needs to fight for our lives. Father Paul cautiously comes towards me. He has his Bible in one hand and rosary beads in the other. His eyes are fixed on me and remain in a state of astonishment.

"Margret, this has to stop. This is not God's work. You have to release this girl and get her medical attention immediately!" he firmly says to her.

"NO, NO, NO! You need to expel the demon and release him back to the pit of Hell where he belongs! GET HIM OUT OF THIS HOUSE ONCE AND FOR ALL!" Mother is not influenced by the priest's request as she yells so loud that Satan himself could hear her from the depths of Hell.

"No, Margret!" he says and then begins walk to me.

I can tell by his unbending convictions that he is going to release and save my baby and me. As he reaches down and tries to figure out how to remove the tight shackles, Mother changes her tone from utter hysteria to the calm and cold woman that I am most used to.

"Okay Father, we will do what you wish, but just be prepared because after this jezebel is released against my will, I will then have the duty to protect another child. I think that I will need to make a visit to Mr. and Mrs. Stewart's residence," she says emotionless. How can this woman go from a crazed lunatic, shrieking at the top of her lungs to calm and collected in only seconds? The priest's expression changes from determination to release me to anxiousness and fret but not for me. He looks toward Mother, and she smiles with arrogance. "I am sure that they would love to know what happened between you and their son. What was his name, Father? Was it Peter? No, that doesn't sound correct. Hmm, what is that ten year old boy's name? Oh I remember, it's Matthew. Peter is only eight. How did I get them confused?" Mother's statement is sharp and uncanny.

I look at the priest and watch him slowly stand and take a few steps away from me. I try to reach for him, but my arms feel like someone is pressing them to the mattress. The priest is now concerned about keeping his own sins concealed. Mother's manipulation of Father Paul has ceased his rescue attempt. His hopelessness now matches mine.

Mother comes to the back of me and puts a leather strap under my chin that is similar to a belt. She uses it to keep my head still. She begins to scream at the priest to begin an exorcism. She has the strap so tightly around my face that even if I had the strength to get up I could not.

The priest reaches into his pocket and retrieves a small bottle of holy water. He starts to sprinkle it on my naked body. He prays and chants for the devil to release me and to take the baby that he created with him. Despite the restricting leather that is cutting into the flesh of my neck, I begin to scream as loud as I can and continue to beg the priest to have mercy on me and my unborn child. I am unsure if my voice is even loud enough for a human to hear. My begging distracts him, and I can see that he struggles to perform the ritual that Mother is blackmailing him to complete.

I see tears roll down his face, and I continue to plead in hopes that I will shake him to the point that this ends and he forces Mother to release me. He continues to chant and speak in Latin. The belt is so tight around my neck that I begin to choke. The room grows dim, and then suddenly it is bright again. The light show that I see continues to repeat itself. The lack of oxygen has caused me to black out, but in the darkness of my mind I can hear the ceremony continue. Father Paul's voice is my focal point, and I use it to concentrate and bring myself back to the light. I hear Mother rejoices because she believes that the episodes of me blacking out and then coming back along with all the paranormal activities that have now seized the dark chamber are a sign that the devil is being cast out of me. I can hear the chants from the mouth of the Priest, and they seem so distorted; they sound more like lingering whispers than a powerful expulsion of the serpent. A gust of wind encases my body and assaults the Priest. The unexplainable wind attacks him, and he is distracted and appears afraid. Joining the Latin chants rolling off the Priests tongue is the familiar ancient, frightening chants of the dark room. The pungent smell that has afflicted discomfort on me penetrates the air and causes this man of the cloth to gasp from the offensive odor. Mother laughs wickedly because she believes the demon is slowly seeping out of my veins, and she screams at the beast to leave her home and never come back.

This ridiculous sacrament will last until she strangles me. There is no demon inside of me, and no amount of holy water is going to draw out anything except for my last breath. The awareness of my surroundings begins to fade, and I do not know if I can find the deliberation to climb out of the darkness again. I feel my body beginning to spiral downward, and suddenly I see a light above the priest's head. I fear that it is the light everyone says that you see when you die. I fret that my fight is coming to an end. God is sending me and my baby into the light.

The bright light above his head begins to dim and change form. It grows into the cloud-like fog that I hallucinated when I was first thrown into this hellish room. The fog gets closer to me, and I see the woman from before. She smiles gently at me, and she holds a baby in her arms. The baby is turned to her chest. I hear a soft voice say,

"Just hang on for a little longer."

The voice lingers on and repeats itself. She then turns the baby towards me, and I can see that it is a little girl. I hear the voices of the lilies singing, and she extends the baby to me as if she wants me to take her.

Suddenly, I hear a loud noise, and the vision is gone. My hearing is smothered from the position of the belt, but I can hear other voices screaming. The priest stops chanting, and I can vaguely see him look behind him. The wind ceases and the rank smell vanishes. What is going on? Are the masked men here to cut my baby out of me? Mother screams at the priest not to stop, but he is sidetracked with whoever is behind him. I hear Mother's voice yell,

"Rose, you need to go! Stay out of here! Continue on, Father!"

Rose? Rose is here to save me. I try to call for Rose, but I am unable to utter a sound from the pressure of the belt that pulls my jaw closed. I can see the priest quickly move to the side, and then I see Rose's beautiful face above mine. Rose is here to save us. There is a God.

"Margret, let go of the belt!" Rose commands her. Mother has gone completely mad. Her rage dominates her, and the insanity is unrelenting.

"Stay out of it, Rose. We have to remove this evil spell from our home now! This is it Rose, this will sever the Ocean Point has with evil and set us free of the curse. She told me she would go away if I did as she asked. It is almost done! Go away Rose! GO AWAY!"

"It is over, Margret. This is not the way to rid the evil, and you know it. You know that there is only one way, and this is not it. This house was cursed decades before this girl was born. You cannot listen to the voices of the past Margret! This is not the solution! You need to let go of this and release her now," Rose says as she calmly tries to convince her to release her grip.

Rose's words mean something to Mother. She lets go of the strap. My jaw is now free, and I feel a rush of air fill my lungs. I gasp as I try to take in a normal breath. I hear footsteps run to the other side of me, and I can see from the corner of my eye that someone has pulled Mother away from me. I make an effort to sit up, but my strength is too diminished. Rose demands that the priest give her his coat. She places the coat over my naked body. I begin to cry hysterically. Rose touches my face and says,

"It is all over now. It is all over."

Her eyes convey that something more significant is happening, something that will change my life forever. She reaches down and touches my stomach lovingly and smiles. I hear screaming and commotion behind me. I turn my head towards the uprising and see my father. He has Mother pushed against the dirty wall beside me. He has his hand to her throat, and she is unable move.

Her demeanor is chilling. She is backed into the stone wall, and her expression of madness has not changed. It is like there was a demon inside of me, and the priest exorcised him out of me and into her. Even being physically powerless against my father does not seem to alter her disposition. She looks at him with a sinister smile. His dominating action appears just to humor her. Her dark eyes are more monstrous than I have ever witnessed before.

I see flashes of light around the room and then hear many footsteps come rushing into the room. My surroundings appear fuzzy, and my body seems limp and motionless. I hear two loud snapping sounds. I feel my raw wrists being removed from the metal shackles. Hands are on my body, and my first instinct is to flinch. I am not able to comprehend all that is occurring around me. Even with the confusing fear that I have fallen victim to, I cannot move. My body is lifted into the air, and excruciating pain surges throughout every fiber in me. I have become so frail that I am unable to even produce a moan from the physical anguish that I feel. My body is placed on a stretcher, and I am surrounded by paramedics and policemen. I recognize some of the officers from the night they apprehended me from safety and delivered me into this evil. I see expressions of dismay and regret on their once stern faces.

Mother is handcuffed with her arms behind her back, and the officers are handcuffing the priest. Rose comes to my side and holds my hand as the stretcher begins to roll out of the room. I see my father standing somberly in a corner. His head is hung low, and he seems to be bothered by being in this room. It seems that it is more than just what has happened with me. My newly awoken intuitive power tells me he has been here before.

We arrive outside, and the fresh air surrounds me. I have never appreciated the simple act of taking a breath as much as I do now. I will appreciate each breath that I take as each day passes for the rest of my life. I finally realize that I survived this nightmare and that it is over. The worry of my baby's health begins to fill my mind with foreboding thoughts. I can no longer jiggle my expanding stomach with my hands to entice my baby to respond. My muscles are depleted and I cannot aid me. I have not felt the precious movements from within me in quite some time. I will soon find out my concerns are valid.

As they load me into the ambulance I see the officers come around the corner, and they are escorting a stranger to a police car. I do not recognize this man. Is he one of the masked men? I dismiss this thought because of the man's physical stature. The man in handcuffs is very old but not feeble. He is tall, and his body has hunched over with age. His hair is white and long. It appears that it has not been cut in many years. It wildly sticks out all over his head. I do not see his face. When Rose notices that I see this odd man she tries to distract me, but I am drawn to him and cannot take my eyes off of him.

The old man turns and sees me. He looks right at me, and I am captivated by his face. Who is this bizarre looking person? I feel an odd and disturbing connection to this man. I am unaware of his identity, but I know that I am terrified of him. He stares at me and displays the expression of a lunatic. He begins to try to get away from the officers. His eyes have not migrated away from me, and he combats the officers' domination over him. He attempts to charge at me. He acts like a wild animal. He begins to grunt, groan, and make horrible howling sounds. The officers struggle to keep their prisoner under control.

I realize that this is the monster that entered my room that dark evening and put his hand on my bare skin. The creature-like noises that he makes are the sounds that have been stamped to my memory. Even when the officers regain control of this unusually strong man I still feel in danger. It is so odd. My feeling of danger is not just physical. It is also an emotional twinge that I do not understand. Why is this seemingly mentally insane stranger connecting to me and frightening me more than Mother ever has? Why is he still here after so many months?

Rose reaches to me and holds my face close to her chest, in an attempt to shield me from the madness of the crazed man. The old man's screams become louder and more volatile. In one maddening second, his monster-like howls end, and he becomes silent. He looks straight into my eyes, and the familiarity I feel with this man terrifies me.

"Coral..." he says in a slow, raspy voice that makes the hair on my arms raise.

How does he know my name? I am so caught up in the draw and magic of this seemly wicked man. I feel a sharp, sudden pain in my stomach. I motion to Rose to signal to her that something is wrong with the baby. I am too weak to tell her of the burning sensation that my abdomen is experiencing. Concern for my pregnancy pushes the actions and questions about the strange man out of my mind, and the enigmatic trance that he captivates me with is broken.

The paramedics begin to fervently execute medical care. They put an oxygen mask on me, and I can faintly feel the prick in my arm as they begin an IV. As the commotion of the men that attempt to save my life is being carried out, I still cannot help but watch the old man as they force him into the back of the police car. There is a supernatural pull that this man has me caught in and there is a connection that I cannot break. He sees me watching him and peers out of the back window of the car. He smiles at me. It is the most spine-chilling, deranged smile that I have ever seen.

The medical workers are delaying our travel to the hospital as they diligently work to stabilize my grave condition. I see Mother come towards us in the distance. As she gets closer, I can see that she is handcuffed and being escorted by officers. I am so relieved to know that she was unable to manipulate or blackmail her way out of the crimes she has committed as she usually does. I finally feel safe knowing she cannot come for me and my baby. Her usually well-behaved hair has fallen from the bun that always clutches it to the top of her head. Strands fall wildly around her face and down her back like those of the deranged stranger's. Her hair is very long, longer than I ever imagined. This is the first time that I have ever seen her hair down. Despite her troubled appearance, she marches across the estate as if nothing has even happened. Her expression is calm, and even with her hands pinned behind her back her posture is still straight and tall. This woman is simply unbreakable.

As she gets near the car with the strange old man in it and sees him in the back seat, her regal behavior disappears. For some unknown reason, seeing the trapped old man has given her a reason to combat the officer. She begins to scream and fight with the officer. He does not expect her sudden outburst and is caught off guard. He scrambles to control this once calm woman. She kicks and shoves the officer even without the use of her hands. Something inside of her snaps, and she is now hysterical. She manages to escape his hold and runs to the police car where the strange man is. She begins to slam her body against the police car until the policeman can physically subdue her again. She sees me in the back of the ambulance and begins to scream at me.

"This is your fault, yours and that harlot's! You both are the devil's wives!"

I am in such awe about the things that I have just heard and seen. I want to question Rose about my mother's mad rants, but I am too tired and physically ill. Besides, Mother is not in her right mind. I disregard the things that she says. The ambulance starts, and the doors shut. Through the square windows in back doors of the ambulance, I watch the police put Mother into another police car, and then I see two men in handcuffs being escorted by officers to a third car. I can tell by their physical stature that these are the masked men that assisted Mother in kidnapping me, torturing me, and holding me hostage for all of these months.

I feel so much relief as the tires of the ambulance begin to move. As we pull out of the driveway, I can see Ocean Point looking at me. The house is alive and is doing its best to intimidate me, but the old mansion no longer scares me. I tell the house that I survived it. It did not break me. It cannot have my baby and me. Its reign over me is over.

Recovery

Over the next month my new home is a hospital. When I arrive, my baby and I are in critical condition. During the evening of my exorcism and rescue, my body goes into early labor due to the severe malnourishment, dehydration, and the extreme stress that was inflicted on me. The doctors work for hours to stop the labor and give my baby a chance of survival. I am not far enough along in my gestation period for there to be any hope of my baby surviving if born this soon. Luckily, the labor is stopped, and since then the nurses and doctors work around the clock to ensure that we will recover.

It takes a week for me to become lucid and aware of what is truly happening. When I arrive, I am dehydrated and severely malnourished. My body is full of infection and poison. My rat family that was constantly snacking on my feet and legs has caused a dangerous infection. The constant companionship that I thought I had with my eight-legged spider roommate was not what I thought. He would wait until I was asleep, and he and his friends would attack my skin and release their poison into my blood stream. My wrists are infected from the rusty shackles that constantly cut into my skin. The back side of my body is covered in bedsores from the lack of mobility.

Over the weeks, I drift in and out of consciousness, overhearing the medical professionals in conversation. Many times I can hear the sound of defeat in their voices as they consider all of the options to heal my baby and me. I wish that I could say that I fight to keep us alive, but the truth is that I am so emaciated that I am unaware of my crucial and dire condition. I can hear Rose pray over my body at nights. If I was in my right mind this display would frighten me, but I am too ill to ever acknowledge the significance of my condition.

After a few weeks, the antibiotics that fill my veins with medication slowly I begin to prevail against the stubborn strains of infections, and my comatose state slowly begins to dissolve. I become more coherent as each day passes. I then begin to overhear the conversations of the nurse and doctors that seem hopeful and optimistic. Often, I even hear the word "miracle."

The feeding tube that they insert into my body aids in my recovery and carries the proper nutrients and vitamins to my baby's ravenous appetite. Slowly, my body starts to function normally again, and my unconsciousness comes less often. I am finally able to speak again. Initially, my words are jumbled and inaudible. No matter how hard I try, I cannot articulate what my mind wants me to say. My words are trapped in my brain and just cannot find an exit.

I begin to feel my legs and arms again, and sometimes I can even raise them inches off of the bed. I know that no matter how feeble I feel, the slightest body adjustments I am able to now conquer still cause me agonizing pain from the sores that cover my back. I begin to consciously assist in the fight to regain my strength and health. Occasionally I feel the weakened movements of my little baby inside of me, and it increases my desire to heal. I feel fortunate that my precious little one is still developing inside my womb. If I had to grieve my baby's death, I would have wished for death myself.

The last month has been a consistent battle between life and death. Now I have finally gotten to a place in my recovery that all of the aches are tolerable, and I have my voice back. Even though I am still thinner than I need to be to carry a baby, I am no longer withering away, and my body is not in starvation mode any longer. I am comforted in knowing that my little one gets the food that it needs to grow and be healthy. They have now removed the feeding tube, and I am gradually becoming able to eat solid food again. In the beginning, the food would make me so sick that I would immediately vomit. I would be so famished that I would overeat, but now my stomach seems to be enjoying the return of a solid meal.

Now that my health has improved, I anxiously wait to see Rose. I need her to find Angel for me. Mother said that he is in jail, and I need her to take me to him. I need to tell him how sorry I am and tell him about the amazing miracle that we created. I anticipate her daily visit soon. I take the last bite of my green pea soup, and like clockwork Rose enters the room.

"Good afternoon," she cheerfully says. I do not waste any time on small talk.

"Rose, I need you to find Angel for me. I need to see him." Her eyes look down, and I instantly know that she has bad news to tell me. She hesitates, but I do not allow her to collect her thoughts to answer me. "Rose, what has happened? Where is he?"

My chin begins to quiver from the doom that seeps into the room. She looks up at me and reaches for my hand. I jerk my hand from hers to display the urgency that I feel to know what has happened to Angel.

"The night that you and Angel were discovered, the policemen took him down to the police station. Your mother made such a fuss and lied to the sheriff. She told him that Angel kidnapped you and raped you. She even produced false hospital reports stating that you were sexually assaulted. They arrested him on kidnapping and raping a minor. In the process of these untrue allegations, they routinely ran a background check. That poor boy has been in a lot of trouble before, Coral. There were outstanding warrants for other crimes, and he was detained. He was given ten years in jail for all of his wrong doings," she says and pauses as if there is more to the story but has to take a moment to collect her thoughts.

My pulse races, and I feel like what is left of my heart is going to explode. I cannot spend another moment without Angel, never the less ten years away from him. We have a baby coming, and I need him by my side to protect me and our unborn child. I reach down and rub my stomach. I subconsciously soothe my little one and reassure it that no matter how hopeless Mom feels that she will figure out a way to get to Daddy.

"Coral dear, there is more. As you know, this country has been in a heated war, the Vietnam War. So many of our soldiers have perished, and many young men have fled from the draft that the government offered Angel a deal. They told him that if he joined the army and went to war that they would release him from prison and throw out his sentence."

She says this with a solemn tone and then looks at my round belly. Her thoughts are with our baby, and I can see the compassion that she has for me and my unborn child. The war is very heated, and daily soldiers are dying on the front line of the gruesome battle. The odds are against Angel to ever come home alive I am shocked and silenced. Tears begin to drizzle down my face. I am so affected by Rose's distressing news that my breathing becomes shallow, and I have to exert great effort to receive air. I feel like I am imprisoned in the dark dungeon again, and Mother has the strap around my neck that is cutting off my needed supply of oxygen. Rose reacts to my condition and hurries out of the room to retrieve a nurse. The pair rushes to my bedside and begins to try to calm me in hopes that my breathing troubles will cease. Slowly, I am able to take air into my lungs, and the wheezing subsides.

I lie back and close my eyes. All I can think about is Angel. I imagine him in a soldier's uniform standing on the front line of battle with bullets and grenades going off around the man that I love. I can see his bravery that I admire driving him to protect his country and take risks that are unsafe.

I try to envision us together and he being by my side when our baby is born, but everything is blank. I cannot see us together in my thoughts. Not being able to envision Angel is the same as throwing me back into the darkness that almost took my life. If I have to face all of this without him I fear that my sanity may be at risk. This terrifies me even more. Is this a sign of what is to come or a sign of what will never be?

This news has devastated me, and I have no idea how to cope with the fear of never seeing Angel again. I fought so hard to stay alive for our child. Now that we are finally safe, Angel fights another battle that tears us apart again. Rose and I sit in silence, neither one of us knowing what to say. She is at a loss for comforting words, and I just do not want to speak. There is a knock at the door, and a doctor enters the room.

"Ms. Berringer, I hope that today finds you feeling okay," he says in a professional manner lacking the compassion that you wish for in a doctor.

He pulls a chair near my bed and sits down. It is obvious that he is not here to examine me but here to have a discussion. Seeing the grim look on his face, I do not expect uplifting news.

"Ma'am, your body has been through severe trauma. We are very fortunate that you and your baby have prevailed considering the condition that you were in when you arrived here. The chances of you making a full recovery seemed doubtful. You sitting up in the bed as effortlessly as you are is a remarkable step forward that I am proud to see."

He gives a long-winded description of the hurdles that I have faced and succeeded to jump. Even with his encouraging words I sense that the positive pep talk is going to change its course quickly. He folds his hands and briefly looks to the floor. I hear him release a slight sigh before he looks at me and begins to speak again.

"As delighted as we are with your continued improvement, the staff made up of specialists here at the hospital is greatly concerned about the health of your unborn baby. We stopped labor many times to give the little one a chance to recover and make up for the lack of nutrients that it requires for proper development. This is a hard task to accomplish. It is even more challenging to make up for lost time. The first two trimesters of a woman's pregnancy are the most crucial." He continues to speak to me, and his voice changes as dire news builds in the back of his throat. "We feel here that we have done all that we can to increase the chances of your fetus to thrive, but we have overwhelming doubts for the health of your unborn baby. We do not believe that the chances of you delivering a healthy baby are good."

He says these words without breaking between his sentences like he needs to rush the forbearing news out quickly before I display a reaction that may interfere with the unemotional environment that he strives to maintain. His pause is short, and he concludes by saying,

"Ms. Berringer, the bottom line is, if by chance you are able to carry this fetus to full term, in our expert opinion there is little hope that the child will not suffer from extreme physical and mental disadvantages."

I look at the doctor, and his demeanor has not deviated. He displays the lack of compassion in his catastrophic theories. I sit silently on the bed with the palm of my hand resting on my belly. I hope that the little baby growing inside is unable to hear such a dismal diagnosis regarding its life. I wish that I could cover my baby's ears to protect it from the doctor's words. Rose looks at the stern physician and asks,

"So what are you saying, Doctor?" She attempts to clarify the doctor's intentions of this terrible diagnosis.

"Well in our opinion it would be best to eliminate the pregnancy. We estimate that Miss Berringer is getting ready to enter her sixth month of gestation, so we are currently in a window of an opportunity. We can medically eradicate the fetus."

I hear the words "eliminate" and "eradicate" and become enraged. What kind of doctor is this? Does he think he gets to choose who is worth living and who is so pathetic that he or she should die? I have spent my entire life being told that there was something wrong with me and that I should not have been born. I have spent my entire life proving that I am not someone that can just be discarded. The last five months of my life, I have been trapped in a dark hole hanging on to the hope of escape and someday holding my precious baby in my arms. Now this mad scientist thinks that he can take all of that from me?

I look straight into the doctor's emotionless eyes. He expects me as young as I am and just recovering from such a horrific experience to take heed in his expertise and follow his orders.

"You need to leave now," I say in a low voice. My tone warns him not to say another word to me. My eyes do not leave the locking glare I have engaged with his.

"Ms. Berringer, your fetus is too small and has been traumatized. I do not think that you understand the hardships that you and the baby will face if you bring this child into the world."

He pleads with me to listen to his advice. His voice becomes more demanding and focused on the war that he now knows I am ready to battle. What does this man know about hardships? I want the doctor to leave my room and keep his advice to himself. This baby inside of me deserves a chance. So what if it is not born perfect? It is my child, and I will love and protect it no matter what.

I was born perfect and have spent my entire childhood with a mother who took all of her energy to destroy my body and mind and make me feel like there was something wrong with me. There will not be one harmful thing done to my baby, period. I am done listening to the insensitive words of this doctor. I begin to scream with more rage than I knew I was capable of.

"GET OUT! GET OUT! GET OUT!"

Rose is taken back. She stands and tries to coax the doctor to leave. I continue to scream. He stands and shakes his head like I am a fool. I scream the same words over and over and do not plan to stop until he obeys my commands. I have never commanded or asked anyone to do anything before, but this doctor will listen to me and leave us be.

Finally the door shuts, and he is gone. My yelling ends, and I strangely feel at peace. I rub my stomach, and I do not feel scared or sad over the doctor's doom and gloom news. I feel a quick, little punch from inside my womb and know that this baby and I are going to be fine one way or another. We are going to get through this time and life together. I am going to give this baby with the love, affection, and joy that I was denied.

I expect Rose to turn to me and continue to argue the doctor's point with medical reasoning and scientific facts, but once again Rose surprises me with her unyielding compassion and kindness. She walks to my bed and places her hand on my firm belly and says,

"Okay Child, looks like we are going to get a new bundle of joy." I smile at Rose and am filled with appreciation for her unconditional support. "The doctors told me this morning that they are going to release you in a few days. We have a lot of work to do at home to get ready for this little blessing," she says with anticipation of bringing us back to Ocean Point.

Her words halt my appreciation. I had always assumed that once I was released Angel and I would reunite and be a family together away from Ocean Point. Now that he is gone, what am I going to do? I will not go back to that wicked house. I will not raise my baby under the roof of a house that is full of more evil and malice than Hell itself.

Rose seems so excited about making plans for the baby and me to return to Ocean Point. She jabbers about what the color the nursery should be and the tiny clothes that she plans to knit for the new arrival. I feel slightly bad about the news that I am getting ready to deliver to my sweet Rose, but I am steadfast in my decision not to return to the mansion. Still unaware of my future and the details that will entail in me starting a new life outside of the controlling house, I tell her very adamantly,

"I will not be returning to Ocean Point."

My declaration interrupts her vivid plans, and she is instantly hushed. She looks at me, and I can see that she is not overly surprised with my declaration. I believe that Rose thought that if she filled the room with words describing the happy future that she wishes for us to have that I would forget about my past life at Ocean Point. These are just wishes and delusions that will never come true. No matter what good intentions we have for this child the house will suck us back in, and the cycle will continue. Her gaze softens, and she says,

"Child, your mother is gone. She will not be coming back for a very long time, maybe never."

I have been so engrossed with getting well and the health of my baby that I have not even questioned what happened to Mother, the crazed old man, Mother's goons, or my father. Regardless of whether Mother is stomping down the halls at Ocean Point or not, my child will not be born and raised in that house.

I am convinced that something is uniquely wrong with my former home. The rooms are filled with horrible, abusive memories. They are full of dust and grime, and it is not where I want my child to be. I want to raise my baby with sunlight shining through the windows, flowers in the front yard, bright colors painted on the walls, puppies trotting down the halls, and love overflowing in every square inch of our home. Someday, Angel will come walking through our front door and join his family and render the love and protection that will make a family strong and long lasting. Ocean Point will not allow the reunion that I deserve. I have to start anew. I have to find a suitable home for me, Angel and our child.

I remain silent and unbending. I look at Rose, and she knows that I am not going to change my mind. She drops her head, and I can see that she is hurt and disappointed. As much as I love her, this has to end now. I have to find happiness and peace. Ocean Point is stained with heartache and unearthly energy that I cannot allow to harm my new family.

"Rose, I think that it is time that I know the truth about my family. I need to know about the secrets of Ocean Point. I need the truth about Mother, Father, me, and even you. I need closure. I need to understand why these things happened so that I can make sure I do not make the same mistakes with my child. I need to heal inside and be whole. I cannot do this if I leave without the truth," I say to her as a demand instead of the way that I used to ask her for truth. My new condition has given me the backbone that had been broken daily under Mother's reign.

"Child, it is time. It is time."

Her words are remorseful as she confirms my need to know what has been untold. I am fretful that our pending conversation may bring up emotions that Rose has never been able to recover from.

"Coral, this talk that you and I are going to have cannot be here. It has to be at Ocean Point. There are things there that you need to see and feel, and this is not the place," she says to me unwavering. As much as I dread the thought of ever laying eyes on Ocean Point again, I am sure that Rose is correct. My pain and abuse began at Ocean Point, so it needs to end there.

The few days that the doctor anticipated for my long awaited release turn into a week. My body was still producing too many white blood cells which indicates infection. After an extended release date, the day is finally here.

I began physical therapy several weeks ago. The goal was to get my joints and muscles built back up so that I would have the strength to start walking again. I have been taking a few steps a day. Now, I can stand with ease and control my legs with effortless movement. I begin to get myself ready to return to the ominous Ocean Point. I do my best to keep the dark images and emotions that the mansion lends to me out of my psyche and look for the courage within me to return for my final visit.

Rose had brought me some clothes from my closet. Looking at the outdated and ridiculous clothing, the fabric brings back the memories that I have been trying to repress. I refuse to wear this reminder of my former life back into the dark misery of Ocean Point. Nothing would make the creepy castle happier than seeing me return in the uniform its master forced me to wear. The spirits would think that the innocent and naive Coral was returning home to live in the darkness forever. I look at my body in the mirror of the bathroom, and even though I appear dangerously thin, I do not look as starved as I was went I arrived here.

It is apparent that I am with child. My belly is round and protrudes from my scrawny frame. I acknowledge that my stomach is not as big as it should be. Regardless of the tininess of my growing child, until it stops punching and kicking me I will fight for its life. I hold the clothes up and wonder if the drab dress would even fit my now even more petite frame. I believe that even with my stomach larger than before that this dress will swallow me whole.

I have no choice but to slip the daunting dress over my head. The garment falls over my body and loosely hangs. Feeling the itchy, outdated fabric makes me think of Mother. I am glad that she is gone and locked up where she belongs, but it cannot end here. I need to understand why.

I hear the hospital room door open and am happy to see Rose. She pretends to be cheerful that I am leaving, but I know she is dreading having to share the dark secrets of my ancestors.

I notice a shopping bag in her hand. She hands the bag to me, and I look inside to see a new outfit. It is so refreshing to know that Mother cannot rip this outfit off of my body as she has so many times before when Rose would surprise me with a gift. I pull the lavender colored outfit out of the bag. I hold it up in front of me, and it is a maternity set. It is so cute with pleats under the bodice to allow my expanding belly to grow. The pants that match the top are the trendy capris like Lucy wears.

I wrap my arms around her chubby midsection in thanks. The normal appreciative embrace turns into a hold that Rose seems to not want to end. She hugs me like this is the last gift she will ever give me. I can feel the apprehension in her embrace. Part of me is alarmed at the reality of the truths that I am going to hear, and the other part of me feels pity for Rose. The position that she has been selfishly placed in is beyond her job description. She should not be responsible for delivering the secrets that have predicted my past, present, and future.

This is the role that my cowardly father should play. I hope he does not think that just because he was a part of my rescue from Mother's evil hands that things are going to get better between us. I have been here for over a month, and not once has that self-centered man bothered to check on his daughter. My mother is locked away in jail, and my father hides out in a quaint cottage disregarding that his daughter and grandchild were almost killed by his wife. I do not know where to go within myself to forgive such blatant neglect from the past until now. Forgiveness is an impossibility.

The Curse

ose and I begin our quest back to Ocean Point. I recall seeing the intimidating house through the ambulance windows a month earlier. I had cursed the structure and told it that I was not frightened of it any longer. At the time, I was at my weakest but seemed to have more courage than I do now. The estate looms in my thoughts and has already spread its caliginosity into my day.

I see the entrance to our long, curvy driveway ahead of us, and right away trepidation begins to devour me. As we pull onto the driveway and begin our rise up the mammoth hill, I reassure myself that today will be the last day that I will ever make this trip.

We turn the last curve, and Ocean Point is in my full view. It is in the middle of the afternoon, but the sky is dark, and the clouds are a charcoal gray color that rest on the roof of the castle-like building. For the entire ride here, the afternoon sky was a beautiful blue with white, fluffy clouds. The welcoming sky has turned uninviting and warns visitors not to proceed. The black iron gates slowly open and welcome me back home.

I begin to hear the noises of chanting and small, innocent voices of children. These are the same sounds that I fell asleep to while trapped in the dark room below the west wing. I am healthy now and have no reason to hallucinate. Could these sounds be real? If these mystifying voices are real then why do they feel the need to remain at Ocean Point, and why am I the only one who hears them?

The aura in the car has changed. I sense that Rose dreads the exchange that she and I are about to engage in. We exit the car and start towards the house. As I step through the large, antique front door, I am frightened but at the same time relieved that the next time my feet cross this entrance that it will be to leave and never return.

Rose seems to be lost with the choice of where to begin our life-changing conversation. She shuffles in and out of every room much like Gretchen did in her final years. She is nervous, and I feel sorry for the position that she has been forced into due to the lack of character that my parents have. One is in jail for abuse, and the other is hiding out in the backyard, leaving this sweet woman who has done nothing but be loyal to this dysfunctional family to the task of cleaning up its mess.

Rose tells me to follow her, and we head up the massive, wooden staircase as if we are going to my bedroom. I am surprised when we continue past my bedroom and shocked when I realize that we are heading to the west wing. Of all the years that I have lived here, the only time that I have ever walked the wooden floors on the forbidden side of the mansion was when I was fourteen and snuck into the wing. Before my feet cross over to the prohibited area, I stop. I do not know if it is from the memory of the night that I saw the demon or if Mother's reign over me still exists even with knowing she is locked away. Rose notices that I have stopped. She turns to me and says,

"Come on, Child. It is safe here now."

I do not understand what she means, but I follow her. Even with the reminder of my childhood fears, I become excited to finally see the history of my family. No matter how deranged my parents must be, surely my ancestors have some amazing history to share.

I follow Rose into the darkness, and I vaguely see her arm extend. The hallway lights up as she turns on a light. I am astonished at what I see. The dusty hallway that I recall is spotless as if Gretchen was still alive and twenty years younger. There are massive pictures with antique, gold frames lining the walls down the hallway. The crown molding that frames the walls and floors is the same rich gold color. The gold is so sparkly that you would think it was real gold. It probably is.

I am behind Rose and want to stop to view the pictures of my ancestors, but she walks at such a hurried pace. I do not have time to drink in the history of the blood that runs through my body. I have a strange suspicion that she is deliberately keeping me from seeing the portraits.

We continue on at a very swift pace. We pass so many doors that I lose count. I wonder what is behind each of the hand carved doors. Why are the doors in the west wing different from the ones in the part of the house that I was allowed to live in? It does not make any sense. I had no idea how long the west wing really was. It seems like we have been walking forever. We finally arrive at the end of the corridor, and Rose stops at an entrance to a room that is unlike any of the others.

This room entrance has two huge doors instead of one like the rest. They are hand carved and made of a dark mahogany wood. The tops of the doors have the same kind of round top that the door to the secret room that I was hidden in does. It looks like the same hand had taken days to artistically create these entrances.

She opens the doors, and I feel a chill cross over my body. I begin to hear laughter as I have before, but this time the voice seems to be female. I look at Rose, and she seems to be unaffected by the sounds that radiate through me. Why does she not hear this laughter? I step inside the room, and the wicked laughter ends.

The room is absolutely breathtaking, but I intuitively have a terrible feeling as I stand in the elegant bedroom. The walls are painted a deep, rich red and are adorned with the same gold crown molding that displays nothing but extreme wealth. There is an accent wall that is covered in opulent designer wallpaper. The bed is gigantic and has four large, hand carved posts that match the doors. There is a luxurious bedspread that covers the mattress, and above the bed there is a painting. The man in the painting haunts me as I look at him. Rose sees my eyes fixed on this painting. She points to the picture and says,

"That is Zyrous Taylor, and the story of your family and my ancestors' pain begins with that man right there."

She continues to point at the man with dark, wild eyes. He has full, wavy hair. His features are boney, and his expression is stern. I can see the resemblance between Mother and this spooky looking man. His face gives off an iciness that I have never felt before from a picture. I can see that this man disturbs Rose as well, but it is more in an angry way, not the uneasiness that he leaves me with. I force myself to break the gaze with Zyrous. He seems to look straight into my eyes.

I peer around the glorious room and notice that it is immaculate. I try not to let my bewilderment with the small details interfere with the family lesson that Rose is going to share with me. I think about all of the meaningless Bible and history lessons that Mother has forced me to listen to. Not one of the senseless lessons has mattered as much as the information that Rose will soon deliver.

I see another picture in the same kind of frame hanging on another wall, and it is of a woman. This woman is very pretty. Her expression is very different than Zyrous's. She appears to be a very meek woman. If I had to pinpoint the feeling that I believe she exudes, it would be grief. Then again, I have never seen an old-fashioned portrait where the person in it looked happy.

"That, my dear, is Martha Taylor, Zyrous's wife and the mother of his children," she states but does not seem to have as much animosity towards her as she does Zyrous.

Rose escorts me to a fabulous sitting area in the bedroom. The furniture is antique and covered with a plush, cream-colored fabric. The couch and loveseat seem to be in mint condition as if no one has ever rested their tired bodies here before. We sit down in the sitting area, and I can feel Zyrous's devilish eyes in my back. In front of me, I can feel

Martha's sorrow.

"Coral, I am going to tell you all that I know about your family, all I have heard, and all I have experienced. There are parts of what I am going to share with you that will disturb you greatly, and with some of the information that you will soon learn, I have concerns of your ability to handle it in your current state. The truth of your life and your ancestors is more sinister than I think you have ever imagined," she says to me so straightforward and without emotion that I now doubt my ability to take on any more misery than I already have.

I have waited so long for this moment of truth. Despite my sudden second thoughts, I am not turning back now. I am going to be a mother, and I need to know the secrets of my family. I can finally put this history behind me, understand my childhood, and ensure that my baby will never experience the wrath of this house and family. This is the closure that I need.

"I know that you have heard the rumors about Ocean Point and your family, particularly your ancestors. For more years than I have been alive, this giant house on the bluff has been known to be cursed, possessed, or haunted. Many would say that these are old rumors or silly folklore, but my dear, this house has been witness to more evil than most would believe. Ocean Point is alive and cursed. This house has a heartbeat and breathes the same air as you and I. I myself have felt its warm breath on the back of my neck since childhood."

She explains this with such intensity in her brown eyes that I barely recognize the woman who is usually jolly and full of smiles. It is clear to me that this part of Ocean Point's history means something very personal to her. I want to ask her if she hears the same laughter, chants, and voices that I do, but I remain silent, concerned that my interruption may distract her.

"Zyrous Taylor is the man responsible for every horrid thing that has happened to this family dating all the way back to the 1700s. He was a vicious, heartless, and merciless monster. His sins and brutal actions caused the dark and wicked spirits to rise and curse this house and the Taylor family for centuries.

Your family has always been a family of privilege, but Zyrous Taylor is the reason that the Taylor family acquired such extreme wealth. In the 1700's, slave trading was a very lucrative business for the white man. Most people believe that the trade was only in the south, but Newport eventually became one of the most profitable cities in the black slave trade industry. The white man would go to Africa and kidnap entire families then pile them onto ships and bring them straight to Newport. The African families would either begin tedious labor here on the island or be sent to the black slave auctions and be sold mostly to southern states.

So many of the Africans would perish on the trip to America from dehydration or the numerous diseases that would run amuck on the crowded vessels. The ones that survived and arrived on American soil faced atrocious abuse and neglect, and I am sure that many of them wished that they had perished on the ship once they realized what the future had in store for them, especially if they had a master like Master Taylor.

Zyrous saw the profit in selling my ancestors and eagerly became a master himself. That's what Negroes back then called their owners. These masters did despicable things to the Negro slaves. They would whip, burn, brand, mutilate, hang, or just out right slaughter them for punishments.

As a child, I would hear stories of the women slaves of the past, and when they misbehaved or just weren't working fast enough the master and his staff would whip the women with leather until their dark skin would break. They would then rub turpentine or red pepper into the wounds. The treatment was inhumane but unfortunately not uncommon.

The slaves were worked for fourteen to twenty hours a day without food or water. Many of my ancestors died from starvation or dehydration. Others would die in large numbers from the diseases and illnesses that would take control of the small slave quarters. The master did not provide medical care for these ailing slaves, and the other slaves were left to care for each other without adequate supplies. Most would perish.

Master Taylor had no remorse for the deceased Negroes. His punishments were harsh, but his lack of respect for his departed slaves was ruthless. He would instruct his white assistants to pile the dead bodies in a stack. They would either burn them or load them up and take them into town to the dead slave dumping site.

Most of the time, it would take days or weeks for the bodies to be removed. The unfortunate, murdered slaves would decay in a pile, and the family members were forced to see this unforgivable neglect and disrespect for the dead."

Rose tells me these awful events, and even though she did not have the life of her ancestors, it is as if she feels the pain of each of them.

"Master Zyrous became one of the most successful slave traders in the country. At the time, Ocean Point was not the prestigious estate that it is now. The mansion was just the middle part of the house, but it was still one of the largest estates on the island.

The east wing and west wing were added on later. The east wing was built for entertaining, and the west wing was built for the family suites and the slave quarters. The slaves built this house with their own hands, and the worst part is they built their own quarters and torture rooms.

I can only imagine the angst that the strong, black slave men felt as they attached the heavy chains and shackles to the stone walls knowing that the wrists and ankles of their own family members would be trapped in them." She pauses to make sure that I understand the importance of the story she is telling. "This is the master's room where we are sitting now," she says and gestures her hands in a way that forces me to look around the plush room. "Beneath this room is room after room piled on top of each other, and that is where the black slaves were housed. Under our feet is where they slept on the cold stone ground and were tortured, beaten, starved, and raped.

Initially, the slaves were housed in a small house at the edge of the property, but as Master Taylor acquired more slaves the space was just too small. With the small house being so far from the mansion and so close to the ocean, many of the slaves escaped or attempted escape. If one of Master Taylor's slaves escaped, it was instant death with no trial. His favorite execution was being burned at the stake right in the backyard here."

She explains this to me, and when she mentions the small house at the edge of the property my thoughts automatically wander to my father. I am sure that the tranquil little cottage he has been hiding in for more than a decade is the original slave quarters. I immediately feel disappointment in him all over again.

"So this is when the construction of the west wing was started. He designed the west wing for a very specific reason." She stops again and looks down, and then after a moment of mourning, she raises her head and points to a door in the corner of the room. The door is strangely camouflaged with the wallpaper that covers the wall.

"There is a passageway that is on the other side of that door, and it was designed so that the master could have easy access to his property at will. When I say the word property, I am not referring to the structure that was deeded in his name. The property that I speak of refers to the Negro slaves that he owned. He would slip quietly through that door late at night while Miss Martha slept and visit the female slaves. He would beat and rape them. If they resisted his violent attacks, he would kill the women either instantly or wait to viciously kill them in front of the other slaves. He would gather the female slaves and force them to witness their mother, sister, or daughter be whipped, beaten, and eventually burned to teach them a lesson.

I have listened to these stories so many times from the proud black women that I have known in my lifetime, and do you know the one thing they always would tell me?" She stops her story and smiles. I realize that she is not really asking me a question. She is building her story up and drawing me in. "They say that rarely did the black female slaves scream as they were being beaten. Regardless of the unbearable pain, they remained strong, and that my dear is something that every woman, no matter what color, should be proud of."

As heartbreaking as Rose's recreation of the past is, I enjoy the fact that she is able to find a sense of strength and pride in the women of her color.

"They tell the story that the rooms closest to Master Zyrous's room were where the women were housed so that he did not have far to travel. These black women were his property, and they knew it. Most complied just to spare their lives. The most upsetting part for me is that many of the black female slaves were children, and it did not seem to matter to the master. He took these children's innocence time after time.

He was so menacing that he would even have fancy parties in the east wing, and after the men were full of spirits he would offer the women to his guests. These drunken men would sneak away from their wives at the socialite events and stumble down the passageway. They would attack and rape the Negro women and children all for their amusement.

The walls of this mansion have been witness to appalling images and have not forgotten what this family has done. The next morning if any of the women were dead, he would order the black male slaves, sometimes even these women's fathers, husbands, or children, to haul their loved ones outside and toss them into the pile of the rest of the decaying Negro bodies that lost the battle against Master Taylor. It was a gruesome scene."

I know the rooms that Rose speaks of. These are the rooms that Lucy and I found on that winter day so many years ago. That was the first day that I stepped into my very own torture chamber. Now I know that the very room I was held in for so many months had been the scene of the terrible actions that my ancestors inflicted on the innocent. It makes me ashamed of my heritage.

"These rooms wind all the way down and end at the very room that your mother held you captive in. Your hands were trapped in the very shackles that my ancestors were held hostage in as well. The room where you were imprisoned is the last room before the outside, and only steps from that doorway is where the dead bodies were tossed out like trash.

The staff here in the past years had reported a foul smell that would engulf the room that they were in while cleaning the west wing. I believe that it is how the dead Negroes remind the family of the torture and disrespect that was inflicted on them."

As she speaks of the foul smell that has traveled to the west wing, I can vividly recall the rank and foul smell that at times seemed to seep underneath the door of the slave quarters that I was trapped in. I remember the smell at times being so overwhelming that I would vomit. After my pregnancy progressed, the smell would be unbearable. I always just blamed my nasty rat family or my waste bucket, having no clue of the ghastly murders that occurred under this roof.

"Well, Master Zyrous Taylor's good fortune eventually did change. You see, he took a liking to one of his black female slaves named Eshe. She was a beautiful black woman and was very strong. It was said that she could do the work of three men. Master Zyrous wasn't just fond of her because of her hard work. He also took her on as his mistress. Yes, he raped many of the slaves, but there was something different about

Eshe.

She had no choice but to comply with his lustful intentions. He was the master. She gave into Master Taylor's sexual demands knowing that she did not have a choice. She played whatever role the master wanted her to, but the master did not know that she was in love with a black male slave named Nanji. He was a skilled carver. His hands carved most of the doors here at Ocean Point. Master Zyrous admired his work and worked Nanji hard. There are a lot of doors in this old mansion.

Neither Eshe nor Nanji were ever for sale. Master Taylor saw their value and kept them for himself. The two were secretly married to each other, not legally of course, but they had a bond stronger than most folks that were married. They had a love affair that would be impossible for most.

Master Taylor would breed his strongest slaves to produce children that he could sell. Even though he never bred Eshe because he wanted her all to himself, he bred Nanji. Nanji had skills that he thought would be valuable to market in his offspring. Eshe had to endure the reality that the man she loved was forced to breed and bring forth children from other women. Many times she was obligated to help raise them until they were old enough to sell. Nanji had to accept the fact that his beloved Eshe was repeatedly raped by the master.

The life that these two had to live was beyond the definition of cruel, but they managed to accept their realities and continue a love affair that others envied. They kept their bond a secret because if Master Taylor would have found out about the two he most likely would have murdered both of them."

Rose pauses as she seems to reflect on the love story of Eshe and Nanji. When Rose speaks of them my mind wanders to Angel and the hardships that we have to endure to be together. I can feel Eshe's passion and longing for Nanji. I can only imagine how hard it must have been for Nanji to know that the woman he loved was being raped by his master, and there was nothing he could do about it.

"Well eventually Eshe became pregnant, and knowing the paternity of the baby would be impossible until it was born. Eshe was a very clever woman and hid her pregnancy from the master. When she gave birth to a baby girl, it was clear that the baby was a Taylor because of her light skin. Eshe and Nanji loved the baby regardless of who the biological father was and hid the baby along with the help of the other slaves. They named her Halla which means 'a gift from God.'

One night, Master Taylor came for Eshe unexpectedly and found little Halla nursing on her mama. He ripped the baby girl out of Eshe's embrace and held the newborn in the air by one leg. He pulled a knife out of his pants, and he split the helpless little baby's throat. He held Baby Halla in the air until she bled to death and did not have any life left in her. He said that he would not have a mulatto child carrying on his bloodline.

Eshe had to sit there and watch her baby girl be slaughtered like a pig. It is said that you could hear Eshe's screams all the way into the east wing. He took the baby's limp, tiny body and threw it on top of the stack of decaying bodies outside of the door where you were held.

The next morning when Nanji found out what Master Taylor had done, anger filled this man's soul. He waited for Master Taylor, and when he saw him five of the male slaves could not hold Nanji back. He beat Master Taylor almost to death, and he would have thrown him on the pile of decaying slaves if Master Taylor's army of white men had not heard his cries for mercy from Nanji's hands. These were the same hands that Master Taylor had placed such extreme value on, and now they were almost the hands that took his life.

Master Taylor ordered Nanji the most painful death imaginable. He cut off his hands for hitting him and then beat him, whipped him, and burned him until he was almost dead. They let him lie there for hours, suffering and slowly dying. Eshe and the other slaves were helpless while they watch their beloved one suffer in agony.

Finally, when the white men thought that he was near death, they hanged Nanji by the neck from a tree in the back yard. They forced all of the other slaves to watch this just to teach them a lesson. They left his body hanging there until it decayed almost to bones."

Rose becomes silent, and I can see the effect that retelling this story has on her. She glances at the picture of Zyrous Taylor hanging on the wall, and I can see pure hatred in her usually soft, loving eyes. I cannot imagine how hard it has been for her to dedicate her life to serving this family for so many years after what was done.

"As I said before, Master Taylor's good luck was about to change. Eshe was not only hiding her love for Nanji and her new baby girl. She had a secret that has affected and changed the lives of every Taylor since then. Eshe practiced Hoodoo. Hoodoo is very common in Africa, and the slaves brought their beliefs with them when they came over on the ships. A lot of Africans practiced Voodoo, which is a religion based on

Christianity. Hoodoo is a practice of magic and spells. Many people get the two confused, but they are very different.

The black slaves knew to hide their practices from their masters because the white man considered Hoodoo to be black witchcraft. If they were caught conjuring they would be instantly hanged or burned at the stake. Eshe was so skilled in her practice that she was considered to be the Hoodoo expert at Ocean Point. Her power was great and well respected by the other slaves.

As I said, Hoodoo is the practice of magic and spells with a theory all of its own. It is known that by combining the power of the spirit with the power of nature that the conjure doctor is able to move mountains. Since the slaves were not given proper medical care, they would come to Eshe for remedies, and through the power of conjure and sacrifices she would heal the ailments. Hoodoo is mostly used to heal and change bad fortunes into good, but there is a very dark and scary side to this practice as well. When Hoodoo is driven by revenge, a Hoodoo doctor can cast spells and curses that are impossible to break.

The rage that Eshe had growing inside of her became suffocating. Late one evening, Eshe along with several other black slaves conjured a spell. The story is that she and the others chanted all through the night asking every dark spirit to rise and aid them in casting the darkest spell ever known. She pulled the dark from the Hoodoo and put an evil curse on the Taylors.

The curse was to affect everyone born that had a drop of Taylor blood in them. The curse called out to the dark spirits and wished for painful and unexplained deaths, mental illnesses, immoral behaviors, and unattractive offspring. She conjured that the men would become weak and walk the immoral life of a demon, and the women would become bitter. Her spells went even further to ensure heartache on the Taylor family for generations to come. She added a spell that caused grief and torture to anyone outside of the blood line that was connected to a Taylor or brought any joy, love, or happiness to one.

Eshe was so full of wrath that throughout the evening of chants she did not leave out one wicked spirit to call on. She even cast a spell on anyone who was born under this roof to suffer the same pain and anguish that her little Halla did. It appears that the only people who have a connection to this family and go unharmed are the servants. She also cast a spell to remind the Taylor family of their wrongdoings to her and her people by always giving them a sign of why death continued to knock at Ocean Point's door. She conjured that before each death a black raven would make itself seen. Unfortunately, Child, many black ravens have circled the estate in past years."

Rose tells of Eshe's curses and spells with such conviction that even a disbeliever would consider them to be true. I am captivated by Eshe's story. It is hard to believe that this could really be true and actually have happened, but so many of the aspects of her story fit into the very same things that I have felt and heard since I was a child, especially when I was trapped in the slave quarters. I heard the chants of the conjure, the voices of children, and screams of torture. Could this actually be possible? Does this explain why my mother and father have abused and neglected me? Is it from Eshe's curse? Does this mean that the fears and experiences that I had a few years back could have been real and not the imagination of a scared girl?

Could it be true that a demon was following me in the hallway? Is it possible that the gardens were alive and seducing me to enter only to confuse me and scare me? Did the trees really attempt to kill me as the icicles stabbed the ground around me?

All of this time I have dismissed my fears of Ocean Point, and now after hearing the story of Eshe, I am not so sure that these events were not just in my overactive imagination. Even with knowing the horror of the real possibility of the house being cursed, where is the connection of my treatment from my own parents? I need to know more than what happened hundreds of years ago. I need to understand why my life here has been so scandalous.

"As you know, I was born into this house just like you were. My distant ancestors were caged below us and treated like animals. These stories of Eshe have always been a part of this house's history. When I was a child, my mother would tell me that these stories were just rumors made up from idle minds to stir up trouble and pain. As many times as my mother dismissed my fascination with the legend of Eshe, when she was on her death bed she looked straight into my eyes and told me that she knew that the stories of Eshe were true. She admitted that she had seen her in the hallways and would hear Halla's cries in the night. I guess that she just had to release the fear of the darkness in her heart before she met her maker."

"Rose, what happened to Eshe?" I ask.

"Child, nobody really knows. There are different stories about what happened to her. One is that the pain and darkness took a hold of her, and she just could not go on any longer. It was rumored that she jumped off of the cliff at the edge of the estate into the ocean and disappeared. Another story is that Martha Taylor, Old Zyrous's wife, knew of her husband's affection for Eshe. When she found out about baby Halla, she killed Eshe in fear of another offspring from her husband's seed.

The one that is most often told and most incredible to understand seems to be the one that most believe to be true. After some time had passed, the constant mourning of Eshe's lost love and child became too much. Her pain had turned black, and the revenge of the curse on Ocean Point and the family was not enough.

They say that Eshe alone conjured again for hours, some say days, being revisited by all of the dark spirits that aided her curse on the Taylor family and Ocean Point. During this conjure, she connected with the most powerful one of all whom she asked to resurrect Nanji and Halla from the dead. Once her family was back together, they disappeared into the walls of Ocean Point. The stories say that they live in these walls and watch the pain and sadness that her spells inflict on the family.

The legend is that the heartbeat and breath of the house are Eshe, Nanji, and Halla. I am not sure what I believe, but I do know that I have witnessed firsthand the despair that this family has endured. I know that the story of Eshe is true. I also believe that there is evil living in this house. I hate to think of her in this way, but Child, sometimes when the people whose hearts are made of gold are stripped down to nothing, they change," Rose says, and then she rises and starts to walk towards the door that leads to the secret hallway where the slave quarters are. "Come on, Child. You need to come with me," she tells me and motions for me to follow her.

"Rose, I don't know if I can go with you."

I am hesitant from the intimidation of going into the duplicates of the room that I was tortured in. I have been doing everything in my power to forget what happened to me in the slave quarters, but I am not sure that I am tenacious enough to live my nightmare over again. I also regress because I now know that these spirits have some sort of special connection to me because they speak to me, and no one else can hear them. This haunting knowledge is frightening to me. The combination of being ashamed of my ancestors and the thought of reliving the torture that both the slaves and I endured in the blackness of the quarters makes my feet not want to move.

"Coral, you wanted to know what happened here, and now you know some of the story. I think it is important for you to pay your respects to those who suffered," she says, and I can see that my hesitation has disappointed her and almost made her angry.

I want to show respect for her and her ancestors, but I am not sure if I can handle seeing those rooms. I stand and walk towards Rose, knowing that I need to find a way to be strong even if for no one else but Rose. As I prepare myself to relive the past of the tortured slaves, I keep thinking about what she just said. I know some of the story. Is there more to this story than just Eshe? Is there more about my family that Rose has to tell me?

She opens the door, and we enter the secret passageway. She reaches for a gas lantern that sits on a ledge and turns the light on. There is a small amount of sunlight that comes through the small windows of the passageway, but the sunlight alone would not be enough.

As we descend down the passageway, I envision Zyrous holding the same lantern as he sneaks down to fulfill his sick, manly urges. Rose does not realize that I have been here before. This is the same passage that Lucy and I found the day we went exploring, and I heard the screams of someone being tortured. Now that I know the story of the black slaves, I wonder if it was the house reliving the past and not Mother torturing someone. That was my original thought back then, but now that seems silly. Who would Mother have been abusing other than me?

The passage is dark and full of spider webs. I wonder if my little spider friend that betrayed me is somewhere in this hallway. There are several flights of stairs that extend down in a circular pattern before we even reach the first room. I am assuming that this was designed to conceal Eshe's screams as Zyrous assaulted her. It is hard to know that Martha, his wife, was laying asleep in the bed right above us while her husband brutally tortured Eshe and the other slave women and children.

We stop at the first door, and unlike before, these doors are not locked. The chains are on the ground with the giant, rusty locks on top of them. She opens the heavy door, and the creaking sound it makes is so daunting that it sounds like a scream. An immediate gush of dusty air blows through us, causing us to cough. It seems that these doors have been sealed for centuries, and the dust was just waiting for a chance to escape the cramped space. What if the gust of dusty air was a warning from Eshe to stay out of her room?

We enter the room, and it is very similar to the room at the bottom of the house where I was held prisoner. There are chains hanging from the stone walls and several piles of old, worn-out quilts scattered throughout.

"It is hard to really know, but I believe that this was Eshe's room. The blankets on the ground were the only bedding that was provided for the slaves. The only lights were candles that would quickly burn out. Sometimes it would be days before they would be replaced. The slaves had to sit in the dark. If they needed to move, they had use their hands to guide against the stone walls, that is if they were not in punishment and chained up over there," she says as she points to the heavy, restricting chains that dangle from the jagged stones. She moves to the center of the room. She stops and looks at the floor. "This is believed to be where Halla was slaughtered."

She points down to a very faint, reddish-pink stain on the concrete floor. I reach down and rub my stomach. I feel overwhelmingly sad. I can imagine how these slaves must have felt alone in the darkness of these cold rooms. I had experienced the same when my amber light burned out many times when I was jailed just as they were.

Rose is somber and thoughtful. I want to move around the room and see where Eshe might have slept, nursed baby Halla, and made love to Nanji, but I am cautious. I am also afraid of disrespecting her space if in fact this was her room. Rose turns to leave the room, and I follow. Just as I step over the doorframe, I can hear a very faint voice. I do not understand what it says. I look at Rose, and she seems unaffected. She apparently does not hear the muffled words that I do.

We begin down the stairs again and enter a room that appears that children dwelled in it. There are childlike markings on the walls, and the quilts that scatter the floor are smaller. The most haunting discovery in this room is in the corner. There is a small pile of old dolls. My heart feels heavy as I can visually see the little girls and boys trapped in this darkness hanging on to the dolls for security. Are the children who slept here the ones who spoke to me when I was chained in the same kind of shackles that dangle from these walls? I can hear the scurrying rats rustle around and imagine how frightened the little kids must have been of the disgusting rodents.

We exit the room and continue to descend further down. We pass room after room that housed the black slaves. I am sure that we are getting near the bottom of the house, and I fear that Rose is going to want me to revisit the room where I spent months being tortured. The closer we climb down, the more anxious I become. I suddenly hear the alarming sounds of chanting, the same noises that filled my room below. It is an unforgettable sound that you cannot forget. Once again, I look at Rose, and she does not seem to hear these sounds. Why am I the only one that hears these noises? Is it because I am a Taylor and was born in this house, and this is a part of the spell that Eshe casted? One landing from the bottom, we stop, and there is another door. Rose opens the door, and we enter. The chanting lyrics stop.

"This is believed to be where the slaves practiced Hoodoo. It was thought to be safe to where the noises of the conjures did not reach the master," Rose says and then begins to walk around the room as if she has been here a hundred times. The room is colder than the others, and it has a feeling of light and darkness at the same time. "This is where it is told that the curse was casted and where Nanji and Halla were brought back from the dead. Somewhere in this room is where the reunited family crawled into the walls of Ocean Point," Rose explains.

The stories seem like ancient folklore that most would find unbelievable, but as levelheaded as Rose is, it seems that she believes these stories have validity. The conjure room is on top of the room that I was held in. It is an unsettling feeling to know that all of this dark magic was performed right above where I lain helpless. I am glad that I did not know of these past events when I was trapped below, whether they are true or not. The fright of knowing these tales added to being unable to move would have given even more anguish than what I was already going through.

We leave the room and luckily begin to climb back up the stairs toward Zyrous and Martha's suite. Rose struggles to climb the stairs. The experience has physically worn her out. There is still a small amount of light from the setting sun that shines through the tiny windows. The thick, stale air makes it difficult to breathe. I think of how tired the slaves must have been after working fourteen hour days and then having to climb these stairs just to get some rest.

We enter the elegant bedroom again, and I can feel Zyrous's eyes on us. I have hatred for this man whose blood pumps through my veins. I want to take down his menacing picture and throw it from the top of Ocean Point. I continue to walk past the sadistic creature and hope that he is getting the punishment that he deserves in Hell.

I walk behind Rose, and we are now back in the west wing hallway. She closes the two hand carved doors. After the doors shut, I take my fingertips and run them across the masterful artwork that Nanji created. An odd feeling of fondness comes over me as if I am channeling his affection for Eshe, Baby Halla, and the pride of his work. Rose sees my fascination with the artistic doors.

"They are beautiful, aren't they?" she says and smiles with the pride of her ancestor's skills. I look down the hallway, and I am again confused with the immaculate condition that the west wing is in.

"Rose, who has been cleaning this part of the house?" I ask, remembering what filthy condition it was in the day that I snuck into the same hallway. Rose stops walking, and she turns to me. Her eyes grow serious.

"Before we discovered you in the slave quarters and months before that, I noticed your mother's gradual decline into the shadows that she is now trapped in. It was obvious that something very evil had taken an even tighter grip on her than it had before. I grew very worried about her and her mental state. She has been living with the curse for years, but something stronger and more powerful was beginning to happen to her.

She knew of the legend of Eshe but spent most of her life denying the stories to be true. Your mother's entire life has been cursed, and down deep she knew it but could not accept it. I think that is why she let the house deteriorate the way she did. I think she was trying to punish Eshe and make her not feel welcome. She shut down the west wing, thinking that Eshe and her family may remain where they belong in the slave quarters. Also, she was hiding her own secret back here as well." Rose pauses and looks away distantly.

"What secret, Rose?" I ask, now awestruck that there is more to the story.

"I will explain that part of your history in a little while, my dear," she says. Her voice and face tell me that the hardest part of the reveal has not even begun yet. "Anyhow, after your mother locked you away, she began to do bizarre things and began to speak to people who weren't there. One day, I could not find her, and I grew worried. Against my better judgment and the rules of the house, I went to look for her in the west wing. I found her on this very floor on her hands and knees scrubbing the grimy marble by hand.

When I called her name, she acted like she didn't even know I was standing right next to her. She was again talking to someone else. Her words were illegible, but I could see by her demeanor that she was following orders. I looked in every room up here, and they were all restored and cleaned spotless. When I finally got her to stop her conversation with the invisible person who was ordering her, she looked up at me and said that Eshe wanted the west wing clean. She kept saying it over and over like a mad woman.

I do believe that the stories of the curse may be true. I always had a little doubt, but seeing your mother on the floor cleaning and being commanded seems like a punishment that Eshe would find amusing. If Eshe is breathing through these walls and the spell is alive, then this is not the only time that Eshe has punished your Mother," she says, preparing me for the rest of the story that I know she dreads. Rose resumes walking but abruptly stops and turns to me. "There was one more thing that your mother said Eshe commanded her to do. She said that Eshe told her to unlock all of the doors to the slave quarters."

Rose's words are chilling. I do not see Mother believing the rumors of the past, but to think of her scrubbing the floors and following someone else's orders leaves me with no other conclusion but that Eshe is real and alive in the walls of Ocean Point.

Family Tree

Rose seems overwhelmed and exhausted from my tour of the slave quarters and suggests that we get something to drink and eat. She urges me to eat something, saying that by now my baby should be hungry. As much as I want her to continue the stories of my family and get to the part that gives me the explanations I need, I agree with her suggestion. I am starving, and it is important for my baby to get to a normal weight and prove the physicians wrong.

We wander down to the kitchen, and the house seems unusually quiet. There is no Rollins in the kitchen mixing together spices and sauces. Gretchen is not shuffling in and out of the rooms. Most importantly, there is no Mother stomping down the hall with her pointy boots looking for a way to punish me.

It is just Rose and me, and now I wonder if Eshe, Nanji, and Halla are with us as well. Rose makes us both a sandwich and retrieves a bowl of cut up, fresh fruit from the large, commercial-sized refrigerator. I have no desire to eat my meal in the stuffy dining room that was the scene of countless unpleasant meals shared with Mother. I was not even allowed to be a person at all of the family dinners. I was more like an unwanted figurine that was ordered to remain silent and motionless. I recall many times being backhanded simply because I was breathing or chewing too loudly.

After hearing the story about Eshe and especially with the evidence of Mother's recent possession, I cannot help but to speculate if she has been carrying out Eshe's wish with me for many years. Has Eshe been controlling Mother's thoughts and actions? It seems that the strict discipline that Mother enforced with me would be consistent with how the black slaves would have felt, restricted and controlled. If this is true then why would Eshe punish an innocent child? Is it because I am a Taylor, and because her Halla was hurt, all generations of this family are cursed to feel as she and her family did? I wish that the darkness that now controls her would allow her to feel my sympathy for her, Nanji, and Baby Halla.

We eat at the breakfast nook in the kitchen and remain quiet. Both of us seem to be caught up in our own thoughts. The sandwich hits the spot, and the fruit is a refreshing change from the hospital food that I have been consuming for some time now. Rose slowly puts our dirty dishes in the sink. It seems like she is taking her time. Something tells me that she dreads the rest of our conversation more than the stories of the curse and the brutal abuse of her ancestors.

She doesn't say a word and motions for me to follow her. Again, we ascend up the staircase. I wonder where she plans to deliver the rest of the family secrets that I have been trying to figure out for years. Instead of continuing down the hallway towards the west wing like we did before, she stops at my old bedroom and opens the door.

It feels strange to be back in this room again. I have changed so much in the seven months since I fled from the attacks and abuse. As I stand in this room again, it does not feel like I ever lived here, let alone spent most of my life in this room. I glance around the now foreign room, and almost everything is exactly like it was when I ran barefoot and battered out of Ocean Point all of those months ago.

My bedding has been changed and made up since the scuffle that I had with the monster that crawled into my bed. Other than that, what little possessions I was allowed to have remain the same. I think of the dainty little diamond bracelet that I found in the buried room in my closet, and I hope that it has not been discovered and is waiting for me to retrieve it from the bathroom closet where I carefully hid it.

No matter how much has changed since I ran away, I still cannot halt my mind of reflecting on that awful night that I escaped from this cursed house. Reminiscing on the events still gives me chills. I wrap my arms around my chest as if I am cold. Rose sits down on my bed. Sitting next to her is a box. Usually if she has a box it is wrapped in pretty wrapping paper, but this box appears businesslike. It is just a plain cardboard box that is worn and tattered like it has been hiding in an attic for many years. I can tell by Rose's posture with guarding the mysterious box that she is not ready to reveal what is inside.

She motions for me to join her, and she pats the spot next to her. As I pass by my closet, I feel a strange sensation to want to go through the hidden door and into the adjoining suite. I feel a pull to the other side of the closet. I smell the lilies as I did before, and the scent attempts to entrance me. I desire the safety of that oversized, comfortable bed and soft, luxurious pillows. I want to rest as peacefully as I did on that afternoon when I discovered the room. I want to sleep the night away, having only pleasant dreams of the day Angel and I will be reunited.

Rose makes a noise and breaks the spell that I seem to be influenced by. If the lilies are magical and have the power to enchant me, I do not think that it is Eshe's spell that captivates me. It is something brought to me from an untainted realm. The smell of the lilies has disappeared, and my need for them has been replaced with the thirst for knowledge of the untold. I join Rose on the bed.

"Coral, what I am about to share with you now will most likely disturb you more than the stories of the Negro slaves and maybe even more than Eshe's curse. I need you to promise to me that no matter how angry, hurt, or confused you may become that you will allow me to finish and tell you everything that you need to know. I have wanted to get these secrets out of my soul for so long," she says to me with a sad and concerned voice.

There is something in the way that she acts that shows me the sincere regret she has and been carrying with her for way too long. Is she concerned that her part in Ocean Point's history will change my love for her? I become disturbed to think that anything could be worse than a Hoodoo lady casting spells on your family and now living in the walls of your home.

"I have to start this history back many years ago when your mother and I were young girls. As I have shared with you before, Margret and I were very close once. She was my best friend. Your mother was very different than she is now. She was kind, loving, and had a heart of gold. She was never an attractive girl, but her charming personality seemed for the most part to distract you from her physical imperfections. Her parents, William and Annabelle Taylor, adored Margret. They sent her to the best schools where she learned the art of being a sophisticated lady. She also was very good with the books. She was incredibly smart and well-read. It seemed that Eshe had taken it easy on this generation of Taylors, allowing them to create a happy home. The only part of her curse that I could see then was the part about having unattractive offspring."

Rose is serious as she relays the history of my mother's childhood, but I cannot help but giggle at her accidental joke regarding my mother's unattractive appearance. Rose realizes what she has just crudely implied, and she begins to laugh as well. Hearing her robust belly laugh makes me think of how much I am going to miss Rose. When she gets tickled, she covers her mouth with her hand, and the laughter comes deep from her stomach and rolls all the way out of her covered mouth while her chubby body jiggles. Her laugh is infectious.

"Old Ocean Point was very different at this time as well. There was a huge staff of servants, and every room in the house was kept immaculate. The air that circulated throughout the house smelled of fresh flowers that were picked daily from the flourishing gardens. Expensive and beautiful artwork decorated the walls and was always a conversation piece for the guests who were lucky enough to be invited to a Taylor soiree.

Oh Child, the parties that were thrown in this mansion were the talk of the town. The Taylors spared no expense when putting on an event. They were remarkable events. Miss Annabelle was very active in charity work, and Mister William was revered as one of the most successful businessmen in New England. They were associated with very influential people. You would be impressed to know the names of guests that have been under this roof.

The grounds were kept in pristine shape with a staff of eight gardeners. Miss Annabelle loved flowers, and the backyard was full of blossoming foliage that was flown in from all over the world. Mister William had the gardeners create a maze of green plants and bushes in the backyard just for Margret to run and play in as a young child. The mazes were so elaborate that they had to be tended to daily.

The mansion and gardens were a far cry from the day that the Negro slaves were held prisoner here. One would have never dreamed of the vile incidents that took place on the very soil that we as children ran freely on. Some of my best memories are running through those mazes with Margret when we were just children.

The Taylors were very kind to the staff. They were generous with pay, and they made the staff feel like they were part of the family. They even allowed my mother and the other black servants to set up a memorial in honor of the slaves that were once a vital part of Ocean Point. Before I was born my mother and her fellow maids and cooks planted a small flower garden full of roses and all sorts of colorful flowers right outside the door of the slave quarters' entrance.

Miss Annabelle did not like the idea of the former slave quarters still remaining in her home and begged her husband to hire workers to remove the reminder of the past and replace it with more updated rooms. Mister William wanted no part in this renovation. He was not a superstitious man, but he did see Eshe's curse inflicted on his parents and grandparents. Even though he never admitted to his belief in the legend of Eshe, he feared making any changes that would disturb the restless spirits of the brutalized slaves. The rooms have been left for the most part as they were centuries ago."

As Rose explains to me of the Ocean Point that she knew as a child, it is exactly the way that I imagined it to be. I recall Rollins in the kitchen preparing meals and bragging of the days that he cooked for dignitaries. His rants about serving kings, queens, and presidents were not the foolishness of a senile man as Mother wanted me to believe. Why did she so desperately want to hide her wonderful childhood and experiences? With her strong belief in our family name, it is confusing that she wanted to keep the regal life of our family a secret.

I envy Rose for living here during such a wonderful time. I have envisioned the gardens blooming with exotic flowers as Rose speaks of. I have fantasized that the haunting gardens and mazes that once played mean tricks on me were at one time a child's playground. Why did so much change? When I was a girl, I would look out my bedroom window and wish that I could chase butterflies in the glorious gardens below me, but the gardens were neglected, and I was held captive in pain, secrets, and within these walls that contained me.

"It seemed that Eshe's curse may have been just folklore and silly rumors. Maybe she was allowing this generation of Taylors to enjoy some peace and to thrive. The talk of the sinister secrets died down in the community and among the staff that had witnessed Eshe's wrath years prior. Many began to doubt the validity of the spells and just summed up the strange occurrences before then as just coincidences. The elder black servants that had been a small part of the slavery and really understood their heritage and the power of a Hoodoo lady did not believe that she was gone. She was not, and in time Eshe's wrath once again warmed the hallways with sinister evil that dripped down the walls. It was clear that Eshe still lived among us.

Around the age of fifteen, your mother met a boy. He was so handsome, one of the most handsome boys on the island. His family was also a family of means. The two ran in the same social circle but had never met. Margret fell in love with this boy at first sight. The very popular boy did not even notice your mother and honestly did not even know that she existed. He definitely did not know of her feelings for him.

The problem was that he had more adoring fans than just your mother and was always seen with the prettiest girls in town, usually a different one each week. From the beginning, I did not trust this fine-looking boy. Margret just did not seem to be bothered with the rumors of his scandalous ways and still found a way to believe that someday he would be hers.

This did not stop her from daydreaming about him and longing for him to notice her. Even though she wasn't much to look at, her parents sent her to charm school, and there she learned how to woo a crowd. She was loved by everyone who met her. I think she thought that her personality and natural gift of charm would override her plain looks and that the handsome boy would fall madly in love with her.

There was eventually an event at Ocean Point that the boy and his parents attended. It was either by chance, or sometimes I consider that Margret was clever enough to arrange the event here at Ocean Point herself. Even though this boy came from money, his family had nowhere near the wealth of the Taylors. Not many in that time could ever compare to the lavish lifestyle that the Taylors were accustomed to. During this glorious time for the Taylor family, they were such significant players in Newport that if they invited you to one of their events, rejecting the invitation would be a mistake.

The day of the charity function came here in the east wing, and the boy that Margret was now obsessed with stood in the foyer. One would assume that Margret would be nervous and shy around this handsome boy, as most teenage girls are this way around their crush, but she wasn't. She strolled right up to him with more confidence than a beauty queen would have and began a conversation. To everyone's surprise, Margret and the boy started dating after that day. They would be seen at the elite gatherings together, and it became clear that they were an item. I felt so sorry for your poor mother because the rumors began to fly around this close-knit community that this boy was handsome enough to have his pick and that since he chose Margret, it simply had to be for her money.

Margret paid the rumors no mind despite her physical deficiencies. She was tall and lanky and did not have the curves that the women were desired to have. Her facial features were thin and long. She seemed not to be able to gain control of her unmanageable hair, and she dressed very conservative.

She disregarded the rumors and continued to shower him with

affection and gifts. She truly believed that these rumors were just the talk of girls that were jealous of her and wished that he was their boyfriend. I think down deep she knew that her boyfriend was not honorable towards her, but her desire for him outweighed his indiscretions."

As Rose paints a picture of Mother, I have a hard time seeing the woman I know as a cheerful girl full of hopes and dreams. I struggle to understand how a woman that now believes that all men are weak and that the devil himself jumps into their minds could ever look at a boy the way that she did this attractive fellow. Maybe one of the reasons that Mother always wears her hair slicked back into a perfect bun is because she still cannot keep control of it. I can see the frustration that she must feel for not being able to control anyone or anything in her life. She even punishes her hair for not following orders by keeping it tightly restricted in a bun. I try to figure out the ending before Rose tells me, and all I can see coming is that this boy hurt her so deeply that she has never recovered. Since, she has punished my father and me for the mean treatment by her first love.

"The boy of your mother's dreams proposed to her on her eighteenth birthday, shocking everyone in Newport's high society. Of course, she gladly accepted, and I am sure that at this point she justified all of his wrongdoing as boyish mistakes. Her father was thrilled. He did not run in the same circles as the youngsters and had not heard all of the rumors. He saw this boy as a suitable match for his little girl. The striking boy wanted to marry quickly which left all of us believing the rumors of greed to be true. They did not marry immediately as they both wanted. The wedding was delayed for two years because that is how long it took Miss Annabelle to plan the lavish wedding for her only child.

Miss Elizabeth knew how to throw a party, demanding only the best that money could buy. With so many prominent people on the guest list, there had to be an extremely lengthy and advanced notice. Margret and her mother flew to Paris to get her wedding dress made by the top designer in the industry. Her dress alone cost more than most people's homes during those times. Her father built an enormous gazebo in the gardens just for his daughter's ceremony. The two odd lovebirds were married right outside in the backyard. The day of the wedding, there were thousands of flowers imported from the Caribbean that covered the wooden posts. There were so many beautiful flowers hanging from the beams that it appeared the bride and groom were standing under a waterfall of flowers. There was not even a speck of the white paint from the structure showing."

I am taken back knowing that Mother was married before my father. I know this man she is speaking of is not the man that I have known. There is an apparent age difference in my mother and father, and I am sure that he would not have been old enough then to marry. I am intrigued with the life that Mother had before meeting my father. Knowing the history now, it is clear that something happened to her first husband. Did Eshe's curse come back? Did her curse take the love of Mother's life from her, and this is why she is full of so much hatred and malice?

"The big day came, and Margret was ecstatic. She got the man of her dreams, and her wedding was considered the grandest event that Newport had seen in years. There were over six hundred guests in attendance. The estate was full of the most powerful people in the world. I do not think Margret really even cared how spectacular her wedding was. She just was smitten with this man and could not wait to become his wife.

She put the big, fluffy gown on, and I think that was the first time in her life that she ever felt pretty. I could see it in her face. She looked happier than I had ever seen her, and even with her unusual features, her happiness made her beautiful that day. I was so happy for her despite my reservations about this boy's seemingly ill intentions.

The event went off without a hitch. Everything was perfect. Margret was glowing, and the guests were having a fabulous time. This was the best day of her life until a little while into the reception. I think that this is when the curse of Ocean Point reared its ugly head once again, and since that day it has spread its darkness more aggressively than ever before. I do not know why Eshe would have chosen this day to return darkness and despair to the Taylors. Maybe it was the extravagant wedding or the overall happiness that the family was feeling, but I do believe that it was the moment that changed the course of your family back into the darkness.

Dinner had been served, and the bride and groom had their first dance. It was time to cut the mile-tall cake, but the groom was nowhere to be found. Margret handled her new husband's disappearance with such grace and elegance that I do not think any of the guests even knew there was a problem. The staff knew what was going on behind the scenes. The superstitious minds of the workers immediately began to scurry around and speak of the return of the curse. The rumors got so farfetched that many thought Eshe had sucked the groom into the walls of Ocean Point. I knew different. I saw this boy for what he was, a money-hungry, cruel man, and I knew that this was not going to end well for Margret. I have never believed that the curse of Eshe made this man immoral. I think that he came into this house as sinister as he left," Rose says and pauses.

She has a strange look in her eyes like she has a personal connection with Mother's scheming first husband. Her eyes are full of so much anger that you would think she is telling her own story and not Mother's. I am afraid that this man's actions may have touched Rose in a way that she has not put to rest even after all of these years.

"In front of her guests, Margret remained calm, but as soon as she slipped out of the ballroom she became overwrought as she searched for the man that she just married. Her big day soon turned into a very sorrowful day. After searching suite after suite, she finally found her new husband. He was in one of the unoccupied guest suites in the heat of passion with her maid of honor.

Poor Margret was heartbroken, but she did not openly blame or get angry with her husband. She was enraged with her friend and became insistent that she was responsible for his immoral acts. She was convinced that he was trapped by her manipulation.

I think down deep she knew the truth, but this train of thought was easier on her heavy heart. This thought process has stayed with Margret all of these years, and as the story goes on you will understand what I mean.

After discovering her new husband in the arms of another woman only a few hours after getting married, she had to pull herself together. They had still not done the tradition of cutting the cake together. I don't know how that girl did it. She put on a show for the influential guests at that party, and no one ever suspected that anything had just happened. I think that is when her husband realized that he could do whatever he wanted, and Margret would always protect him."

At this point in Mother's story, I would expect her first husband to already be gone. Rose still has not revealed this man's name. Her deliberate attempt of concealing the name of the mystery man confuses me but has pulled all of my attention to every word she speaks.

"After a very short amount of time, it was clear to everyone, and this time even Margret, that her new husband did not feel any attraction for her and that his attraction was the Taylor fortune. The rumors never ended about the numerous affairs, parties, gambling, and drinking while Margret sat at home and waited for him.

Her father at this point had become ill with another Taylor unexplainable disease and was suffering immensely. His illness prompted him to turn most of the Taylor family business over to his new son-in-law. The financial security that Margret's husband now had enabled him to quit playing the game of doting husband and not care what Margret knew of his behaviors outside of the marriage.

Margret's desperation to make this man love her consumed her. All of her attention was on him, and she even neglected her father in his final days. The obsession for this man to love her had taken control of her. One morning at breakfast, she shocked all of us, even her uncaring husband, by announcing that she was pregnant. He grew angry and stormed out of the room with Margret chasing after him. I believe Margret thought that a baby would make him love her and might would keep him at home more.

If this indeed was her plan, it did not work. This caused him to stay gone more and come home even more intoxicated. During what should have been a special time in her life, she was lonely and felt isolated. During her pregnancy, her father passed away, and this left her husband with complete control of the Taylor money. Timing was perfect because he had just blown all of his family's money on bad deals, women, and partying. He left his parents destitute and did not seem to care.

The evening that Margret went into labor, her husband, as usual, was out. The family's midwife was called, and shortly after her arrival a baby boy was born. She named the baby boy Jefferson. Jefferson's father had still not arrived when Margret labored to bring his first son into the world. Around sunrise, he arrived home and was drunk. He stumbled throughout Ocean Point in the obnoxious manner that we had all grown accustomed to. When he entered the bedroom and saw that Margret had given birth, he did not react the way that she had hoped he would.

Poor Margret was exhausted from giving birth and was cradling her newborn baby. She was so excited to show her husband his first son. He looked at the two in bed and callously said that he was going to sleep in another suite because he had a meeting the next morning and feared that Margret's son would keep him awake. He never once acknowledged that little Jefferson was his son as well. She was crushed, and the entire house could hear her uncontrollable sobs throughout the night."

I have a brother that I do not know about? Why would they hide him from me? I am beginning to understand Mother's pain a little bit better, but I still have not heard enough for me to forgive her.

"The next morning, the staff was allowed to visit the new mother and Baby Jefferson. Her eyes were swollen almost shut from the endless tears. It had appeared that she had not slept the entire night. She began to talk strangely, almost as if the physical and emotional drain had made her delusional. Her words were jumbled and did not make sense. She kept pointing at the window, and she seemed terrified. She held her baby strangely as if to protect him from us. All of a sudden, she began to scream and point out of the window. We all turned and looked at the window that seemed to be tormenting Margret, and flying back and forth was a black raven.

Immediately, I knew from her body language that she displayed when we entered the suite that she was holding her dead baby. I reached for the baby boy swaddled in a baby blue blanket, and Margret resisted and began to fight me, trying to keep the baby in her arms. One of the male servants assisted me and held Margret until she was helpless and released the baby to me, I looked down at the tiny baby, and he was blue. Life had left him."

Rose tells this part of the story, and I can see that the experience upset her. Maybe this incident alone is why Rose has remained by Mother's side as her constant, loyal employee even when she did not agree with Mother's insane behavior. I have no idea why hearing of my mother's hardships and pain could cause me to have any sympathy for her considering that she just tried to kill me and my baby, but I do feel for this woman. I hurt for her loss, and I hurt for the cruelty that she had to endure from her husband. I am also sad to know that I had a brother that passed away that I never got to know.

"This is not the last time that Margret saw the black raven at her window. I thought that after the experience she just had with the lack of human compassion that her husband showed her during the birth and death of their child that Margret would finally put her offensive, uncaring husband out of the house.

I was disappointed when she kept trying to make her husband happy but couldn't. His drinking and womanizing ways got worse, and her desire for another baby got worse. I think that at one point she did not mind her husband to come home drunk because I think then she knew that she would have a better chance of him performing the acts to conceive a child.

Altogether, your mother conceived and lost five children. Not one of the babies lived past three years old. The curse was attacking Margret, and it could not be stopped. Everything that the curse said it would do it did within the five lives of her children. There was sudden death, deformities, and long, painful suffering inflicted on the innocent lives. I was always frightened of the rumors of Eshe's curse, but after seeing how dark and evil the spells really were as I watched these children die year after year, I do not doubt the power of a Hoodoo lady.

Even with seeing the black raven so many times and suffering the deaths of all of her five children, this is not what changed Margret into the evil woman that she became."

I am dazed at Rose's revelations regarding my mother and all of the siblings that the curse has denied me of knowing. Hearing the story of these five little lost lives gives me an explanation for the five tiny graves that I found in the cemetery. I recall my overactive mind when I was younger and under Mother's cruel and senseless abuse actually entertaining the idea that the buried little bodies may have been my brothers and sisters. My instincts were right, but my thoughts of Mother murdering them were false.

Now I question if the sweet little voices that called to me to play with them while I was hidden in the slave quarters were not slave children but instead my own siblings. I remain unsure of where I fit into this family. Rose keeps talking about Mother's husband then and the five children that she gave birth to and lost, but when do my father and I come into the picture?

"The day your mother changed and let the darkness take her soul was the afternoon after burying her fifth child, David. Most would think that watching your baby being lowered into the ground would push you over the edge, but the death of David was not the trigger that changed Margret. It was a knock at the door.

All of the guests had just left from paying their respects to the loss of young David, and there was a knock at the door. Margret just happened to be walking by and answered the door. When the door opened, she saw the woman that she caught her husband with on their wedding day, her former friend and maid of honor. As upsetting as it was to see a former friend who betrayed her, the only thing more appalling was seeing a little boy standing in the doorway that was the spitting image of her husband.

The little boy was absolutely precious. He had blonde hair and bright blue eyes. He had the most adorable dimples that everyone fell in love with. Instantly, Margret knew that this was her husband's son. If this hurtful realization was not enough, the boy appeared to be around three years old, the same age as the son that she had just buried.

The mother of this little boy told Margret that she could not take care of him any longer and that it was time for his father to take on the responsibility. The little boy's mother just left and abandoned her son with Margret."

Rose pauses and looks down. She seems to be shaken emotionally and is having a hard time finishing the story that confuses me, fascinates me, and leaves me to still wonder where I fit into this family. How could I have lived my whole life without knowing that my mother was married before? Even worse, how could I have never known that I had five brothers and sisters? How did Mother have the ability to love, want, and mourn for my siblings but has never loved me? Why was I not her little miracle and a blessing from God because I beat the curse?

"Coral, what I am about to tell you about this little boy is probably going to anger and upset you, but you have to promise me that you will remain calm and hear the entire story. You have come this far, and you need to know everything," she says to me as her eyes plead with me. The tone in her voice has changed from being factual to being remorseful. "Joseph is the name of the little boy that was left on the porch."

She says this and then stops speaking and waits for my reaction. I do not understand. The boy has the same name as my father? Many people have the same name, so I do not know what the big secret is. Rose sees that I have not made the connection needed for her to continue with the story.

"Child, the little boy is the man that you call 'Father' today."

I try to process this part of a very confusing family tree. If the little boy is my father, then Mother is not my mother. I feel lost. If Margret is not my mother, then who is? I become upset, and tears stream down my cheeks. I feel betrayed by everyone. Why would everyone who claims to love me play such sick genetic games with me? Furthermore, if I have no blood connection to Margret, and she is not my mother, then why has everyone allowed her to mistreat me and torment me all of my life? Why would Margret want to raise a child that is not hers? Most importantly, where is my real mother? I do not even raise my eyes up, and I coldly speak in the same tone that I spoke to the doctor that wanted to eliminate my baby.

"Who is my mother?! Where is my mother?!" I begin to scream at Rose.

I am angry with her for going along with such a horrible lie. I know that she is an employee, but she should have protected me and made this stop. She should have been a better woman and not gone along with what every evil game this family or curse has played on me. Where is my real mother? Is she hiding in the quaint little cottage with my father? I feel like I just lost my identity. I have no idea who I am now.

"Child, you have to let me finish. You need to know all of the facts before you make judgments. You are going get all of your answers with me now. Okay, child?" she says to try to calm me down. She reaches for my hand, and I quickly jerk it back to display my anger. "Please Coral, I know that you are hurting, but you need to hear the whole story," she begs. I do want to know more, so I do my best to simmer my anger so that I can at least find out who my mother is and why everyone has lied to me.

"Margret did her best to try to love Joseph as her own, but she just couldn't. Her husband, Alan, adored the little boy. He was his pride and joy and gave him the love and affection that he never gave the children that Margret bore for him. Alan was not the only one that had affection for the little guy. Margret's mother, Annabelle, took to him as if he was her blood grandchild. The staff would spend their breaks playing with little Joseph. He brought joy and laughter back into a house that had been devastated with the five deaths of Margret's children.

In Margret's eyes, it seemed like everyone was replacing her lost children with this bastard child born from her husband's betrayal. I think that this was partially true. Everyone saw little Joseph as a blessing because of his good health compared to Margret's innocent children that had to suffer and perish before their eyes. I hoped deep down that she would look at him as a gift from God and could find a way to love him. She was being given another chance to be a mother. I guess that the pain of losing her own children and the cruel way that Alan felt nothing towards the children she gave him but adored Joseph kept her unable to feel anything but jealousy.

Her resentment toward the little boy grew every day. By this time, Alan was out of control. He was making bad business deals and losing money left and right. The rumors of other women got worse when he was accused of sexual assault. His drinking became a daily routine, and he became nasty when he drank. Margret still tried to protect him and raise his son that was not even hers. Finally, she put her foot down and took the family business back over. She put her sadness aside, took the family money, and turned everything around. Margret turned out to be quite the businesswoman and was able to regain so much that was lost."

The connection that I have to this family is still foggy, but I acknowledge that Margret's first and only husband was actually my grandfather, my father's father, named Alan Jefferson Berringer. This means that my mother is actually my grandmother-in-law. This twist to my crooked family tree as of now leaves me motherless, and my father was never the husband of the woman that I have called "Mother" my entire life. Unfolding this part of my heredity also excludes me from having any Taylor blood in me. The curse obviously has not missed me even without me being a Taylor, so hopefully the reveal of my biological mother will soon be known and make sense with the lies and secrets.

"Margret became the woman that you know today during this time period. She began to abuse Joseph in some of the same ways that she has abused you. The former slave quarters that you were held hostage in is the same room that she put Joseph in time after time. He was only six years old when she started the heartless punishments with him. It was appalling to think of a six year old little boy being shackled alone in the dark for days. We did not know that she was punishing little Joseph as viciously as she was. When the little man of the house was gone for days, the staff was told that he was away at camps or educational trips. Alan was always out or intoxicated, and Annabelle's health had declined so rapidly that she was now bedridden. Margret took control of the house and everyone in it. Everyone feared her.

Joseph was different than you, Coral. He could not handle the mental and physical torture. He began to change. He withdrew himself from the world and eventually stopped speaking. He was constantly scared and was tormented with nightmares. We should have seen what was going on, but we would have never dreamed that Margret was capable of such brutality. Back then, she was more cautious and hid her treatment of Joseph. By the time you came along, she had such dominance over everyone that she did not care who knew how she treated you. In her mind, she truly did not believe that what she was doing to you was wrong. The Margret that I knew was gone, and her body was the playground for Eshe's curse. She became Eshe's servant and delivered the evil and darkness of the curse with her own hands. The darkness took control and has never let go.

Joseph's mental health grew worse each day. He began to try to take his own life. After the second attempt at ending his own life, he was institutionalized. With Margret becoming the cold, cruel woman that she became, Annabelle now decrepit and slowly and painfully dying, and little Joseph's mental instability, the staff was sure that Eshe was back and ruling the future of the family. Many of the servants became frightened, not because of a superstitious legend, but they were convinced that they had heard voices. Some even claimed to see Eshe and little Halla. Many dedicated employees quit. The remainder of us were running the house ourselves, but Margret expected the same work to be performed. She refused to hire anyone else, so we all worked like the Negro slaves did centuries ago."

As I listen to Rose, I have a new understanding of my father after knowing that he had gone through the same harsh punishments and abusive childhood that I had. Even with acknowledging how difficult both of our lives have been under Margret's thumb, I just cannot comprehend how he could allow this disturbed woman to raise me knowing what she did to him? I would never let her near my baby.

"Years went by, and Miss Annabelle passed away. Alan was so out of control that Margret was forced to withdraw from the charities and social events that the Taylors were accustomed to. His shameful behavior was a disgrace to the Berringer and Taylor names. Compounding the social stigma were the servants who fled the house with fear of the curse and took new positions with other Newport families. This is when the rumors of the sinister spirits and Hoodoo curse began to travel rampantly throughout the community again.

Despite the mental illnesses that Joseph had been struggling with since a young boy, he grew up to be a very intelligent young man. Leaving Ocean Point and entering a long-term residential treatment center saved his life. He went to school and had top-notch grades. It was time for him to start college. His doctors felt that he was cured of the mental instability that he suffered and released him to go to live a normal and prosperous life. His grades were good enough to get into the prestigious Vanderbilt University in Nashville, Tennessee. His grades were above average and allowed him entrance into many colleges, but the personal relationship that Annabelle had with the Vanderbilts, who owned a home on the island and attended many Taylor events, made Joseph a wonderful candidate for attendance at Vanderbilt. With his good grades and personal relationship between the families, he left for Nashville to begin his education."

The timeline that Rose explains is very believable, and I begin to get the full picture of Ocean Point. I can plainly see the deterioration of the family and Ocean Point coming in the near future. It is evident that Eshe's curse does not destroy the family overnight. It takes many generations of Taylors before her spells come to full destruction. The scariest part is that even with the latest events under the estate's roof being guided by the curse, I do not think that Eshe is satisfied or done. I do not believe that she will ever leave Ocean Point. This is her home. I question if this is what she wished for all along, a slow, painful decay of the house, souls, and spirits.

"About a year into your father's college education, it appeared that he was adjusting to life outside of the mental facility very well. He did not come back to Ocean Point, but he sent letters to the staff that had taken the boy into our hearts from the first time that we saw his sweet little face. He wrote about having friends, and he seemed to be coming into his own. We were proud of his success.

One day, we got a letter from Joseph that would change this family forever. We had already seen happiness, joy, misery, sadness, and death, but nothing prepared us for the coming events. He told us that he had met a girl. He had fallen head over heels in love with the southern belle. He informed us that he was going to come back to Ocean Point so that she could meet his family over Christmas which was only a month away. We knew when he wrote about his family that he was speaking about us, the servants."

I now anticipate the knowledge of who my biological mother is. I just want her to blurt out the identity of my absentee mother. I recognize that Rose has held this inside of her for so many years, and no matter how angry I am at her, I promised to be patient. I am going to give her more respect than anyone in this house has ever given me.

"Christmas was here, and the staff worked overtime to get the mansion ready for a guest. We had not seen a guest in too many years to count. We were so excited with the anticipation of Joseph and his new love's arrival. Finally, the front door opened, and in walked a rare beauty. The object of his affections was an absolutely stunning girl. She had long, wavy, strawberry-blonde hair and bright blue-green eyes that exuded kindness and a sweet innocence of a child. She would light up any room that she entered and was so naturally flawless that she turned heads everywhere she went. The most endearing quality of this girl with the undeniable southern accent was that she did not even know how beautiful she was, much like you, Coral."

Rose stops speaking, and I can see tears in her eyes. Why is she crying? It is evident that she is speaking about my mother. Why does this make her sad? I become bothered by her disposition when speaking of my real mother, the one I never have known. Rose reaches in the box sitting between us and pulls out a picture.

She hands me a picture of my real mother. When I see her pretty face looking back at me, I begin to tremble. I know this woman. She is the woman that had come to me when I thought I was hallucinating. Once, she came to me when I was in the room on the other side of my closet. I woke to her gentle face and in her embrace. She came to me twice when I was held captive in the slave quarters. She was watching over me, and I remember her telling me right before Rose arrived to rescue me to "hold on." I begin to cry uncontrollably because I now know that my mother is dead. I know that I will never know my mother. I know that I will never know what it feels like to have a mother that holds me and protects me. Rose does not try to console me. She allows me to cry freely without attempting to harness my anguish.

"Rose, was my mother's name Lily?"

I ask this because of the significance with lilies that has always seemed to soothe me and been present every time my mother has visited me. My question seems to stun Rose. It takes her a moment to respond.

"No Child, her name was Caroline, but her favorite flower was a white lily."

"How did my mother die?" I somberly ask. Rose seems to ignore my question and continues her story.

"We all instantly fell in love with Caroline, but of course, Margret could not stand her. She was convinced that she was not good enough to be a Berringer. She used the word 'undeserving' in describing sweet little Caroline. It was clear that she came from a poor family, but her charm outshined Margret's even when Margret was at her best. The charm wasn't taught at some expensive school. She just had a natural ability to win people over.

During the visit, Joseph announced that he had proposed to Caroline, and this news made Margret boil with rage. Joseph paid no mind to her open disgust with the girl from the wrong side of the tracks. During this visit and announcement, Alan had just left a forced stay by Margret at a rehab clinic, so he was more lucid than usual. He encouraged the two to move into Ocean Point and marry here in the gardens just as he and Margret had.

This support that the now sober Alan was extending to his only son enraged Margret more than I had ever seen up to that point. Margret began to argue the value of Joseph finishing his college education and that he should not just drop out over the first pretty thing that walked in front of him, but Joseph had more to share than just his engagement. He had dropped out of college months prior and began doing nonprofit work for the environment and the needy. Needless to say, this did not impress Margret. Even without him having the privilege of a Taylor bloodline she had built in her mind the importance of the Berringer bloodline.

The two young lovers desperately wanted to be together and knew that the best option for starting their new life together would be to move into Ocean Point. The security that the mansion provided them enabled Joseph to continue his work without the added pressure of supporting a household and his wife. He had received a donation from Vanderbilt to continue his work at a non-profit organization that studied sea life. Joseph never finished college, and that is why he became the marine biologist that Margret told everyone he was. His charity work was too much of an embarrassment to her now shady family, so she lied to make sure the family still looked prestigious to others."

I begin to glance at my closet. I know now that the room in there was my parents' suite. I slept in my mother's bed, smelled her favorite flowers, and woke up with her beside me. Rose sees my interest in the closet that separates the identical bedrooms with painted lilies on their walls. Rose narrows her eyes like I have been caught breaking the rules. I can see that she is curious if I know about my mother's room or not. Neither of us elaborate on the current questions that are on both of our minds.

"Alan wanted an elaborate wedding for Joseph and Caroline like the one he had here at Ocean Point. He was so clueless to the damage that he had caused to the family's name and reputation due to his improper and vulgar behavior. There would be no way that there could be such an elaborate and well attended ceremony with the rumors of the haunting of Ocean Point and his careless decisions.

That did not matter to Joseph and Caroline. They were not driven by materialistic things as the rest of the family was from past to present. Their love is what mattered, and a small, simple celebration in the garden was all they wanted. Margret was relieved with the couple's wishes due to the embarrassment that she thought Caroline brought to the family."

Rose again reaches into the brown box and pulls out another picture. I look at the picture and see that it is a picture of my mother and father on their wedding day. They were such an attractive couple, and I can see myself in both of them. My mother's dress was simple and elegant. She was so beautiful that she did not need a fancy dress. She was petite like me, and the white satin dress hugged her feminine curves perfectly. I notice hanging from her wrist the delicate diamond bracelet that I found in her room. I am taken back knowing that I have worn the very same bracelet that once was wrapped around my mother's wrist.

I see my mother and father in a loving embrace, and I can feel the love between them. It reminds me of Angel and me. Seeing such a loving couple makes me miss Angel terribly. I physically hurt with the separation that is out of our control. As I gaze at my parents, I wonder how I could have ever believed all of the lies about my birthright. How could I ever have believed that Margret was my mother? She is gangly, plain, and completely opposite of my genetically blessed parents and me. I guess when you are told something all of your life you accept it as the truth and don't have any reasons to question it. My quarantined life at Ocean Point aided in keeping me oblivious to the possibility that my whole life could be a lie.

"The week before the wedding, something changed in Caroline. Her constant bubbly personality seemed to turn to distraction. Everyone said that she was just getting wedding jitters and that it was natural for the bride to be nervous, but I sensed something different.

There had always been a definite sadness behind her bright eyes. I knew that this girl had not had an easy life, and I was sure that she was lugging around some past pain. Honestly, that hint of sadness made her even more endearing. It was evident that Caroline had a lot of depth in her soul, and it was expressed in her remarkable eyes. Margret sure didn't make her life easy here at Ocean Point. She was jealous of her beauty. When she looked at Caroline, she saw every woman who had caught Alan's eye. She still remained steadfast in her convictions that women that looked like your mother were to blame for Alan's immorality. Margret did horrible things to Caroline to try to scare her away. She even offered her money to leave town and never come back. Caroline did not accept the money and tolerated Margret's petty actions and insults. Even with the constant reminder that she was undeserving of being a Berringer, she married Joseph in a simple backyard ceremony.

Caroline seemed to become sadder with each day that passed, and I grew very concerned. It wasn't long after they married that the newlyweds announced that they were expecting. Joseph was delighted and publicly doted on his expecting bride. This fueled Margret's resentment towards Caroline even more. Watching Joseph treat Caroline the way that she had longed for Alan to react to her pregnancies made Margret fill with more hatred. Margret was beside herself knowing that Caroline was going to give birth to a Berringer.

This baby was you. You have asked me so many times when your mother, or Margret, began to hate you. The answer, my dear, is at conception. You were the reminder of her short comings. As the story continues, you will begin to understand Margret's hatred for you even more.

Alan had fallen off of the wagon again, and Margret spent most of her time paying people off and chasing after him and trying to keep his wild ways under control. Margret was not around much. She was so distracted with her ill-behaved husband that she left Caroline alone for the most part.

The day you were finally born, it was one of the happiest days I have ever seen at Ocean Point. The staff was scurrying around, anxious to take a peek at the new baby girl. Flowers began to arrive by the dozen, and the fragrances filled the house. Caroline's favorite flower, as I already said, was the white lily, and the house was adorned with the fragrance of the graceful flower. Come to find out, all of the bouquets were from Joseph.

We did not see any black ravens that day. Margret was so enraged from the joy that your little life spread through Ocean Point that she began to throw the vases of flowers across the foyer like a child having a temper tantrum. Even with all of the chaos that she was stirring up, everyone seemed to overlook her and focus on the new little girl that was breathing life back into an old mansion that had seen only heartache for so long.

Your parents and you would play on the beach and make sand castles. You and your mother would have picnics in the gardens. You would run through the mazes in the gardens and chase butterflies. There was a time that you had the kind of life that I know you thought you were denied of. If I had one wish left in this old body of mine, it would be that you could remember those lazy summer days. You were loved Coral, truly loved. I have always believed that the love you received then has given you the forte to become the woman you are today despite what we all did to you.

I was again beginning to think that the family's illnesses, hardships, and deaths were just coincidences. Eshe was just an old folklore that we black folks needed to hear. When I saw the healthy and happy little girl that you were, I knew that Eshe and her curse would never allow this blue-eyed, strawberry-blonde little girl to thrive and have such a wonderful life under Ocean Point's roof."

Hearing Rose describe my early childhood should make me happy, but instead, I am full of grief. I do not remember those days. The gardens that I remember frightened me. The only butterflies that I remember were outside of my window, and the only mother I know loathes me.

"For the first time in a while, Ocean Point seemed to be full of happiness again as it was when I was a child, but unfortunately, it did not last long. When you were almost three, you and your mother and father decided to take an afternoon cruise on the family sailboat. This was not unusual. The three of you would take pleasure cruises often.

This particular day, the sky was clear, and the sun was shining bright. The blissful, little family sailed off into the blue sea. About an hour into your leisurely cruise, a terrible storm suddenly surfaced at sea with no warning.

I remember that day like it was yesterday. Thinking back to it always leaves me with a horrible sense of distress and helplessness that I have never gotten past. I recall glancing at the window, and the beautiful, sapphire-colored sky had grown murky and black. In the distance, I could hear thunder, and I could see bolts of lightning pierce through the sky over the sea. It was a fear-provoking vision. I knew that my precious Coral was out there. I paced back and forth in hopes to see the three of you come running up the path.

I watched out the window for you, and when I saw that old black raven making circles around Ocean Point, I was instantly grief-stricken. I was hysteric, and my fellow staff members could not console me. We all stood on the sun porch and watched the spell-driven bird flap its black wings for hours. All of us stood together holding hands and grieved for what was soon to happen. We all knew that death was knocking on one of Nanji's hand carved doors.

Out on the sea, as soon as Joseph saw the heavens grow dark, he immediately began to turn the boat back to the mainland. The storm came too rapidly, and it was too late. Rain poured over the sailboat, and the vicious waves crashed into the small vessel. Joseph struggled to keep control. He yelled for Caroline to take you to the safety of inside the cabin. As the two of you stood to climb down to safety, your tiny foot slipped, and at the same time a massive wave rushed over the sail boat. Your small body was thrown into the angry ocean water. You helplessly floated in the middle of the violent waves. All they could see was your orange life jacket bobbing up and down in the cold, angry water.

There were not many things that your mother couldn't do, but one of them was that she could not swim. Despite her inability, when she saw her baby girl floating away from her she dove straight into the ferocious water to save you. I don't know how she did it. God must have been looking down upon you, but somehow she managed to get your freezing little body near the boat. Joseph reached out and Caroline pushed you as hard as she could until you were safely in Joseph's reach and pulled back into the boat. Joseph then reached out for Caroline's hand, but she just stared at him with the most heartrending look that could be imagined.

He began to scream at her to take his hand, afraid that the waves would wash her away, but she still did not reach for him. Instead, she mouthed "I love you," and she unsnapped her life jacket and perished in the water. It took Joseph years to relay what really happened on the boat that day."

I am so full of emotion. I grieve the loss of a mother that truly loved me, but I cannot even remember her. I am mortified as I envision the predators of the ocean feed off of her flesh. I feel completely destroyed to know that I will never know the mother that loved me enough to risk her own life. There must be somewhere deep inside me that remembers and loves the woman who carried me inside of her. My hearts breaks, not from anger of the senseless lies, but from a true longing and absence of someone who lives inside of my heart but I just cannot remember. Another part of me is irate with her. How could she leave me? How could she leave me with these unstable people in the house that she had to fear just as I did?

"Joseph was devastated and never recovered from losing his Caroline. He suffered from great mental illness with the death of your mother. All the hard work and progress that he made to recover from his childhood illness came back to him ten times worse. The day that they recovered your mother's body from the sea was his final breaking point. I had never seen a man so emotionally crippled to that degree in my life. I have seen a lot of heartache and illness in this house, but nothing has come close to the suffering of this man. He was mentally unable to care for you any longer, so the staff began to look after you and raise you ourselves.

Questions consumed Joseph about why Caroline took her own life. I think that is what wrecked him more than the fact that she was gone. It seemed like Eshe's curse was delivered on him as well. He went in and out of mental hospitals and struggled to remain sane. One day, he returned home from another stay at a hospital and tore his and Caroline's room, which he had not stepped in since that day at sea, apart out of anger and despair. During his rampage, he found her diary stuck underneath their mattress, and what he read in his wife's handwriting changed Ocean Point forever.

The diary spoke of her childhood and the terrible things that her own father did to her as a little girl. There was more hurt living within her than any of us knew. As he read her diary, it was apparent that she never was completely able to recover from her past. We soon found out what happened to trigger her unpleasant memories of the past and push her so far into a place of despair that she took her own life.

She spoke of Joseph and how in love she was with him. She explained how he was her savior and that her time as his wife and your mother was the only time that she could ever say she had happiness. When he reached the end of the diary, he finally understood what changed the happiness that she felt into so much torturous pain that she just could not go on. What poor Joseph read in that diary was more than he could handle."

As I listen to the love story of my parents, I think of them as a modern day Romeo and Juliet. Even with knowing the love between them was beautiful, it does not give my heart a slight bit of peace. The sting of being given my real mother today and then immediately having her taken away is unfair. Why could they not tell me of her years ago? I do not understand how my outcome would have been any different. It is clear that my father could not care for me and that I would have eventually ended up in Margret's custody anyways. Why the secrecy, betrayal, and lies?

Rose takes a long pause. I can feel the tension as it builds in the room. I become fearful of what she is going to say next. I cannot fathom what else there can be that causes her such a struggle to continue to tell me about my bent family tree and explain to me each of its twisted branches. She begins and stops her next sentence several times, and she begins to cry as she tells me the rest of the corrupt events.

"Caroline wrote that the night before their wedding, Alan came into her room. He had been drinking, and he attacked Caroline and sexually assaulted her. Her shame and humiliation kept her from telling Joseph. The situation was even more impossible to cope with because her rapist was her husband's father. I cannot conceive how hard it must have been on her to keep such an unbearable secret all wrapped up inside of her. That unfortunate girl had experienced years of sexual abuse and had learned how to cope, but this was different and was her breaking point."

Rose stops again and is so distraught that I am not sure she can continue. She stands and walks to the window and peers out as she wipes the tears from her now bloodshot eyes. It seems that she needs to distance herself from me to deliver the conclusion of the unbelievable history.

"The diary continued, and the words that Joseph read next altered this house forever. Caroline wrote that Joseph was not your father and that instead Alan was, Coral. Joseph's very own father was the actual father of his little girl. At that moment, not only did Joseph lose Caroline, but he lost you as well."

The words that leave Rose's mouth are too much. This cannot be true. How do I know that this is not another lie? If this is not another sick lie, then the truth of my genetics is revolting. If my DNA is composed of the people that have been revealed to me, this means that the man that I was told all of my life was my father is actually my brother.

It is not bad enough that I was lied to and never knew my biological mother, but now Rose is trying to tell me that my father is my brother, and the man that I thought was my dead grandfather is my biological father. She is telling me that I was conceived through an immoral act that was placed on my mother. Does this mean that Margret is right? Am I the child of the devil? Was I born from the serpent? Do I have evil inside of me from the evil seed that created me? I immediately think of my innocent unborn baby. Will it be born evil as well? I begin to scream and cry. I want to run out of this morally warped house and never turn back.

If I have to run to Vietnam and find Angel, I will. I do not want my baby anywhere near these criminals. I dash for the door, but Rose steps in front of me to stop me. I shove and push her, trying to remove her from my path, but she does not budge. She seizes my arms to gain control of my body as I cry and tremble. She looks me straight in the eyes, and her intense stare gets my attention. I begin to calm down.

"Coral, you have to sit down. There is more," she sternly says.

What more can there be? My entire family tree has been scrambled, and each branch is as crooked as the next. Out of defeat in knowing that Rose is not going to permit me to leave until she completely destroys me,

I return to the bed.

"By this time, there were more accusations of Alan's attacks on other women, and the authorities were getting ready to react. There was also an ongoing investigation alleging Alan's involvement in a money laundering scandal and tax invasion. Alan was in serious trouble, and the constant drinking had begun to take a toll on his health. Half of the time he did not even know who he was.

When Margret heard this shocking news regarding your paternity, she made decisions for everyone, and there was nothing that anyone could do. Joseph was in no mental condition to fight her, and neither was Alan. The servants that had been caring for you had no legal rights, so everyone was at her mercy.

Margret, still protecting her monster husband, took this news as the last straw. When Margret found out that you were the daughter of her husband, her hatred reached a new level. She came up with an insane plan to fake Alan's death. She even had a fake funeral and burial in the backyard. An empty casket is buried beneath that stone that has an evil name engraved on it. She was so clever and had enough money to keep people quiet that her plan actually worked.

Joseph was so overwhelmed with this new knowledge that he was admitted into a psychiatric center for many years. Joseph has never been able to return to the ocean since the day he lost his Caroline. His noble projects at sea ended, and that is when the lies about his work started to spare you the truth and allow Margret's plan to continue. All of this was Margret's idea. She had Joseph declared mentally unstable. She managed to get a power of attorney over him, and that is when you became her daughter. She was claiming to protect the family name, but she was really protecting her husband and your father, Alan.

She was unstoppable. She was determined to raise you with high morals and standards, but what she did was inject you with the mental anguish that she felt. She blamed you and your mother for every pretty woman that her husband ever cheated on her with or assaulted. She was so deranged that she still believed that he was provoked and that your conception was from the devil. She was convinced that innocent Caroline seduced Alan.

Margret had an unbreakable love for a man that never loved her back. She still does to this day. You, in her mind, were the product of every sin in this house. You were a reminder of the children that she lost and the women that her husband preferred. You are the image of the woman that she feels is responsible for the final downfall of her husband.

I stayed at Ocean Point for only one reason after these incidents happened. It was to protect you. I knew that I couldn't take you away. Margret would never have allowed it. Even though she had nothing but hatred for you, she had become so mentally ill herself either from the loss of her children, Alan's horrific treatment, or maybe it has been the curse all along, but regardless, she needed you. She needed to vindicate herself and the wickedness that now ruled her decisions. Torturing you would give her closure."

Rose retelling the horrors of my childhood and after all of these years giving me the explanation that I have needed to hear has given me an understanding of why I was treated the way I was. I spent my entire life thinking that something was very wrong with me, but the truth is that it was everyone else who had the issues. I was just the punching bag that Margret needed. I do not feel sorry for Margret any longer. I feel sorry for the children lost, my brothers and sisters, but she never deserved to be a mother. I would never wish hardship or pain on the babies lost, but I believe that they are better off in Heaven than with Margret and under the roof of this house. Just when I think that the story is over and that the history of this unscrupulous family is finally told, Rose begins to speak again.

"There is another part of this story, but it is my burden. I have been affected by the curse as well. Caroline was not the first and only woman that Alan attacked in this house," Rose says, and she timidly looks up at me. I see a terror in her as if Eshe herself is standing behind me. I already know where this story ends for Rose. "When Alan's drinking problem became a real illness for him, he began to come to my room in the night. He would force himself on me night after night. He was so strong that I could not fight him off. I wanted to tell my mama, but at that time jobs were few and far between, especially for a black woman back then. I knew if the truth came out that she would be fired. I kept his continual attacks to myself.

After a few months of this violent, unwanted relationship, I conceived a child. I had to tell my mama, and immediately she had to send me away. She could not afford to lose her job with the Taylors. I was forced to give the little girl I had up for adoption. Her name is Alyssa, and she is your sister, Coral."

Rose tells me her secret and then pulls another picture from the box. She hands me a picture of a radiant, light-skinned black woman. She is absolutely angelic in appearance. She has the same blue eyes as Joseph, but her skin is so much darker than his that the blue in her eyes appears the color of a blue sapphire. She has the same kindness in her eyes and smile that Rose does. Seeing my sister seemingly unaffected by Ocean Point or the evil seed that we were both created from gives me hope for my unborn baby to not be inflicted with the same heartache and evil that Joseph and I experienced. As hard as it is for Rose to know that she had to give her little girl away, there has to be a part of her that is relieved that Eshe, Ocean Point, or Alan could not drag her into the darkness.

I instantly feel a connection. This is the first news that I have heard today that actually gives me joy. I know that what happened to Rose is horrific, but if you can get past the pain, this is a wonderful gift for Rose and me. I look up at Rose. She has tears in her eyes, but I can see so much pride in them as well.

"Your sister is waiting for you, Coral," she says and smiles. I am confused. She reaches back into the box and pulls out a large envelope. "Since your mother's incarceration, your father, I mean Joseph, has been granted control of the family companies and money. He has opened a bank account in your name. There is enough money in the account to take care of you and the baby for the rest of your lives.

Also, there is a bus ticket to Charleston, South Carolina. Your sister, Alyssa, lives there and is expecting you. She is a nurse and has room in her home for you to stay until the baby is born or you figure out what you want to do."

I did not know what I was going to do after I left this house, but I knew that I was not going to sleep one night under this roof with my baby in my stomach. I get up and go to the bathroom to find my mother's bracelet. I am pleased to see that it is exactly where I left it. As I put the elegant strands around my wrist, it dawns on me that Rose did not tell me what happened to Alan, my rapist father.

"Rose, what happened to Alan? Is he still alive?" I ask her in a very casual manner.

Rose looks down and begins to shake her head. Was she hoping that she could leave this detail out? With all of the other menacing things that she told me, why would his whereabouts be any worse? I return to the bed and sit back down.

"After Margret faked his death is when she let most of the staff go and started allowing the mansion to be neglected. One reason was a lack of staff to maintain such an enormous home, but the other reason was, I truly think, that by this time the disbelief she had in Eshe's curse had become true in her mind. With watching her family be destroyed generation after generation, I think that she began to think of Ocean Point as belonging to Eshe and her family, not the Taylors or the Berringers. I think that she was trying to punish Eshe for what she had done to her family, especially her husband.

Coral, I am sure after your tour of the west wing that you assume that it was abandoned because of the slave quarters and the fears of the curse. Well, that was not why. Your mother was never afraid of Eshe. She was equally as dark and sinister herself. I believe it is possible that in the end Eshe had possessed Margret and lived within her controlling her every move. If this farfetched idea is not the truth then there is no doubt that Eshe made Margret her slave just like Margret's ancestors had made her one.

The history of Master Zyrous and what he did to the slaves in the west wing did not affect her either. She would always say that was just the way it was back then. She had no remorse for the brutal treatment that her ancestors inflicted on innocent people.

The reason, my child, is because she has hidden Alan in the west wing for all of these years. Margret has punished and tortured him daily. She has been his warden and has made him pay for every crime that he has ever committed. He was treated like the black slaves were and was even at times held captive in that same room that you were imprisoned in."

The events that occurred when I was a child come rushing back through my mind. I try to make sense of how this man has been living in the same house as me, and I did not know it. Alan is the man in the picture that frightened me when I snuck into the west wing. Alan is the demon that followed me in the hallway. He is the one that peered at me through the window when I was lost in the gardens. He is the man that I heard Mother torturing when I snuck into the tunnels. He is the wild, crazed man that I saw from the back of the ambulance. Oh my God, he is the stranger that crawled into my bed my last night at Ocean Point.

My own biological father was going to molest me. I suddenly feel nauseated as I recall the feeling of his hands on my bare skin. I run to the bathroom and begin to vomit. Rose comes to comfort me with a warm wash cloth. She gently wipes my mouth. I can see that she suffers for me, and I know that she loves me. I wrap my arms around her and squeeze her as tight as I can. We cry together.

I do not want to leave her here alone, but I have to leave Ocean

Point. I have to heal and protect my baby. Whether Eshe's Hoodoo curse is real or folklore, I cannot stay in this house that is the scene of all of the sins and abuse that I and everyone else who has ever slept under the roof of Ocean Point has had to endure.

Suddenly, something clicks. "C.O.B." I know that there is one more thing that I have to do before I leave. I have to pay my respects to my mother. I have to find a way to be grateful to her for saving my life and forgive her for leaving me. I ask Rose to follow me.

I take my last long walk through the hallways of Ocean Point. We exit through the back door. It is becoming dusk. I take Rose's hand in mine and lead her to the opening of the pathway of the gardens. We arrive at the entrance, and I feel Rose's eyes on me. I am sure that she is surprised that I am aware of the mysterious path. She does not say a word. She just grips my hand tighter, and we enter.

I feel the emotions of the neglected weeds. I even feel sorry for them. At one time, they grew and were magnificent, but because of the darkness of my family even they have been neglected. I can feel them try to fill me with fear, but not even the angry foliage is going to stop me from going to where my mother's body sleeps.

If Eshe is here and wants to harm me, then I will allow her to attempt to take her wrath out on me. I am not afraid. I believe that the love I have inside of me for my baby, Rose, and the mother that I do not remember is stronger than the dark and evil spirit that Eshe became. I continue on, daring Eshe to try to stop me.

We arrive at the small cemetery. The first thing we see is the huge monument for Alan. Disgust fills me to know that the man whose blood flows through me is not worthy of such a display. To make my anger worse, he is not even underground. He is still alive and breathing while people he destroyed are gone and buried under my feet.

First, I walk to my brothers' and sisters' tiny graves. I stand in front of the row of small stones. I wipe the dirt off of each of their names. I begin to pull the weeds off of the ground that they lie beneath.

Rose stoops down beside me and begins to toil along with me. As we clear off the taken children's graves, I feel a deep ache for the babies. I wonder if they knew that our father was evil and did not love them. I hope that their innocence protected them and that they never knew what he was.

I kneel at each grave and silently say the names Jefferson, Thomas, Annabelle, David, and Abigail. I introduce myself to them individually and tell them that I wish I could have known them. I tell them that I will never forget about them and that I think about them every day.

Just as I begin to rise from the last stone, I feel a cool and tender breeze. It lifts my hair slightly. I look at Rose, and I can see that she too feels the unexpected, gentle gust. I begin to hear the children's laughter and voices that visited me in the slave quarters.

It was my siblings who came to comfort me in the darkness. As eerie as this might seem, it is one of the happiest moments of my life. Rose and I look at each other, and we smile. We both know what just transpired but do not stay a word. After tonight, I have learned that some things are just better left untold.

We travel to my mother's grave, and the children have gone to play somewhere else. I hope that the spirits of all of the children here, both the Taylors and the slave children, find a way to have peace and play together. I hope that God has taken their memories and pain away so that they are finally free to run through the gardens and chase butterflies like I once did.

I stand in front of my mother's grave, and as before, on top of it is a blanket of lilies. The smell travels through me and gives me the warmth that my mother did when she visited me all of those times. I now know that Joseph still brings her the flowers that she loved the most. I hope that she can feel his love for her and knows that no matter how hopeless she may have felt that she had a man who loved her with everything he had. I pray that she knows what Margret did to me, not to hurt her but so that she understands why I have never intentionally visited her before today.

As I sit in front of my mother's grave, the anger and bitterness that I felt for her has vanished, and my heart is full of love. I may not be able to give this love to her, but I promise that I will give it to her grandchild. Everyone was a victim, my mother, Rose, Joseph, me, and even Margret. Not one of us is either right or wrong. Everyone just did their best to survive. Some of us did, some of us did not, and some of us wish we had not.

I do not know what comes over me, but I begin to crawl across the lilies that cover my mother's grave. I lie on the flowers, knowing that her body is beneath mine. I wish that I could hear her heartbeat like I can Angel's when I lie on his chest. It is silent. I feel close to her, and I know that she sees me and always has. She has been with me every day of my life. Now, my wish for her is to go and find the peace that she deserves and know that her little girl is finally safe.

A little time goes by, and then I stand and look at Rose, telling her that it is time to go. We hear a noise to the side of us, and it is Joseph. He keeps his distance from me. I can see that he is afraid. I can also see the toll that all of this has caused on his already weak mind. I look at him and see him as a six year old little boy chained to the same wall that he helped rescue me from. He did not deserve any of this any more than I did. The one thing that we have in common other than the same sick father is that we both had a love larger than life, and we both lost it.

I walk towards him to ease his nervousness. I see something in his hands. I stop in front of my brother, and he hands me a book. The book is worn, and it looks like it has been read a hundred times. I open the cover of the battered book and see that it is my mother's diary. I acknowledge what a huge gift this is from him. He has been reading these pages and holding this leather cover in his hands for so many years to try to keep Caroline close to him and alive. I am grateful that he is willing to give me his prized possession and maybe the only thing that he has left of his Caroline. He looks down at my wrist and sees Caroline's bracelet. He reaches and takes my hand. He lifts my wrist up and runs his fingers across the chains.

"This is the bracelet that I gave your mother on our wedding day. It was the happiest day of my life," he says as tears roll down his face.

I take Joseph in my arms, and I hold him tight to me. I do not say a word. I just hold my brother and let him know that I am not angry. I forgive him. He sobs openly, and I can feel his anguish that is now the only emotion he knows. I pull away from him and look into his eyes.

Sorrow fills my soul because I know that Joseph will never recover and find happiness. His life ended the same day that my mother's did.

Rose and I leave Joseph at my mother's grave and begin towards my final departure. We get into the car with the bus stop as our destination. The car begins to move, and I look back at Ocean Point. The sky is now dark, and it looks like a storm is beginning to brew. I see lightning behind the large castle. I wonder if it is truly lightning or if the house is so enraged that my baby and I escaped its darkness that it is its anger producing this display of flashes and not a storm at all. I hear the iron gates close behind us with a loud, angry clang. I know that Eshe's curse has been broken at least for my baby and me.

I watch Ocean Point dissolve into the darkness as the vision of the sinister mansion vanishes. I put my hand on my stomach. I gently rub my hand across my growing baby and say,

"You are safe now, Lily. Mama is here, and I am never going to leave you."

ABOUT THE AUTHOR

Tamara Helene Arrington lives in Nashville, Tennessee with her three amazing boys Julian, Connor, and Parker. She started writing *Untold* when she was fourteen years old with a pencil on a yellow legal pad. Twenty-seven years later, she had an accident which left her temporarily in a wheelchair, and during the horrible time and circumstances out of her control, she decided to finish the book that has never left her mind or heart. She took her misfortune as a sign and finished *Untold*, the first of the Berringer Family Novels.

What happens to Coral next? Her journey doesn't end here! Look for book two of the Berringer Family Novels in early 2013!

A BERRINGER FAMILY NOVEL

unveiled

Tamara Helene Arrington

Made in the USA
Charleston, SC
02 November 2012